The
Ghosts
of
Africa

The Ghosts of Africa

A novel by
William Stevenson

Skyhorse Publishing

Skyhorse Publishing books may be purchased in bulk at special discounts for sales promotion, corporate gifts, fund-raising, or educational purposes. Special editions can also be created to specifications. For details, contact the Special Sales Department, Skyhorse Publishing, 307 West 36th Street, 11th Floor, New York, NY 10018 or info@skyhorsepublishing.com.

Skyhorse® and Skyhorse Publishing® are registered trademarks of Skyhorse Publishing, Inc.®, a Delaware corporation.

Visit our website at www.skyhorsepublishing.com.

10 9 8 7 6 5 4 3 2 1

Library of Congress Cataloging-in-Publication Data is available on file.

Cover design by Eve Siegel

Print ISBN: 978-1-62914-443-6
Ebook ISBN: 978-1-62914-963-9

Printed in the United States of America

Whenever I take up a newspaper
I fancy I see
Ghosts between the lines.
There must be ghosts all over the world . . .
And we are so miserably afraid
Of the light,
All of us.

Ibsen, Ghosts

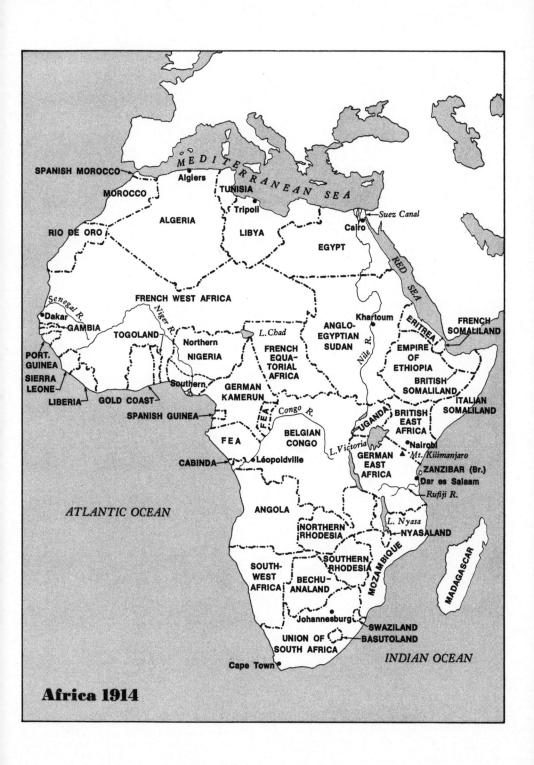

SPANISH MOROCCO →

MEDITERRANEAN SEA

Algiers

MOROCCO

TUNISIA

Tripoli

RIO DE ORO

ALGERIA

LIBYA

Suez Canal

Cairo

EGYPT

RED SEA

Senegal R.

FRENCH WEST AFRICA

Dakar

GAMBIA

Niger R.

L. Chad

Khartoum

ANGLO-EGYPTIAN SUDAN

ERITREA

FRENCH SOMALILAND

PORT. GUINEA

TOGOLAND

Northern

NIGERIA

FRENCH EQUA-TORIAL AFRICA

Nile R.

EMPIRE OF ETHIOPIA

SIERRA LEONE

Southern

GERMAN KAMERUN

BRITISH SOMALILAND

LIBERIA

GOLD COAST

Congo R.

ITALIAN SOMALILAND

SPANISH GUINEA →

F.E.A.

BRITISH EAST AFRICA

UGANDA

FEA

BELGIAN CONGO

L. Victoria

Nairobi

CABINDA →

Léopoldville

GERMAN EAST AFRICA

Mt. Kilimanjaro

ZANZIBAR (Br.)

Dar es Salaam

Rufiji R.

ATLANTIC OCEAN

ANGOLA

NORTHERN RHODESIA

L. Nyasa

NYASALAND

SOUTH-WEST AFRICA

BECHU-ANALAND

SOUTHERN RHODESIA

MOZAMBIQUE

MADAGASCAR

Johannesburg

SWAZILAND

UNION OF SOUTH AFRICA

BASUTOLAND

Cape Town

INDIAN OCEAN

Africa 1914

By Way of Prologue

ONE OF THE persistent mysteries of the Second World War concerns the plan of a group of high-ranking German generals to assassinate Adolf Hitler in 1944. This attempt, now known as the July 20th Plot, failed by the thinnest margin, injuring rather than killing Hitler. The results were the barbaric executions of the conspirators by torture, a purge of many innocents, and the continuation of the war to its savage, destructive conclusion.

The question that remains unanswered is why Allied intelligence agencies, secretly appealed to by the generals, refused to give substantial aid to this effort that could have brought the war to a rapid conclusion and avoided further devastation. The reasons were undoubtedly many and complex. A fundamental concern was the integrity and intention of the conspirators. In that regard, Allied intelligence sought the advice of an elderly gardener living in humble quarters in the German countryside. His reply was firm, decisive—and negative: let Germany suffer the full penalty for the Nazi nightmare it had unleashed on the world.

Who was this obscure man? Why was he so trusted and respected? He was known to Winston Churchill as Paul Lettow, formerly a German military commander. He had been one of the most dangerous adversaries ever to confound the British. Their regard for him came not from the Second but from the First World War. His extraordinary character inspired this novel, and his fascinating actions from 1914 to 1918 form its historical foundation.

Part One

The Cannon Blooms

I

From a dispatch in The New York World *by a special correspondent with the British fleet off the German East Africa Coast, November 1, 1914:*

Aboard H.M.S. *Goliath.*

During a briefing today, a staff aide of the English military command released this statement:

"There are persistent rumors that the German army commander will oppose the landings by the British Imperial Forces ordered to peacefully occupy this German colony. The commander is reported to be training thousands of native askari soldiers in defiance of the Governor, who accepts the belief of all the colonial powers that blacks, once trained and armed, will develop a dreadful capacity for killing white men and in time will plunge the Dark Continent back into bestiality and ignorance. Since the European war broke out three months ago, white settlers in both English and German colonies had avoided becoming embroiled in the conflict on the very grounds that nothing must shake black respect for white superiority. . . ."

2

THE TRAIN burst from the gorge with an explosion of black smoke and glowing cinders, galvanizing hundreds of gazelle whose arched leaps were etched against the golden morning sky and the purple massif of Mount Kilimanjaro.

The Kommandeur sat on a box of ammunition in the last flatcar. His bush shirt carried no badges and had been crudely dyed khaki, the fashionable new military color, which matched the thick dust sculpting his face into the mask of an eagle. One blue eye nestled in scar tissue. The other was guarded by a monocle. His sandaled feet rested on a worn cavalry saddle. It carried his needs: a rolled poncho, a ration of dried meat called biltong, a knife, and a battered dish in which he washed and cooked.

His name was Paul von Lettow-Vorbeck, known as Lettow, a lieutenant colonel of the German Imperial Army who had had twenty years of active service. He was accompanied by black soldiers, askaris from his *Schutztruppe*, the Protective Force of German East Africa. They walled the flatcars, their rifles slanting out over the Masai plain dotted with thorn trees. The askaris wore crowns of feathers woven into their tight black curls for camouflage. Like the Kommandeur, they were spare, no more than skin on muscle on bone.

The engineer, a bearded Sikh, swayed with the train as a naked African fed logs into the firebox. Two more blacks were braced to relieve the fireman if he faltered.

The engineer's mouth fell open, and a betel-stained grin split his beard. He hauled on the brake to pace the horseman who galloped alongside.

The Kommandeur jumped at the first snatch of brakes and replaced the monocle with a black eye patch secured by an old shoelace and previously hidden in his reddish-blond hair. He leaned out beyond the flatcar, two askaris bracing him, their hands like talons on his thighs. The horseman swerved and, with Lettow to steady him, fell sideways into the flatcar. The driver let the riderless horse run clear of the track and then inched open the throttle until the pistons thrust the train back into the pounding rhythm that had drummed in the ears of the *Schutztruppe* since midnight.

"Orders from Governor Schnee," gasped the horseman, a big red-bearded settler. "You're to stay on Kilimanjaro."

"Only the Kaiser gives me that order."

"Then you'll fight?"

"If the English invade, I fight."

A light, brilliant on the horizon despite the rising sun, blinked worriedly. Lettow pulled a canvas-backed notebook from the pouch slung around his neck. An old black turned his back and leaned forward to make a desk for the Kommandeur. A silver-gray monkey, perched on the old man's neck, watched. The horseman shifted his bandoliers. They all waited for the distant heliograph to stop its bursts of Morse.

"The Governor appeals to all settlers to keep the peace." Lettow snapped shut the notebook. "That includes you, Prinz."

"I'm at war."

"Not according to the Governor."

"Confound the fool! The war's three months old in Europe. Already they call it the first war of the world."

"Not here. Not yet. Your job's protecting your farm against the tribes—"

"And against the Uganda Railway Volunteers." Prinz spat. "Bloody Americans, most of 'em. As a reservist, I claim the *right* to fight!"

"And destroy your own empire?"

"It's not mine anymore," Prinz snapped in reply. He glanced back at the ghost of Kilimanjaro along the horizon. Tom von Prinz had been born an Englishman, Thomas Prince, and he had been raised on a farm on the English side of the mountain. Then Queen Victoria gave Kilimanjaro to her first grandchild, Kaiser Wilhelm II of Germany, throwing Tom Prince's loyalties in doubt. The English army had rejected him, and in anger he had joined the German army to fight in the Kaiser's colonial wars. For his savage victories, Berlin had teutonized his name and awarded him the ennobling "von." With clear military logic, Prinz believed the Germans should occupy the sixty-mile stretch between Kilimanjaro and the Uganda Railway so they could move up the railway to seize Uganda and gain some strategic advantage over England's vital sea lanes, her jugular vein passing through Suez.

The Kommandeur guessed what might be in his old friend's mind. Lettow's own thoughts had already moved in the same direction. The burgeoning war in Europe was, for him, a diversion. He had watched from a distance the slow escalation: an archduke assassinated in the Balkans; the Austrian Empire demanding German help when Russia stepped in; then suddenly England, France, Belgium, Serbia, Italy, Japan, and Russia declaring war against the Kaiser's Second Reich. By August 1914, the long-awaited world war had started, with only the United States still uncommitted. Lettow's own battleground, equal to all of western Europe in size, was German East Africa, a few degrees south of the equator. It rose from a sweltering coast to cold highland mists to mountain ranges and great inland lakes as treacherous as the broadest ocean.

Lettow, military commander of this vast area, led fewer than three hundred professional white soldiers and three thousand black askaris to control forty warrior tribes numbering six million men, women, and children. The freedom of these black Africans was the Kommandeur's fundamental, although officially unvoiced, concern. The Governor of German East, in complete contrast, had signaled his agreement to let an English armada land an expeditionary force to "pacify" the tribes. Thus the pride of England's Indian empire had been shipped across the Indian Ocean to land its best fighting regiments at Tanga.

The little potbellied locomotive trailed an arc of wood sparks. Along the sides of the flatcars rippled torn banners proclaiming the Great Imperial German East Exhibition, which ironically had co-incided with the outbreak of the war in Europe. It was to preserve the great accomplishments celebrated by the exhibition that Governor Schnee declared, *"There's no war here!"*

The American girl, Kate Truman, stood in the Customs shed at Tanga, waiting impatiently for a grubby German official to finish his lengthy examination of her travel papers.

"You were studying tropical medicine in *Berlin?*"

Kate nodded.

"Why not stay in Berlin? All we've got in Africa are the diseases."

"The research clinics here are the best, it's said."

The Customs man grunted. "You liked living in Germany?"

"Very much."

"Remember that—if your President tries to get into the crazy war there."

"I'm sure Mister Wilson would never dream of such a thing."

Kate raised her eyes at a sudden commotion at the far end of the shed. The crowd there seemed to be testing the barriers. The

Customs man looked at the gathering mob with obvious annoyance. Then he glanced back and asked, "Are you related to Major Truman?"

Kate nodded again, fear catching her by the throat.

"*Mein Gott!*" Sympathy spread over the fat perspiring face. "His execution is tomorrow, no?"

"No! That's not possible!"

"Anything's possible with that Prussian pig who runs our army," retorted the Customs man, his attention abruptly turning to the onrushing figures in white dhotis and yellowing nightgowns. "I'm sorry, *Fräulein*. There are rumors of an English invasion. Go that way—" He shooed her agitatedly behind him.

Kate moved against a tide of panicked Asians and Arabs seeking passage on what they believed would be the last steamers out of Africa. She brushed aside pleas for money or for any token of American or Swiss connections that these traders and their families might barter for an exit permit. More traders broke away when they spied her. A man in a white turban and with daggers in his belt screamed at her. An Indian *babu* clerk, clinging to respectability in white suit and Panama hat, began suddenly berating a Moslem woman covered from head to foot in black. Slipping beyond this melee, Kate escaped to the sunshine outside the shed. The blinding glare and the heat struck her like hammers. The cloying smell of cloves mingled with the sweaty aroma of the *homali*-cart pullers who were too poor to consider escape. Now she felt she was back in Africa.

She raised her green parasol and surveyed the railroad station of glass and girders draped with banners announcing in gothic letters of red and black the great exhibition of last August. Since then, German armies had driven back the French and Russians on two fronts. Europe was aflame. How sad now seemed that exhibition of such great promise.

She stood at the dockyard gates, a pretty young woman in a long white cotton dress that concealed any evidence of breasts or ankles. Her raven-black hair was cropped unfashionably short. Her blue eyes summoned a near-naked black pedaling a bicycle to which was attached a basket chair on wheels.

"*Wapi?*" demanded the pedicab boy, and Kate replied, "Kaiserhof," the only hotel she knew by name. She settled beside her bag in the wide seat and tried not to stare at the long black muscular back bent over the handlebars. Lifting her gaze above the rhythmically swaying shoulders, she saw the land rise and merge with the sky. Nowhere but in Africa had she seen such shades of color. Flametrees threw umbrellas against the torrential light. Jacaranda tossed down a drift of ice-blue blossom on the pink crushed sand of the washboard road. She wiped her brow and lifted her skirt to let the breeze cool her moist thighs. Despite her outward calm, tremors of excitement vibrated through her body. She seemed to see Mount Kilimanjaro's foothills, a hundred miles away, lurking like purple ghosts in the haze between earth and heaven.

That was where her brother was reported to be imprisoned. Chuck, older by a year, was supposed to go on trial for his life. But the Customs man had spoken of immediate execution. It was absurd. She fumbled inside her cloth holdall and carefully extracted the photograph with its inscription: "In the event of hostilities, this identifies the holder as Catherine Truman, who is to be given the protection of forces under my command."

The signature was as spiky as the man. In Berlin her friend Helen Lange had warned that the Kommandeur—Colonel Paul von Lettow-Vorbeck—was in disfavor. Helen wrote for *Die Frau*, the daring feminist magazine. "You'll be invading a man's world," Helen had cautioned. "You'll have to cater to a Prussian soaked in the tradition of a military elite." She had quoted Marwitz: "They renounce all personal advantage, all gain, all comfort, all desire. They sacrifice everything for the honor of Prussian weapons!"

"This is *not* an invasion," repeated General Ha-Ha Splendid Aitken, supreme commander of the British Imperial Expeditionary Force B: "It's a *peaceful occupation*."

"So you say, sir," retorted a junior Black Watch army captain. "The Kommandeur of German East might take a different view."

The bridge of the English warship *Goliath* seemed awash with generals and admirals. Their heads turned to see who the impertinent intruder might be. His name was Myles Hagen.

"Who is this Kommandeur?" rumbled an admiral, looking not at Hagen but at the supreme commander.

"Some Hun with a bunch of armed niggers," huffed General Aitken.

Hagen corrected him, undeterred by the hostility on every side. "The Kommandeur's a bush commando. He learned peasant warfare in China and guerrilla tactics against us in South Africa." He wanted to add that the Kommandeur was in league with black

Bolsheviks and Zionist Jews. But Hagen was accustomed to being ignored. As an intelligence officer, he was lower than a gunpowder monkey when flag commanders got the smell of battle in their nostrils. Biding his time, he clasped his hands behind his back and joined the others in gazing at the armada of troopships and escorts rolling in the oily swell.

It was the morning of Sunday, November 1, 1914. It had taken Force B three weeks to stagger across 2,500 miles of ocean from Bombay. "A mere couple of inches," the Viceroy of India had said, looking at the chart of the hemisphere. None of Force B's commanders had maps of inland Africa. None of the troops had ever laid eyes on Africa; nor were they seeing it now, being occupied in heaving their guts up in the black ovens 'tween decks.

General Aitken was supremely confident. England's war minister had wirelessed the grand design, signing himself Horatio Herbert, Lord Kitchener. "If the Germans should resist, the full might of the empire will be mobilized to crush them. This piece of Africa is vital to the plan to pulverize the Second Reich." When Kitchener spoke like that, his generals listened, for this was the soldier who had fought his way up from ambulance boy; the inventor of concentration camps; the legendary British agent in Egypt.

While General Aitken meditated upon the manner in which he should enter Tanga (on a white horse, like Kitchener at Khartoum?), another general was saying to Hagen, "If this Kommandeur fella disobeys the Governor and fights, get rid of him!"

"I might have to do that," said Myles Hagen. "Or you'll still be hanging around Tanga when your 'Hun' has bled the empire dry."

The general gave a derisive snort. There would be no struggle for Africa. Lord Kitchener and the Viceroy had said so, speaking for the King, Emperor of India and the Dominions Overseas, Ruler of the United Kingdom of Great Britain and Ireland, Defender of the Faith.

Four hundred kilometers south of the English armada, the svelte 375-foot cruiser *Koenigsberg* crept into the Rufiji River, between petrified forests where century-old crocodiles mimicked driftwood in their ancient war with man and his ancestors. The *Koenigsberg* had been last glimpsed by English spies during the Great Imperial German East Exhibition, when all white settlers in Africa were invited to see the progress made by Germany in her civilizing mission to enthrone *Kultur* among the heathens.

The *Koenigsberg* had vanished from harbor when the code word EGIMA warned all German vessels of the outbreak of war in Europe. She had sunk an English cruiser and raided English convoys despite the Governor's wirelessed pleas not to provoke the English. So far as the *Koenigsberg*'s captain, Max Looff, was concerned, there were no geographical limits to war at sea. No damned German colonial administrator was telling him where to wage it. Nevertheless, he had taken refuge in the Rufiji. Now he stared expressionlessly at the narrowing channel as the cruiser with silenced engines glided near a mud bank where hippos thundered into the chocolate waters with shovel mouths gaping, tails slapping the water with machine-gun thuds.

Strange sounds drifted over the stilled warship: wild echoing cries of unfamiliar beasts and birds of prey. All three hundred sailors were aware of the trap Looff had voluntarily entered. Here they must lie, baked by the sun, breathing pestilential vapors in an eerie landscape, vulnerable to all the enemies of man until summoned into action again by Looff's old comrade, the Kommandeur.

3

KATE TRUMAN had glimpsed the warships of Britain's Cape of Good Hope squadron searching for the *Koenigsberg*, and even some rusty tubs of the invasion fleet escorted by the formidable *Goliath*, during the voyage to Tanga. The spectacle now seemed remote as the warfare in Europe. In the sweltering lobby of the Kaiserhof, she faced a desk clerk who parted new veils of polite hostility.

"We cannot accept non-German guests."

"I know the ban exists in Germany," Kate protested, "but you're not at war here."

"A state of apprehension of war exists." The clerk looked more closely at the Deutsche Ost-Afrika steamship line's papers of recommendation. "The ban," he added slowly, "especially applies to relatives of Jewish spies."

He obviously recognized the family name, although she had never before heard her brother identified as Jewish. She did not stop to argue. She had no recollection of marching through the lobby back to the waiting pedicab.

A man in a starched white suit twinkling with brass buttons ran after her, caught up with her at the hotel's entrance. She saw a weathered face under a cork helmet with a sweeping stern like an otter's tail. He bowed stiffly.

"That rudeness was unforgivable. Accept my apologies. Major Wolfe, ma'am, at your service."

"At *my* service? That's rich." She hesitated. "You could tell me where to find the Governor."

"He's normally in the capital—Dar es Salaam." Wolfe looked away and then back at Kate. "However—"

"Well?"

"His Excellency is here in fact, negotiating to save us from the horrors of war. You will find him at the old fort, conducting a day of punishment. He does not believe, ma'am, in neglecting his duties."

"Would you instruct this man?"

"Of course." Major Wolfe spoke in Swahili to the pedicab driver and then helped Kate into her seat. The physical contact brought a blush to his cheeks, darkening the tan. "Forgive me, Miss Truman. I claim an artist's and a poet's privilege. I should have known you would be beautiful—"

"How did you know my name?"

He straightened. "Your brother has been in our custody." He raised a hand quickly. "There is no cause for alarm. He is safe with the army."

Kate rose from her seat. "These stories—"

"Don't listen!" Wolfe began to back away.

"They say he's to be shot."

"Please. The trial has not started yet. You should not be seen talking with me. While we have jurisdiction, your brother will never come to harm." Wolfe was watching a group of men at the top of the hotel steps. "Trust me!" He saluted and ran up the steps.

Frightened by Wolfe's sudden agitation, yet oddly reassured by his words, Kate motioned the driver to set off. *Major?* He talked like a romantic and called himself a poet. Kate compressed her lips, remembering how her romantic imagination had also led her astray about the Kommandeur. Perhaps it was because she had learned to call him Paul as if he were an ordinary man with ordinary tastes.

A year ago, during her first voyage to Africa, on the steamship *Praesident,* Kate had considered him the most intriguing man she had ever encountered. He kept aloof from the German and English settlers returning to the colonies of East Africa and spent his time pacing the deck or whittling chunks of wood while sprawled in a chair. He walked stiffly with his left side hunched forward as if to protect his damaged eye. Over this right eye he usually wore a black patch.

Her chance to learn something about him came after the ship rounded the cruel spear of land that points out of northeast Africa toward Asia. The appalling heat of Suez and the Red Sea drove passengers to sleep on deck. Kate placed her mattress close to his.

About five every morning, Kate had noticed, the ship swung its bow. The engine stopped, then started, and the vessel resumed course. During one of these early morning maneuvers, Kate found herself standing at the stern rail beside the mysterious German. She asked him what was happening.

"It's supposed to be a secret."

"I'm accustomed to secrecy," said Kate with some asperity. "My father's with the American embassy in Berlin."

He had smiled at this naive guarantee of her discretion. "There's bubonic plague among the lascar sailors. Those who die are thrown overboard"—he corrected himself—"are, ah, committed to the deep before anyone is awake. The ship turns to save the bodies tangling in the propellers."

"So far as plague is concerned, I've avoided rats and I drench myself in Keating's Powders."

Surprised by her apparent callousness, he said, "You must have been to Africa before?"

"No, but I was warned."

"If the English in Mombasa heard of a plague, they would keep us in quarantine for weeks. The owners can't afford that, so they keep the secret."

"So shall I," said Kate.

"What's your reason for keeping it?"

"Silkworms."

The man had laughed then. Laughter transformed him; he seemed rather like a schoolboy. He ran fingers through his thick reddish-blond hair and peered at the green band along the horizon where the sun would shortly rise.

"I'm afraid the cocoons will hatch in my cabin," said Kate. "I don't want silkworm grubs running all over the ship. If we keep to schedule, they'll still be cocoons when I give them to my brother."

"He's going into silk, eh?" The German seemed on the point of making some other observation. Finally he said, "Well, in Africa we'll try anything to stay alive."

During that first voyage in 1913, the ship had touched land at Mombasa. The English port came as a shock after the dreamlike passage south along a coastline of untamed shrubbery and golden endless beaches. Suddenly Africa swarmed up the gangway with a noise and glitter that was frightening. Beaded women waved woven baskets of gaudy fruit. Naked boys dived for coins, their bodies flashing and glittering like flying fish. Mothers chased fractious children while red-faced fathers twirled their handlebar mustaches. Half of these settlers would be dead in a year from disease or fangs. They would ride the Uganda Railway to wherever land had been allotted them, in tsetse fly or malaria belts or among lions turned into maneaters by a diet of Indian rail workers. Or so the German had told Kate.

The ship left Mombasa on a night tide when firelight flickered like a snake's tongue over bronze bodies squatting silently on the wharves. Aroused by the rattle of anchor chains, Kate made her way to the stern where her German stood quietly smoking. A sweetish smell mingled with the tobacco smoke. She wondered if it was opium. For days she had speculated about his profession. Could he be an addict, a Catholic missionary whose only relief was opium? A Catholic priest could not marry. Now what had put that idea in her head?

The ship shuddered as the engines fell into a pounding rhythm. The air was perfumed with nutmeg and cattle-dung fires, a sweetness and pungency that swept the senses.

"My name's Lettow," he had said abruptly. "I'm known as Paul." It seemed a strange, delayed introduction, almost as if he thought she knew it already. He hurried on to comment about the anchored dhows whose lateen sails were brushed by a ghostly light. His voice was almost lost in the swirl of water under the stern. He spoke of the tyrants who had swept down this coast out of Arabia, leaving the ruins of forts and cities. For the black men, the Zinj who were now the black natives of Africa, there had been thirteen hundred years of unspeakable cruelty. Their shackles had been loosed for less than a century. The blacks had a lot of lessons still to forget, said Paul. Their women still made themselves ugly, as their elders had done, to escape the slavers and buccaneers. They still stretched their necks and mutilated their breasts and submitted to circumcision even when the original causes were all but gone.

Kate was entranced. She thought of a German word to describe him: *sanft*. She defined it as hard but gentle, a kid-glove smoothness drawn over a core of penetrating resolve. She was not innocent in matters of sex, and the undeniably phallic image made her blush. She remembered what he had said about female circumcision. Was he a missionary, one of the harsh ones of Presbyterian vision who discouraged any doglike copulation and taught the heathen women to lie on their backs in submission? He didn't seem prudish. It was when she gave voice to certain of these questions that an abrasive note was struck.

"I'm a student of nature," he had reluctantly responded at one point.

"Africa's the place for that!" she said teasingly.

"Of human nature."

"Are you, then, one of these Social Darwinists?"

He seemed to turn cold. "Using Darwin to justify the concept of supermen? No!"

"The most daring new thinkers in Germany hold such views."

"Dangerous views they are! You share them?"

Now Kate matched his evident anger. "Why would you suppose I do?"

"Anyone acquainted with such lies about racial superiority must be—how do you say?—in the swim? Young people in the swim parrot what's in vogue. Your kind interpret Darwin to say man grows through wars and violence into superman."

"Not my kind! I have my own interpretation."

Whatever this was, she had never explained it. The captain had interrupted, and the threatened altercation was averted.

She passed the rest of that day with the remaining passengers. They were mostly Germans with narrower vision than Lettow. They planned to grow coffee or sisal, and their enemies were "the natives" and Jewish Zionists who sought the promised land in Africa. Such enemies, they said, made brothers of all colonists, German and English. They were confident of their ability to keep out of the lunatic rivalries in Europe. If conflict came, they would be safe here. They felt themselves to be rebels against the warmongers of Berlin.

Lettow dodged any further personal discussion, which for Kate was tantalizing. Her father, feeling his task as an American consul should include ferreting out the facts of German military preparations, had encouraged her to flirt with the men likely to possess privileged information. The German Crown Prince had described Kate as having cat's eyes; while looking into them, he had spilled navy secrets. Prince Henry of Prussia talked about the massive transfer of armies by rail just for the privilege of studying her shell-like ear. The Dutch aviator Fokker confided his design for a German army bomber. But her shipboard quarry evaded her by whittling wood.

She would have one last chance to invade his privacy at dinner before she left the ship next day at Zanzibar. Now the ship moved so slowly and so close to shore that Africa could assault her senses with colors like none she had seen before, with sights and sounds to tantalize her imagination. The mystery of man's origins had seemed in Berlin an academic puzzle. Here she could see, or thought she could see, the conflict between good and evil at an animal level. Man had descended from those apes she saw tumbling across a golden beach. Suddenly she was less certain that man's destiny lay onward and upward. She smelled, or believed she could smell, the rank odor of wild beasts mingling with wild coffee and clover and geraniums. She felt the presence of elephants moving with saintly tread between the galleries of trees, the leopard gathering itself without stirring, the bat-eared fox peering from mossy rocks pricked by violets and yellowstars. The lemon dove whispering shyly from the pepper tree was not likely to be heard above the wash of the sea, but she believed in it, as, indeed, she believed she saw her first jackal hunching to spring, or kestrels and owls and cape rooks and sky cuckoos nestling in a giant fig tree fifty meters wide at the base and said by the captain to be old when Moses crossed the Red Sea.

There was no sign of Paul Lettow at dinner. Kate had wheedled an invitation to join the captain's table, where Lettow usually sat. She put aside all pretense and asked if he would appear later. The captain gazed at her doubtfully and said, "The Kommandeur has left to join his men."

"Kommandeur!" Kate dully repeated the military title.

The captain fished in his wallet and pulled out a photograph. "He said you might need this."

Kate stared at the picture. He looked, well, fortyish. Really, much too old! Her impulse was to tear it up; then she read the request that she be given *Schutztruppe* protection. Of course! An African soldier who could not read would recognize his commander's photograph and take it to his white officer. Nevertheless, she positioned her hands to tear the photograph.

The captain was startled out of his habitual calm. "My dear young lady, you really may need it!"

"I am visiting my brother for Christmas," Kate said. "Then I return to Germany. I cannot imagine a reason for coming back to Africa."

"Few of us ever can," the captain had sighed.

Now, back again after the year's interval, Kate thought lazily how much she had grown up since then. Her pedicab tottered between tipsy Arab houses with fretted balconies. She heard the wail of a muezzin among the minarets and the chants from a dazzling white Hindu temple. Women squatted, black-cloaked and hooded, eyes flashing behind crocheted slits; they contrasted strangely with the bare-breasted black women harnessed between the shafts of trolleys, their sex glistening wetly between partings of their bustled reed skirts.

The pedicab rattled through an arch in the fortlike wall at the top of the town. Kate gasped. She saw a platform and on it a gibbet against a blazing sky. A black man stood above her with his head in a noose.

The pedicab driver swung down from the saddle and grinned back at her as if to say, *What luck! We're just in time. An execution!*

The courtyard inside the fort was packed with a silent crowd facing a marquee and ignoring the man on the gallows. He stood curiously at ease, the rope loose at his neck. On the far side were men, powdered and starched, dignified by tricorn hats.

Governor Heinrich von Schnee was finishing a speech. "The natives are ignorant. They are unclean. They are savage. Our task is to save them, not to teach them war. The provocation of wars in which black would fight white must stop! We must not use blacks to fight white wars. Germans and English must cooperate in teaching the natives to obey!"

A line of Africans shuffled across the square. Kate had a sickening impression of blacks stripped and stretched over a wheel to receive the lash. She heard the crack of a whip, the victim's grunt, the sigh of the crowd.

An interminable, rising whine filled the square. A girl fell back from the wheel. The ground trembled and the marquee swayed.

"That's a shell," thought Kate, and the delayed *crump* fanned her cheeks. Smoke billowed through the fort and brought into sharp relief the man on the gallows. He was shaking his head to free the noose. Togaed tribesmen sprang to the scaffold and slashed the cords binding his wrists and ankles. Out of the confusion and smoke emerged a bearded European hustling the condemned native toward her.

There was only one route of escape, down the crooked lane into the warrens of the town. The pedicab driver was gone.

"Get in!" Kate ordered the European.

The man stared. He looked like a rabbi in his black *kupa* hat and black cotton suit. The released man was restoring circulation, dancing and swinging his arms. "She's right, Jacob!" The big arms made circles in the dusty air. "You'll help us, missy?" The accent was unexpectedly from the American South.

"Yes!" said Kate. "For pity's sake, hurry."

"Bless you," said the European, climbing into the basket seat beside Kate. "I hope you know what you're doing! You know who and what he is? Cornelius—?"

"Yes," lied Kate. She could hear shouted orders and boots crashing through the smoke screen. "Please do make him hurry."

The black took the handlebars and wheeled the pedicab to face downhill. He no longer looked like a convict who should be twitching at the end of a rope. He began to pedal, slowly at first so that guards running out of the fort ignored him, seeing only an elderly bearded European with a respectable young woman in a Tanga pedicab.

"Thank God for the stupid English," said Jacob as the vehicle gathered speed on the downhill descent. "Though why they should start shelling their best friend, the Governor, only God knows."

Kate caught him staring curiously at her bag. She said in explanation, "I just arrived," then added, without knowing why, "They turned me away at the Kaiserhof. They said I was Jewish."

"And are you?"

"Not really," Kate replied.

There was a short silence. Then the man said, "I'm Jacob Kramer. I'm not a rabbi, despite my *kupa*, but I've been known in Africa for more years than I care to tell as Jacob the Jew."

Further talk was made impossible by the growing surge of noise bouncing from the coral-rag walls of the narrowing streets. Kate clung to the side of the wheeled chair and heard Jacob shout to the man he had called Cornelius. She was fascinated by the ripple of powerful muscles under the dark, glistening skin. He had the build of a Masai, hardly a student from a Southern Baptist seminary. Yet, from his speech, she was sure he came from one.

The shelling had stopped, but the crooked lanes buzzed like an angry hive. Kate recognized the dock area. She would have asked to leave, suddenly aghast at the jeopardy in which she might have put her own mission—to save her brother. But Jacob forestalled her.

"You must come to the military hospital. It won't be safe for whites here, not after those shells."

"Who fired them?"

"English warships. Reminding the Governor to cooperate."

"Isn't shelling an act of war?"

"Whoever holds the gun makes the rules." Jacob laughed bitterly. "The might of the British Empire lies out there."

The pedicab was bouncing over sunken railroad tracks. Above the noise from the freight yards rose a spine-chilling chant. She looked past Jacob, along the steel rails glimmering toward the station. The deep-throated singing of men on the march grew louder. She saw askari soldiers coming down the track, many with plumes and feathers in their hair, some dignified by loincloths, others pathetic in torn jackets. They marched barefooted with rifles reversed. Their voices drove down like hammers on the hard consonants of the words they sang, underlined by snare drums and punctuated by dented bugles:

> *Tuna-kwenda, tuna-shinda,*
> *Tuna-fuata Bwana Kommandeuri.*
> *Askari wana-endesha,*
> *Askari wana-endesha,*
> *Tuna-kwenda, tuna-shinda.*

Jacob said quietly, "That's the askari marching song, the '*Heia Safari.*'" He translated:

> We go, we win,
> We follow the Kommandeur.
> The soldiers drive on,
> The soldiers drive on,
> We go, we win.

"The Kommandeur's soldiers!" exclaimed Kate in disgust. "What right has any white man to lead them into wars?"

"If they don't fight with us, they would fight each other. Better some good should come of it."

"What possible good—" began Kate. She saw Jacob's face close tight. The chanting had become louder and the rhythm made her sway. She heard Jacob speak from a long way off. The pedicab stopped. The marching columns passed on either side.

"You look faint." Jacob was holding her arm. The voices had receded.

"I'm all right. A touch of sun."

"Or of fright?" suggested Jacob.

"I thought I saw men riding across a plain." She was surprised by her own words. "Some were dangling in the stirrups. The column wound on for miles, skeletons marching. It must have been the chanting."

"The marching songs of soldiers all give rise to nightmares," said Jacob. "I, too, have visions, child. A massacre such as the world has never seen. If poor natives must be sacrificed to stop such a catastrophe, that is the good that will come of it."

4

KATE TRUMAN sat on a cot in the military hospital and watched the moon swell out of a misty sea. A train clanked along the dockside. Men with guns were outlined along the veranda outside her window. She tried to suppress a rising sense of hysteria.

The matron who had put her in this cubicle had been eager to talk. Magdalene von Prinz. A pretty name. But they had not talked. Kate had been overwhelmed with fatigue and she must have slept several hours, as if the fear and uncertainty were too much. Now she felt the panic rising again.

She jumped at a sudden clatter of freight cars shunting along the harbor. She heard a woman cry out in pleasure. Along the veranda, askaris padded to positions behind the posts, crouching and scanning the moonwashed sea. A huge man in jackboots, bandoliers crisscrossing his tunic, crashed past with an arm around the waist of a woman whose head was thrown back in laughter. There was, in the way the man held her, a tension that Kate had seen too frequently in Europe since the slaughter began.

Another man passed, his face sharp in the cold moonlight. She had known it was Paul Lettow before she picked out the features. She was shaken by the way she responded to his presence after almost a year.

She heard him say, "I'll see Cornelius alone, Tom."

"As you wish." The other man disengaged from the woman.

"How is he?" asked Paul.

"Calm. And grateful," replied the woman. Kate recognized the voice of Magdalene von Prinz.

"The Governor suspects nothing?"

"Nothing. He's too busy scraping the mess out of his pants from the shelling."

"Did it do much damage?" persisted Paul.

"To property, a lot. To human beings, not much." Magdalene's voice became sarcastic. "We've put some wounded natives in a ward. Nobody white got hit. The English will turn you into a general yet."

The voices faded, but soon Kate heard the scraping of chairs in the adjoining room. The wooden walls were thin and perforated for ventilation. She heard Paul speak and responses from Jacob and then Cornelius.

"I come in response to your message. The Governor arrests me. Are you surprised I suspect betrayal?" asked Cornelius.

"You were arrested by the Governor," Paul said quickly. "Not by my wish."

"Then who governs?"

"I do, from the moment the fighting begins. I'm sorry if the English failed to stick to schedule. I was not expecting this fraudulent offer of 'peaceful invasion.'"

The voices were lost in the crash of freight cars. When quiet returned, the voices had gone. Perhaps the speakers had feared they might be overheard, Kate thought.

The door to Kate's room opened. Magdalene von Prinz said, "My Lord! I nearly forgot you. You were sleeping so soundly, dear. Half the staff has run away." The words came in a rush. Magdalene turned. "Tom, this is the American who helped the escape."

Prinz leaned awkwardly forward, wriggling his massive shoulders to shift the ammunition belts. "You? Such a dainty to rob the gallows."

"I happened to be there—"

"She was heroic," interrupted Magdalene.

"I'm not sure we'll thank you two or three years from now," growled Prinz. "Hanging's too good for Bolsheviks like Comrade Cornelius."

"Tom!" His wife pulled away. "He'll hear you."

"He's gone. Struck a good bargain and wants to spread the word." Prinz clowned, cupping a hand to his ear. "You probably hear the tom-toms now. The only reason I go along with these black revolutionaries is the Kommandeur made the deal. If he made a pact with the devil, he'd wind up the master of hell."

"That 'devil' influences my tribes, Tom!" The soft voice from the unlit corridor was Paul's. As he walked in, his features in the yellow light from the single oil lamp seemed a demonic reddish-black from the dust of the journey. He stopped when he saw Kate.

"You!" There was an awkward pause. "An unexpected honor."

"Not intentional," said Kate curtly. "My bro—" She was stopped by Paul's sudden grip on her arm. With his other hand he adjusted the black patch over one eye, then groped in his dirt-caked shirt for his monocle.

Tom von Prinz knew the gesture. Gently, he led his wife out and closed the door.

"Do they know who you are?" asked Paul.

"I don't think so," said Kate. "Does it matter?"

"Yes, very much." Paul stood away from her. "Please sit down. I—this is a shock."

"I expect it is," she said drily.

"You introduce an element that complicates things dangerously." Paul slammed a fist against his side. "You must be the woman I was told about—"

"Who helped Cornelius? Yes. I was looking for the Governor to appeal for my brother."

"Don't go near the Governor! Don't leave this room until I've had time to think. Give me your word."

"No," said Kate.

"I've no wish to surround you with my *Schutztruppe*."

"Then give *me* word of my brother."

Paul regarded her closely. "He's safe with me—"

"Safe with a military tyrant? You don't even have to go through the mockery of a trial."

"A trial is what he has most to fear! *Schutzengel!* That's the word the Governor uses for you Americans. Guardian angels of the English." His voice softened. "Please, Miss Truman, get some rest. Things are seldom as bad as they seem."

She was stunned by the spark of excitement she felt when he touched her cheek. She watched him leave. She felt angry with him for generating the current of sexual attraction she called *zuetz-zuetz*, but angrier at herself for having recognized it.

Magdalene slipped back into the room. "I've never seen our Kommandeur so agitated. He knows you, then?"

The question was posed so prettily that Kate could not take offense. Magdalene von Prinz looked about half her husband's age, with her glossy black hair tucked inside a white nursing cap. The temptation to confide in her was strong, and Kate was relieved by the interruption of Jacob Kramer.

"*Mazel un b'rachach!*" he said in Yiddish. "Good luck and prosperity! Take my word. It will go well with your brother."

Kate shot him an agonized look and he stopped.

"Brother?" echoed Magdalene.

"Have I said too much?" asked Jacob. He seized Magdalene by the arm. "Forget those words, my dear. All will become clear, no doubt. They have need of you, the orderlies, and I must be off, too."

Long after they had gone, Kate remained standing by the window. Why had Jacob presumed she would understand the Yiddish phrase?

Paul inspected the racks where Tom von Prinz and the other reserve officers parked their bicycles.

"You can't *pedal* to an audience with the Governor!" protested Prinz.

"Why the devil not?" Paul selected a Krupps Fahrrad. "I might want to spy out the land later. I've a hunch the English will land scouts before daybreak."

He bicycled to the mansion that automatically became the Governor's palace whenever Schnee visited Tanga. Black servants in white gowns ran down an imposing curved staircase and caught the cycle. Paul mounted the steps two at a time, wondering about the blaze of ceremony at such a late hour. Flares sputtered outside the main hall. The Governor stood by a Grecian urn, flexing a swagger stick between plump hands.

"You disobeyed my orders, Colonel!"

"I discharge my duties, Excellency!"

"Duties? Your duties are protection of property, not inviting trouble from good English neighbors." Dr. Schnee clipped pince-nez on his button nose in his fury.

Paul clenched his fists. Only then did he see the Governor's wife and, standing beside her, a figure in English military uniform. Ada von Schnee moved quickly forward.

"This is Captain Myles Hagen. He is here to lay down the terms of occupation." Ada's voice was harsh.

"Not occupation, madame. Cooperation. We wish only to land troops to help put down rebellion." Hagen turned and flashed Paul the frank smile of treachery. "We meet again, Colonel."

The Governor pirouetted. "Again? You've met?"

"After a fashion. We fought," said Paul.

"Fought?" echoed Schnee. "When?"

"When chivalry and honor flourished," Paul said. "South Africa. Boers against English."

"When the Kaiser saw fit to become involved where he wasn't concerned!" added Hagen, turning away and following Ada inside.

At the entry to the reception room, Ada swept round quickly. "He's here to drive the wedge." She fixed her periwinkle eyes on Paul. He had learned to trust Ada since she had advised him to heed the settlers who resented bureaucrats like her husband. Ada knew those settlers intimately—too intimately, some thought. English-born, bred of imperial rulers, she had married Schnee while he was fresh out of Berlin's oriental seminary. Now, while he drank to keep pestilence at bay, she consoled herself with the farmers. She would crudely boast of "muscles hardened on my back and on my horse," for she would ride miles in search of a friendly bed. The tropical heat that drained most European wives inflamed her. The vivid red long since drained out of her hair by years of stress in hot climates, she was still so vibrant with energy that Paul felt the sexual tension in her as he brushed past.

"Our offer," Hagen was saying, "expires in two hours."

"What damned offer?" demanded Paul.

"His Excellency has the samples," Hagen replied. He drew some papers from his pocket after a moment's hesitation, implying that he was conferring a favor on the Kommandeur by letting him see them too. "These leaflets were scattered this evening over your German settlements."

"Scattered. By what means?"

"By aeroplane, Colonel."

"This machine has flown over my territory?"

"As part of the peace-keeping effort."

"I'd call it aggression!"

"As you please." Hagen shrugged. "Our English flying corps wished to convey an offer of help to your isolated communities in view of the native uprisings."

"So now the single aeroplane becomes a flying corps! Captain Hagen, I consider a state of war exists between us."

Schnee's pince-nez quivered. "You forget yourself, Colonel! I am commander-in-chief—"

"In peacetime, yes, Excellency," snapped Paul. "Captain Hagen has just given further evidence we're no longer at peace!"

"We do have a gentleman's agreement," murmured Hagen. "The Governor, who represents the Kaiser, agrees that peace-keeping operations may be conducted against any force disobeying him. Our offer depends upon you withdrawing all native troops from Tanga. Immediately."

Paul returned the Englishman's insolent stare. "There will be no withdrawal."

"Then you disobey your Governor. We must treat you as a lawbreaker, your soldiers as bandits." Hagen nodded curtly to Paul and saluted the Governor. "I beg to take leave, Excellency."

"I will see you to your transport," replied the Governor, his face drained of blood.

Ada walked with them as far as the top of the steps, then returned to Paul. "You've given Hagen the perfect excuse to hunt you down like a common criminal."

"He'll do that anyway. The man's full of bluff. He speaks for nobody but himself."

"He came as spokesman for the biggest invasion fleet in his empire's history."

"Whose commanders will disown him tomorrow if it suits their purpose. Your Heinrich's a fool, Ada. Never conclude an agreement with a spy!"

Monocle in place, Paul read the English leaflet. "Listen. '*German colonists! White must unite with white. Protect our racial superiority! The black children of Ham were directed by God to hew wood and draw water. Do not give them arms! Reject your Kommandeur's proposal to place weapons in black hands! March with us against those who would subvert the Bible!*'" He crumpled the paper and shoved it into his pocket. The grit on his hand made him aware for the first time of how dusty he was. He wiped a film of dirt from his face, then grinned. "No wonder Hagen addressed me like an outlaw. I look like one."

"An impression you'd do well to encourage. Let the English think you're harum-scarum, a ragamuffin."

"Hagen knows better."

In the garden Hagen whistled for his horse-drawn gharry. He turned in surprise when the Governor asked, "You are familiar with the book by Norman Angell called *The Great Illusion*? And the Jewish conspiracy?"

"The book is not unknown to me." The Jewish conspiracy was anti-Zionist nonsense, and the book argued that war in the twentieth century was impossible. In both England and Germany movements had sprung up to propagate the latter faith. "I believe the author might be correct in theory."

"Do you?" asked the Governor eagerly. "Let me confide. So does the Kaiser! He fears the Zionists here, too."

Hagen pretended to be distracted by the arrival of the gharry. Was it possible the Kaiser regretted starting the war in Europe? It would be like the posturing idiot to put out peace feelers in this way.

"Even today the Kaiser is wrestling with a military clique whose idol is General von Bernhardi," said Schnee.

"Who preaches the manifest destiny of the German race is to rule the world," Hagen added.

The Governor coughed. "Too much importance is attached to that. Bernhardi has explained that is not quite what he meant. Now, Captain Hagen, I am certain if I transmit a full account of our talks directly to the Kaiser we shall receive a reply satisfactory to us both."

"A direct order from His Imperial Majesty?"

"Precisely as you propose. Neutrality in Africa."

Hagen fingered the outline of a cigarette case in his breast pocket, his senses abnormally sharp. He was enormous in presence as well as size, and the cigarette case was mute testimony to his indomitable will. Inscribed inside the heavy metal case were the words *"Never surrender."* Hagen, said his friends, was suicidally heroic. To stop the bullets and spears that must otherwise someday pierce his vitals, they had given him the cigarette case to carry over his heart. Already it bore the marks of many missiles. Too often, though, he went almost as naked as the savages he fought. Bandits pursued by Hagen through Malay jungles had likened him to their own hogs wallowing in red mud. He seemed covered in red, from his red thatch of hair running into buggers-grip sideburns down to the red pelt of belly and groin. His redness had been striking awe in mutinous subjects of the empire for eighteen of his thirty-eight years. He had split men's skulls, slit gizzards, choked tribal chiefs with his hairy-backed hands. He spoke strange dialects. He had been trained to rule in an English world where the King of Burma could be dethroned because the emperor in London disapproved of his drunkenness. Hagen, said his enemies, would bend over for a sodomizing maharaja or go down on a nigger queen if doing so would enrich the empire. What the Governor had just revealed unwittingly to this politically sensitive soldier was that Paul was still a formidable political obstacle.

With sudden insight Hagen said, "The Kommandeur made no mention of today's unfortunate shelling."

"The Colonel came from Kilimanjaro. You saw the state of his clothes, the mud plastering his face. A fine example, I must say, to his men."

"Don't bluster, Excellency."

Schnee sighed. "Your admiral signaled apologies and said his captains thought they had seen the masts of the *Koenigsberg* in the inland basin. What they did accomplish was the escape of a criminal about to hang. A dangerous revolutionary, well known to your Nairobi political intelligence. An American Negro who passes himself off as a Masai. A 'sport' or mutation, a genetic deviation from the norm."

"Ah!" said Hagen before the Governor became intoxicated by his own rhetoric. "Cornelius!"

The Governor read outrage in Hagen's voice. Reassured, he said slowly, "I could, I suppose, get the Kaiser's support in a joint Anglo-German operation to put him back on the gallows."

Hagen cocked his head, more alert now than ever. He heard the click and croak of life in the nearby mangrove swamp, the hysterical laugh of hyenas, the clear chime of the clock he had glimpsed in the house. The clock was a seventeenth-century Thomas Tompion. With luck he would liberate it very soon. He said softly, "May I respectfully submit, Excellency, that what we are really talking about is the execution of someone else? Someone whose fate will show who runs German East? In peacetime you are supreme military commander and the Kommandeur takes orders from you. In war he takes military command. He says we are at war now. You say no. There is a quick way to get rid of him."

"What are you suggesting, Captain Hagen?"

"Request from the Kaiser a clear instruction that the trial of Major Chester Truman is to be placed under your jurisdiction. Then make it a show trial and demonstrate that the American was conspiring with Jews and black rebels to subvert white authority in Africa. See that all the names come out in evidence—Cornelius, Jacob the Jew— and force Major Truman to reveal their connections with Colonel Paul von Lettow, a traitor to Germany."

"I need time," said the Governor. "Can you delay the landings?"

"No. The less time your Kommandeur has to pack Tanga with troops, the better chance we have of avoiding bloodshed."

A disturbance at the top of the staircase made the Governor look up with a guilty start. He heard the muted voices of Ada and Paul. He shook Hagen's hands and said piously, "Whatever we do must be with the interests of English and German colonists at heart, and in the Christian knowledge that we have our black brothers in our care."

"Of course," said Hagen.

5

"*Adui tayari!* The enemy is ready!"

The ancient Swahili call to battle sent a thrill of apprehension through the Tanga hospital where Paul had concentrated his defenses.

"The enemy is ready!" echoed an old askari, standing in the doorway of the medical director's office.

"Enemy's ready when you are," relayed Major Wolfe, his sense of humor stimulated by the prospect of action. He watched Paul scramble from his bed.

"Blast Hagen!" Paul said cryptically. "If he controlled their operations, this wouldn't happen yet."

Wolfe blinked. "Cornelius holds a line across the peninsula with his tribesmen. If the English land where you predicted, he'll keep them confused all day."

"What time is it?"

"Four in the morning."

Paul buckled on his gun belt. "Make a note in the war diary. A prophecy for tomorrow, Major. Tuesday, November third. By this day the black man will have smashed the myth of the Great White God."

Wolfe shuffled papers and said sarcastically, "These telegrams of support came in. None seem to be signed Black Sambo."

Paul riffled through the colonists' messages. So! *Some* civilians were all for a fight. They were the Boers and the army veterans. How many would stand the ultimate test of a prolonged campaign, only their wives and children would decide. He hefted the bandoliers and felt the sinking sensation that, for him, preceded African warfare: the sense of evil in everything, the sun remorseless and inescapable, the mist dripping in forests, dark and humid, where every mortal being moved in fear and turned against another in self-preservation. He lit a cigarette, and the sweet smell of opium was enough to calm the twitch in his scarred cheek.

"That American girl, the sister of Truman—" began Wolfe as Paul walked to the door.

"What about her?"

"Don't jump down my throat," protested Wolfe.

"I want her presence kept secret," warned Paul.

"The place is buzzing with rumors."

"You know how clever the English are with rumors. They started one that Truman was being shot tomorrow."

"And scared her out of her wits," said Wolfe, unprepared for the ferocious way Paul thrust his face back into the lamplight.

"So you've taken a squint at her, Major? Your English grandfather lost his head for sticking it in the wrong place! King Charles might have enriched your royal Bavarian blood, but he's not an example I'd like you to follow."

Major Wolfe stared into the empty space vacated by the Kommandeur and blew out his cheeks. On his desk was a sketch pad on which he had penciled from memory a portrait of Kate. He covered it quickly as Paul came banging back through the *kus-kus* tatties hanging in the doorway to cool the sticky night air. "Well, what about her?" Paul demanded.

"Shouldn't we hand her over to the English before there's any fighting?"

"You really think she'd go?"

"No," sighed Wolfe.

"Put her to work with Jacob analyzing English forces. His head's full of information, but it's no good to us stuck underneath his hat. Can she nurse? The casualties will be heavy. Can she use a gun?"

"Hold on, sir—"

"She's compromised already, Major. She's safer with us. And if she's with us, she'd better learn to fend for herself. Maybe she looks a butterfly to you, Major. Perhaps she's got whalebone in her corsets. But if I'm any judge, there's steel in her spine."

This time Wolfe followed his commander to the *kus-kus* and rested a hand against the freshly drenched mats of woven roots. The passing wind cooled his burning cheeks and he concentrated on finding a phrase to rhyme with "steel butterfly." He sometimes found the Prussian's armor quite impenetrable.

Paul moved swiftly along the darkened veranda. The hospital had been built on stilts beside a beach extending along the Tanga shoreline for two miles to the peninsula of Ras Kasone, the place where Skaramunga said the English were landing.

It was Skaramunga—"God's Soldier" in Swahili—who had reported the enemy's readiness. The old askari was Paul's gun bearer, cook, guide, valet, and bodyguard. He had come running straight from Cornelius, concealed with his men in the Ras Kasone swamps. Now, with the silver-gray vervet monkey perched on his shoulder, Skaramunga padded barefoot behind the Kommandeur. The monkey was not, as many thought, an indulgence. Paul used it to spot the enemy. This it could do with greater speed than a native tracker. Many misunderstood such idiosyncrasies on Paul's part. They thought of him as a Prussian, and they thought in clichés about Prussia. War was Prussia's national industry. Prussia was hatched from a cannon-ball. Prussia demanded *Obrigkeit*, slavish obedience, and *Kadavergehorsam*, submission of the mindless body to degrading military drills. One Englishman knew from experience not to believe his own propaganda about Prussians, and that was Myles Hagen. Now Paul needed to know if Hagen was masterminding the invasion. If he was, the danger to Paul was greater than losing this single battle.

One of Paul's junior officers waited near the steamer wharf. Lieutenant Wiedemann had not been happy at being sent to German East for attachment to what his brother Fritz jeeringly called the Ministry of Tourism. Fritz, fighting in the trenches of Europe, thought of the *Schutztruppe* as a glorified police force, of German settlers as war dodgers, and of Africa as corrupting. Lieutenant Wiedemann saluted Paul and reported that seven hundred German askari had taken up positions within Tanga, his tone implying they would be better occupied seeking out the enemy in the bush instead of skulking inside houses. He was silently critical of the way the Kommandeur dressed like a poor peasant. Even in the pale sea glow, the lieutenant could see Paul's face smeared and the steel of bayonet and rifle covered in grease. Disgusting!

Paul had to repeat an order, delivered so casually that Wiedemann pulled himself up with a jerk. "Capture their machine guns?"

"That is your task," Paul said patiently. "I need at least one working model of their Mark I Vickers. You're familiar with the Vickers?"

Wiedemann recited, "Fires five hundred rounds per minute on recoil with gas boost—"

"The point," Paul interrupted drily, "is that it requires two men to carry it. So make sure you have at least someone else with you."

"Yessir."

To ease the formality, Paul said, "The Vickers is formidable, but there's no such thing as an ultimate weapon."

Wiedemann stared. Did the Kommandeur really believe he was fearful of English weapons?

"When I was young like you," said Paul, taking over a bicycle brought up by Skaramunga, "I spoke with the inventor of the machine gun, Maxim." Paul took a tin of blacking from the askari and began daubing the bicycle's frame with it. "I said to Maxim the machine gun was inhuman, it cut men down like a scythe. Maxim laughed. Know what he replied?"

Wiedemann, still at attention, regarded his commander with unbelieving eyes. "No, sir."

"Maxim said, 'The gun's so terrible, it will make war impossible.'"

There was a pause. Wiedemann gave a polite laugh. Paul sighed and straightened up from the bicycle. "Take this, Lieutenant, and don't look aghast at the boot blacking. It might save your life by masking the glint of moonlight. I know you were trained for cavalry, Lieutenant, but don't look down your nose at the bicycle. It's swift, silent, and surprising to the enemy. In my kind of warfare, bicycles are worth more than horses. And in my kind of fighting, I've no room for spit and polish. Now, if you'll endeavor to bend your knees and elbows, perhaps you'd black out my bicycle in the same fashion?"

The tows had been slipped too soon, and the English lighters grounded a distance from the beaches. Myles Hagen was in the first boatload. His sense of grievance might have been greater if the supreme commander of Force B were not sharing the risk and discomfort with him. General Ha-Ha Splendid Aitken had overridden Hagen's objections to landing along the peninsula.

"For the love of Pete!" Hagen saw English officers rocking another flat-bottomed barge to make the occupants jump out. The fading moonlight glinted on steel. Turbaned heads clustered in resistance to muted orders.

Hagen turned and saw a Malay trooper from Malacca peering saucer-eyed at the gently lapping waves. "The water is warm and cannot harm you," hissed Hagen, catching the man off balance and tumbling him in. "Follow the example of your brave brother," he whispered hoarsely to the remaining men.

"But our brother is drowning," observed one.

"Not at all." A corporal's round nut-brown face rose above the gunwale. "He is bathing, silly fellow. *Laksum*, this is no time for taking bath-la!"

General Aitken waded ashore, making himself a solitary target. He threshed back again and glared at the men, who were unmoved. They spoke so many different dialects, thought Aitken helplessly. They followed so many damned silly taboos. Which was it started the Indian Mutiny? Hindus, offended by cow fat to grease the cartridges? Or Muslims, inflamed by pig grease? They were all foreign to his experience.

Pinggg! A bullet skated across the bay. *Ratatatat!* Hagen flopped into the water and ducked his head at the opening bars of battle, thinking some trigger-happy Rajput had let fly with a machine gun. An eerie green flash split the horizon, and the swift false dawn illuminated men sliding down the sides of the grounded lighters.

Everything smelled of disaster to Hagen. Men were running into the swamp, jabbering like monkeys. They were Nepalese mountain gunners, Bombay grenadiers, Kashmiris, and Gurkhas. Deadly fighters in familiar terrain. But Africa was not familiar.

After leaving Schnee, Hagen had returned to the *Goliath*'s wardroom to find the Force B commanders ready to go. He had expected opposition to his proposal for speeding up the invasion. Instead, the commanders were ahead of him. Much too far ahead.

"Our scouts report the peninsula totally undefended," Aitken had said. "Before the Hun gets wise, we'll have occupied it. With a firm base, we can put down any resistance from this Kommandeur."

"Don't do it!" said Hagen. "If I know Lettow, he's packed the territory with bush-wise tribesmen."

"We'll walk over any bunch of niggers," said a voice.

"For God's sake," Hagen insisted, "remember New Orleans."

"Where the wine grapes grow?" asked Aitken.

"*New* Orleans. America. We landed the flower of the Peninsular armies there after they thrashed Napoleon. They were going to walk over the natives, too."

"Make your point," barked one of the admirals.

"We lost four thousand men in the first ten minutes. The Americans lost eight."

The silence was broken by General Aitken. "We'll meet for lunch in the Kaiserhof. Tiffin in Tanga! Splendid!"

By lunchtime Hagen was stuck with the General among mangrove roots as big as bear traps. The swamp echoed to the grunts and groans of bewildered men. Most of them were insanely costumed: turbans, short cutaway open-fronted Indian jackets, white shirts, cummerbunds, knickerbockers, and puttees. Nearby squatted a Sikh staring stupefied at an old crocodile, belly down in a tidal channel, the teeth in its gaping man-length jaws gleaming in gums oozing pus. The Sikh wore a blush-rose turban, white pajamas, and Persian shoes of crimson leather. He was a picture of oriental elegance and ease, and how he had come to this particular spot, Hagen could not imagine. But he had no doubt about the intentions of the eighteen-foot crocs slithering down the muddy banks. To shout a warning would invite a bullet from the German askari snipers hidden in the trees, already armed with Lee-Enfields seized from the unguarded arms stockpiled on the beaches.

A young English subaltern had groped through the sodden embrace of vegetation toward the edge of the rubber plantation at the neck of the peninsula. Hagen, using glasses, winced when he saw the youngster's brass buttons with Zulu shields and crossed swords twinkling in the sunlight that fell through the trees. A Maxim gun chattered and the top half of the subaltern flew high in the air, and his pelvis and legs squirmed among the fleeing sepoys.

It would be a feast day for the crocodiles. Hagen swallowed bile but continued to watch as part of the subaltern's torso struck the brackish water. A six-foot tail of bone and armor smacked the torn head and sent it flying. Other crocodiles drifted astern, jaws open, throat membranes closed against the water.

An angry buzz drove the running English sepoys to the serpentine creeks. German sharpshooters were picking off hollow cedar logs hanging in the trees and put there by native beekeepers. Whipped into fury by the fusillade, the wild bees swarmed out and sought the nearest victims for their rage and venom. Bees settled on bare limbs and men cried out in sudden agony and fear. A young officer of the Loyal Lancashires ran screaming with his arms around his head, his eyes black with seething bees, and threw himself into a creek. The water erupted and crocodile jaws clamped tight around his thighs, leaving a flesh-pink froth.

"Sound the retreat!" ordered General Aitken.

"In the face of a few hundred enemy rifles?" demanded Hagen in a sudden and perverse fury.

"My estimate is three thousand." A bullet whistled away the General's outraged dignity. "Back to the beach!" he shouted and wriggled backward into a clump of elephant grass.

Hagen followed the withdrawal in disbelief. There would still have been time for a late lunch at the Kaiserhof.

Kate had been awakened by the sound of gunfire. She stared uncomprehendingly at the rafter poles above her cot. She felt stifled by layers of hot air. She was still gathering her wits when Magdalene von Prinz burst into the room.

"I need an extra pair of hands to help my nurses."

"At once. I've worked in hospitals before."

"Good!" Without ceremony, Magdalene dragged her off.

The wounded began to trickle in toward noon. Kate was appalled. She worked alongside Magdalene, bandaging, making splints, cutting with scissors and knives. She felt inadequate, but whenever she looked up, she saw in the eyes of the black nurses an astonishment and trust that made her go on.

An askari lay on the floor of the main ward. Half his stomach had fallen out of a ragged tear between his navel and groin.

"Dum-dum," she heard from the bearlike man bending over him. "The bastards!" The big man wore a white soutane, and his head was crowned with a mane of white hair. His hands were at the wounded man's neck, gripping it with thick claws, thumbs pressing inward beneath the angles of the chin. The askari's eyes rolled and the head fell limp.

A young Englishman on the adjacent mattress said, "My God, murdering your own men!"

"Dum-dum," repeated the white-haired man in the gown. "Is that the way you English fight?"

"Cowards and Boers, perhaps," said the Englishman, raising himself on one elbow. "But not us."

Kate looked in horror and disbelief at the dead askari. "But you're a priest," she said to the man who had broken his neck.

"I'm also a doctor. Neither calling would cleanse my conscience if the poor fellow were left to die in agony." The man got up heavily.

"Count Kornatzki, look here." Calling from across the aisle was Tom von Prinz, probing the purple coils and yellow layers of fat issuing from another dead askari's belly. "It's a dum-dum did this."

Kornatzki lumbered to his side. Prinz was bellowing at the wounded Englishman that he knew dum-dum bullets when he saw them—regular English cartridges with the steel point snipped off so the bullet ripped and tumbled through the victim's body. The Englishman was shouting back.

Kate saw men with murder in their flaming eyes. Outside on the battlefield homicide was legal. Here they could only scream at each other. She turned and fled into the dispensary.

A black woman was lifting her arms to hang up a native *kanga* robe, and the muscles in her breasts tightened as she turned to look down at Kate. Four black girls in white uniforms swiveled big oval eyes in Kate's direction, their hands still moving methodically between pans of water, enamel dishes, surgical instruments, and bandages.

"What the hell difference does it make?" asked Kate. "Blunt bullets. Sharp bullets."

The four black nurses paused. They were Chagga from the slopes of Kilimanjaro. They had come with their men. One askari sat with his bleeding head between his hands, patiently waiting for treatment. Beside him was the baby of his *bibi*, his woman. He looked up when Kate lurched threateningly in the infant's direction. The injured soldier sprang to his feet.

The nurses froze. The tall woman dropped her *kanga* and moved swiftly to intercept Kate. She had striking gold-flecked eyes, was still naked from the waist up, and her breasts jutted in a beam of sunlight as she drew back an arm and slapped the white girl.

Kate groped for a chair and sat down. The Chagga girls and the askari gazed awestruck at this black woman who had the audacity to hit a white. She stood in front of Kate, took Kate's head, and held it against her hard, flat belly. She stroked Kate's hair.

Kate closed her eyes, comforted by the strong earthy smell of the woman's body. Bewildering images of the past few days burst across her vision. She shuddered and recovered her self-control. She felt the woman's body relax, and she looked up the long slant of the light-brown breasts and the graceful neck into a face of haughty beauty.

"I'm Lanni. You understand—I had to stop any panic." The eyes glanced across at the Chagga girls, and she said something quickly to them in Swahili. The girls became all dutiful attention again. "If Kornatzki sensed any failure of discipline, we'd all be out of here in a flash." The woman picked up a triangle of white cotton and flung it over her shoulders, knotting two corners in front.

"Kornatzki? The priest?"

"Count Kornatzki. Our medical director. He might have been a dedicated missionary once. Even he may have forgotten."

"I forget nothing!" It was Kornatzki who came charging into the dispensary. He lifted his white soutane and examined his black boots, gleaming wetly. His skirts were stained rusty-red. He sat down suddenly and began to remove the boots. "Young woman, what did you mean, invading my wards—?"

Lanni said quickly, "She's the sister of Major Truman."

Kornatzki paused in the act of handing one boot to the black orderly with him. "So! You rescued Cornelius?"

"Yes," whispered Kate. She saw Lanni's eyes widen.

"Brave thing to do, lass. You've got nerve. Why break down over blood and guts, then? All right, I know. Being a spectator's not the same as taking part, is it? Lanni! Put her to work! And no more hysterics, please! Not in my hospital. I don't want my old auntie nagging me now."

Lanni led Kate back to the wards. "His old auntie," she said, "is the Kaiser's mama."

Count Kornatzki took from a cupboard the striped knobkerrie he called his "Never-Love-Thine-Enemy" club. It had been the weapon of countless Uganda kings until a benign old monarch introduced more democratic methods and used it as a speaker's gavel. A rival had brained him with it. The savage successor had been killed later by Kornatzki, who kept the club as a reminder of the realities of life.

With the club hanging from his wrist, the medical director moved into the adjoining clinic where Paul was entering by way of a window. The Kommandeur swung his other leg over the ledge and dropped inside the room.

"Unorthodoxy can go too far," growled Kornatzki.

"The most orthodox rule I know is that the shortest distance between two points is a straight line." Paul dropped his rifle on a table. His face was streaked with black powder and blood, his jacket dark with sweat. "We've pushed back the first wave."

"I suppose this is siesta?"

"In England they call it the tea interval." Paul looked over his commandeered desk. "Where's Major Wolfe?"

"He went an hour ago. Left a pile of messages brought by runner from the *Koenigsberg*."

Paul had unlocked the war diary, a brass-bound volume kept inside a padlocked ammunition box. Kornatzki coughed and said, "Colonel—?" He coughed again, and his gravelly voice dropped to a more intimate level. "Paul, my boy, why exactly is the Truman girl here?"

Paul lifted his head sharply. "What's she done now?"

"Nothing. Except." Kornatzki stopped. "This is hardly the time to share my thoughts about militant feminists, but I've a feeling in my gut that Miss Truman's one."

"I put her in Wolfe's charge," said Paul, ignoring the stuttered words. "She was to help Jacob."

"Jacob the Jew is deciphering material from Mombasa."

"Just what I need. The English are mounting a second expedition from there." Paul's right arm was shaking, and he held out a trembling hand for Kornatzki to see. "Got a tame witch doctor who can fix this? It's the same old pain."

"There's an essence in the top right-hand drawer Chief Obwe swears by. It might knock you out, though."

"Nothing more will happen before tonight," said Paul, opening the drawer. "Then, night operations and English killer squads."

"Hagen's trademark?"

"If Hagen takes charge." Paul sniffed the bottle of native medicine and made a face. He replaced the stopper without touching the contents, leaned back in a chair, and rested his feet on the desk. "Hagen didn't plan today's fiasco. He was the political brains, though. No formal declaration of war. Just a burst of wireless messages to London announcing the start of a pacification exercise. By tonight, unless I've lost my touch, I'd bet on the generals pleading with Hagen to dispose of me."

"One assassin can save a lot of bloodshed."

"Yes," murmured Paul. "Either way."

He closed his eyes.

Kate took a break. Nobody stopped her leaving the hospital grounds. The sun was low in the sky and burned fiercely against her face. There was no wind, and the heat made her dizzy. But she had to see. Both sides had now vacated the battleground. Its size surprised her. It was so small, hardly more than a New York City block.

She made her way awkwardly along the waterfront and came upon skinny brown bodies with English army scarves wrapped around their faces against bees. Each man had been stabbed in the back with his own bayonet. Her stomach reacted—she vomited. She forced herself to stare down at a boy in *Schutztruppe* uniform, his tongue forced out between lips drawn in a mirthless, gaping smile, his eyes covered already with flies. She remembered the black woman who slapped her face to stop her hysteria. "I won't do that again." Not a tear would she shed for a man again.

Another shadow joined her own. She felt a strong hand on her shoulder. "Don't mourn the dead," said Paul. "The living need you."

"Half the wounded are English," she said. "Why not shoot them? Better yet, bayonet them. Stick them like pigs. You can save bullets and food and medicine." She took a breath. "You want me to help patch them up? Make them fit to kill?"

"On the march, both our own and English askari kill the badly wounded, Miss Truman. There are sound reasons—"

"Of course!"

"Your brother would tell you these native practices are difficult to stop."

"My brother is not an army man!"

"Don't say that!" Paul's voice had lost all softness. "You understand? The title of major stands between him and the firing squad."

She stared into the scarred face. Her body shook with an unexpected sensation. The images of mutilation faded into pleasuring waves of color. She shaded her eyes against the sun and felt the voluptuous tides recede when he took his hand from her shoulder. She thought she heard him say, "Do as I tell you, if you want your brother to live."

With an effort of concentration, she asked, "What should I do?"

"When we evacuate Tanga, come with us."

She did not respond but looked at the battlefield dead, trying to absorb the sense of his words.

"This is strange warfare," said Paul. "You'll not find it in any military manual. We sell space to buy time. Those who get killed are the coin of this trading."

She turned to hide her sudden revulsion. She had considered making love to this man to save her brother. But it would be like bedding with death. She lifted her head quickly and smiled, all actress now, and was surprised to see in his face some hint of aroused emotion.

6

MYLES HAGEN sat in the back of a pedicab with the oilskin hood raised against inquisitive eyes. The wheeled basket chair tilted and turned, giving Hagen views of German strongpoints around the railroad station and the hospital. He had stained his face and hands so that a casual observer would take him for an Indian merchant in his mildewed solar topee and crumpled off-white suit. If the *Schutztruppe* caught him in this twilight period between peace and war, Paul Lettow would shoot him and deny all knowledge.

"Gideon?"

"Yes, *bwana?*"

"Turn down this lane and pedal slowly by the hospital."

The Kikuyu wheeled round. He was a Nairobi Intelligence Service agent, mission school clever. Near the hospital entrance, on a rise, he stopped and Hagen raised his dull black-cased binoculars. By God! There was Paul now!

"Let's get out of here. Fast!" whispered Hagen.

Paul lowered his glasses, smiling. He was leaning against his bicycle on the headland opposite Hagen, watching one of his own German officers masquerading as himself. He said to his companion, "Lieutenant, lesson number one. No matter how well your enemy knows you, you can always make him use that knowledge to his own disadvantage."

"Yes, sir," said young Kurt Wahle, not seeing at all. He was looking in the other direction, with a good view of English barges unloading mules, motorcycles, and more troops. "Sir, do we fight or lick their boots?"

"Junior officers don't question strategy, boy."

Kurt Wahle listened with half an ear to the Kommandeur's reprimand. He stood astride his own bicycle and wondered what good it was against the enemy's advanced weapons. The *Manual of Arms*, of course, would make any bicycle sound formidable, a giant leap in technology, turning a five-hour cross-country trek into a fifty-minute joy ride. He shifted attention back to the Kommandeur. "The question, sir, is not mine."

"Then whose?"

"Thunderbolt's, sir."

"Dammit, Wahle, you must learn to come to the point. Take me to him."

Young Wahle denied himself the pleasure of asking who it was first strayed from the point. Instead, he slid back onto the saddle and wobbled off along an antelope track. Paul had picked out the boy as a born bush fighter. He was nineteen, pimply, with mousy hair, a cutaway chin, and a painfully bobbing Adam's apple. He might have fitted into the Heidelberg academic scene as a botanist, but he had sailed with his father to see the Great Imperial German East Exhibition and now they were both caught here. The father, a retired general in his sixties, had offered to serve under the Kommandeur, though a mere colonel. Young Wahle had made two journeys into the interior, and Paul calculated he would prove an imaginative commando, if his need for adventure did not kill him first.

Cornelius waited among the mangroves whose arthritic roots clawed into the sea. Thunderbolt was the code name given him and his forces, identified as often as not by nothing more than a zigzag flash of white lime on a dark forehead or arm.

"We had an agreement," said Cornelius softly. He sat on a rotten stump, positioned so that nobody could approach without triggering an explosion of birds.

"Indeed we did," confirmed Paul.

"My leadership depends on you keeping that promise. The tribal chiefs need visible victories. In return, you will get men unlimited."

"That was the understanding."

"Then what is this?" Cornelius stood up in the jungle gloom and recited phrases that Paul recognized as typical of a Berlin telegram. He was not altogether astonished. The warship *Koenigsberg* was relaying wireless signals by *ruga-ruga* couriers. The mercenaries performed faultlessly, running with cleft sticks held vertically for extraordinary distances—but as ready to deliver an imperial decree to an Englishman as to a German or a Thunderbolt agent.

"From the Kaiser's lackeys to the Governor," said Paul. "You don't give that credence, do you?"

"It says there's to be no resistance to the English. No power to the tribes. No pardon for Truman. No yielding to your authority."

"My reply will be victories. Berlin can never resist them."

Cornelius watched the Kommandeur's face in the sunlight filtering through the tousled heads of trees that dropped from salted roots. "You had better clarify this problem of the supreme German authority in the colony, just as I must. The tribal chiefs wonder if I might betray them and if you might betray me."

"You are obsessed with fears of betrayal." Paul gestured impatiently. "I'll tell you where treachery lies. If the Governor persists in sending messages through the *Koenigsberg*, he'll betray her position."

"On the other hand, if he hadn't used the *Koenigsberg*, I would never have heard about the Kaiser's interference." Cornelius let the implication hover. "How do I know the Governor won't overrule you even now? Then my men are trapped."

"Stick to the plan. By my oath, there will be guns and ammunition for every Masai warrior."

The reference pleased Cornelius. Like many American-educated blacks, he felt at a disadvantage among other Africans, but he still belonged to Masailand. It covered both German and English territories. The Masai kept their own standing army of *moran* warriors, six-footers with the faces of fiends. Stoically, they taught their sons to face pain by flaying their foreskins and testicles during initiation rites.

Cornelius was wearing the Masai-style goatskin blanket over one shoulder, and he carried an eight-foot spear. A two-edged sword, the *simi*, hung at his waist in its red-stained oxhide scabbard. In wielding these weapons, he was as expert as his Masai blood brothers. He said, less tensely, "Has Israel prepared the treaties?"

"Israel never sleeps," Paul replied in a tired voice, feeling the crisis recede. Israel was the code name given Jacob Kramer. The word meant nothing here to whites or blacks.

"He feels death snapping at the heels of his people," murmured Cornelius. "As do we."

Returning to the hospital, Kurt Wahle said to Paul, "I was interested in his remark about the Jews, sir."

"He studied theology."

"Beg pardon, sir. He's read more than the Bible."

"Karl Marx, no doubt."

"And Professor Merker. Merker says the Masai are the original Jewish tribes who came south—"

Paul had a great urge to deflate young Wahle's ego but held his tongue while the boy skidded his bicycle around a termite mound. "Merker claims," said Paul coldly, "the Masai have astonishing tracking skills, something I don't associate with Hebrews. Best rely on your own prophets, Lieutenant. Goethe"—he waited for Wahle to catch up—"Goethe says if you want God's help against adversity, walk erect."

Wahle gave a fair imitation of a dim-witted smile. "That's a bit difficult on a bicycle," he said.

By nightfall Cornelius had been joined by veterans of the *Afrika für die Farbigen* uprisings. They kidnapped a pair of young Loyal Lancashire riflemen and, in a parody of kitchen English, told the boys what would happen to prisoners. Then, after a pretense at a scuffle, they let the riflemen escape.

"Friggin' 'ell," reported one. "Big black bastids, they wos. Everyone 'ere eats English flesh and calls it pig's bottom. Chops it orf a white man which they keeps alive while they eats 'im bit by bit. The best parts are kept fer the chiefs, who likes balls and cocks fried when they 'aven't been chewed orf by their wives." This story quickly spread among the bogged-down invaders. "That there jungle's full of bleedin' lions and tigers and bollock-naked cannibals," said the instant experts. Three hours after dark much of Force B was exhausted by the disturbances caused by Cornelius's men rattling cans and flashing lights and by the nameless fears fertilized by the tales of atrocity.

"You had Hagen in your sights and didn't shoot him!" exclaimed Count Kornatzki in disbelief. "You're mad!"

"Hagen's more useful alive when he's full of misinformation," said Paul. "And I don't like shooting a sitting duck."

Kornatzki scratched his beard. "You'd be lost without Hagen.

You love him. Every soldier needs an enemy. Hagen's the necessary enemy for you."

They were talking in the military command post Paul had installed at the hospital. The tree frogs outside filled the night with tiny staccato bursts of song.

"You require the love of a woman," Kornatzki continued. "It's a paradox. You wouldn't love Hagen this way if you loved a woman." His face lit up. "Speaking of which—"

Lanni brushed through the *kus-kus* curtaining the doorway and glanced inquiringly at Kornatzki with eyes that sharpened his wits. Kornatzki had known a lover of hers in Berlin who called her after Balzac's *la fille aux yeux d'or*. Golden eyes. He knew the strange story of her grandfather in Zanzibar, the Iman of Oman, who had cast out her mother, a princess, for marrying a common German. The girl combined the qualities of the Nilo-Hamitic tribes that roamed south from Araby and those of her Prussian father, who had been an explorer. Kornatzki thought of her romantically as one of the Lost Legion of Marc Antony. She had the prominent cheekbones, the curved nose, thin lips, and long lean legs characteristic of the Nile. She was now wearing a black Arab *burka* that enabled her to move unseen in the darkness outside.

She said softly, "Hagen's on the grounds."

Kornatzki looked sharply at Paul and muttered, "This time! With your first shot!"

"Wiedemann, by the window!" Paul extinguished the lamp. "Lanni, next door with the American."

Lieutenant Wiedemann had been indulging his favorite dream of service on the Western Front, away from gossiping old soldiers like Paul, away from somnolent, decaying Africa. He poked his old-fashioned Mauser rifle haphazardly through the open window and felt, to his astonishment, a weight on the end of the barrel as if it had turned into a fishing pole with a mammoth catch on the line.

Hagen and a Gurkha crouched on the veranda, covered by Gideon the Kikuyu. They had been landed ashore after Hagen argued that lives could be saved during the lull in fighting if the Kommandeur were eliminated. On this score Hagen commanded attention because he had an impressive record with killer squads in conjunction with young Lawrence in Arabia, who was carving out a promising career with the Eastern Mediterranean Special Services Intelligence Bureau, the so-called Arab Bureau, by which the British Empire hoped to eliminate some of its enemies.

When the Mauser rifle was poked casually through the window above Hagen's head, he responded as if his work for the bureau had been tailored to this end. He knew the Mauser's weaknesses as an outdated weapon. His fingers hooked over the barrel at a point near the muzzle. When he pulled down, the leverage almost jerked Wiedemann through the window. The Lieutenant's finger squeezed the trigger. The rifle exploded in Hagen's face, and the bullet whined past his ear.

The Mauser was notorious for emitting black smoke. Wiedemann fell backward into the clinic, blinded and choking. Count Kornatzki replaced him and groped until his strong fingers dug into Hagen's mane of hair. The sensation of personal combat took Kornatzki back to his struggle with the warrior king for the knobkerrie. The kerrie was on Kornatzki's desk, and it was Wiedemann who recovered it and vaulted onto the veranda.

Myles Hagen tore free from the hands at the window and fell onto his back, still dazzled by the muzzle flash. Through mists of pain he saw the knobkerrie, but not Wiedemann's face. The club was too distinctive to be mistaken for any other than the one Hagen had long coveted. He saw the club swing, and he kicked violently at Wiedemann's ankles.

The crouching Gurkha slid the curved *kukri* knife from its sheath and moved with precision as Wiedemann was thrown off balance. Wiedemann was bent back by the momentum of the swinging club he carried, and his neck was stretched to receive the classic death blow of the *kukri*—striking through the larynx and all the great blood vessels and bone of the neck. The Gurkha pirouetted gracefully and sank to his heels. Above him swayed the suddenly headless trunk, spraying blood like a fountain. Wiedermann's body completed its spasmodic circle and folded, as if to lay the knobkerrie at Hagen's feet.

Tom von Prinz had completed his rounds of the sentry posts when the uproar began. He thumped along the ward where Lanni had taken Kate, just as the door at the other end burst open. Hagen and the Gurkha darted between the cots shrouded in white mosquito netting. Prinz, not daring to fire among wounded men, swung his rifle like a club and chased the Gurkha, now leaping from bed to bed, his *kukri* slashing the nets.

Kate saw Paul appear from the clinic and Hagen spring at him with the club. From inside Kornatzki's den, the count was roaring like a wounded bear. Hagen hesitated, unprepared for the sudden tackle from behind. It was Kate, diving for the Englishman's legs as she had so many times in childhood tackled her brother at football practice.

The ward was lit only by the moonlight outside. Paul backed against the doorpost. He saw tipped beds and shrouds of mosquito netting, then Tom von Prinz shaking and clawing blindly at the little Gurkha clinging to his head. Kate was astride Myles Hagen on the floor. Lanni was hitting the Englishman's head with a chamber pot whose contents she had already poured over him.

"Get up!" Paul said, gesturing with his pistol.

"Don't let the Geordie near you!" yelled Prinz. "Conk him with the pisspot."

"A brother limey," Hagen interjected, dripping urine.

"I said get up!" Paul's voice cracked like a whip. "Tell your *jemadar* to release my officer." He lifted the pistol toward the Gurkha clinging to Prinz like a spider monkey, his knife's blade against Prinz's throat.

"On your guarantee of safe conduct," Hagen said promptly. "I came to resume negotiations."

Paul's laugh was without humor. There was a horrid halitus emanating from Hagen, drenched in Wiedemann's blood as well as in urine. "You'll be lucky if we hang you for nothing worse than murder."

"Never mind me!" Hagen straightened up, a cunning expression on his face. "Hang Truman! If you don't, your Governor will. A signal's on its way now from Berlin."

There was another roar of pain from Kornatzki's clinic. The count shuffled out, clutching his crotch. "The bastard got away," bellowed Kornatzki and then stopped. He peered into the ward and saw the knife gleaming at Prinz's throat.

"What signal?" Paul asked in a steel-edged whisper.

"Instructions to Governor Schnee," continued Hagen. "Dispose of the trial either by military court under the Kommandeur or, if the Kommandeur defies authority, under the Governor. I'd rather deal with you than with Governor Schnee. You and I should work together to keep Africa under control."

Kate listened with growing astonishment. She was pressed against a wall by Lanni's warning hand. It seemed obscene that two men who seconds earlier were dedicated to killing each other could now talk together of killing her brother.

"If you resume fighting tomorrow," Hagen was saying, "we all lose in the long run to the blacks. You know who'll take our place?"

"I think you'd better take your thugs out of here," Paul said softly.

"Let me finish. Germany and England will be replaced by the Zionists." Hagen wiped his red beard with the corner of a bed sheet. "Lord Rothschild has resurrected the issue of African land for the Jews. A commission is on its way from England."

Gideon the Kikuyu had lost Myles Hagen in the scuffle. Now, creeping back through the clinic, he glimpsed his commander through the ward doorway. He still gripped the bolt spring of the bayonet with which he had attacked Kornatzki's sex organs. His shadow flickered across the floor and caught Kate's eye. She cried out and flung herself forward as the Kikuyu lunged at Paul. The renewed commotion triggered nerves already tense. Prinz somersaulted the Gurkha over his head. Paul was knocked sideways by Kate and at once fired his revolver at Hagen, who leaped back. Gideon was carried by his own momentum past the Kommandeur and skidded down the ward among patients still disentangling themselves from the nets. Shooting began outside. In the pandemonium only Paul was aware that Kate had attempted to join Hagen in his escape.

"I got Count Kornatzki," Hagen reported to General Aitken aboard the *Goliath*. "I never knew a German to give up the luxuries of the court for a dog's collar and a syringe the way he did."

"I'd rather you'd got the Kommandeur."

"Kornatzki's not a bad second. He was the effective governor of German East, in terms of real power. He could get anything done through his network of medicine men."

"Witch doctors!"

"Not in the sense you think," objected Hagen. "Folk medicine's powerful stuff. I don't dismiss it."

"So you kill Kornatzki. He doesn't seem all that important to me," said Aitken with a sigh.

Hagen shrugged. "Kornatzki was on British territory last month, delivering vaccine against smallpox in Uganda. A fine spectacle. English and German flags flying side by side and our French comrades green with envy. Why? Because Uganda's divided between an alliance of English and German Protestant missions against the French Catholics!"

Aitken shook his head in honest bafflement. He knew Hagen had a direct line to Winston Churchill, who was running the Royal Navy and threatened to take over African operations, too. You never knew with Churchill. He'd got a bee in his bonnet about Uganda ever since visiting there. He was also directing the key British intelligence agencies, which was why you dared not fool around with Hagen.

"Well," said Hagen after the long silence, "I'd better get below and read telegrams."

"And write a few?" suggested General Aitken jealousy.

"You'll get copies," promised Hagen, knowing the supreme commander's neurotic fear that things might be said to London behind his back. "I'll even give you a recap on Kornatzki, poor chap."

7

Telegraphie des Deutschen Reichs

Telegramm

Majestaet des Kaisers und Koenigs

Berlin. November 2, 1914 . . .

Myles Hagen had smiled over his copy of an intercepted telegram to the German Governor requiring an urgent reply. Captain Max Looff cursed. The *Koenigsberg* was in enough danger without having to break wireless silence again to give the English another chance to fix his position. Looff gambled that the Royal Navy would concentrate the Cape of Good Hope squadron around Tanga, one day's steaming from the Rufiji delta where the corsair lay. The delta was so big, covering an area greater than metropolitan New York, that searchers must explore every serpentine creek.

The English cruiser *Chatham* was lying far offshore to give masthead lookouts a wider range of scan. Most of the delta trees were in partly salted water, which made them grow like tall telegraph poles with the only foliage clustered at the top. By a monstrous piece of luck, a lookout had seen such a tree move. It turned out to be the *Koenigsberg*'s mainmast, camouflaged with palm fronds. Signals had been flashed to the Royal Navy cruisers *Dartmouth* and *Weymouth*, which had been monitoring the *Koenigsberg*'s wireless. As darkness fell, the three warships covered the Rufiji's mouth with eighteen six-inch guns. They were still uncertain of the Germans' exact location, but their wireless direction finders were ready for the briefest of German transmissions.

Max Looff had sent copies of Berlin's earlier messages by *ruga-ruga* to Paul and the Governor. Now he sat under an awning to speculate on what had given Berlin this unaccustomed verbal diarrhea. One signal had advised the Governor to take responsibility for Major Truman, the American spy, but it was neither an order nor an authorization. Max Looff guessed the Kaiser was playing the Kommandeur against the Governor, with imperial support ultimately going to the man who came out on top.

A flicker of what seemed to be lightning caught Looff's attention. Seconds later he heard the rumble of exploding shells and curious waterspout noises like the spattering of a torrential rain. He had the *Koenigsberg* in malarial swamps, twelve kilometers inland, well beyond maximum English range. Still, it was best to be cautious. He ordered all lights out, despite the effect on already low morale. Then he told Radio Officer Niemeyer, "Ignore Berlin's request for acknowledgment. Enough damage has been done."

Myles Hagen had always broken the rules. One was a ban on personal diaries. As intelligence chief, Hagen kept meticulous notes in a code of his own invention. He wrote assessments in the guise of bird watcher's notes. In the dark hours before Force B launched a fresh assault against Tanga, he wrote in this book, scattered with sketches and nature notes and entitled with typical schoolboy humor *The Bird Watching Notes of an English Country Gentleman*:

Aerial scavengers seen over the battlefield: white-necked raven, Egyptian kite, hooded kingfisher . . . Paul von Lettow is utilizing the ambitions of tribal chiefs and Zionist plotters to serve his own wild dreams. He wants to turn Africa into *Das Land wo die Kanonen blühen*—which freely translated means the land where the cannons bloom! For this most rigid of Teutonic knights, Africa blossoms as the perfect theater of war where professional soldiers can fight without interference from politicians. His military record shows his arrogant disregard for civilian authority. He is a man immune to sentiment, bred for war, uncomfortable with companions other than warriors. He has specific objectives, of course. One is to make Uganda into Jewganda, as the English settlers call it whenever would-be Jewish pioneers show their noses. Like any emperor bent on conquest, he makes expedient alliances with those he can bend to the yoke. These allies include:

Cornelius Jeremy Oakes. In 1890, when aged sixteen, he was spotted among the Masai by American missionaries. Contrary to some belief, he was not born in the U.S.A. but was sent there. A Negro Baptist Seminary in Virginia and Lincoln University in Pennsylvania educated him. I suppose the missionaries are to be congratulated for having understood the superior mental powers of the Masai, who almost certainly are the "master race" descended from Marc Antony's Lost Legion (they drill like centurions—*but why circumcision?*). He returned to Africa near the end of the Boer Wars against England and inflamed the tribes through his oratory and vision of a black Zionist movement "to take over Africa, arm it, and make it defend Negroes the world over." Cornelius later organized the first Africa National Congress (1912) with funds supplied by Senator John Morgan of Alabama, who had his own reasons for wanting to speed the reverse migration of Negroes out of the U.S. to Africa. Cornelius became disenchanted when the first wave of immigrants sailed on a chartered steamer, the *Liberation*, under a bizarre American black, "Chief Sam," who selected them mostly from threatened Negro communities in Oklahoma. It soon became obvious Chief Sam was being used by rednecks to lure blacks out of Africa. Cornelius then joined Chilembwe, another U.S.-trained black radical. Since then they have been in constant touch with Zionist Marxists and with rebel chiefs in German and British Africa. Cornelius Jeremy Oakes is a savage Bolshevik with a veneer of Western culture and the foulest of hearts. Like the revolution that eats its young, he is the black revolutionary who will eat his own tribal disciples when he gets hungry enough and especially if we cheat him of the rewards promised by the Kommandeur.

Paul von Lettow sees Africa as the battleground where he can first destroy the British Empire—a brilliant, imaginative, and, of course, quite mad concept. Bits of that fragmented empire would be given Cornelius in return for his help. Later in these notes I shall focus on other German allies in the land of the blooming cannons.

Then Hagen rode in yet another invasion barge for Tanga.

Paul lay sleepless on a cot in Kornatzki's clinic. He was suffering one of the wretched nights that often followed stress. Pain radiated from where he had fractured a spinal vertebra while serving with the Dutch Boers. Opium softened the pain, which he feared only because it could someday catch him at a critical moment in battle.

Lanni, sensing his agony, rose from her sleeping place on the veranda. She found cigarette papers and began rolling him a cigarette with opium mixed in the tobacco. She said, "The American. She's walking out there."

"She's not accustomed to hot nights."

"She's crying."

"Then comfort her," Paul said abruptly.

"No." Lanni lit the cigarette for him. She listened to Paul swearing quietly in the darkness, and finally she gave him his clothes from a chair. "Let the girl comfort *you*. Don't speak of comforting her."

"What have you told her?"

"Nothing."

"Keep it that way." He picked up his shirt. "She's a rebel, but only a white rebel and of small use to you."

"Unless she helps us win," murmured Lanni.

Paul found Kate Truman on the hospital beach. The boom of the surf concealed his approach.

"It's unsafe to be here alone, Miss Truman."

She gave a start. "I thought your enemies had run away, Colonel."

"They'll be back. And they still have snipers who don't distinguish between Germans and neutrals."

"What a goose I am." She let him walk her away from the silvered sea. "I see what men do, yet I still expose myself to their guns."

"Not an unusual impulse."

She looked at him sharply. "I hate your guns."

"So much," he asked, "that you wanted to run with Hagen to safety?"

"You see too much." She hesitated. "No, I did not intend to run away. I wanted Hagen to give a message to an American friend—a man I knew in Berlin."

"About your brother?" Paul rested a hand lightly on her shoulder. "You were wise. I know the friend you mean. Your brother will need sympathetic publicity. Don't be surprised. I guessed what you might try to do." ·

They were far from the surf now. Kate marveled at the softness of the night, a magic that softened reality. Then she heard the grunt of animals in the bush. Shivering, she remembered the bodies ungathered.

"Don't endanger your brother by being impatient," Paul said. "Give me time—"

"To decide if he's useful." She added angrily, "I'd rather not discuss this now." A vibration, a low, grumbling roar, shook the night air. Kate trembled.

Paul recognized the arrogant authority of the pride. "Lions," he said. "Nothing stops the lions, not even war."

"Lions! Here in the town?"

"Tanga's just a bite in the wilderness. The lions work as teams, stampeding livestock into the jaws of the females. They maraud through the native *shambas*, the plantations."

Kate shivered and stepped back into the deep shadows cast by feathery coconut palms.

"Kate. *Kätzchen*. Tomorrow I shall order the retreat."

"What did you call me? *Kitten?*"

Paul laughed awkwardly. "It's how I think of you. *Tapfer*. Gutsy. Feisty. Full of fight. But still a kitten in need of protection."

"That's a strange notion in the light of events."

"Call it a fancy. However, I'd like you to travel upcountry with me. For your brother's sake. I know how you feel about retreat—"

" 'Enemy advances, we retreat,' " she quoted. " 'Enemy tires, we attack.' "

"Where did you learn this?" asked Paul, thunderstruck.

"From a military paper. Sun-Tzu invented the tactics in China. You wrote the paper. I should have remembered because I did some research on you in Berlin after you left me your photograph."

"Which you nearly tore up."

"So you did some research too?"

"I'd never met a steel butterfly before."

"Is that what you thought?"

"It's what I suspected. Though you were crying a few minutes ago."

"I cried for what happened here a few hours ago."

Paul said slowly, "The stupidity of men is sometimes depressing. Sometimes it would be better to die in battle."

Kate said after a long silence, "Do you still condemn Social Darwinism?"

"You have a remarkable memory. But you never told me your interpretation of Darwin."

"You flatter me by remembering. It was, of course, the ship's captain who interrupted us."

Neither spoke for a moment and then Paul asked abruptly, "Well, then? Are we on opposite sides of the argument? War seems to me a necessary evil. Let the experts on human nature decide if we've inherited violence from our ancestors."

"*You* were the student of human nature, so you said."

"My work requires me to study how men react to violence. Our scientists here search for the roots of violence in man's history. Some say we kill because our ape-man forebears had a lust to kill. Others say Darwin never did claim war was in our blood."

"If war's your work, you can't believe in progress through team-work."

"A soldier defends the fruit of teamwork."

"What are you defending here?" she scoffed. "German culture?"

"Yes." He moved as if to escape an unpalatable topic. "A good soldier today travels far to fend off an attack. This is too subtle to discuss here and now!"

Kate said swiftly, "There'd be no need to defend if there were nobody attacking."

"And nobody would attack if we lived by love instead of vio-lence," Paul recited. "I'm familiar with the litany. I question its practicability."

"But we do have a choice. Evolve through love. An act of imagi-nation. It distinguishes us from animals."

Kate's impassioned statement met with another silence, as if again she had angered Paul.

The edge of night had been moving imperceptibly back from the sea's horizon. A raven swooped from the tree as the first turtledove began its soft morning cooing. In a few seconds the dawn chorus of birds would break into full song. Paul's mind began to race with the accelerating day. He noted almost absentmindedly the jerky flight of a Kilimanjaro sunbird. Out of the sea mist rose a flare.

Kate felt a weight of sorrow descending upon her again. "I sup-pose I'd better get back where I belong, among the women." She turned and saw Cornelius move out of the shadows.

"The women are warriors, too, in this kind of fight," said Paul. He also had seen Cornelius and walked to meet him. "Old men forget—"

Whatever it was that old men forget was lost in the terrifying screech of a shell and the subsequent explosion. Lanni ran from the hospital veranda and grabbed Kate by the arm while the sky erupted into flame.

Young Kurt Wahle was stationed in the German settlers' cemetery when the English began their morning barrage. Beside him was a muzzle-loaded cannon made in the railroad workshops from a steam pipe reinforced with a jacket of iron railings bent into rings. The cannon was mounted on a trolley and was to be fired as a signal be-tween Cornelius's tribesmen and the few Germans directing askari positions inside the town. A procession of English troops began pass-ing Kurt's hiding place. Mules and porters emerged from the swamp. Wahle saw a pony swerve out of the English column and jog toward him. The trap would be sprung too soon if the enemy spotted the homemade cannon. Wahle kept the pony in his sights until he could pick out a small figure in the saddle. Beads of perspiration broke out on young Wahle's forehead. He had never in his life shot a living thing. He strained so hard to see the soldier that the image blurred. He blinked and saw that the rider was a fresh-faced boy, a bugler perhaps, his broad-brimmed hat tied by a lace under his bony chin. The pony had got out of hand and seemed intent on jumping the cemetery wall. Kurt Wahle's finger trembled on the trigger. The boy was twelve, thirteen at most.

The gun crew stirred uneasily. There were three of them, askaris with heads camouflaged in crowns of twigs and leaves. They would be discovered, the ruse disclosed, if he delayed shooting the boy.

Wahle swallowed. A peaceful morning, a boy on his pony, birds singing. It was the spring of the year, though in Europe the long first winter of war had set in. The spring of life and the onset of death, he thought. "A time to love and a time to hate." Ecclesiastes. He squeezed ever so gently, laying the barleycorn of the foresight between the wings of the backsight, imagining the boy's heart fluttering like a bird's under the drab shirt.

Nobody stirred behind the cemetery wall when the rifle cracked. The boy rocked forward and was then suddenly flung backward by the pony's terrified bucking. The single shot was drowned in the chatter of machine guns opening up from inside the town as the boy's companions crossed the cutting where Prinz's men lay hidden. Above the high arch of the railroad terminal, a heliograph flashed. Wahle saw the signal and ran to the far side of the cemetery. He raised his hand, palm outward, and saw an answering flash of white from inside a giant fig tree on the verge of the swamp. The air shimmered and assumed the substance of smoke. He ducked and ran back to the howitzer. He waited five minutes and then, with lungs bursting, yelled, "Fire!" The cannon let loose its raucous signal. At last Wahle could rest his head against the cemetery wall and vomit, his eyes wide with horror and fixed upon the boy's dead body, its open mouth already filling with flies.

Paul, chain-smoking in the girdered room of the railroad station, saw the brush-fire signal and heard the distinctive roar of the howitzer. Now the rebel tribesmen under Cornelius would begin the task of chopping into the columns of porters. Within the hour the advancing English troops would be trapped inside the town, their supplies and their paths of retreat to the beaches completely cut off.

All the long afternoon English forces hacked their way forward. The Imperial Eagle was finally replaced over the Kaiserhof by the Union Jack. German snipers dodged from rooftop to rooftop, picking off English officers who were easily spotted in uniforms distinguished by badges of rank that glittered in the sun. By five o'clock it occurred to the English that they were being divided into small and killable units by an enemy who fought according to unfamiliar rules. But the discovery came too late.

Kate stood on the veranda and looked toward the cemetery. The ground was black where trees had flamed like torches. Vultures, their pink necks twisting greedily, hopped over decomposing bodies. Out of the lazily swirling smoke walked a tired old man trailing a rifle. His hair was matted the color of the red earth. Kate recognized with a shock young Kurt Wahle, stumbling and swinging his rifle at the vultures starting to rustle their wings and pitch forward their great beaks.

Behind her appeared Cornelius, cloaked like a Masai. "Miss Truman, an American—" He stopped when he saw her staring at the vultures, transformed into majestic vessels riding the putrescent air. He said consolingly, "The vulture's immortal. Nobody finds the carcass of a vulture. By taking us, they make us immortals, too."

But Kate was reaching out to the young lieutenant mounting the veranda steps. Wahle lifted his head and fancied he saw contempt on the faces above him. A storm of emotion chased across his own streaked features, and his mouth became suddenly ugly. Couldn't they understand it had not been a question of the boy bugler's life against his own? The child had almost given the alarm, betraying Cornelius.

A group of German askaris trooped openly across the cindered road, and Cornelius said angrily, "The English spared the hospital, but your askaris—"

Kurt Wahle understood. If the English had known that combat troops hid behind the red cross, they would have bombarded the hospital. His askaris were now inviting such a reprisal. He whirled and his face darkened. A stranger's voice issued from his corded throat. Kate recognized the Brandenburg-Berlin accent that marked its practitioner as accustomed to command—the *Potsdamer Ton* of barking contempt for the rest of the human race. Kurt Wahle called the askaris *Schweinhund* and *Rindvieh*, swine, vermin, dogs. Thus

they were ordered to leave the hospital premises by a young lieutenant trying to blot from memory his murder of a child.

The man standing inside the clinic said, "That must be Miss Truman with, ah, that screaming maniac?"

"Yes," said Magdalene von Prinz. She called Kate, who left the
veranda with Cornelius. "This is Mister Pope—"

"Quentin Pope of *The New York World*," said the newcomer
quickly. "I got your message."

Kate was aware of the glances between Cornelius and Magdalene
but nonetheless continued. "You came with the English fleet?"

"And stumbled into native insurgents." Pope grinned ruefully.
"My paper would be interested in your brother's trial, Miss Truman,
but—"

"Then stay and report it."

He watched her face. "Very well," he said.

Myles Hagen waited beside a stream whose bloody waters turned
smooth as crimson velvet in the dying light. Somewhere in the
swamp an English soldier dolefully played on his harmonica "Where
Is My Wandering Boy Tonight?" The spunk had gone out of the
troops.

Hagen cursed their commanders for walking into every trap. Even
at the end of the day's fighting, it had been obvious why the Germans had suddenly reopened a supply route to the landing beach.
It always demoralized an army fighting with its back against the
wall when you took away the wall. Now General Aitken was asking
for an armistice and time to re-embark. The business of war offended Hagen when it was so badly mismanaged. Men died for
nothing. They died from pigheadedness. They died as the Muslims
would die, bivouacked for a second night among fever trees. Hagen
had tried to warn the beardless English subaltern who commanded
them. The junior officer thought the trees, green-blossomed with
feather-fine foliage, provided the cleanest shelter.

"But they grow on moist ground, and mosquitoes breed there,"
said Hagen. "I know the trees don't produce malaria, but the bloody
water does." The subaltern had doggedly refused to move, and it
was true, the fever trees made a beautiful bower. The gravestones
would look pretty there later.

Quentin Pope came out of the ravine.

"Where's the girl?" demanded Hagen.

"Changed her mind. Won't come."

"Held against her will?"

"She's held all right, but by her own feelings."

"Not falling for Lettow? Women always do."

"Not in these circumstances," said the American. "She wants me to stay in German East, report the trial."

"That," said Hagen cautiously, "would be a break for you, Quentin."

Pope considered. He was one of a breed of writers making their names on American newspapers and periodicals. He was older than most, and the competition was tough. The great war in Europe was opening new fields for Irwin S. Cobb of *The Saturday Evening Post*, Oscar King Davis of *The New York Times*, Harry Hansen of *The Chicago Daily News*, Seymour B. Conger of the Associated Press. And, of course, Herbert Bayard Swope, who was Pope's colleague and rival on *The New York World*. This might be Pope's one chance to cross the lines and see at first hand, exclusively, the glamorous figure of a German Kommandeur who must become a legend, to judge by Hagen's reluctant admiration.

"You'd like a neutral in the German camp, wouldn't you?" said Pope. "You'd make it easy for me?"

"My explanation will be you got left behind. You can still send your dispatches through me—we'll find a way."

Pope laughed outright at the intelligence chief's air of innocence. "We're not in the same business, Hagen. I'm accountable for what I report. I nail it up for all the world to see. Who can challenge your secret reports? My dispatches won't suit your propaganda. I report facts publicly. Facts you might wish suppressed."

"I was warned about you Vermont Yankees." Hagen shrugged good-humoredly. "Hard as granite and wintry like your climate, with a passion for truth. So what is truth? Talk to me five years from now when Paul—when Lettow—has destroyed us and your precious liberalism."

"Five years?" Pope had started walking toward the sand dunes.

"Today's only a beginning. England's biggest military defeat in history. But not the end of the war, for war it is or will be." Hagen looked down on beaches where torches already flickered. Beachmasters were collecting arms and equipment for shipment back to the Force B fleet. "We can't just leave with our tails between our legs. The Battle of Tanga was a black victory. A victory for black tactics, black arms. Cornelius will see to that. It would be the end of the British Empire if we let it go at that."

Cornelius watched the Kommandeur drawing his fingers together, bending them into a clenched fist. "We'll pull back on Kilimanjaro, concentrate the reservists there, bring in some of the settlers along the English border," said Paul. "Your guerrillas should aim to control the countryside at night only. Let the enemy wither in the camps and townships."

Count Kornatzki groaned on his cot. The men were grouped around him in the clinic. The medical director's wounds from the Gurkha's bayonet attack were superficial, but they were clustered in the region of his groin.

"The enemy's not going to wither," said Kornatzki. "Don't fool yourselves. I've seen Jacob's latest analysis—"

Jacob Kramer, impassive on the edge of the lamplight, passed over some crumpled sheets covered in minuscule writing. The sheets were stained from concealment in sweaty loincloths. "Those are the actual details," said Jacob. "The general picture is unchanged, except it's blacker."

Cornelius shifted his cloak. "We've just proved black Africans can fight the biggest empire in history."

"Don't get carried away," warned Paul. "The English will be back. They'll come back with crack regiments from the best imperial fighting forces. They'll keep coming back, no matter how many more Tangas they suffer. You can't stand alone against that empire, Cornelius. You need us."

"But why should we serve his purposes?" demanded Count Kornatzki. "I'm not opposed to revolution. We're all revolutionaries here. Rebels against Berlin, against the Kaiser even. But indiscriminate warfare? Do we want to destroy what scraps of civilization have been built by our settlers? The land will be laid waste—"

"Either way, it will be laid waste," murmured Paul. "You're lucky to be alive. Be thankful for small mercies—"

"Thank God my mercies were small, or they'd have been cut off." Kornatzki clutched his crotch again. "Though it's the loss of my kerrie I most resent."

Cornelius said quietly, "Hagen carries that kerrie now. It marks him, though he doesn't know it. We'll get it back for you."

"And put some fire in my belly?" challenged Kornatzki. "I'm an old man—"

"Old men forget," said Cornelius, turning his dark eyes in Paul's direction.

The Kommandeur rubbed the area beneath his eye patch. "Sometimes you overhear the most remarkable observations."

"Sometimes I remember I was a prize student of Shakespeare." Cornelius quoted: " 'A good leg will fail. A straight back will stoop.' "

Paul added swiftly, " 'A black beard will turn white. A fair face will wither.' "

Kornatzki was twisting his head from one to the other, his full white beard and white mane shining against the dark army blanket.

" 'But a good heart is the sun and the moon,' " finished Jacob, " 'for it shines bright and never changes, but keeps its course truly.' "

Later, Paul unlocked the war diary. He stared at a blank page. So much had happened since the last entry. "Africa," he began to write, "will never be the same. Tanga was the birth day of black independence."

Part Two

A Touch of the Leopard

8

From the war diary of Colonel von Lettow, Tanga, November 3, 1914:

Cornelius can quote *Henry V*, but I had to quote him a Masai saying today: "When the leopard wishes to destroy a bigger enemy, he draws in his claws and lures that enemy into territory where the natural advantages are on his side. That is the touch of the leopard. . . ." Our retreat over two hundred kilometers to the Kilimanjaro garrison of Moshi still bothers Cornelius. He still fears my ultimate aims. My aims, of course, are quite simple, with Kilimanjaro at the heart of them. Queen Victoria gave it to the Kaiser in a gesture of contempt for both the mountain and the King-Emperor of the Second Reich. The mountain is my symbol of power.

First, our enemies would force Prussia back into a land of peasants. They surround Germany, would destroy the Second Reich as they did the First, and then disperse us. When I speak of this with Jacob, he looks uncomfortable and says, "The Diaspora is for the Jews." Well, of course! Germans and Jews shared the same dangers. A knight of Zion is an appropriate adviser to a knight of Prussia.

Second, I would rather build an empire than lay waste whole cities. If war must be waged, and this is the human condition, I would rather wage it here in a savage land than over fields cultivated by generations of Europeans. The time approaches when disputes between nations can be settled on battlegrounds isolated from civilian centers. Africa will prove an ideal continent for war.

Third, the creation of a powerful German Empire depends upon the destruction of the British Empire. If Germany had not been attacked, the necessity for this would be less apparent. The unacceptable alternative to struggle, for Germany, is dispersal. Jews like Jacob understand this.

Fourth, I must provoke the Viceroy of India to continue massive intervention here. Lord Curzon, as Viceroy, is our most powerful adversary. "So long as we rule from Africa East," he has written, "we are the greatest power on earth. If we lose Africa, we drop straight to a third-rate power." To speed this event, I have conceived of a German-African empire in which *blacks may rule*. Africans can be trained to govern and defend themselves. Black leaders of totally opposed purpose—like Cornelius with his radical dream and the tribal chiefs with their lust for personal power—can be welded into a working national unity if they see the chance of safety and prosperity under a German flag. Free people must undergo a bloodbath for their own self-respect, since freedom is worthless unless won by sacrifice. I can offer dignity, liberty, and independence to those who fight with me. What can Curzon offer? He is haughty in the powers of his own autocracy, greeted everywhere with the most elaborate deference, and mesmerized by bureaucracy.

Grandiose Viceroy Curzon, of course, is the ideal of petty Governor Schnee. A comparison of the two becomes ludicrous— but I vow never to slip into Schnee's bureaucratic ways.

Major Wolfe, my deputy, normally kept this war diary. He is talented as artist and poet and in the past decorated our entries most amusingly. I am now taking over sole responsibility because I must record my observations to learn from my mistakes.

9

Major Wolfe reminded Kate of his distant but famous ancestor, King Charles the First of England. She guessed Wolfe was in his late twenties and, by some miracle, he seemed unaware of his good looks and the devastating effect of his chestnut curls and well-trimmed orange-red spade beard. When she confided her doubts about traveling upcountry with the army, he advised, "Don't ask too many questions. The Kommandeur will explain things when the political danger is gone. Avoid the Governor."

When she took her place on the last evacuation train out of Tanga, she found herself sitting within sight of Governor Schnee, although hardly near him. He was flanked by his personal police and aides. At each wayside station, girls besieged the train with garlands, and German farmers sat long-legged in the saddle. From the dour expressions of the Governor's party, the waiting throngs had come to cheer not the Governor but Paul.

"They should save their breath," muttered Major Wolfe. "They'll need it later to curse him."

"But surely Paul's won them a victory, a noble victory?" said Kate ironically.

Major Wolfe lifted an eyebrow. "I mean curse the Governor. He's left the farmers undefended."

"What will happen to them?"

"Some will trek inland to join the Kilimanjaro bastion. Their homes are already under attack. Von Prinz—" Major Wolfe glanced at Magdalene, who was sitting nearby beside Quentin Pope. Abruptly he changed the subject. "You talked with the Governor about your brother?"

"I tried. It was a mistake. He believes I helped Cornelius escape. I'm also confused—I thought Cornelius was fighting on the German side."

"So he is, but so was your brother. Neither, it seems, fits into the plans of His Excellency. We can all fight on the same side and still fight among ourselves." Wolfe examined the backs of his hands. The fingers were long and artistic. He flexed them and sighed. "Why do men prefer conflict when they're deprived of daily involvement with women?" He glanced at her shyly. "I daresay if the Kommandeur had a pretty girl like you, a lot of the desire for combat would go out of him."

Kate looked in Paul's direction. She had heard Wolfe call him a leopard, the only creature that kills other than for food.

"Despite the triumph at Tanga," Kate replied, "we are now fleeing."

"He who fights and runs away lives to fight another day," said Wolfe, smiling to acknowledge the weary cliché. "It's not the Schlieffen Plan, though, I grant."

Kate knew of Count von Schlieffen's plan. Who did not? It was one of Germany's best-publicized secrets. What a long way Paul was from the grand Schlieffen design: Schlieffen's "battle commander" would sit in comfort before detailed maps while every resource of modern technology fed him the facts of battlefield action. Schlieffen had envisaged the majestic movement of armies by large numbers of long trains under the direction of railroad generals working to splendidly conceived timetables. Such calculations, worked out years beforehand, had now smashed Germany's enemies in Europe, avenged the defeat of the Teutonic Knights, and slaughtered the Russians at Tannenberg.

Here in Africa there were virtually no maps, few trains, and only this rickety railroad climbing laboriously into the mountain. Signals depended on barefoot runners and heliographs. Generals? A black revolutionary. A Jewish visionary. Count Kornatzki and his witch doctors. And Paul, eye-patched, stiff with scars, two pistols in his belt, setting himself against the English, whose empire in Africa was four million square miles, a third of the entire continent.

A shower of wood sparks descended on the train as iron wheels locked. Carriages jolted against one another and sounded like firecrackers. Kate fell forward against Major Wolfe, who was moving to join the askaris already scattering along the track. The train quivered to a stop, then reversed a few yards.

Quentin Pope's concerned face appeared out of the dust on the track. "Better come down, Miss Truman." He helped her out of the fast-emptying carriage, then explained, "There's been some sort of raid."

Kate saw Paul's askaris firing at the dust plumes left by cavalry. The horsemen were in loose formation and moved parallel to the blue foothills of Kilimanjaro.

She recognized the mountain with a shock of surprise. She had never before seen the snow that covered the highest peak, floating unexpectedly above withered candelabra trees and fleshy cactus. A sudden explosion consumed the eternal snows in a sun-blooded mist.

"Uganda Railway Volunteers," announced Paul some five minutes later. "Bandits, in plain language." He stared disgustedly at Pope. "*Your* bandits. Come and see!"

Pope looked in sick surprise at the remains of a man splayed between two thorn trees. He had been extremely fat. He must have tumbled from his horse and fractured one leg, which was bent at a grotesque angle. Paul's askaris had finished the job with rifle butts. The man wore a cowboy hat in which fragments of his head lay splattered, as if reluctant to let death interrupt a long friendship.

"He was laying a mine," said Paul. "We just detonated it. We were meant to be part of the explosion."

The American newsman knelt and examined the dead man's belt; its buckle was stamped with a star and the word *Texas*. Among the papers lying beside the gory hat was a dog-eared copy of *Musketry Regulations* folded open to a section of bayonetry.

Pope walked away angrily, back to where the train's engine hissed and shuddered in a cloud of steam. He had no sympathy for the dead American's motives. He was sickened, though, by sheer violence of a quality he had never imagined. As he approached the passengers' carriage, he saw Magdalene von Prinz. A memory flashed through his mind of Tom von Prinz locked in intimate embrace with Ada von Schnee. Pope had surprised them while he was calling on the Governor in Tanga and had blundered into the telephone room of the residency. That image superimposed itself upon what he had just witnessed and heard. He felt an unexpected surge of compassion for a woman like Magdalene caught in such ugliness. He found it impossible to avoid looking at her frequently as the train resumed its journey.

They stopped for a late lunch at Wilhelmstal, the summer capital, centered among green pastures that covered a region as big as Bavaria. In the stationmaster's bungalow a table had been laid with starched linen and gleaming cutlery. Bottles of white Moselle stood in ice buckets. The tiny room was hot, but the windows sparkled from hasty washing, and the settlers' wives bustled about, fresh looking in their best print frocks.

There was a sudden cry from Magdalene von Prinz.

"Damnation!" exclaimed the Governor's wife. "Someone's told her."

"I thought she knew," apologized the informant, a *Hausfrau* who had been gossiping with Magdalene.

"What have they done to the farm?" Magdalene accosted the Governor. "I want to go there, now!"

"You must wait until your husband reports," replied the Governor.

"So Tom knows already?" Magdalene turned to the Governor's wife.

"Yes," Ada said calmly. "I didn't tell you because—what could you do?"

"I could go home."

"To a burned ruin?"

Magdalene's back stiffened. She looked around the circle of wives whose joy had turned so swiftly to distress. "Who will lend me a horse?"

"You can't ride out there alone!" snapped Ada.

"I'll ride with her," volunteered Pope. He saw their surprise and said, as if he felt the need to explain himself, "I'm the only one here without duties or obligations."

"Quite impossible!" declared the Governor. "You're a noncombatant."

"Noncombatant!" snorted Count Kornatzki. "So you do recognize there *is* a war—"

"The situation's delicate; this man's American. Madame von Prinz must remain here, and furthermore—" The Governor fingered his pince-nez and prepared to flood the room with oratory.

"Furthermore, American intervention is becoming intolerable!" interrupted Paul. The spring-loaded split doors crashed shut behind him.

There was a ripple of excitement among the Wilhelmstal wives. This was the man they had come to see, the hero of Tanga, not a fusspot Governor whose wife cuckolded him with their husbands.

Paul removed his bush hat and brushed it against his jacket. He removed his eye patch and left a circle of white on his dust-coated face. "Excuse me, ladies! Heinrich, sit down and we can have lunch."

The Governor gave a small start and then a hesitant, protesting smile. "I don't think—"

"Do not think, Excellency," said Paul. "Sit!"

Kate watched in astonishment. She had not seen Paul in this mood. He was telling Magdalene how he had sent Tom to investigate after news reached Tanga that their farm had been attacked. He finished abruptly. "You'd better go now, Magdalene. Lieutenant Wahle will take charge of an escort."

He clasped his hands. "Well, then! What do we have here, ladies? Light magic from the Moselle, I see. And game pie." He beckoned Kate to sit beside him. All through lunch he made small talk, captivating the local wives, bringing smiles to the ruddy faces of their husbands. Then, when the fruit appeared, he tugged papers from his frayed jacket.

"This is something you missed, Mr. Pope, when you examined your dead countryman."

Ada said quickly, "Time, I think, for the ladies to retire."

Chairs scraped. There was a general flutter of hands and napkins.

"Not you, Miss Truman," said Paul. "You shall hear this."

The Governor busied himself with the brandy. Kornatzki dug his fingers into an abandoned bread roll. Ada shepherded the wives away.

"The Governor was right to hold your brother, Miss Truman," said Paul when the door had closed and the small group was alone.

Kate's hand flew to her mouth.

Paul pushed the papers toward Quentin Pope. "These were found near the dead American. They call on the natives in this territory to give aid to the so-called Uganda Volunteers in return for American gold."

"What has this to do with Miss Truman's brother?" demanded Pope.

"His Excellency had Major Truman arrested with the purpose of reminding foreign adventurers of the consequences of introducing dangerous games within German colonial territory," Paul said coldly. "I shall expect you to report his trial fully."

Kate, stunned, found herself staring across the table at Kornatzki. The medical missionary's eyes were fixed on hers. What was he trying to say?

One of the Wilhelmstal wives rode with them to the next station, distracting Kate from her depressing speculations. The girl chattered like a school child. Oh, yes, they were all accustomed to jump on and off any train that came by, and sometimes one paid and sometimes not. Her neighbor had once taken a vacation to Germany with a ticket issued for travel between Wilhelmstal and Tanga! "Most of us wives come out here very young," she said, blushing. "But we are not so backward. We have been busy making meals for the *Schutztruppe* since the great victory at Tanga." She became bolder. "Is this a real war or no? All of us hope not. We live as good neighbors with the English farmers. We must, isn't it so, in a place like Africa? Why kill each other because the King of England quarrels with the Kaiser?"

Before she left, the girl thrust a basket of apples into Kate's arms. "Tell your brother," she said quickly, "we all think him innocent."

Kate's stomach lurched. Then everyone knew! She thought of those pretty young wives on their best behavior at lunch, so polite, questioning her about Berlin. They had only been putting her at ease.

Climbing back over the wooden slats dividing the open carriages came Paul, his damaged eye bared, his torn jacket flapping, his head white from ash scattered by the engine. He shouted above the screech of brakes. "That, Mr. Pope, is what I mean by atrocities!"

Pope shielded his face from the westering sun. A smudge of smoke lay along the horizon.

"That," said Paul, "was the Prinz farm. Well, then? You want to see for yourself what the English do to our settlers?" He gestured toward a knot of tall Masai warriors beside the track. "You'll be in hands I can trust."

Kate saw Pope hesitate, baffled by the Kommandeur's changed attitude.

"Please go to her," said Kate, who was amused when the American's face darkened in an uncontrollable blush.

"It's a devil of a long way," said Pope feebly.

"There's your transport." Paul indicated a bicycle being lowered from the engine driver's cab.

Pope glanced at Kate. "It's my job—"

"Miss Truman is perfectly safe with me," said Paul. He put out a hand to the figure detaching itself from the spearmen.

"Lanni!" Kate exclaimed in astonishment. Behind the octoroon stood Cornelius like a centurion with a toga over his shoulder. The Governor had turned away.

Lanni climbed into the carriage. She was dressed in a Masai cloak with a short daggerlike sword hanging from the belt at her waist. She smelled of charcoal and animal grease, the smell of the nomad. Her amber eyes flashed her pleased recognition of Kate.

Pope had been given no time to digest the scene. A bewildered expression settled upon his face when Cornelius addressed him in American-accented English. It was not a disagreeable face, thought Kate. Pope wore the mask of the disenchanted. His incipient dewlaps and his small paunch were territory surrendered in a campaign against worldly disillusion. He would shed weight and years if he found a cause to restore his faith in dreams.

Kate's eyes followed Pope's erratic progress along a dried-up riverbed long after the train had resumed the slow climb toward Moshi. Until they fell from her sight, she watched Cornelius and the Masai jogging behind the American's bicycle with no sign of effort.

An elephant, hanging its head low, stood near the railroad tracks and captured Kate's attention. She was surprised that an elephant could be red in color. It resembled the huge conelike termite hills, and it stood obstinately still while the train rumbled over a wooden trestle bridge. The riverbed below was dry, and in it lay the carcass of another elephant, a vulture thrusting its scavenging beak under its tail.

"Drought," said Major Wolfe, appearing back at her side. "At this time of year, the elephants migrate and make things worse. A terrible sight."

"Terrible?" Kate stared disbelievingly at him. "You people waste your sympathies in odd directions."

"Herds of elephants devastate the land," persisted Wolfe. He was glancing anxiously about him. "It's terrible if they cause famine, surely?" He seemed to settle something in his mind. "Miss Truman, none of us likes the other kind of devastation. We're all of us falling backward into war. The process is like a bad dream. The Kommandeur hates war as much as anyone. Don't judge him harshly. His outburst at lunch was necessary. And now we've got the American journalist out of the way."

"I don't understand." She felt fear clutch at her heart. She was alone on a German troop train winding slowly into an unknown land. There was no path of escape, even if she decided to run.

"Your brother," said Major Wolfe quietly, "must never go on trial. The Kommandeur is determined to prevent that. Your brother was caught on Kilimanjaro with tribesmen who were already branded enemies of the German civil administration. They ran into a patrol of settlers, former soldiers who protect the borders. A German was killed. To protect your brother, the Kommandeur pretended he was an army major of Uganda Railway Volunteers serving the English. It was a device to get a military trial. Otherwise your brother would have been convicted and executed for murder long ago."

"What was he doing on Kilimanjaro?"

"I thought you'd know the answer to that."

Kate shook her head. "What is it you want from me?"

"Your patience. Perhaps your help."

"What help?" asked Kate, seeing a pit yawning in front of her.

"In your brother's escape," replied Wolfe.

Paul kept a distance between them during the rest of that long day. Kate glimpsed him whittling away at a piece of wood when the train took a sharp curve and she could spot his trim figure perched in another carriage. Her feelings about him were now more mixed than ever.

They halted for the night in the Kilimanjaro highlands. Ada took

Kate under her wing. "My precious Pumpernickel can look after himself tonight," said the Governor's wife, laughing at Kate's bewildered look. "Maybe you think of him as the Governor, but he's the Pumpernickel to me."

Major Wolfe overheard and looked worried. When Ada von Schnee called her husband the Pumpernickel in public, trouble was brewing. She used the word in its Westphalian sense of "blockhead." Wolfe helped Ada select one of the trunks in the baggage wagon, and while a porter carried it down the embankment, he asked her discreetly, "What's the problem, Ada?"

She shot him a shrewd look. "The old fool is planning to win over Max Looff and the *Koenigsberg* crew."

Wolfe whistled softly. Navy Captain Looff was technically the senior service officer of the colony. If the Governor plotted with Looff, they could between them remove Paul from his military command. "But Max is physically beyond reach."

"Not beyond the reach of runners," said Ada. "The messages have gone out already."

The porters pitched camp. Ada, on the pretext of a sisterly concern for an inexperienced visitor, shared a safari tent with Kate. There, clad in riding clothes, her hands thrust mannishly into the pockets of her unpressed cotton jacket, she told Kate: "I want you to know, my dear, I'm delighted you're with us. Colonel Lettow needs you. Don't look astonished, child! Already you call him Paul. So do we, when he's not on his military dignity. Others call him Simba, the lion. But they're blacks. Blacks aren't supposed to count. Except, you'll see, the ones with real influence are blacks—like Skaramunga, the gun bearer. He started this lion thing at Tanga. What Skaramunga says today, the black *effendi* officers say tomorrow and the tribes for miles around by the end of the week. Mark my words, that's more powerful stuff than any number of propaganda speeches by my Pumpernickel."

Kate listened in growing bewilderment. Ada sounded like a matchmaker presenting the potential groom's qualifications.

"Paul was one of the Kaiser's favorites," continued Ada. "One of the elite *Fluegeladjutanten* with a field marshal's baton in his packsack, as they say. Then he was posted to China. It was the time of the Boxer Rebellion. . . ."

Paul had been sent to punish the Chinese for the assassination by rebels of the German Minister in Peking. To the embarking troops the Kaiser had said: "Give no pardon, take no prisoners. Be like the Huns under Attila." The speech was widely reported abroad under

caustic headlines: "KAISER ORDERS 'HUNS' TO SLAUGHTER 'SLIT-
EYES.'" The repercussions included the popularization of "Hun"
to describe a German. Paul found he was saddled with the reputation
of Attila. A decade later he was sympathetic to the Chinese rebels
who ended centuries of imperial rule with the revolution of 1911.
The theme of revolution on Ada's lips sounded strange, and Kate
regarded her with renewed interest and Paul with the increased
understanding Ada had intended.

The tracks were slippery from the rolling mists when the train
tried to get underway next morning. Kate watched the engineer spin
his wheels until the boiler ran out of steam and carriers had to pass up
buckets of water to cool the engine.

"Not all our enemies wear uniforms," said Paul, joining her beside
the track. He pointed to a flock of guinea fowl running like little
men with their hands in their pockets along the embankment. "Those
monsters peck for insects under the tracks and undermine our trains.
I'm not joking! White ants destroy the creosote coating of the railroad ties. An epidemic of caterpillars can blanket the track. When the
locomotive runs over the first lot, crushing the caterpillars to pulp,
the wheels start to slip and lose their purchase."

He laughed at Kate's disbelieving look. "The driver has to be
bribed with good Scotch whisky," he continued. "He comes originally from the Indian State Railways, like most. As a good Hindu, he
shouldn't drink alcohol. But his tastes were formed among the British,
who disguised the whisky as cold tea to satisfy his scruples. They're
all the same, these 'Herr Engineers.' Lubricate their tonsils and they'll
make the trains work in the face of any enemy."

He tilted his chin to where a vehicle crawled toward them along
the shining tracks. "Here's my army jigger. Would you ride ahead
with me?" The jigger was a four-wheel-drive Mercedes-Benz with
flanged wheels to grip the rails.

The Mercedes was not in any evident hurry. Paul had taken Kate's
arm to help her walk forward of the engine when one of his Jaeger
scouts spoke to him. The man was a thin-faced Turkana wearing a
fez, with a flap of cloth to protect his neck, and loose shorts. He was
pointing, and Kate heard the word *simba* repeated vigorously.

"There's a pride of lion in the *korongo* there." Paul pointed to a
fissure in the landscape.

"He's not going to shoot them?" asked Kate, glancing at the scout's
sporting rifle.

"No. The lions are in the gulch. If you want, we can see them from the lip above." Paul's voice had a fresh, schoolboyish tone. He was already anticipating her assent, instructing his askari to keep guard over the train. He wanted no sightseers.

The gulch was twenty minutes' fast walk through the bush. Paul moved along the abrupt edge and motioned Kate to lie down, dropping on his stomach beside her. The Turkana melted into the bush. Her eyes searched the pebbled floor, but she could discern nothing. Then Paul nudged her with his elbow. She squinted obediently into the hot glare of the tawny ground immediately below. Shapes resolved out of the haze. Golden bodies streaked with black softened into shades of yellow and brown. Lions! The pride matched its speckled retreat, a sun trap of brush and rocky soil. She had never imagined lions like this, lying on their backs with their feet in the air, toasting their lightly furred bellies, their cubs frolicking in the underbrush.

A big black-maned lion rested his magnificent head on his forepaws, dozing. A lioness rippled through the tinder-dry grass and nuzzled him until his eyes flew open. The eyes were molten gold, and when Kate felt their impact, she thought at once of Lanni. The lion was turning his head. The fur was loose like an emperor's mantle around his shoulders. The nose was long and aristocratic. The crown was that enormous mane.

The female cuffed him. He yawned. She flicked his ear. He uttered a low, bored growl. She pushed her nose against his cheek and nudged him onto his back. He stretched and lazily pawed the air. The lioness tensed, crouching as if to spring, her smooth head tilted, ears flattened, tail twitching. Her sudden concentration infected the pride. The cubs stopped playing. The whole world fell silent.

The lion spread his groin to the lingering sun. Instantly the female doubled back. Her tongue slid out and over the root of his tail, over the furry gold pouch of testicles, over the hardening gold ridge sheathing his penis. Her head swayed with the rhythm of her licking. Saliva glistened and dried in the harsh sun. The lion raised his head sleepily and let it fall back again with a rumble of content. But the female was not petting. Her tongue rasped up the center line of his belly. She growled, pawing the upturned male and baring her teeth. He shifted, exposed to the sky and to the watchers above. Out of the sheath slid the moist, hard penis like a greased cannon. The vivid redness of it startled Kate. It challenged the natural surrounding colors, drawing upon itself a shocked attention.

The lioness dodged a movement of the male's forelegs with claws suddenly extended. He twisted and crouched. She slipped from beneath his hindquarters and flattened her belly to the ground, spreading herself. The male watched her tail rise until it stood erect. Hardly seeming to move, he covered her in a series of motions: graceful and aggressive, gentle and relentless, limbs entwining and claws hooking. Each melted, color and shape, to become one undulating pelt.

Kate, tense in the awestruck silence, felt Paul's body close against her, as tightly locked by the beauty of the spectacle as the bodies of the creatures below. The sun's heat pierced her. Her mouth, instead of turning dry, filled with saliva. She watched the lion lick the lioness with his tongue, his head alone breaking the symmetry of their two bodies. Kate's mind filled with the man and the desire to love and to be loved like that. The brutes were beautiful. There was no brutality in the aura of mutual concern, each caressing and caring for the other. Kate was startled by this passion of spirit, this expression of love between animals from which custom borrowed such offensive adjectives implying human degradation: swinish, bestial, goatish, ruttish. There was nothing ugly here.

Paul drew her attention to the Turkana scout, now silently beckoning. As she pulled back from the edge of the *korongo*, she caught a last glimpse of the lioness lying content under the lion. He had raised himself on stiff forelimbs, bestriding her, bending his black-maned head to caress the back of her glossy head with his tongue. The tongue was thick and long and he used it with loving restlessness. But it was the female's tongue, thought Kate, that first aroused him.

There was silence between them on the walk back to the train. The slippery tracks flickered as if on fire under the burnished sky. Men were singing. Young German officers. Kate recognized one of the *Soldatenlieder* that dwelt so heavily on death: *"Und unser allerschoenstes junges Leben . . . Liegt in dem Krieg wohl auf das Schlachtfeld hingestreckt. . . .* And our most beautiful young lives stretched out in wartime on the field of slaughter."

Paul began to snap orders. The singing stopped. Kate glanced at him in surprise. She had supposed he was still moved by the mating of the lions, and she was disappointed by the sudden harshness in his manner. He said roughly, "I want you with me at the garrison before the Governor arrives." He raised his arm in the direction of the Mercedes now stationary before the smoking locomotive. "Come."

She was tempted to refuse, but she wanted to restore the good feeling between them. She saw the young officers look at Paul with bewildered expressions. He took her arm and said in a changed voice,

"I've no stomach for these maudlin songs, this faith that war cleanses the soul."

She saw something then that made her heart turn over. She said with a boldness that surprised her, "The lions know better." Then, seeing him turn away in sudden shyness, she added, "I hated to leave the lions. It seemed—like sacrilege."

His look, Kate thought, was of pure gratitude. " 'Divinity is reached by modern man through physical love,' " he quoted.

"Then why do preachers make war noble and love unclean?"

He shook his head angrily. "Preachers! The whole of church art in Germany is devoted to violence. That's where these patriotic dirges come from. Hymns to the virtue of pain."

"And love of war?" she asked softly.

"Kitten." He paused. "Do you mind that I call you *Kätzchen*?"

"If I may call you—" again she surprised herself—"Simba?"

He was laughing, but she caught apprehension in his voice. "Don't unman me, *Kätzchen*."

She felt unexpectedly close to him, for he had been open to the meaning of the lions, and she recomposed the scene in the gulch from the moment when the female initiated the ceremony.

10

QUENTIN POPE reached the gutted farm after a bizarre bicycle ride. He had come to Africa looking for a story to rival that of a predecessor, Henry Stanley, whose old desk at *The New York Herald* had inspired Pope before he moved over to *The World*. His romantic visions of the African bush had fed upon the vast body of literature produced by explorers of the decade. He had not been prepared for a bumpy, back-breaking, boring bicycle safari ending in the ashes of razed farmland.

He noted a lively chestnut mare, three white stockings and a blaze, tethered near one of the few buildings untouched by fire. As a youth, he had worked with horses for an entire summer on a cattle ranch in Colorado. The sight of the mare roused a wistful sense of that time, mingled with an awareness that his former physical fitness was missing. His thinning sandy hair was a warning of time running out. Pope had fought his way from police courts and city hall to the privileged circle of the international press, but he envisioned himself an author-adventurer in the tradition of the great reporters who regularly vanished for months into distant and exotic lands to emerge into a dignified life of lectures and distinguished writings. He half believed he could still achieve his ambition if he could find the self-discipline to get back into shape.

The walls of the main house were of mortised cut stone and remained erect. As he walked toward the scorched façade, Pope could picture the mullioned windows overlooking terraced lawns. He stopped and retrieved a partially burned book, its German Gothic print still readable, a copy of Goethe's *Faust* opened to a page where he read: " 'Tis I for whom the bells shall toll / And timeless night descend upon my soul."

The compact with the devil! He turned and saw Cornelius watching at a distance and he moved on, walking around the shell of the house to a stone buttery still miraculously intact. Magdalene stood in the doorway, her face smeared, her riding clothes stained.

"Mr. Pope!" Her greeting seemed almost exuberant. She had the relieved expression of a woman who has anticipated disaster so long, it comes finally as a friend. Pope had seen that look among the wives of drowned fishermen.

She shrugged off his words of condolence.

"A fire's like fate, striking in one place and leaving another untouched. Look, that was my husband's first leopard. The skin's still intact when so much else is damaged and destroyed." She had turned up a lantern in the windowless buttery. As they moved inside, the glow revealed racks of wine and a few family treasures she had salvaged. Outside, the brush fires burned fiercely against the darkening sky.

"Didn't you come with that young lieutenant?" asked Pope.

"Yes—you remember."

"Where is he?"

She gestured vaguely. "I made him organize a burial party. Some of the laborers were killed when the native huts caught fire." She talked with a nervous compulsion. "My daughters are in English schools in Nairobi. Isn't it ridiculous? Perhaps the English will make them celebrate this 'victory.' "

"Are you sure the English did this?" asked Pope.

"No, I'm not sure." Her voice caught. "Tom will say they were responsible. He won't look for other evidence. He has to believe the English guilty, he hates them so."

The memory returned to Pope's mind of the English wife of the Governor making love to Prinz. If Prinz hated the English, he had a strange way of showing it. It occurred to Pope that Magdalene might have a shrewd notion of Prinz's true character. She had come as a young bride to Africa, and, like the wives of so many settlers, she had little choice but to accept her man and overlook his faults, supporting him morally despite private misgivings. Africa was unforgiving of quarrelsome strangers.

She said, "Mr. Pope, I think I need your shoulder."

Her hot tears soaked his tunic. After a moment, she raised her head and laughed self-consciously. "I'm not supposed to cry. Tom doesn't allow it. A bad example to the natives. Tom will know what to do when he gets here. They call him Bwana Sakarani. The Wild One. He is that. It's difficult to be in love with a wild one. Love him, but not be in love."

Cornelius coughed before entering, but still they were slow in breaking apart. "The bwana is making camp for the night at Kisiwani," he reported tonelessly. "He will be here *saa nne na nusu*." He quoted the time, ten-thirty the next morning, by the Swahili clock, emphasizing the time of arrival as if to say Magdalene need not worry. Pope resented the patronizing manner of the man. The lamplight deepened the knife scars on either side of the thin Hamitic nose and gave a golden gloss to his skin. He concluded, "Lieutenant Wahle is posting guards and will be staying in the servants' quarters that remain intact. Many of the servants are returning."

"Is he dependable?" Pope asked after Cornelius had withdrawn.

Magdalene gave him a curious look. "You don't know about Cornelius? Well, why should you? He is in partnership with the Kommandeur. Paul's pact with the devil."

The phrase reminded Pope that he still held in his hand the copy of *Faust*. He showed her the smoke-blackened book.

"I'm so glad!" She took it from him. "This belonged to my father. How strange. Yesterday I would have had difficulty remembering if it was in our home in Berlin or here. Now it becomes very precious and important." She folded it in her arms. "Mr. Pope, I am sorry for that exhibition a moment ago. No, not sorry for what I said. I say what I mean. I think crying, though, is something one does not impose on others."

The Mercedes railcar gobbled the miles, its flanged wheels hugging the track along cool mountain slopes. Driving it was a young Jaeger, a German scout, anxious to make up time after the long delays. A red-fezzed askari stood on the running board on either side. Kate was in the upholstered rear seat with Paul. Two more askaris stood on the back platform, greasing their bayonets to dull the steel. The heat of another day had died, and now the top of Kilimanjaro was silvered by the moon. The askaris kept glancing up toward the peaks. Even the driver occasionally turned his head in that direction as if to get his bearings.

Kate felt Paul's intensity as he talked about the mountain. Kilimanjaro had captivated him since at school he'd read how England's Royal Geographical Society ridiculed the German missionary Rebmann, who first reported its existence. "You make it sound like a family heirloom," said Kate. "You pronounce it the Swahili way. Kilima Njaro. The English spell it as one word."

"The English sing a hymn about Zion's City—"

"'Glorious Things of Thee Are Spoken,'" filled in Kate.

"Our words to the same music are 'Germany Over All.'"

Kate smiled sadly. "If you sing in harmony, why fight?"

"Would it were that simple. If Tom von Prinz were to sing his English national anthem, his men would think he was singing the Uhlan victory song. Only the melody of 'God Save Our Gracious King' sounds like 'Heil dir im Siegeskranz.' We all think in symbols, like tribes with totems." Paul was watching the changing moonlight on the peaks. "Really, you could control the strategic centers of east and central Africa from here. I wasn't surprised last year when Hans Reck discovered a fossilized human skeleton not far away and said it proves this is our birthplace."

"It could be our graveyard," suggested Kate. She saw the street lamps of the garrison flickering into life, pinpricks of progress in a savage land. The vision of Germans and English burying each other here made her shudder. "You'll bleed each other," she said, "until nobody's left."

"Except Africans. They fit the mountain into a different mold. They see the land in terms of tribal territories, not our neat and arrogant geometric divisions. If I work within the African concept, I move with the people. But that will not bring peace." Paul straightened as the native huts converged around them and the European bungalows appeared ahead. "'The people's wars will be more terrible than those of kings,'" he quoted. "Those words were written by an Englishman named Churchill, but I doubt if anyone in England remembers them. Winston Churchill. A very young man with a very old head."

Moshi, the garrison town serving Kilimanjaro, seethed with foot soldiers and riflemen on quick-trotting ponies. The Mercedes approached the station, and the streets came together like spokes in a wheel, spilling two-wheeled bullock-drawn tongas, rickshaws, camels, donkeys, and spluttering automobiles into a traffic circle. Tin-roofed bungalows rose one above another, their gardens releasing the scent of roses and flaming poinsettia, chrysanthemums and bougainvillea in a fragrant mix of temperate and tropic blooms.

The brick station would have fitted into most of the German market towns known to Kate. But when she descended to the platform, it was thronged with Europeans in dented pith helmets decorated with eagle feathers and ostrich plumes. The driveway was packed with horses and mules jingling with water bottles, skillets, and pots, weighed down by bedrolls and kit bags, led by barefoot urchins waving sticks of bamboo. Carriers shuffled past, kicking up a fog of red dust, turning the lights into orange gobs. Behind the jogging, grunting, failing column of tottering coolies came servants, gun bearers, and stablemen leading ponies laden with still more chop boxes, water filters, and tin trunks, like a religious procession carved by a German medieval monk. Out of it swung a carriage drawn by a pair of Abyssinian grays. A cavalry officer rode ahead and bent over his saddle to speak with Paul. While they talked, the cavalryman twisted his bearded face to study Kate. Then he swung upright, saluted Kate, and spurred his mount forward into the mob.

"God be thanked!" Paul said as he rejoined her. "The Governor hasn't warned the SK."

Kate let him help her into the carriage. She tried to remember what the SK was. Secret police? She was distracted by physical sensations where Paul touched her. It had been like this in the railcar, as if their bodies had totally independent wills and had decided they needed to be in contact. She wondered if he, too, was conscious of this spark between them.

Paul was speaking to a man in the uniform of the railway posts-and-telegraphs. Of course! Kate now understood with clarity what she had only known before from books—that in Africa the railroads carried the wires and mails and tracks and pumped into white communities the lifeblood and nervous impulses of Europe. Before the railroads came, a white man was lost if he wandered more than a few miles inland.

The Abyssinian grays pawed the baked earth. Paul said, "We're going to the fort." He gave an order and then added, "We'll call on your brother—"

Just like that! Kate clenched her hands; beyond that she revealed no reaction to Paul's offhand statement. Instead, she tried to let the sights and sounds flood her senses. The squat, sullen walls of the fort frowned on hovels whose occupants came out on hearing the dogs bark. Orders were shouted along battlements. A pair of nail-studded doors creaked open. Paul saluted the rigid sentries. More orders in a cobbled courtyard. There was a smell of damp brick. Boots struck against stone. Here, thought Kate, the Kommandeur is preceded by an invisible steel arrow. No wonder the Governor felt emasculated and in need of his own police force.

She was escorted to a cell-like room after Paul cautioned her to be ready within the hour. Her lumpy carpetbag was waiting on a narrow cot under a barred window that looked on a parade ground lit by flares. Hot water steamed gently in a zinc tub. A tray with delicately cut sandwiches had been set beside a pot of tea. A lamp cast a warm glow.

On the cot beside her bag was a small stack of documents, a short note on top. "This was carried by the dead American." She examined the rest. Papers identified him as a Uganda Railway Volunteer, re-cruited by the Stockbrokers Battalion of the Royal Fusiliers. She came to a red handbook folded back at a section entitled Musketry Regulations: "How to Use Your Bayonet." The lines fell into a macabre blank verse in her mind:

> The bayonet should be directed at the target's throat.
> The point will enter easily and make a fatal wound.
> Usually exposed are face, chest, belly, and thighs,
> Or kidneys when the back is turned.
> Bone protects the genital triangle so
> Aim at the soft area, three inches below the navel.
> Six inches of bayonet is enough to incapacitate
> And allow for a prompt withdrawal.
> If bayonet goes too far, it is often impossible to pull out.
> In such a case a bullet should be fired
> To break up the obstructing organs.
> IN!
> OUT!
> ON GUARD!
> If you rigidly follow the drill, there will be no time to think.
> Bayonetting is not an unpleasant business
> If conducted automatically.

An English manual like this in Chuck's possession might have justified hanging him. The genital triangle . . . there will be no time to think. . . .

But she'd had too much time to think. Kilimanjaro dominated Kate's thoughts. If the mountain held her brother captive, she wanted to know all about it.

Paul had said: "The people of the mountain think it's the place where man was born. Some German explorers have fossilized evidence that the first manlike creatures emerged near there. You don't object to Mister Darwin's suggestion we're descended from apes?"

"I'm more conscious of it here than ever," Kate had answered.

"There's a saying: 'Somewhere the Sky touches Earth / And the name of that Place is The End.' "

That place, thought Kate, was described in another book left here for her: an account published in 1893 of a climb by a French missionary, Alexandre le Roy. He had written:

Kilimanjaro rose high and clear, celestial and benign. Great fires of dry grass were burning. The long spirals of white smoke rose slowly in the evening air like incense burners placed at the foot of the mountain. The high forest was most amazing, enormous trunks of the ancestors of the forest covered with swellings, pitted with crevices, overgrown with creepers, orchids, ferns, mosses, bushes and a whole layer of parasitic vegetation. . . . Thunder strikes the distant peaks, the lightning passes in endless flashes, the darkness descends, the rain falls like an avalanche, the wind howls with infernal violence and the earth itself trembles as to break open. One walks with the idea that one is at the gates of hell, in a corner of that forest Dante described.

The mountain seemed to loom like a magic fortress of Kate's childhood nightmares. "An enchanted mountain," the Arabs called it, "hiding itself or changing its place, only to reappear and hide again." It had been thrown up during the earth's great upheavals of fifteen million years ago that also created the lava plains of Masailand. There was an old Abyssinian legend that King Solomon's ring was at the very top where elephants in the past had come to die. Above the 2,000-meter line there was shelter for rare birds: the green tinker with low, rasping, clinking cry, the monkey-eating eagle, the widow bird named Fischer's bulbul after Gustav Fischer, who had discovered strange ruins there. Into the cloud forest climbed lion and leopard, white-maned Kilimanjaro bush pigs, giraffes and honey badgers, Kaiser's rats and tree mice. Perhaps, thought Kate, such a reserve of wildlife would provide the right conditions for testing the rival theories of Darwin's disciples. It no longer seemed strange to her that men should wage a war around such a mountain, the highest solitary mountain in the world.

She jumped at the sudden knock on her door. Paul appeared. She followed him through dank tunnels and spiked gates. She was out of breath and reminded herself that at this altitude the air was thin, the mists cloying. Across another yard dark shapes moved in a sort of fog, and then came another tunnel. Huge iron gates clanged shut behind them.

"We're on our own," said Paul. "If I've made a mistake, the Governor will have me swinging on a rope by morning."

Governor Schnee no longer doubted that if it were put to the vote, German East would elect Colonel Paul von Lettow to the rank of General with full military and civic powers of command. The train journey had demonstrated this. If only Lettow would put a foot wrong. The man had too much charisma. The word had lately come in vogue, being stronger than the German word *Charme*. The Governor cursed the Tanga victory and the accident that had conferred on Lettow a scarred eye, the swashbuckling black patch, and that curiously impressive necessity to hunch his head and shoulders as if advancing into a storm.

Schnee's train drew into Moshi two hours after Paul's. The garrison commander and a small honor guard slid with exquisite precision into view, arriving exactly where the Governor must step down. Flares lit the dark faces of askaris in battle kit along the red carpet winding into the main hall. German officers stood with ceremonial swords drawn at formal salute. The Governor unpursed his plump lips and squared his narrow shoulders, squeezing the sphincter muscles in his buttocks to control any nervous twitch of face, and descended in a manner that prompted Count Kornatzki to mutter "tight-assed bastard."

The ride to the fort with Major Wolfe deepened the Governor's apprehensions. Streets were dusty with the passage of wagons and mules. The red glow of forges spilled out of alleyways. Carpenters hammered, wagoners tapped, ostlers moved among the whinnying horses. Always, somber undertone to sharp cries and clatter of hooves, there was the soft shuffle of the army's barefoot carriers. To the Governor's protest that nobody slept, Wolfe replied carefully, "There are reports of English troops moving along the border, Excellency."

"Then I must communicate with my colleague in Nairobi, the English governor, at once!"

"The telegraph lines are down between here and the English," Wolfe said swiftly.

"Runners, then, Major!"

"I'll see to it, Excellency." Then, heading off more objections, Wolfe added, "Professor Etrich is here, of course."

"Igo?" The Governor's face lit up. "Wasn't he to demonstrate his monoplane—?"

"Tomorrow at dawn, Excellency."

Schnee sighed. He had been looking forward to a good night's sleep. "A postponement, Major? Why must aviators always leave at dawn?"

"Conditions then favor a successful launch, I believe, sir. I was thinking the machine might be used to drop your message to the English."

"Ah, yes, I see. A capital notion!" The Governor settled back, a martyr to duty. The coach and escort drew up under the fort walls. "And what are the arrangements for the trial of Truman, our American spy?"

"That has not been the Kommandeur's most urgent concern, Excellency."

"It has *my* highest priority, Major Wolfe!" The Governor acknowledged the salutes as his carriage passed into the fort. "Charges read, evidence heard, sentence of death. A morning's work and still time for a drink at noon."

"But we're in a state—"

"State? What state are we in, Major?"

"The state of emergency, Excellency. Telegrams were sent down the line. The Kaiser's orders at the Kommandeur's request."

The Governor turned to Ada for the brandy flask and caught her smirking. Quickly she adjusted her expression. So that was why Paul suddenly went ahead. She kept her eyes on the Governor's purpling face while she poured the brandy into the screw cap of the flask.

"Major, it is more important than ever that the Truman trial take place immediately. You hear? Immediately!" His execution would prevent this madness turning into full-scale war, thought the Governor. It would show the Kaiser what was really at stake.

Kate was still luxuriating in the sweet familiarity of her brother. He was the same untidy handsome devil: black hair uncombed, chin deeply cleft, eyes dark with passion, and the wide mustache made popular by some Mexican guerrilla leader. Chuck was summer on Cape Cod, winter at Walden. He was maple syrup in the snow. He was the simplicity she missed in Berlin. He was a language she had not spoken for so very, very long.

"How much do you know?" Chuck asked after Paul had left them alone together.

She told him while he paced the monkish cell carved from solid rock. She saw now why his hair was so long. It concealed a livid scar on his neck, running under the collar of his vaguely military tunic. But Chuck had been too much a loner to become an army man. His skill was in linking men and machines, in "messing about" with flying machines.

"I'm no longer the boy adventurer you knew, Sis," he was saying. "When you came to Zanzibar, I still dreamed of finding the world's biggest diamond, of blazing a trail by aeroplane to the inland lakes, of developing new resources. Then I met Jacob. He'd already done some of these things. He made me look at a different challenge. Our Jewishness."

Kate stiffened.

"I was excited by his dream of finding a sanctuary in Uganda— an antechamber for Jews to the Holy Land."

"What has this to do with us?" demanded Kate.

"Hear me out, Sis. I never was happy about the way we changed the family name."

Kate concealed her dismay. Fierce family rows had broken out over the choice of "Truman" by Grandpa Goldstein. He had migrated from Germany to St. Louis in Missouri with his sweetheart. Their first-born, Joseph, the father of Kate and Chuck, had moved his new young family to the fringes of the most solid of American society institutions on Fifth Avenue. Joseph Truman, an investment broker, doggedly refused to make known his Jewish origins, but he had never denied or cut the German ties. Indeed, after his lavish contributions to President Wilson's election campaign in 1912, he had been appointed to the American Embassy in Berlin. Kate and Chuck had attended Berlin University, from where Chuck went on to Oxford with an unexpected Rhodes scholarship.

"Who is this Jacob Kramer?" asked Kate, not bothering to hide her displeasure.

"Let him tell you. He foresees what's in store for our people unless they form their own government to give them protection, to protest against persecution abroad. He was inside English concentration camps in the Boer wars. Children were dying from neglect. Jacob got sick and fell into a delirium, saw Jews instead of Boers, saw human skeletons waiting in line to enter Christian chambers from which they would not return—"

"You let a mad old Jew trick you into this?" Kate said in alarm.

"Wait till you discuss it with him, Sis. He sought me out in Zanzibar. He'd been asked to help Jewish migration, not from a comfortable distance as a rich diamond trader giving to charity, but by direct action He had a premonition he'd not come out alive. So he wanted my advice—someone brought up a non-Jew. What purpose, he asked, would there be in sacrificing himself now just to gain self-respect? Yet if he refused, would he always wonder if he'd been a coward—or worse? I told him to do what he believed was right. Because courage was the key. If courage goes, I said, all goes." Chuck smiled. "By the time I'd answered Jacob, I'd answered myself."

Chuck had agreed to work on a secret survey with Jacob's Zionist friends and with Shai, the Jewish underground intelligence service. They began with Leasehold Number Sixty-four, set aside for a Zionist national home by some English empire builders who planned a chain of white settlements, protected by the Union Jack, from the southern to the northern corners of Africa. This proposed Jewish state was in the marvelously clear air and highland climate above the Rift Valley. But the Zionist settlers were not eager to become part of an empire, however paternal, and other would-be settlers violently objected to Jews who, they said, were notoriously useless on the land. Some Jews nonetheless had settled nearby and in ten years had made their region the biggest wheat-growing area within British-controlled territory.

Chuck's companions had their eyes on Ugandan territory. They had detrained from the Uganda Railway during the August bank holiday weekend when war in Europe broke out. Unaware of the conflict, English settlers were enjoying the holiday and paid scant heed to the Zionists, who were ridiculed, however, in *The East Africa Standard* for seeking to build Israel in "Jewganda."

"We blundered into German territory on the following Tuesday," said Chuck. "The English settlers had just found out about the war and came after us as spies and saboteurs. The Germans weren't much kinder. We split up and some of us escaped. Two of us walked straight into the Kommandeur's men. I was marched in to see him, and he moved fast to get me out of the Governor's clutches by saying I was in proper uniform."

"Why should Paul protect you?" asked Kate.

"Paul, is it?" Chuck grinned. "Then you must remember old Paul the Hun?"

Kate shook her head. She still had to come to grips with her brother's Zionism. "Brer Fox"—she reverted to the name they had taken from childhood readings of *Uncle Remus*—"tell me, Brer Fox, is it your Jewishness that threatens your life?"

"No," he said. "If the Governor gets his show trial, my execution will be unavoidable because I'm American."

Kate's confusion grew. She argued, "When I left Berlin, the Kaiser's greatest fear was American intervention. Surely, if you were tried and—and found guilty—there'd be such a gigantic fuss! Protests from Washington. Front-page headlines—"

"Exactly what the Governor wants. If I were caught spying for a foreign army, serving a Jewish cause, working with black revolutionaries, the Governor could play upon the fears of his English neighbors and of the Kaiser, who nurses a neurotic fear of some international Zionist conspiracy."

"So the Governor would win the Kaiser's approval and English support?" She watched her brother with eyes catlike and electric blue in the guttering lamplight. "How can I help you escape, Brer Fox?"

"Keep out of it, Sis. Let Paul worry—"

"No! Paul's interest is military."

"Don't dismiss Paul. Don't you remember my letters from Oxford?"

"The young German officer who was a Rhodes scholar?"

"That's it. You practically fell in love with him just from my descriptions."

"I'm not in love with the original, if that's your hope."

"You could do worse," exclaimed Chuck.

"How can any woman love a man whose only love is killing? No soldier should expose himself to the danger of falling in love."

"Why not?"

"It would unman him," said Kate and stopped, thunderstruck by her unwitting echo of Paul's exact phrase.

Kate remembered now. She had known him only by the nickname that Oxford undergraduates invented: Paul the Hun. He had arrived at Oxford at the same time as Chuck. Both were beneficiaries of a grant awarded by the English empire builder Cecil Rhodes, who had made a fortune in African gold and diamonds. She remembered Chuck's comic leters about Rhodes's scholarships "for men of high character to create the best of all possible worlds, a world ruled by English-speaking gentlemen." As an afterthought, Rhodes had included the Germans, and the Kaiser had sent Paul to Oxford "to get inside the English mind for a year."

Now, in the rush of memory, Kate recollected her brother's thrilling prediction that Paul, a favorite of the Kaiser, would rise to high rank. It had made an impression upon her because Father was then already angling for the Berlin post. Kate could see now that the period had been a golden age before the *Nacht-und-Nebel*, the night and fog, of war descended. Perhaps she should have recognized the first hint that Germanic *Kultur* would cast a shadow upon that glorious age from Chuck's own description of the sort of man the German system was organized to create out of Paul: ". . . a dictator with powers of life and death, should he be placed in command of troops. In war, living alone, guarded always. If he shows himself, his lieutenants will shift to lee. None will dare address him except on matters relating to duty. No soldier will speak without removing his hat. One will uncover one's head to him as to one's God. . . ."

Kate was increasingly bewildered. Despite his background, Paul was no perfectly tuned military machine. Was she modifying her opinion because she needed him to save her brother? She had condemned him as a warmonger, a lover of battle. Now, to protect Chuck, was she willing to see Paul as a cultivated and wise leader? Perhaps this was the perpetual barter of life: one surrendered ideals for the sake of security.

She was startled by the rattle of bolts. The heavy door creaked open and Paul entered. "I'm going to make you more like a kitten, *Kätchen*." He used the German name for Kate, playing with the words. He tossed clothing onto Chuck's cot. "Your brother will leave here with me. Jacob will explain the rest while he cuts your hair." Jacob walked in, carrying towels and a pair of barbers' scissors. "We don't have time for argument," Paul said, cutting short all protest. "The Governor's hatchet man is already on his way."

Magdalene von Prinz cranked the gramophone once more and the cracked record played the song for the burial of a dead soldier: *"Ich hatt einen Kameraden."*

She returned to the damaged sofa set in front of the dying fire. It no longer seemed important that all her earthly possessions were crammed into the tiny buttery, such a cramped shelter compared to the spacious farmhouse now destroyed. She had spent the earlier part of the night in a restless search for family papers and then returned exhausted to where Quentin Pope had restored order.

He had produced a meal, a New England game soup made of venison and onions discovered in the storeroom where racks of wine had also survived. Magdalene made no secret of her surprise that he could cook.

"I had to learn despite being married," he told her and was mildly surprised when she changed the subject and asked, as the record clicked to a stop, why soldiers celebrated the death of a comrade.

"Tom's favorite soldiers' song," she said, "is some English version ending, 'Then worms will come and eat you up.' He thinks it funny."

"War does strange things to people." Sitting with her on the sofa, neither commenting on the absence of anywhere else to sleep, he remembered London in the first feverish weeks after war in Europe broke out. "Getting off" between the sexes happened in trams, buses, in the underground, on the street. Two perfect strangers would become lovers at a glance, as if the war threatened to snatch away all future chance of happiness.

"So you're married, too?" Magdalene looked up at his face, brooding and ruddy in the fire's glow.

"Was. She went back to her parents in Vermont."

Magdalene curled her feet up, set her glass of wine on the baked earth floor, and carefully placed her head in Pope's lap. He sat very still.

II

Furor Teutonicus was the way Kate would have described the violent rage of the man dancing in front of her an hour after Paul had taken her brother from his cell, leaving her with Jacob. She stood in the darkest corner, clothed in borrowed breeches and bush jacket, feeling literally light-headed from the extremely short haircut given her by Jacob.

She knew she was in the presence of the secret police chief, Hackmann, who perfectly fitted Jacob's description of a hatchet man, with small ears curled tight against a bony skull bristling with short pinkish bristles. His path had been blocked by Jacob, who was objecting to Hackmann's manners.

"I'm *Mister* Kramer to you. And let me remind you, I'm honorary American consul in Uganda."

"You're a Jew," snarled Hackmann. "Jews belong to no country. There's no Jewganda, Jew!"

"Nevertheless," Jacob replied calmly, "you will abide by normal rules of international conduct. I represent the American government on behalf of Major Truman."

Commissioner Hackmann lowered his head like a frustrated hunting dog. His lips were moist and already salivated over the nearness of his quarry. His tiny red eyes darted uncertainly toward Kate, who remained silent, obedient to Jacob's instructions.

"I am here to convey Major Truman to the civilian court," grumbled Hackmann, his body slackening into the posture of the practiced toady.

"In the middle of the night?" Jacob looked in the direction of the frock-coated native guards waiting outside. "Under armed escort? This bears the stamp of the Governor. A quick trial and execution—"

"I take orders from the Governor," Hackmann said. "His Excellency is acting within his rights."

"Not Major Truman's rights," replied Jacob. Timing the gesture carefully, he withdrew papers and held them just beyond the policeman's reach. "There are certain requirements before the trial can proceed."

"Damn the requirements! Stand aside, Jew!" Hackmann started forward again.

Jacob placed his small frame directly in front of the burly figure. Hackmann drew a revolver.

"I warn you," said Jacob, holding higher the fistful of papers. "Physical violence against a representative of the United States government is a serious offense."

"You're no consul, blast you! You're as fraudulent as 'Emin Pasha.'"

"Who was nevertheless Governor of Uganda."

"And remained a Jew!" Despite his anger, Hackmann's voice was changing to the shrill defiance of an official unsure of his grounds. Jacob saw this and pushed forward, forcing Hackmann to back into the open doorway.

"I am here at the Kommandeur's request," said Jacob, "to report all proceedings to Washington. Until you come here with the Kommandeur's express permission, Major Truman and I will continue to confer alone."

Kate watched the repulse of Hackmann with a mixture of apprehension and admiration for the old man. Jacob must be nearing seventy; he was frail; and she was certain he was not an honorary consul for anyone. He had a fierce will, though, and that frightened her. He had re-created her brother, it seemed. Now he was re-creating her. After the door had been bolted again and the clatter of boots receded, she asked, "How long must I do as you tell me?"

"Until your brother is safely away. Perhaps by dawn." Jacob escorted her to a chair. "Do you want me to continue?"

Again she felt compelled to give him the answer he clearly wanted. "Please go on."

"This is a good *slik*, a good hiding place," said Jacob appreciatively. He resumed the account he had started earlier, arousing Kate's suspicion that he hoped to convert her to Zionism as he had Chuck. "I told you about the horror I found in the English concentration camps. I was sent to investigate, being a neutral American and someone of substance in South Africa. The Boers had been fighting guerrilla wars to preserve their independence, and they made Kitchener—now the war minister in London—look an ass. So he burned their homesteads and pushed their dependents into what he called concentration camps. Women, children, and old men were put behind barbed wire without medical, toilet, washing, or canteen facilities.

"The prisoners were herded into cattle wagons for the new camps. The railroads were arranged to speed delivery of inmates. Extermination got rid of those who could not work—extermination by neglect, malnutrition, smallpox, pneumonia, scarlet fever, and diarrhea. Their sleeping places were encrusted in excrement. Children died like flies. Fine men testified to these atrocities thirteen years ago—men like the stretcher bearer Gandhi, and Edgar Wallace and Conan Doyle and Winston Churchill. The young Spanish-born painter Pablo Picasso has portrayed the English oppressors as brutal, half-witted soldiers in jackboots.

"The Boers were persecuted because they lacked a government to speak for them. I saw how Jews could be wiped out by these same new legalities and these same new technologies."

Kate interrupted. "Yet you turned to Germany?"

"A temporary ally. We all need them. Germany has been the enemy of our enemies in Russia—where the danger has been the greatest. Today Germany fights Russia. A young girl like you knows nothing of the persecution of Jews in Russia, which is far worse than the treatment of Boers by the English. The standard greeting among Russians is '*Boje Tsaria Khranee!* God save the Tsar!' It is followed automatically by '*Bev Jidoff!* Beat the Jews!' "

"That German police chief—Hackmann—said something about Emin Pasha," said Kate. "Who was he?"

"A good thing you ask! Emin Pasha was a Jewish physician from Berlin who made us aware of the possibilities in Africa for a Zionist sanctuary. He was an adventurer and took the Moslem name when he joined the English colonial service here. Thirty years ago 'Emin Pasha' was besieged, and there was an international race to rescue him. Really at stake was Uganda! It appeared on German maps as part of the Kaiser's sultanate and on English maps as governed by 'Emin Pasha' for England. A *New York Herald* reporter, Henry Stanley, finally saved him, and he works here now for the German colonial service. The Kommandeur and Count Kornatzki have said they would support his claims to make Uganda a Jewish homeland."

Kate shook her head disbelievingly. "Uganda's so very far away, weeks from the Tanga region. Before the railroad it must have taken several months' journey on foot."

"Uganda's really a state of mind," argued Jacob. "Churchill called it the most suitable of all countries for a practical experiment in state socialism. Theodor Hertzka proposed a 'Freeland' there that would guarantee all inhabitants the right to do as they pleased. At this very moment there are three battalions of Jews fighting as part of the English Royal Fusiliers because they believe in English promises of a Zionist national home."

Kate was unmoved. She respected Chuck's decision to embrace the Zionist cause. But she identified herself solely as an American. There seemed nothing more idealistic about seeking a Jewish homeland than there was about being a patriotic American. If she rejected Jacob's plea, she admired his courage, and she decided not to add to his burdens. She said that her concern was for Chuck. She knew her masquerade would be over soon. What then?

"You must watch over the Kommandeur," Jacob replied. "We need him."

Kate shook her head. "I'm grateful for his aid to Chuck. Beyond that he means nothing to me. It's you who needs him."

Jacob gave her a searching look. "Germany will need him someday."

A soft rapping at the door interrupted them. The bolts were withdrawn, and they heard the soft chattering of Bamboo, the monkey, then saw Paul's gun bearer, Skaramunga. An urgent voice addressed itself to Jacob in Swahili.

"Time to go." Jacob took Kate by the arm. "It will be near daylight outside. Skaramunga will take you directly to your own room. Go to your bed as if nothing has happened."

"Where's Chuck?"

"He's safe." Suddenly Jacob took her head between his hands and kissed the top of her hair. "I shall be watching over him, child."

It seemed as if she had struck some sort of a bargain, thought Kate, following Skaramunga down the rock-walled corridors. She turned, expecting to see Jacob coming up behind, but the old man was gone.

"Five thousand English troops crossing the border with native askaris," said Hackmann, adding after a second's pause, "Kommandeur."

"How do you propose to deal with *that?*" demanded Governor Schnee. "They're swarming over the Kaiser's Mountain." He repeated the words, relishing his fancy. "The Kaiser's Mountain."

Paul shifted his gaze from one to the other. "How long have you known this?"

Hackmann volunteered, "For an hour."

"And you saw fit to discuss it with His Excellency first?"

"Well," said Hackmann, beginning to sweat.

"*Well what?*"

"The commander-in-chief—"

"Is me," rasped Paul. "We are at war, Commissioner. Get back to your office. Double check your agents. God rot you, *move!*"

Hackmann scuttled out of the mahogany-paneled dining room where the Governor had been taking an early breakfast.

"How dare you give him orders? This is intolerable," said the Governor.

"It would be less tolerable for you to become known as the Governor who failed to resist an invading enemy." Paul looked up as Major Wolfe pushed through the door. "I'd be obliged if you would write the following," he continued, taking paper and pen from Wolfe and pushing them into the Governor's hands. " '*All adults between twelve and fifty are hereby conscripted for military service and will report to the local akida. The jumbe will carry out these instructions.*' "

The Governor saw the trap. The *jumbe* held the Kaiser's *jum-*

benschein certificate of authority. If the *jumbe* failed to produce the conscripts, the *akida* collector of taxes had power to punish him. This method of raising armies often provoked native rebellions. An uprising now would be blamed on the Governor for issuing the decree. But if he failed to sign, in the face of an English invasion, the Kaiser would want to know why. The Governor pushed the pince-nez up the bridge of his snub nose with a trembling hand. His side-buttoned boots danced under the table, and his buttocks lifted slightly from the chair.

"Write!" ordered Paul, and the Governor's hand jerked forward.

Major Wolfe whisked the signed papers away and murmured politely, "Your landau is ready to take you to the aerodrome, Excellency."

Paul smiled inwardly. Aerodrome was a new word in Africa. He also liked that other innovation just produced inadvertently by the Governor. There was no question, if you called it the Kaiser's Mountain instead of Kilimanjaro, the region became identified with German honor, German duty, and the German Empire. It had been the Kaiser who decided to reinstate the Swahili usage of Kilima Njaro as a retort to Queen Victoria, who had remarked that he could lick the snow off the top like an ice cream cornet, which was why she was letting him have it. Any German who let the English snatch the mountain back again would never survive the Kaiser's wrath. And the Governor knew it.

The Governor's wife was coaxing indiscretions out of Professor Igo Etrich in a muddy field on the outskirts of Moshi. Dawn was not the time Ada would have chosen for flirtation, when a damp mist shrouded Kilimanjaro and the early light was reduced to a funereal gloom. Igo Etrich was the designer of the fabulous Taube. Already the rumors had spread to Africa of the Taube's role in the smashing German victory over the Russians at Tannenberg in August. Ada saw little that was formidable about the flimsy mothlike machine. She found its maker far more challenging, a stumpy black-bearded Austrian.

She had come early on the pretext of bringing the inventor a canteen of hot tea laced with rum. Now, the tea consumed and the time set for the demonstration almost upon her, she squeezed Igo Etrich's hand. "I would so love to surprise my husband with a little advance knowledge."

The professor returned the pressure. With Fritz, the mechanic, he had assembled the demonstration model in record time, each part numbered and crated, and each crate and package miraculously delivered here. He had endured the Governor's postponements with patience. Nevertheless, none of the crowned heads of Europe had subjected him to such delays and disappointments. It was true, of course, they had treated the machine and its maker as a joke. Still and all, the Central Powers and their emperors and generals were not laughing now. The Taube tractor-monoplane fluttered over the battlefields of Europe with a deadlier purpose than any had imagined possible.

Igo Etrich had been warned about the Governor's wife by the colonial minister responsible for sending him to Africa. "Ada is coquettish out of vanity, but it is ambition that makes her use every device to please the Governor and thereby control the colony."

She was pressing her body close to his, urging him to permit her a closer view of the monoplane. If her ambition was identified with the Governor, there could be no harm in yielding a little to her charms. Igo Etrich led her around the dew-moistened golden fuselage and past the ugly Mercedes-Benz engine. He made her duck under the thin wires supporting the slender wing. He stood behind her and, with each hand supporting her above the waist, he allowed her to view the pilot's position.

"That," he said solemnly, "is the joy stick. It means the same in German or English. Like many aeronautical terms, it originates with the Americans. The stick," he continued pedantically, "by which we maneuver— *Ach!* I *beg* your pardon."

"Please," Ada said innocently, "I was looking for your stick of joy."

He said breathlessly, "With this machine the pilot and one passenger may travel four hours without a stop, or a distance of four hundred kilometers."

"And the tank is full?"

"Yes, of course; it must always be so."

Ada turned from the cockpit. "Look out! Here comes my Pumpernickel."

Igo Etrich gasped again. He was aware of clutching the Governor's wife much too tightly at the same moment that he saw the Governor in the back of a motor-driven landau.

"Perhaps you should be warming up the engine," Ada said helpfully. "You are very good at warming up."

These words had an electrifying effect. Igo Etrich executed a smart step to the rear and unhanded Ada. With a gay snap of the heels and a schoolboy shout to Fritz, he leaped into the pilot's seat. Fritz ran to the propeller and grasped the wooden blades. The six-cylinder Mercedes exploded into life. Ada ran out of the slipstream in time to be caught by her husband descending from the landau.

It was the Governor's intention to reprimand his foolish wife. Before he could utter a word, the barrel of a revolver was laid against the back of his neck and a voice with an unmistakably American accent said softly, "One move, Excellency, and I'll blow your brains out!" Nobody else could have heard the threat spoken directly into His Excellency's ear. Ada seemed to notice nothing.

A black-coated figure, holding down his black hat with one hand, sprinted from the mechanic's tent to the cockpit and ejected Igo Etrich at the point of another gun. Chuck Truman shifted the revolver from the Governor's neck and bolted across the grass to vault into the vacated pilot's seat. He gave the Mercedes a burst of throttle and the Taube rolled forward. Beside him Jacob Kramer crawled into the observer's position. The monoplane, gathering speed, zigzagged between the tents and kangaroo-hopped down the field and into the air.

When they brought the news to the Kommandeur, Paul expressed polite disbelief. "Impossible!" he declared. "Hackmann, you yourself visited Major Truman in his cell, did you not?"

Chuck Truman had never flown in Africa. He was not as scared as his situation warranted because he was too busy. The Taube was not maneuvered by ailerons; instead, the pilot had to warp the wings. The wings were supported by piano wire from a vertical pole above the pilot's head. The heavy water-cooled Mercedes intermittently tossed back splotches of oil that obscured vision. The machine bucked and kicked in the early morning winds. Cloud streamed off the face of the central massif and the summit towering nearly four miles above the plains.

Chuck glanced back at Jacob crouched in the observer's bucket seat, with nothing but bamboo poles to separate him from eternity. Jacob knew the location of the pioneer Zionist community on the shores of Lake Victoria opposite Entebbe in Uganda. His objective was to keep flying north until they reached the Uganda Railway and then follow the tracks—and that required first flying around the mountain.

Jacob could see the rocky slopes tilting at crazy angles on his left side. He had never in his life felt so discombobulated. He had been bounced out of his seat early on. The sensation of traveling unaided through the sky had been terrifying, and Jacob clung to the frame of his seat until he discovered straps for the purpose of tying him to the machine. By then they were being whirled across the Tsavo plain, east of Kilimanjaro, and above English territory.

Jacob had known every inch of that soil. Looking down on the sandy expanse between ancient black lava and the Uganda Railway, he thought he saw again the band of hopeful Zionists who had trekked out, encouraged by English politicians but rejected by English settlers. Then he saw that the cavalcade was infinitely larger.

An army of askaris and their *bibis* and *totos*—their women and infants—proceeded on foot and horse and mule up the dark red scar of the railroad embankment and across the lush green swampland. They joined in three thick columns climbing Kilimanjaro's lower slopes. Jacob could trace the marchers back to the fortresslike English station of Simba, named after the lions whose man-eating tastes had once delayed construction of the line. There were trains backed up from the water tower, disgorging more troops and porters and native women and boys, trailing all the boxes and bundles of an African military expedition. The long flat rays of the rising sun threw the upward-sloping landscape in stark relief all the way to Nairobi.

Blue flames from the exhausts of the thundering Mercedes stabbed the pink-and-green-stained sky. Chuck's eyes were weeping from the airstream of the whining prop. As the sun warmed the plain, he saw the flash of guns and bayonets. He grimaced at Jacob, hanging half-way over the ribbed fuselage. They had stumbled across the spear-head of an English attack.

12

Tom von Prinz was aroused in his bivouac by the cry "A letter, a letter, it is burning in my hand! A letter, a letter!"

Grumbling, he rolled out of his cot. He heard the native runner challenged, heard the response, and waited. The postal system was becoming too efficient. The time was two hours after midnight. The runner was the end of a chain reaching back to the nearest railway station and its telegraph key. The runner burst into the inner circle of tents with his message fixed in a split reed.

"Bwana Sakarani—"

It was, as Prinz thought, a telegram. He slit open the cover. The message was addressed to him personally: FOLLOWING DISPATCHED ALL RESPONSIBLE PERSONNEL. MAJOR CHARLES TRUMAN BEING HELD FOR TRIAL THIS NIGHT ESCAPED. ALL UNITS REQUESTED GIVE TOP PRIORITY TO RECAPTURE OF THIS AMERICAN OFFICER WHOSE DESCRIPTION ALREADY CIRCULATED ALL POLICE POSTS. FOR YOUR INFORMATION TOM EXERCISE DISCRETION SIGNED KOMMANDEUR SZ.

Tom von Prinz grinned. The final sentence was a reminder that Paul was only going through the pretense of chasing Kate's brother. Well, good luck to Major Truman! He and his sister were better allies than Cornelius and his black revolutionaries.

Prinz moved out into the clearing. The moon had been late rising and bathed the surrounding scrub in an eerie light. The hyenas near the waterhole had resumed their unnerving laughter. There wasn't much point turning in again. A few hours and day would break.

"*Hapana majibu!*" he told the waiting runner. "There is no answer!" He clapped his hands and raised his voice for the benefit of the still sleeping members of the patrol. "*Sikia-sana!* Rise and shine! Sherr-a-leg, sherr-a-leg, sherr-a-leg! We're moving out. Douse all fires."

Long after, the bush continued to echo with startled outbursts of beasts and birds. One of the satisfactions in soldiering, thought Prinz, was that you didn't have to explain your decisions. He'd made camp because he was tired and didn't fancy a night march. Now he was breaking camp because he was awake. It was that simple. No woman's questions to answer, no explanations. He listened to the men girding up and watched with pleasure the keen young face of his German subaltern checking the gear. What wife in the world would respond with such unquestioning obedience? Well, Magdalene, maybe. He was suddenly in a fever to see her. She'd certainly not hesitate to cook up a decent breakfast even if he was in time to slip under the blankets with her first.

Pope watched Magdalene sleep in the firelight. He tried consciously to print the details on his mind. The black hair fanned out across his thighs. Small black curls clung delicately to the nape of the softly curving neck.

She stirred and seemed to stare at him, her eyes unfocused. She murmured and the long lashes closed again. Like morning dew, moisture gathered in the tiny curve of her upper lip.

Pope disengaged an arm and slowly moved away. He located one of the animal skins and spread it over her, took a light from the fire and put it to the wick of a lantern, carried the lantern to an upended crate where the light would not fall on the sleeping woman, and there he began to write. The compulsion to set things down on paper, the daily logging of events for *The New York World*, created a need like eating and drinking. Pope wrote while the logs shifted in the grate and the lantern glass darkened with soot. He reread what he had written and was taken aback. He had been scribbling almost in a trance, trying to fix on paper thoughts that were difficult to phrase. Now they seemed trite. He sounded like the writer of romantic novels, derided by reviewers as suited only for the simple-minded. He had written about love and how it transcended all reason, caution, or physical reality. He wondered why these words, crabbed squiggles in the dancing flame, so disconcerted him now.

Pope folded the sheets of paper and glanced at the sofa. He was glad Magdalene had nothing about which to reproach herself. They'd both feel less uneasy for having spent the night together innocently.

He got up and put what he had written inside one of Magdalene's riding boots. That way she could hardly fail to find the letter. He hadn't intended to write a letter. It was a spontaneous outpouring of sentiments. The dawn chorus of birds penetrated from outside. He walked to the door and heard a clatter of hooves. When he swung the door open, Lieutenant Wahle was sliding from his saddle.

"Prinz is here!" In his excitement, Wahle forgot his manners. "Magdalene's husband!"

"Thank you, I'm aware who he is."

The Lieutenant boggled. "He's riding fast."

In confirmation, a figure on horseback appeared out of a blackened clump of trees. The horse was coming at a gallop.

Wahle's curiosity carried him into the doorway. His eyes probed the dim interior. The captain's wife was in for several shocks. What a bitch she must be. He'd thought she was different from the general run of settlers' women, who were always making eyes, as if bored by too little work and too many servants. He felt Pope's surprisingly strong arms propel him back.

"I wished only to save embarrassment—" Suddenly Wahle drew himself erect. Prinz was out of the saddle before the horse pulled up in a spurt of dust in front of Pope.

"What the devil brings you here?" asked Prinz.

"The Kommandeur thought I should see—" began Pope.

"Did he, now?" Prinz interrupted. "Curiosity satisfied, then?"

Pope kept his voice calm. "I'm sorry. About your home. If it's the result of a deliberate program of terror, my paper should hear of it."

"Of course it's a deliberate atrocity. An English atrocity!"

"That's yet to be proved, Captain."

Prinz glowered. "I'll prove English involvement, never fear. Where's my wife?"

Prinz brushed past the American and glimpsed Magdalene rising sleepily from the sofa. His misgiving were swept aside by a rush of emotion. "My love!" He spread his arms.

Magdalene hesitated, one foot halfway into a riding boot.

"Thank God we're spared." Prinz hooked the door shut. "Who cares if material goods are lost?"

"You were always extravagant with words," said Magdalene, cramming her foot down firmly.

Lanni aroused Kate from a troubled, exhausted sleep. The black girl wasted no words. "The Kommandeur is addressing his officers. You should be there."

"Why me?"

"The English have launched a general offensive. Now your brother is safely away—" Lanni stopped, then added, "I'm sorry. You fooled everyone and enabled your brother to escape and, of course, you're last to know." Her eyes flashing, she described what had happened. "It was a good thing Hackmann didn't inspect those papers Jacob waved at him," she concluded. "They were forgeries."

"Jacob seems infinitely resourceful," said Kate, unable to keep the distaste from her voice.

"He sharpened his wits against Myles Hagen, the English captain you saw at Tanga." Lanni saw Kate shudder at the recollection of the violence, and she said, as if to drive home some lesson, "Hagen is in charge of the hunting down of Paul. Myles Hagen's keenest pleasure is the hunt and the kill."

Kate regarded her with astonishment. "I'm not interested in the barbarism of soldiers."

"You're interested in Paul's survival."

"No. Not particularly." Kate spoke so coldly that the black girl's eyes glazed over. Kate fell silent, then said suddenly, savagely, "Let's get it clear, Lanni: this is Cloud-Cuckoo-Land. I'm not getting emotionally involved."

Lanni began to paraphrase softly from Heinrich Mann's *Im Schlaraf-fenland*, In Cloud-Cuckoo-Land. " 'A land of thoughtless, perilous innocence with its own laws, out of touch with the reality of the world at large.' In such a place, Kate, you need an emotional touchstone."

"But I've no plans to stay here. My concern was for my brother. That was all."

"You'll find you have other concerns," said Lanni.

"Our aim," Paul was saying, "is to destroy here those armies that would otherwise invade the Fatherland. It may take five years."

There was a gasp from his audience of young professional officers. To qualify for duty in the colony, each one had had to excel in three years' active army service. Other empires might send out wastrels. Germany planted the best of her sons.

"I am pulling out of here," Paul continued, "because we are not concerned in this kind of warfare with positions won or lost. The guns we have now must be reckoned the guns we'll fight with five years from now. What we eat, what we wear for the next five years must come out of our own resources. Five years from now our manpower must come out of the black children of today. Five years to replace our human losses."

Kate stood beside Lanni and studied the young officers, each immaculate in starch-collared white uniforms that contrasted with Paul's open-necked shirt and ragged shorts. They crowded the low-beamed operations room, leaning against whitewashed clay walls or squatting on the red earthen floor. The morning sun had yet to warm the fort's interior, and the air was damp and cold.

"In Africa the hunt is not one-sided. Let me quote you the field manual on an old enemy, the Black Napoleon." Paul opened a worn book and lifted the black patch from his damaged eye. Kate was shocked to see how closely he held the book in order to read, and then she decided skeptically that he found this more dramatic than using his monocle. " 'The Black Napoleon always retreated before larger forces. He attacked only to break up our concentrations and not to hold territory. At the earliest opportunity in battle, his forces dispersed and coalesced behind our lines of advance. He surrounded our positions but never occupied them, preferring to let us wither inside.' Gentlemen, that was how German colonial forces were once beaten by a black rebel. Now we must adopt the methods of that so-called savage."

During this discourse, the sentries drew aside once to admit General Wahle, the sixty-four-year-old cavalryman who had sailed to German East with young Kurt, his son. Unlike Lieutenant Wahle, so pale and priestly, the General was like gnarled oak. His legs were bowed, molded by chargers. His white-maned head reared back from a beer-keg torso. His face was the color of puce, what could be seen of it through a tangle of white whiskers. He stood with arms akimbo, listening while Paul concluded.

"The final victory will go to those who fight the better guerrilla war. Watch for any signs that the English are shifting leadership from white to native officers—these are the ones to fear. And, as I said, never overlook, never disregard Hagen. Myles Hagen is not in favor with the present English command, but he still operates his own formidable forces."

Heads turned as General Wahle growled and then spat out the words: "Hagen! Hagen's a pip-squeak spy, sir. What's this rubbish about retreat? We're not a rabble."

"Correct, sir! Not a rabble." Paul saw several of his younger officers glance at the General with sympathetic curiosity. "Gentlemen, this is General Wahle, retired. He has volunteered to serve with you—"

"No!" rasped old Wahle. "To serve *under you*, sir!"

"Very well. You are invited, General, to command communications and the women's corps!"

Kate watched as consternation fought with pride in the old man's face.

"That includes transport," Paul added. "And support services for Thunderbolt and Israel irregulars whose insignia and codes you will all be briefed on."

"Transport?" Wahle tugged his whiskers. "You were speaking about retreat. That means tearing up the rail tracks."

"And laying down new ones," said Paul.

"What? What's that?" The General cupped his ear.

"We'll pick up and lay tracks where necessary, as we have done already with the *Koenigsberg*. The ship's guns"—Paul paused and grinned—"the guns were modified in the Dar workshops after they were sledged out of the Rufiji and then loaded on a makeshift railway." He waited until the applause died down. "You will all get a chance to study in detail how this feat was accomplished, because I expect you to do better. Major Wolfe!"

"Sir!"

"Finish the briefing." Paul swept up his battered bush hat and reassessed the fresh young faces. "Gentlemen, I've never pretended to be a model of sartorial splendor. If I catch anyone dressed for a dinner dance again, he'll be on a charge. Personal cleanliness, by all means. Individual distinction, no. The enemy must find it impossible to tell you from an askari. No heroics, gentlemen. No playing-field rules. No holding on for death and glory. You will fight and run, smash and grab, kill and not get caught!"

Governor Schnee sat in his quarters talking privately with Commissioner Hackmann. "I daresay you built up quite a file on the Kommandeur in Berlin?"

The police chief pretended not to understand as he considered the implications. He had laid before the Governor a report on Major Truman's escape. No proof of conspiracy, nothing to link it with Colonel von Lettow.

"Have another drink," coaxed the Governor. "Half the stuff will be left behind. No sense baptizing the English in it."

"Treason," murmured Hackmann, pouring a cautious thimbleful of schnapps. "Treason, to abandon the fort without a fight."

"The Kommandeur could be shown up as a traitor if we knew more about his personal life." The Governor blinked owlishly, the morning's indignities drowned in the noonday tipple. "Cigar?"

"I hear the Kommandeur's planning to make tobacco, too," Hackmann murmured, reaching for the cigar box. "A five-year plan of total self-sufficiency. Are *you* prepared to stick it out that long?"

"My policy is to outlast everyone. The telegram from the Secretary of State of the Imperial Colonial Office reaffirms my supremacy. Not a move I'll make that isn't by the book."

Hackmann revolved the cigar between his moist lips. "You have the power to hold the girl. I could arrest her in the first instance as an alien." He squeezed the wet tip of the cigar between thumb and finger, licking his lips as the tobacco leaf split open gently. "Seduction, not rape, Excellency." He waved a lighted match in front of the deflowered cigar. "There was an affair in Berlin that revealed a weak link in the Kommandeur's armor. Miss Truman might be another."

Major Wolfe tried to close his army sketchbook before Paul saw his drawing of Kate. Too late. The Kommandeur was taking it from between his nerveless fingers.

"Very good," said Paul. "But the contours I need are territorial. I need maps to leave behind—false maps, crammed with errors. The English are chronically short of maps. They think we're infinitely better equipped." He had flipped a page and now glanced away hastily from some verse written in Wolfe's careful script. "Draw me some maps, Major," he added gruffly. "Go down and see what the Governor's wife has in the way of copyists. She's organizing some female talent for Hammerstein's operations tonight."

Wolfe felt as if his face still burned when he joined Hammerstein in a canvas-topped trolley. He became stiff and formal after Hammerstein complained about the Kommandeur's refusal to disclose broad plans. "Africa," replied Wolfe, "hardly lends itself to logical concepts. Our enemies are hidebound and hope to dominate events by logical schemes. The Kommandeur reacts to events. That's the secret. He'll never have a precise overall plan."

Captain Hammerstein held his tongue when he heard this sacrilege. "Do you know," he asked instead, "where the women's corps is?"

"In the old research institute. The Governor's wife took it over. Half the town's already pulling out."

Hammerstein could see this for himself. Asian traders with their families trudged behind fast-trotting Muscat donkeys piled high with personal possessions. Many of the women wore the funereal black *buibuis* of purdah or envelopes of printed cotton if they were half-caste Swahili or black. Gold and silver ornamented their necks and ankles or gleamed in their noses and earlobes. Their wealth had come from the *Schutztruppe*, and word had spread that the troops were leaving.

Ada swooped on the two men as they walked into the crowded hallway. "Just what I need," said Ada. "More men." She ran an appreciative eye over Hammerstein—slim, handsome, with curling blond locks and light-blue eyes.

Hammerstein recognized the look and edge nervously away. He regarded women with caution, considering marriage an unmitigated disaster until the time came for procreation. He heard Wolfe burbling on about the women having trained here with Count Kornatzki's medical teams. "Now they'll help us manufacture substitutes for rubber, soap, medicine and fuel. Isn't that so, *sehr geehrte Frau?*"

Wolfe's question was answered by Professor Etrich, who had been tugged by Ada out of the throng. *"Ersatz,"* said the professor happily. "That is my motto. *Ersatz* goods and materials."

Hammerstein's attention was wandering. His roving eye paused to study the fresh young face of a girl.

"That," volunteered Ada, "is Celeste, the niece of the captain of the *Koenigsberg*. She is one of three ladies we have selected for you, Captain Hammerstein."

The words fell upon Hammerstein's ear like a death knell.

"For night operations," Ada added sweetly. *"Military* operations."

13

LANNI HAD heard from the Governor's houseboy that Kate Truman might be arrested and was on her way to inform Paul when Lieutenant Wahle came galloping through the fortress gate.

"Hey! You!" Kurt Wahle's harsh shout brought Lanni to a startled halt. He had reined in his horse. "Do you usually ignore your masters?"

She turned slowly. He had snarled in ki-Swahili. She replied in good German, "I don't recognize boors."

"You black bitch, take these reins."

Lanni was wearing a scanty robe, printed in Hamburg with a pattern of pineapples, the garb of a camp follower. She watched him dismount, and when his feet were firmly on solid ground, she told him in polite but precise terms where he could put reins, bit, halter, saddle, and horse.

Wahle had traveled in record time from the gutted estate of Tom von Prinz, his hero betrayed by a woman. Wahle was exhausted. He raised his whip with no intention of using it and bawled abuse at the girl. Lanni spat at his purpling face. The spittle trailed through the red dust thick on his cheek, and he slashed blindly, the crop striking her shoulder. Lanny wrenched the stock from his grasp. One corner of her *kanga* robe was ripped, exposing a full light-brown breast. She cracked the whip once, etching a line from Wahle's mouth over one cheekbone to the ear. The horse shied and clattered away.

Old General Wahle was crossing the barracks square. Dazzled by the afternoon glare after leaving the dim coolness of Paul's quarters, the General slowly absorbed the scene. He recognized Lanni before he had covered the space between and had already decided that the young scoundrel whose horse now clattered around the square ought to be whipped to within an inch of his life.

Then, with a horrified shock, General Wahle recognized his son. Blood oozed from the Lieutenant's lacerated face; his eyes had a wild look.

"Outrageous . . . a son of mine . . . beyond belief!" The General ran out of words and made as if to hit the boy. The dazed young man, unaware the threatening figure was his father, reached for his pistol. The General, responding instinctively, drew his gun.

Half-raised, the General's pistol went off. Young Wahle fell to the ground. His father, robbed now of all speech and action, stared down. He was standing there still, his countenance stormy and unrepentant, Lanni frozen in disbelief, when Paul pushed his way through the circle of onlookers.

"You saw the whole thing?" Paul asked, escorting Kate from her room an hour later.

"My window overlooks the scene."

"Thank God the boy's not badly hurt."

"You still defend him?" demanded Kate incredulously.

"The boy had potential. I was arrogant enough to force his growth."

"And you forgive the father?"

Paul gave her a strange look. "General Wahle? He doesn't need anyone's forgiveness."

"Look here," said Kate, "if young Wahle is your idea of good potential, and a father who shoots him is to be admired, then you and I live in different worlds. Have you forgotten Lanni in all this? Women have rights, too—"

Paul lifted his hands despairingly. "General Wahle was trying to defend Lanni. Look, *Kätzchen*, we are confronting bigger issues."

"No issue's bigger to you than war." Kate stopped and faced him. They had been walking along the crushed gravel skirting the square. Overhead, kite hawks swooped in the dying light.

"You really don't know me!" Paul leaned with his back against the pink-streaked wall, tilting his face to catch the late mountain sunshine. "We need time to talk."

Was this a man crying for help? Kate looked intently at Paul's head profiled against the rock wall and saw a firm resolve that needed no help. She remembered the way the mating lion had lifted his head.

"Let me tell you something about General Wahle," said Paul. "Some years ago he was traveling with influential businessmen who abused the Kaiser as a dictator. One traveler, Walther Rathenau, said that if the Kaiser went too far, the way to correct him was to apply constitutional limits. All the others agreed and even pressed Rathenau to draw up a proposal. Wahle, silent until then, asked if the others would sign such a proposal. They replied yes, yes, certainly. Then Wahle said bluntly none of them had the guts—they'd let Rathenau stick his neck out and then they'd desert because their names on a petition would mean the end of their social advancement, the end of their patents of nobility, no more plum jobs for their sons. Well, of course, Wahle was right! But it took courage and an obsession for honesty to speak up as he did in such company. He was at a critical stage in his army career—"

"Who told you the story?" asked Kate. She knew about Rathenau, Germany's most influential Jewish industrialist. The anecdote would be more impressive if it came from that direction rather than from Wahle himself.

"The niece of Walther Rathenau was present when it happened," said Paul. "I can vouch for the story because she told it to me. I can vouch for her because we were to marry—"

"You married—?" Kate caught herself.

"No. No, there was a tragedy. But that is not the point." Then he was silent.

Kurt Wahle had been shot in a fleshy part of the leg. The infirmary nurse avoided his eye when he requested a more compact bandage so he could ride. Damnation to all women! he thought. The sting of the whip wielded by Lanni hurt more than the gun wound. Now these nurses, gossiping. He could hear them jabbering behind a screen.

"The General shot his own son, imagine!"

"The little fool struck the Kommandeur's *bibi*."

The nurses ran off, giggling, when they saw him. Ringing in his head were the cadet-school litanies about honor, courage, glory, duty. Women corrupted and undermined the will. Look at Magdalene von Prinz, performing unspeakable acts with the American civilian. Wahle let the rage well up. He must punish the adulterous woman. The garrison was too busy preparing to run from the enemy to notice if he slipped away.

The messenger who rode through the scorched landscape into what remained of Tom von Prinz's farm was covered in red dust. "Saddle up!" he yelled, checking his big brown gelding. The horse reared and plunged, the coat stained dark with sweat. The rider tossed a pouch that Prinz caught and unwrapped.

Quentin Pope, from a distance, saw Magdalene's hands fly to her face. He saw Prinz tug his thick red beard while he read the orders. Then the American newsman walked away and took an interest in the stone fountain set in what had been a manicured lawn. Prinz ordered his groom to fetch the blue roan from the stable, and then he took Magdalene back to the gutted house. Their bed was intact, the shuttered bedroom windows merely scorched, the tray ceiling still whole. The frame of the bed was of rocklike *mvule* timber. From this room Magdalene had scavenged nothing.

"Don't go, Tom," she said.

"Stop it, wife." He laughed, mistaking her need, refusing to think she was capable of rebellion. This was old times, the frantic coupling made poignant because they were clothed and booted—and in danger.

She was moist by reflex, feeling his hands at the flap-fly of her riding breeches. God be thanked, he was dumb in this mood of violent lovemaking. Habit made her mimic the movements. He was quickly done. She twisted her face into the bedding. Once she had adored him when the hunger was great. She felt him shift his weight. He was already projected into his male world, where a man was held in contempt if he let a woman divert him from duty's path. She rolled over, and the place on the bed where he had been was mercifully empty.

Prinz had slung his rifle over his shoulder. It was again a part of him alone. On his belt was the knife in its sheath of leopard skin, in his hand the slouch campaign hat. He mistook her tears for the familiar essences. Her breasts heaving under her stained shirt was the ecstasy he had always known. He bent and kissed her, but his eyes were staring through her now.

"Paul needs you with the main column," he said. "Ride up to Moshi with the American. What's left of our possessions will be collected later." He made no mention of his own task, and she knew better than to ask. She had said goodbye in this fashion too many times before, submitting to men's violence and repairing the pieces later. But she knew she would never do so again.

Quentin Pope, watchful beyond the ruins, saw two more men ride over the horizon and draw up under the olive gums. Their horses, frisky in the lively air, curvetted and neighed. Prinz appeared with his arm around Magdalene's waist. The blue roan was restless and jerked against the stable boy's pull. Magdalene stopped and let Prinz continue walking. She straightened her hair and said something to which he replied without turning his head, merely raising an arm in salute. He mounted the horse and swung it around. The messenger and the two newcomers rode up alongside, the tails of their horses switching lazily. Then they all moved forward, stirrup to stirrup. Prinz waved his hat. The horses broke into a canter and were swallowed in the red wool of their own dust.

Magdalene turned and walked slowly toward Pope. Her eyes matched the jacaranda petals, blue and almost mauve. They were still dazed.

"Tom apologized for not saying goodbye." She looked up at him in a sudden appeal. "I'll need your help catching up with Paul."

"Your children?"

"We'll have to trust them to the English."

Pope recognized the rising panic in her face. "The children will be looked after. I'll see to it. That's something a neutral can promise."

She caught the bitter tone. "I'm glad you're not involved. I hate war! I hate the way Tom glories in war!"

She lifted her eyes to the horizon. Horses and men were blurred disks in a dust cloud irradiated by the sun. She still felt Tom's seed running down the inside of her thighs. Maudlin Tom! He seized his wife as he seized the enemy, making love and war with the same cheap gallantry. These madmen took the memory of the last hour with their women and brooded over it in dawns crackling with the blaze of campfires and guns. It was as flat and meaningless as a photograph, but they pressed it between the leaves of time like meadowsweet plucked in spring and preserved between the pages of army regulations. She was tired of their *ersatz* sentimentality. She wanted a real man, who stayed beside her, not riding into yet another celebration in blood with comrades already looking like ghosts in the sunlight.

In response to Paul's call to gather below the "Kaiser's Mountain," the German womenfolk began a separate trek. Magdalene rode with Quentin Pope through a land sculptured by Boer settlers who had moved here to escape English rule. The rains this season had prepared the soil, which was red and moist, folding open behind the spans of oxen like vaginal lips welcoming the winter seed. The days' slow rhythms were shattered by the old cry, "We are trekking!"

"Tom's seen this before," said Magdalene, guiltily anxious that Pope should understand her husband. "He fought in South Africa when twice the Boers rejected London's rule. They won their independence by force of arms, but when the English discovered what wealth lay under Boer land, they tried again to win control. That was fourteen years ago, but Tom is still bitter. He had a son by a Boer girl he couldn't marry. And the child was transported like a convict to the Bermudas when the children began to die like flies in those frightful camps."

Many among them had been Transvaal Boers of German stock. Now fathers and sons swarmed again in response to the flickering helios, leaving the women to manage the land. These Boers had never accepted the second peace with England. "God damn the English!" they had cursed years ago, paying in blood for the land to the south. "If we had no gold and diamonds in our soil, they'd leave us to starve." And they had trekked incomprehensible distances to shelter under Kilimanjaro. Their old *trekpad* was still marked by the graves of men and the bones of the oxen that died along the way when they had withdrawn into a spiritual laager, the camp physically resembling the defensive circle of wagons that was also the hallmark of American pioneers. Here the migrant Boers were comrades in religion to the Germans and cousins in race. This was *Ons Land*, their land. And so they ventured forth again.

Kate became accepted as the Kommandeur's unofficial adjutant in filing and summarizing reports, a task formerly performed by Major Wolfe. She had no time to query the tasks set before her. She had complained enough that in Germany the women played no public role. Now, here, she saw they were equal partners by force of circumstance. Lanni dealt with the native agents run by Cornelius, and Kate thought no one could be better qualified to maintain the liaison between the tribal chiefs and their white comrades.

It was Lanni who brought her the gossip. "The pigeons arrived safely," the black girl had announced, and Kate had not found it necessary to ask who the pigeons were. Chuck Truman and Jacob Kramer had landed safely in the Rift Valley. The confirmation had been flashed back by drums, by sun-reflecting spears, by smoke signals and runners. Already Kate understood the speed of this "bush telegraph." Africa only seemed vast and empty. In reality, it was all eyes and ears.

"Then my purpose in coming here is fulfilled," said Kate, not sounding convinced.

"Your brother is still fighting. He'll expect you to stay with the Kommandeur. Perhaps you can save the Kommandeur? Not in the same way, of course."

"Save Paul? Save him from what?"

Lanni smiled. "From himself, perhaps?"

14

LANNI WENT to see Paul again and found him in the operations room, now stripped bare. Count Kornatzki was there, supervising medical loads for the long trek ahead. He took one look at Lanni and lumbered out of earshot.

"Commissioner Hackmann's got the legal adviser to say a case can be made against Kate."

"What would be the purpose?" Paul asked, displaying what Lanni thought was an astonishingly reluctant interest.

"The Governor wants to get you back under control, and this is one way to pressure you."

"Miss Truman's the last person he can blackmail me with."

Lanni shrugged. "I wish you could jog the Governor back into his old self. I liked him better when he ran the colony for prestige and profit."

"He stayed out here too long." Paul shot her a shrewd look. "Your own people wrecked his health with their hemp and fermented banana juice."

"They thought they'd get what they wanted that way," said Lanni defensively. She motioned gracefully to Kornatzki, and he joined them. "Couldn't the Governor be curbed for health reasons?"

Kornatzki shook his head. "He was going to Berlin for a checkup at the end of the year. I'm certain he'd never have come back here. Too late now."

Lanni returned to her original concern. "Do something about Kate before that sadist Hackmann thinks of something new. She should be at your side, Paul. I can't be in two places at once. The woman can be your eyes in the *pori*, in the bush."

"Skaramunga meets all my needs."

"Not all," said Kornatzki, taking up the refrain. "Kate Truman's young and strong. She'll put some of her health into you. She's twenty years younger. A good difference when you're fighting a war. She'll give you balance."

Kornatzki had been peering into the square. He said casually, "The girl's out there now. Get to her before Hackmann."

"This is a conspiracy!" Paul began to laugh, but then the smile vanished.

Kate saw the two figures emerge. How well they went together, Lanni's slim grace and Paul's thrusting pace.

"Tom von Prinz is waiting for you in the officers' mess," she told Paul. She smiled as a greeting to Lanni and felt a sudden pang of jealousy.

"Fast work. I'll see him at once."

"Not before settling this Governor business," interrupted Lanni.

Paul turned to Kate. "The civil police might try to hold you. It's nothing to worry about. I'll work out some title for you, *Kätzchen*, one that protects you."

"I can think of one," said Lanni.

Paul made a dismissive gesture, but with such good nature that Kate felt another twinge of jealousy. She had a sense of blundering into an alien land as she heard Lanni murmur to Paul, "*Cia ũthoni ciambaga nguhi.*"

Then Kate was alone with Paul in the sun-struck square. The brilliant light, the arid heat, and the nearness of Paul brought to her mind the lions mating in the *korongo*. Paul touched her elbow, and a sensation of pleasure swept through her body. She felt suddenly light-headed, almost feverish. Perhaps conversation would restore her composure. "What did Lanni say just then?" she asked.

"In Kikuyu? A proverb. It means figuratively 'Great events have small beginnings.' "

"What does it mean literally?"

Paul hesitated, then replied, " 'The buying of a wife begins from a small thing.' "

Kate looked away. For a long moment they were motionless, silent, then Paul said, " 'Da steh ich nun, ich armer Tor! Und bin so klug als wie zuvor. . . . And here I am, for all my lore, the wretched fool I was before.' "

Her face drained of color. She broke the physical contact between them abruptly, as if fearing her own impulses. She picked up the Faustian quote from Goethe. " 'And see that for all our science and art, We can know something. . . .' "

He completed the line. " 'It burns my heart.' "

They stood in the sun as if trapped, as if walking out of it would remove all constraints, so that their bodies would merge and capsize discretion. Kate increased the distance between them with a quick backward movement, a sudden twist. She was like a young colt—she tossed her head and her black hair swung and shimmered. She watched Paul resume his steps, afraid to be too near him, so powerful was the urge to touch and caress.

Inside the mess they behaved as if the earth continued in its normal orbit.

Tom von Prinz came to meet them, carrying in either hand a glass of wine.

"A toast!"

Paul raised a protesting hand. "Not yet. We've work to do."

"I insist. It might be our last." The burly soldier-settler pressed a glass on each of them.

"What's the toast?" asked Paul in a resigned tone.

Prinz rescued a third glass for himself. "To the return of Kilimanjaro to England!"

Paul put down the glass. The room was empty except for Major Wolfe, who strolled unobtrusively to join them from the bar.

"That's foolish, indiscreet, and offensive," Paul said softly.

"I meant it to be!" Prinz's face had turned dark.

"For God's sake, ease off," Paul muttered. He glanced around the paneled room. A few regimental trophies still sparkled in their glass-fronted cases, but there were bare patches where the hunting pictures had been removed. Soon this sanctuary of tradition would be stripped of its memories.

"Well?" demanded Prinz. "When do we hand over?"

Paul regarded him steadily now. "Never." The word was almost a whisper.

The English renegade swayed. "Get off the platform! Everyone knows we're scuttling."

"Not from the mountain." Suddenly Paul's face broke into a smile. "You're taking a force to guard the Kaiser Wilhelm Spitze! It's not the whole of the Kaiser's Mountain, but it's the bit that counts. The German eagle will fly from the highest point in Africa—"

Prinz slapped his thigh, the anger in his eyes changing to proud delight. "I'm the man for the mountain. Climbed it as a boy! Know its moods! The way up is the eastern face of Mawenzi. There I can see the English path of advance. Look here—" He began tracing lines in the dust of a neglected table. "The three volcanic centers are Kibo with Shira to the west and Mawenzi to the east—"

Major Wolfe interjected, "The pride of the German Empire in an Englishman's hands!"

"And the Kommandeur in the hands of an American," added Count Kornatzki, barging through the swing doors from the kitchen. "If we're going to save her from Hackmann's thugs, we'll have to give Miss Truman a position of authority. What should her title be? The Colonel's lady?"

Prinz looked stunned. Major Wolfe turned away and examined the label on a wine bottle.

Kornatzki's thick beard split in a grin, displaying black stumps of teeth discolored by bush fever, while he poured a glass for Prinz, who said shakily, "To the Colonel's lady! I suppose the Kommandeur has asked you, Madame?"

"I was expecting it," she replied.

"One does strange things under pressure of war," cautioned Major Wolfe, recovering his tongue.

"She's still an American citizen," warned Prinz.

"You're right," said Kate, seeing an angry flush darken Paul's face. "Loyalties, Captain Prinz, are vital. My first loyalty would be to my husband."

Count Kornatzki sucked his teeth. Prinz blinked and then beamed. Major Wolfe sneezed and covered his face.

Paul gaped at her in astonishment.

"I'm proposing you marry me, Simba," said Kate. "It's the female who takes the initiative, remember?"

News of the marriage threw the Governor into confusion. Ada said sweetly, "They've tricked you, dear, unless you want to jail the lawful wedded wife of your military commander."

The wedding ceremony had been conducted by Count Kornatzki while the first group of askaris poured out of the fort, many dressed in remnants taken from the abandoned Indian stores. Flares and fires of dried dung shone upon the strange procession, providing, thought Kate, a fit background to her wedding. The askaris had been told to help themselves to whatever would keep them warm during the chilly mountain nights. Their uniforms were rolled up in kit bags and ammunition cases, and they marched out wearing tattered dinner jackets, moldy top hats, wigs of grass and sisal, French-style kepis with flaps of cloth, and topees cocked at jaunty angles.

"This is the last solid bed you'll sleep in for a long time," Paul warned Kate when they retired to his quarters. The room was starkly simple: whitewashed walls, a stone floor, and an enormous four-poster bed.

"Sleep's not what this bed's about," replied Kate, making room.

Kate was surprised by Paul's sudden discarding of his armor. She admitted now, without trace of guilt, that he had always touched off in her these rising waves of sensation. His hand on her shoulder had been enough to drive away the demons at Tanga—the corpses imprinted on her mind had then vanished; the battlefield screams had been silenced. She had been embarrassed that he could exercise such power over her. Now she was astonished by the transformation in him, that a man bred for war could surrender to love.

"The Governor thinks this a marriage of convenience," she said once.

"Of course, it's convenient," he chided. "I need you, *Kätzchen.*"

"I needed you," Kate said. "I pretended I was near you for my brother's sake. Then I pretended I was saving you from cloud-cuckoo excess—" She stopped. "The lioness started it all, that day in the creek; the real facing up to feelings that were there all the time."

But she had not won him yet. Toward dawn Paul was summoned despite Count Kornatzki's elaborate measures to leave them in peace. There was trouble in the stables. Kate panicked for a moment and cried out her need to hold him.

"*Kätzchen,*" he said gently, "don't clutch."

She released him slowly. "I will be good. But just once, let me tell you this. My love is possessive. I want you as a lover, not a warrior. I'll stay controlled. Nobody will know each parting is, for me, a defeat."

He refused to acknowledge what she had said. Instead, he told her to come with him. "Woman of passion," he said, laughing. "Give me a hand, woman of passion."

Their way passed through lines of soldiers marching by the light of flares that shone on cartridge belts slung across naked torsos and on forbidding machine guns carried between pairs of men. The frenzy of movement continued inside the stables. Kate felt an unexpected clutch of sexual excitement, brought on by the restless physical force of the warrior horses, their cropped tails flicking with nervous eagerness, bits jingling, saddlery creaking, heads tossing.

A childhood memory flooded back to her, the long submerged recollection of danger from a black stallion serving a white mare. It had seemed a brutal and bloody thing to the small girl, wandering alone on her uncle's stud farm. The stallion and the mare were bred by men for war. She had seen the stallion grip the mare with his terrible teeth, nostrils flared and scarlet, mane flying, ears laid back, eyes rolling. He had reared above the terrified girl, who watched the stallion's forelegs dig into the mare kicking against his chest. The little white mare fell still while the stallion's hindlegs sank into the turf. Then the black stallion arched his loins and thrust and thrust until he slipped, tearing deep bloody wounds in the mare's flanks. The mare sprang out from under him, and the stallion rose, black and enormous against the crystal sky, and utttered a single piercing shriek.

That sexual act, to a little girl almost crushed by the cresting stallion, had seemed frightening, violent, and cruel. Now the lions had shown Kate a gentle and caring act of coupling. The lions ran free. Was that why they were different? Those horses of her childhood, intended for battle, were bred for the U.S. cavalry. She glanced at Paul and wondered how he would reconcile the urgencies of warmaking with the leisurely lovemaking of two made one in flesh to become one in spirit.

He came to her side. A stableman had been leading a string of horses. "Stallions," said Paul. "They'd have killed each other if they had caught the scent of a mare. You can't expect a raw native recruit to know that."

"Is that what happens in your man's world? The males get along until a single female intrudes?"

"Don't anticipate trouble." Paul led her back. "I've issued orders that all womenfolk are to be brought along. We pull back to the Olduvai Gorge. It forms a natural sanctuary. A laager. Askaris may bring their *bibis*, Moslem porters their boys. The wives of my officers are trained for military service. I guarantee, *Kätzchen,* no man will have cause to begrudge the comfort you bring me."

She walked beside him in companionable silence. She had found the gentle lovingness in him, the way of love that was not violent and cruel. But, like the warrior horses, he'd been bred for war.

"I want us to be like the lions," she said, sitting on the edge of the four-poster and watching the gray light of morning creep over the narrow sill.

"Lions only fight and kill for food."

Kate hesitated, and then she said, " 'And on the horse rode Power.' "

His face darkened. "Finish the quotation! 'Beware the horse of Power that rides over us and tramples on defiance. We all love Power, for we have submission in our blood.' " He paused. "Henrich Mann could only write that about other Germans. Is that what you think, *Kätzchen?*"

She was frightened by his somber expression. "It's a warning to all of us."

He was staring through the window to where the mountain peaks caught the early sunshine. " 'Part of a group,' " he recited, still quoting Mann, " 'moving upward in a cone-shaped mass to that height where Power stands, stony and glittering! To share in Power, triumphing even as it smashes us, for in this way Power vindicates our love!' "

She shivered then and clung to him and knew her wedding night was over.

When Kate awoke, sunlight was streaming into the austere room. Paul was sitting by the bed, whittling a piece of wood. He refused to tell her what he was carving but said she must wait until she could recognize the outline.

He was golden in the sun, and she was overwhelmed with love for this man absorbed in carving wood. She would armor him, refresh his spirit, and no enemy, however cunning, would ever penetrate their sanctuary.

Count Kornatzki hammered with unnecessary vigor on the teak panels of the bedroom door, this way venting his anger against himself. He had prayed that the need to disturb Paul would not arise. He had never in his life been so pleased with a marriage. The reasons, he acknowledged, were selfish. The girl would compel Paul to perfect ideas, make his mark far beyond Africa. And God knows, the missionary-doctor thought piously, we'll need him in Germany when the war is over.

He banged on the door again. It opened and Paul, dressed in bush jacket, shorts, and sandals, stood in the sunlit room. Kornatzki glimpsed Kate kneeling on the bed by the window, and he mumbled an apology. "The English have probed into the outskirts of Moshi. Not regular troops; I wouldn't bother you about them, Paul. The regulars are still straggling around the other side of the mountain. These are the bush fighters, native Indian officers, frontiersmen looking for a scrap, and Hagen leading them."

"Who says so?" demanded Paul, closing the door and already moving so fast that Kornatzki broke into a shambling trot.

"A friend of the Governor—Der Dicke."

Der Dicke had come riding in among the tented wagons drawn in a circle outside the fort. None dared question his presence—he was Von Prittzwitz und Griffon, the renowned Boer expert on tribal affairs whose political intelligence was at the disposal, so he declared, of the Governor. He demanded to be taken to Schnee's marquee and would not believe that he and his entourage were already over the horizon.

Major Wolfe had intercepted him finally. The Major had a nose for mixed loyalties.

Der Dicke rose to a great height astride a thickset black horse. When standing, he was six feet four inches tall, and he possessed a powerful belly and a voice rumbling with false laughter. He leaned from the saddle and gave Wolfe a better view of his shovel-shaped black beard, parted and tied with red ribbons to his head of black hair twisted into locks.

"You'll have to ride forward," Wolfe said calmly, "for about another hour."

Der Dicke swayed in the saddle and his dangling legs quivered with laughter. "You don't have to hide His Excellency from me, man. Now tell me. Where is he, really?"

"The Governor's party moved with the midnight columns. Our marching sections stretch such a distance, the first column left at sunset in order for the tail to depart this sunrise. The civil administration is on horseback, but it cannot move faster than the speed of the caravan, which is that of the slowest who move on foot. Thus," concluded Wolfe patiently, "if you ride hard, you'll overtake them."

All this talk was Wolfe's way of delaying the grotesque figure until General Wahle could be summoned. The last thing Wolfe wanted was to have Der Dicke demand to see the Kommandeur. For all he knew, the Boer was a spy or possibly even an assassin. Wolfe was alive to such dangers because, by a disturbing coincidence, he had this day put on an old safari jacket with the crest of a Stuart rose. It was the anniversary of the betrayal of his English ancestor, King Charles the First, which his family in Bavaria always marked by wearing a white rose. By an even stranger coincidence, Wolfe had discovered and plucked a white rose that very morning.

Wolfe watched coldly while Der Dicke slid to the ground and squinted with bloodshot eyes at the black hulk of the fort. Word had come that he would be received by General Wahle, and this deflated the Boer. He threw the reins over his horse's head. It was an old commando trick, and it made Wolfe trust the man even less. A horse needed to be trained over a long period to behave this obediently; the owner must tie the reins to a log until the horse associated loose reins with immobility. Man and horse must have been together a long time to build up such a trust.

General Wahle was sitting inside a staff headquarters marquee.

"My commiserations, General!" Der Dicke bowed.

"I'm not crucified," growled the old General. "What's the fool talking about?"

"Your boy," said Der Dicke. "Gone! Armed and mounted, they say—"

"By thunder!" Wahle lumbered to his feet. The top of his head barely reached the level of the Boer's shoulder. "The subject of my son has been dismissed. You understand? He no longer exists!"

After Der Dicke had been questioned and then told to wait, General Wahle walked outside and took from his pocket a handful of loose tobacco, which he stuffed into a meerschaum pipe stained black with use.

"Watch this man," he warned Paul, who had come to the square with Count Kornatzki. "Use him for his knowledge of tribal treacheries. Then get rid of him. He claims the English have started to lay down water pipes and new railroad tracks to support an overland invasion."

"You're my chief of transport and communications," said Paul. "What do *you* think?"

"He could be sent by Hagen."

"And if he isn't, and if it's not some trap, what then?"

"He says the English cannot move without complicated lines of communication. He also reports the Masai have been talking about magic strings by which Queen Victoria speaks from London. Telephone or telegraph lines, I suppose." Old Wahle paused. "As your director of the women's corps, I have a more positive suggestion—"

Old Wahle lit his pipe. For a moment he had found it difficult not to see young Kurt standing where Paul stood. Young Kurt, during the southwest Africa campaign, sixteen and already as tall as his mother, with her same gray eyes, with a face burned by days in the bush. Young Kurt, anchored against the charge of an elephant, fearless. What had they done to him at that blasted Prussian cadet school? Now the mother was dead—and so was the boy unless he redeemed himself in a manner so heroic that he would probably be killed anyway. Old Wahle waved away the pipe smoke and with it all further thought about his son.

Part Three

The Kaiser's Mountain

15

From Myles Hagen's The Bird Watching Notes of an English Country Gentleman, *Kilimanjaro, late November 1914:*

> The red-eyed turtle dove coos in the soft evening, a most haunting echo of persistent sadness. . . . I have obtained a copy of a letter sent via the Jewish underground from Jacob Kramer to Louis Brandeis, president of American Zionism, reporting a deal with the Germans to make Uganda available for Jewish settlement in return for Zionist help. *What colossal cheek!* This same Jacob worked with "Emin Pasha," the German Jew who once governed on England's behalf in north Uganda. Jacob was also close pal of Cecil Rhodes—shared his gold and diamond interests. Jacob's wealth comes from New York diamond dealing. His brother in London writes in the *Jewish Chronicle*: "We have never felt secure since a British royal commission on 'the dangers of an influx of Eastern Jews fleeing Russian persecution.' . . . London Zionists view German East Africa as best hope." *Well!*
> . . . I know Paul von Lettow better now than I know myself. I can anticipate his moves. I am using Uganda Railway Volunteers to provoke him into attacking, then closing my larger forces in region he treats as sacred. He signaled his resolve by calling it the "Kaiser's Mountain." Power has gone to his head! *Kaiser's Mountain indeed! What a hoot!*

From the war diary of Colonel von Lettow, Kilimanjaro, November 22, 1914:

> Hagen's so-called Uganda Railway Volunteers bear watching. So far identified are two of Africa's greatest white hunters, a Chicago carnival owner, a Washington presidential candidate, a Boston wildlife photographer, a Texas police chief, and bored scions of the American rich. They sound like clowns, but Cornelius reports they are all first-class marksmen and adroit in the bush.

From Quentin Pope in a dispatch to The New York World (*unpublished*):

> Christmas approaches within sight of Africa's eternal snows, remote Kilimanjaro. This forgotten war will influence future more than congealing battlefields of Europe where armies cling to trenches, dugouts, and craters, locked in mindless slaughter because of mulish immobility of generals. Native soldiers here are rallying to German commander they have begun to call the Lion of Africa.

16

"THERE ARE two diversionary forces," explained Major Wolfe. "This group under Captain von Prinz is going up the mountain. Nothing secret about it. We want the enemy to chase after him—if they can. You, Captain Hammerstein, will operate behind the enemy with the ladies."

Alex Hammerstein's jaw dropped. "Just because you put me in with Ada's girls—"

"That's not the reason." Wolfe bent over a map. They were in a tent outside the fort. The sounds of demolition hung over them. "These particular girls have taken a fancy to you, and that's important."

Hammerstein's gloom deepened.

"There's no danger," pursued Wolfe relentlessly. "There *is* need for diplomacy and discretion. Another reason for appointing you. It's a delicate matter."

"You make me sound a ladies' man."

"Nobody was ever under that impression," said Wolfe with heavy sarcasm. "Now see here, it's an experimental operation. Won't take long. If it works, we'll use it as the basis for expanded actions."

There were only two girls waiting for Hammerstein, and they apologized prettily for the absence of the third.

"She's the real expert on giraffes," said Celeste Looff.

"But we're good, too," piped up her sister Elsa.

"Is the other one sick?" asked Hammerstein, not really caring. He was taken aback by Celeste's retort.

"Don't try that male superiority stuff! We're as good as men, menstruating or not."

Hammerstein turned and glanced about to hide his blushes. He had never met girls like them. It had taken Wolfe an hour to explain the route on the map. The girls already understood. That was partly because they would operate in and around the property of their father, Hector Looff, on the eastern slope of Kilimanjaro. He had created, in one section of his ranch, a sanctuary for wildlife. He called it a game park, a revolutionary concept in an age of indiscriminate slaughter by hunters. Hector Looff's brother was the *Koenigsberg*'s captain, a source of pride for Elsa, who was seventeen, and Celeste, nineteen. Both girls had the lustrous black hair and peach complexions of Alsace-Lorraine. When Hammerstein first saw them, they looked like beautiful long-legged boys in jodhpurs and khaki shirts.

They would have to operate with a Boer corporalship of twenty-five men. The mission was frankly experimental. The Kommandeur planned to mix Boers with regular German officers, but the Boers disliked taking orders from professional soldiers. They would, in this instance, have to take direction from the Looff girls. Nobody had ever heard of Boers submitting to female orders before.

The girls rode out with Hammerstein in the middle of the night to a small hut made of wattle and daub. It stank of cow dung and palm leaves wet with mist. Below the hut were the English lines of communication, strung out along a riverbed and looping round behind them. Somewhere at the head of the lines were Hagen and his volunteers scouting the outskirts of Moshi. The main body of German forces now trekked west from the garrison, leaving rear guards and squads of askaris to give an impression of strong defenses.

The girls were to show the Boers how to drive certain game park animals through the English lines with destructive intent. While they waited for the Boer bush fighters, the girls tolerated Hammerstein's attempts to teach them caution. They had wanted to tie their horses near the rendezvous. He had to show them how to hide their mounts, with reins trailing, behind the brow of a hill. He cautioned them against chattering. Still, they giggled and went on whispering. They knew there was no real danger. Their bush sense was instinctive. One girl was always on the lookout while her sister never left the entryway of the hut, commanding a view of the enemy's territory.

"Do you know how Boer commandos operate?" asked Hammerstein. If the girls must talk, they might as well learn something. They professed not to know. "A commando is made up of two field cornetcies, each with two hundred men. They're usually close friends, so they can't be infiltrated. They use code words nobody outside their region could possibly recognize."

"I bet the English lick them," said Celeste, who had attended the English boarding school in Nairobi.

"Lick them?" echoed Elsa, giggling.

"Because they're ice cream cornets." Celeste collapsed in laughter.

"Lord, save me," prayed Hammerstein under his breath.

The Boers came up so silently, their leader was on them before Hammerstein issued a challenge. "Field Cornet Viljoen," he said. This set the girls off into fresh paroxysms they disguised as a fit of sneezing.

They moved into the open together, and at once two-dozen men rose up out of the long grass. They had left their horses in a dip and were covering their leader in case of treachery. Their comrades were raiding the English night train from Nairobi and the supply columns straggling into German East. Viljoen displayed a hoof freshly hacked from an English horse. The regimental number was burned into it. This was how you got information on enemy units, he said casually. The horse had been killed in a small action. That made the girls stop sneezing. They squatted on either side of the field cornet, with the other men sitting on their heels around them.

"The English command post is over there," said Viljoen. "We cut it by riding east."

Then the girls spoke, swiftly, succinctly. Hammerstein was impressed. "We must ride abreast," said Celeste. "We'll descend from upwind." Elsa rattled off the landmarks by which, even in the dark, they would be guided. Viljoen put himself between the two girls when everyone was mounted. The riders spread out, covering nearly half a mile from wing tip to wing tip, each rider made visible by white handkerchiefs tied to the stirrups. The Boers had ridden together so often they could read each other's minds. They moved at a slow walk down the long slope to where Hector Looff's giraffes stood with ears twitching. Normally the animals gathered at night above a narrow defile. Four of them had been with Hector Looff since Celeste and Elsa were toddlers. The tallest giraffe was called

Mädie. She must have been seventeen feet tall, her head poking inquisitively above the flat tops of the acacia trees.

Celeste saw her first and whistled. Elsa followed. Both girls had stuffed fresh lettuce and sugar lumps in their jacket pockets. "Mädie," whispered Celeste and sensed the giraffe moving softly in her wake.

The men sat waiting on the rise, forced to remain spectators. The heads and necks of the ghostlike giraffes protruded above a natural fence along the creek marking the end of the paddock. Habit was deeply ingrained in the giraffes. If Mädie halted on the edge of her territory and refused to go forward, the herd would also stop—and abort the operation.

"Here," cooed Elsa where the thorns and acacia came to an end. Behind her, Celeste rode up, holding out the palm of her hand. She walked her pony slowly through the break in the fence and past Elsa, not daring to look back. She was aware of Mädie moving alongside Elsa, pausing, and then advancing timidly after her. A shooting star curved across the bright eastern sky, and Celeste kept her eyes fixed in that direction, afraid that if she so much as tilted her head, Mädie would take fright. Then, because Celeste was young and romantic for all her pragmatic ways, she made a quick wish on the star concerning Captain Hammerstein.

Hammerstein waited uneasily, his mind on the two girls somewhere in the dark. He heard a whistled signal on two notes. Viljoen held up a white handkerchief, and each man picked up the flash of white from the next and walked his horse toward the defile, while ahead the giraffes filed solemnly through the embrasure, horned monsters in a starlit landscape.

Celeste, with Mädie's long tongue rasping at her open palm, led the cautious procession. They came to the conjunction of two creeks. From here, if she turned left, she should reach the English telegraph lines within two kilometers. The wires would be strung from living treetops, insulated by broken bottles. Dead wood was useless for carrying lines. Only the living wood was impervious to corruption. The lines were raised high so that nothing would break the links between English commanders and their headquarters in Nairobi. They were safe against all animals save the giraffe, whose powerful, long neck was like the iron prow of an icebreaker.

Celeste backed her pony. Mädie had taken the last tidbits and moved softly away. It was a shock to know she'd gone. When would they meet again? Celeste waited in the shadows while the rest of the herd followed the bellwether.

The men's horses swished through the long grass, rifles ready across their thighs. Elsa was overtaken by Hammerstein and swung her pony alongside. The giraffes were striding at a faster pace, nervous about what lay behind, and soon they broke into a rocking run toward the English lines. There were nine or ten cows attended by three bulls and several calves, held now by a tremulous bond. Each giraffe responded to the other without audible contact, as if the swaying necks and knobbed horns were antennae receiving and emitting signals.

The arc of men advanced again, Viljoen quickening the pace. Ahead of the horses, the herd sped up. Viljoen slapped his mount's neck, and the sound echoed along the line of horsemen. Hammerstein turned while the Boers broke into a fast trot. Elsa was pulling back from the ranks. Hammerstein swung closer. Only the giraffes were running now, straight through the enemy lines.

Hammerstein looked for Elsa's companion and found only a shadowy candelabra tree. "Where's your sister?"

"She went ahead of the herd. There was a panic." Elsa talked as if he must understand the empathy of the animals. "They nearly broke in the wrong direction."

"Then *where*—?" He choked back the fear.

"She got them back on course." Elsa smiled in the darkness. Soldiers were so hidebound. It was a simple roundup, and Celeste would be back any moment.

A shot rang out, then another. Hammerstein strained to see the muzzle flash if there should be a third. But there was nothing; only the thin echoes.

Viljoen came riding back. He had night eyes like an owl. The other horsemen followed him up the long slope.

"Time to go," he said. "English *rooineks* are camped down there." He prepared to give the signal.

"Where's the older girl?"

Viljoen slowly lowered his arm. He peered at Elsa. He twisted in the saddle and called softly to the nearest of his companions. The question was repeated from man to man. The words mingled with the wind's sigh, and finally the reply drifted back. "The girl's not with us."

Shortly after midnight Myles Hagen learned his forces were cut off from Nairobi. He went straight to General Gordon Forget-Me-Not Gaunt, who might have seemed out of place among the unconventional Uganda Volunteers except that he wore sprigs of forget-me-nots embroidered in purple around his gilt oak-leafed tabs. His wife had put them there to make sure he didn't forget her. The flowers matched in eccentricity the leopard-skin bands on the bushwhackers' terai hats.

"I think the German Kommandeur is walking into our trap," said Hagen. "The wires are down. The engineers blame giraffes. Giraffes don't migrate across this part of the country. Which means they were stampeded."

General Gaunt let this intelligence sink in. He was tall and thin and had the stooped shoulders of a cavalry officer. His expressionless stare gave a suggestion of deep thoughts swimming inside his large domed head, which was innocent of hair. Few penetrated his armor to find out if he was as slow-witted and forgetful as his appearance and nickname implied.

"Giraffes? Stampede?" The General leaned under the lantern swinging from the ridgepole of his tent. "Who?"

"A German girl was picked up by a patrol. Name's Celeste Looff."

"I say, you spy wallahs move fast. Magicians! Wires down, no communications, so you pull out the old crystal ball, eh?"

"She wouldn't talk at first," said Hagen, unruffled. "Her uncle's commanding the *Koenigsberg.*"

"Celeste Looff? Dash it, of course, the gel was at school with Emily, my young'un."

"I'm going to talk with her now."

General Gaunt sucked his cheeks. "That young lady's not the sort to betray her own people. Not proper for you to question her, either."

"Perhaps I could take her news of Emily?"

"Yes," the General said. "Yes, that would be thoughtful."

Hagen ducked out of the tent. Give a general some polite camouflage to pull over his conscience and he turned gentle as a lamb.

The first thing Celeste noticed about Myles Hagen was the close-grained walnut knobkerrie. She recognized the beads strung on the leather lace securing the kerrie to Hagen's wrist. So this was the creature who took Kornatzki's club and beheaded Wiedemann! She put on an innocent air.

"You must be dead tired, child," said Hagen, straddling a gun box. "You can cat nap for a couple of hours. Then we'll have to send you to the rear for questioning. Or you can chat until breakfast and get your eight hours' beauty sleep up the line. Which?"

"I'd sooner talk with you," Celeste said sweetly. "You know it won't help to ask me questions, though."

"Of course." Hagen sighed. He knew about the Looffs—Max defying the whole Royal Navy; Hector coaxing crops out of volcanic soil. Stubborn breed. This girl would give precious little away.

He was startled when she said, "I'm sorry I can't explain about the giraffes. My father's research is still secret, which is silly, but that's the way he feels, and so I mustn't answer questions about it."

"What giraffes?" asked Hagen. "We are not," he added carefully, "interested in your father's livestock experiments. And you can take my word for it, nothing you tell me will go beyond these tent walls."

"Well," began Celeste, fluffing her hair, "Daddy's worried about the effect of gunfire on animals kept in captivity, so he made me chase the giraffes out into the bush."

It was the dark hour before the dawn when Hammerstein had caught up with Paul outside Moshi. By daybreak the garrison would be deserted. The Kommandeur was not pleased when told about the missing girl. But the Boer Field Cornet had been correct to refuse Hammerstein's request to try to rescue her. "Take a patrol and reconnoiter," said Paul. "Don't run risks, though. One girl isn't worth one trained soldier. Sorry, Alex."

Hammerstein and his four askari trackers were joined by Skaramunga. "Bwana Simba sends me in his place," God's soldier announced. The silver-gray monkey, Bamboo, sat on his shoulder. Hammerstein was moved by this evidence of Paul's concern after the pretense of harsh military logic. Skaramunga was precious to Paul. Only later did it strike Hammerstein that Skaramunga had used the increasingly popular name of the lion for his commander.

By noon, his eyes sore from lack of sleep, Hammerstein heard the sharp soft cries of the monkey. The patrol was approaching a patch of black lava. Bamboo jumped up and down on Skaramunga's shoulder, dropping his head and then raising it in the direction of a Somali mule trotting through the heat haze.

"Take cover!" ordered Hammerstein, focusing his glasses on the mule, which had zebra stripes painted on the flanks. A mule camouflaged as a zebra was an English trick. Then he saw Celeste bouncing on the mule's back, her legs trailing. Hammerstein showed himself and imitated the whistle he had heard Celeste use with the giraffes. She swerved.

"It's me—Alex!" he shouted, forgetting in his eagerness that only in daydreams had he heard her use his first name. "Captain Hammerstein!"

She jumped down and sent the mule running with a slap on its flanks. "Get me away from here!" she said. "Fast!"

She refused to talk until they had put a good distance between themselves and any English patrols. Then she told Hammerstein about the questioning. "You can identify the man because he had Count Kornatzki's knobkerrie. He knew I was at school at Nairobi. He was a big man, red and hairy. I tried making goo-goo eyes at him, but he's not the sort to be interested." Hammerstein felt a twinge of envy. "Then Emily's father came along and turned out to be General Gaunt. The other man explained how I was setting the animals free, and Emily's papa said I wasn't to be treated as a prisoner. So first chance I got, I stole an army mount." She wrinkled her nose so deliciously that Hammerstein's heart seemed to miss a beat. "I never rode a pack mule before. It's given me a frightfully sore behind," concluded Celeste.

When Paul heard the girl's story, he sent for Der Dicke. Major Wolfe and Count Kornatzki were already in the command tent when Der Dicke thrust his way in.

"What do you know about General Gaunt?" asked Paul.

Der Dicke's eyes shifted from face to face, eyes that gleamed red, like those of a wart hog brought to bay. "Why, Gaunt's a reservist, farms in the Rift Valley," Der Dicke began cautiously. "He's cavalry, not popular with the general staff in Nairobi."

"So they'd palm him off on Captain Hagen and his circus act?"

"Yes, yes, exactly. Could I ask why—?"

"We've made contact with Gaunt's forces on the other side of Moshi. Hagen's there, too. What would *you* suggest I do?"

Count Kornatzki and Wolfe glanced at Paul, trying to conceal their surprise.

"I am consulting you," Paul added flatteringly, "because you are famous for your expertise in bush fighting."

Der Dicke plucked at the ribbons in his beard. "You are too kind, man." He paused. "Knowing the opposition, I'd accelerate the evacuation process. But I would also, Kommandeur, attempt to ambush General Gaunt. He's far forward of regular English forces—"

"And cut off," encouraged Paul.

"Yes, and cut off from reinforcements so long as they lack telegraph lines."

Paul nodded. "Very well. Now, sir, I believe you wished to be of further assistance?"

"In evacuating this region, yes," said Der Dicke eagerly. "You will need ten thousand porters for every hundred kilometers of travel in the bush. The kaffirs eat their own loads, a kilogram a day. They need their women, else they go berserk. Overseers, you'll want to give them *hamsa ishirini.*"

Paul winced at the reference to lashing porters with the hippo-hide *kiboko* whip. He said, "We have a specialist in transport," and picked up a field telephone and cranked the handle. "Mister Singh? I'm sending over your new technical adviser."

After Der Dicke had been escorted out, Major Wolfe said, "God save us, what are you doing, Paul?"

"Working out the exact opposite plan to what that treacherous bastard just suggested," said Paul.

"Mister Baghwash Singh is my name," said the blue-turbaned Indian awaiting Der Dicke. "Railwayman is my profession. Bombay my home. I am for many years working on Uganda Railway for *bloody English.*" The *babu* English phrase poked its way into his lilting German. "My specialty is nigger transport, caravans, loco-mobiles."

Der Dicke took a deep breath and immediately regretted it. An exotic aroma of garlic and red peppers hung on Baghwash Singh's breath.

"We are destroying equipment here," continued the tall Indian. "We are having little to work with."

The Boer listened in glum silence. This man was the cheekiest kaffir yet. But he must know a thing or two. He must know, especially, what was being done to link up the German raider *Koenigsberg* with the Kommandeur's headquarters and where the *Koenigsberg* lay hidden. Without that information, Der Dicke could do nothing to help his fellow conspirator, the hunter Pieter Pretorius.

Baghwash Singh twined his fingers in his thick black beard. Finding nothing in his beard for inspiration, the Indian thrust a finger into a large hairy nostril and beamed happily, his mouth moist and his teeth stained red with betel spittle.

Pieter Pretorius, holding a long measuring rod, stood in a dugout canoe that floated in the muddy Rufiji waters near the *Koenigsberg*.

The capital of South Africa had been named after his father. The elephants of the Rufiji that had died under his guns were known as pretorians and numbered near six hundred. The German police had chased him for years as a poacher. The German governor had tried to take away his land on the edge of the Rufiji delta. He was an anti-English Boer, turned into an anti-German Boer by German stupidity. He was engaged now in plotting the channels by which shallow-drafted English monitors might get within shelling range of the German warship whose seamen were scattered in the surrounding marshland.

Through his own knowledge of these waters, Pieter Pretorius, without awaiting help from such spies as Der Dicke, had located the *Koenigsberg* and the huge sleds being hammered together for hauling along a hundred-mile corridor to the Dar es Salaam workshops. The warship's crew had been reorganized into the *Koenigsberg* Land Force. KLF units were equipped with the warship's 47-mm secondary guns, now mounted ashore. Tropical mold ate across the corsair's decks and bulkheads, the hull was sinking into the green jungle, food and medical supplies were running down, morale fell as the days dragged on, and the men collapsed with dysentery and fevers. The KLF patrols grew jumpier in the relentless heat, scattering when the hippos splattered the river banks with excreta and slapped their tails, sounding like hostile machine guns.

Pieter Pretorius knew the spine-tingling mysteries of the Rufiji sewers, crammed with creatures from another time. He knew how the toughest white hunters broke under the strain of so much that was unfamiliar. He gave the *Koenigsberg*'s crew no more than a few days. Then the tension and the pestilence would curdle their brains.

His gun bearer had taken a *ruga-ruga*, leaping on the man from behind and choking him with one fist thrust into his throat for silence. The runner carried a message from Governor Schnee. Pretorius read it and then buried it. There would be more of the same, of course. Eventually the orders would get through to Captain Looff. The Governor was calling on Looff to exercise his right as senior officer of the Africa Corps to take full command over Paul von Lettow.

Maybe sometime early in the new year, thought Pieter Pretorius, it would be wise to encourage Captain Looff to trek inland. Sometime in, say, March. By then the Captain's brains would be thoroughly addled and half his crew would be dead.

17

SCORPIONS DRAGGED their five-inch deadly bodies out of muddy holes left by a flash flood on the outskirts of Moshi. Regarding them in silent horror, Hagen was forced to admire the tactics of his enemy. Paul had an African sense for the swiftly changing seasons and had pulled his best troops out of the garrison just before the first sweep of mountain rain. It had been Hagen's hope that the German would blunder into a fight with the Uganda Railway Volunteers probing into the town. Hidden on each of Hagen's flanks were two dozen English regulars, ready to close a trap.

The distinctive rattle of German Maxims brought Hagen to his feet. The machine guns were identifiable because in this hot climate they must be fired in squirts of five shots to prevent overheating. General Gaunt stepped out of the shadow of a mango tree, and a sniper's bullet smacked the ground between his feet. "Just where I planned my siesta," said Gaunt. "Don't the blighters stop for lunch?" But while he spoke, the General opened the bolt of his Lee-Enfield. "Oops-a-daisy," he said, sliding the blunt cartridge into the breech. "God rest ye merry—" The brass-encased wad of death rode the greased steel. "O way and up she rises!" he murmured while the cartridge crept into its hole. He clamped the bolt tight and squinted along the barrel. He was a thrifty soul and would never waste a bullet.

Hagen took in the rock overhang, his men scattering, a horse wild-eyed and frothing at the nostrils. This was not the German attack that he had planned to counter. The ambusher was ambushed.

"*Hu-yu! Hu-yu!*" A pair of Masai scouts hopped up and down. "There he is!"

Gaunt's rifle cracked. A man reared up on a pony profiled against the blue sky above the ridge. The bullet had gone through the rider's leg and into the horse's heart. Gaunt hummed tunelessly, searching the boulders for another bargain. Two for the price of one. His barrel ceased its traverse and again jerked. The Maxim stopped stuttering.

A young English subaltern came running, concerned for the safety of General Gaunt, aged sixty, too old for this caper, blood staining his arm where a sniper hit, standing and munching sandwiches as calm as you please. Beyond the ridge Major Wolfe fired his 1873 cannon. Gaunt yelled a warning. The subaltern was blown into bloody pieces.

One of Hagen's volunteers manhandled a Vickers machine gun to the top of a rocky tower. An askari with ammunition belts slung from his neck shinnied up behind. Hagen crossed his fingers. A well-placed Vickers was murder, equal to a thousand native spearmen. Hagen's gunner on the rock was soon firing at a target invisible to Hagen below. Then the gunner shot bolt upright and sailed end over end into the riverbed. Hagen's volunteers and General Gaunt's English troops were now immobilized between the hill and a ford by a small force of Paul von Lettow's men.

"Hit and run," said Hagen.

"What?" asked Gaunt. "What's that?"

"Paul von Lettow's motto." Hagen looked around the deserted *kopje*, a volcanic knob from which a path retreated up into the mountain slope beyond. The German force had left only its dead, heads hanging from rocks or bodies propped up, limbs twisted grotesquely. The corpses were in shirts and cotton trousers, pockets empty. Hagen contrasted them with Gaunt's English officers, striding around in cord riding breeches with leather strappings inside the knee, steel spurs clinking, jackets heavy with papers and badges. He watched Gaunt descend sideways the steplike ridges in the rock, revealing the cavalryman's manner of clattering down stairs so the spurs don't catch.

"The Huns aren't exactly fuzzy-wuzzies, are they?" said Gaunt, catching up again. "One doesn't just dash in and biff 'em, eh? Still, they lost fifteen dead, and with their limited resources, can they afford it?"

"If they get the general in command," said Hagen, "yes. And they nearly did. If you hadn't been quick—"

Hagen broke off and hurled himself at Gaunt, knocking him down while he tugged his own pistol out. Gaunt rolled onto his elbows and saw Hagen dive for a German left for dead. The man was on his knees, rifle up, aiming for Gaunt. Hagen's body blocked the muzzle while he took a snap shot. There was a double blast. Hagen jumped sideways, and the German fell back with a bullet between the eyes.

"Dammit," said Gaunt, rattled to see Hagen had been winged. "You saved my skin, blast you!"

Hagen sat up, laughing. "Blast your eyes, General, you'd better save mine."

"Eh? What? How?"

"I've been outwitted. Headquarters will hold it against me. I wanted you to witness a classic maneuver. What you've seen instead is Lettow's classic counter-maneuver. Look here—" Hagen began sketching in the sandy soil with a stick. "I wanted to trick the German into springing an ambush, and then my men would have closed in."

General Gaunt watched, and there was nothing in his cold mastiff-gray eyes to warrant his reputation for being absent-minded. He had accepted Hagen's invitation to join this sortie because he recognized in Hagen the wild genius that flourished best in odd circumstances. When Hagen finished, the General had only one question to put to him: "How do we fight this German Kommandeur?"

"With his own weapons. They say I'm a savage. Well, General, none of us will survive if we don't learn Lettow's way of fighting. Take no prisoners on the march; they're a burden on supplies. Take no wounded prisoners at any time; they consume time and resources. Cut down on porters and loads. Shoot every 'dead' soldier between the eyes."

General Forget-Me-Not Gaunt stooped to listen. This was hardly decent military behavior that Hagen was advocating. But Hagen was right to condemn the complacency of high-ranking officers. Myths surrounded them. The truth was, the worst defeat the English ever suffered in all their imperial campaigns had been the losses around Diamond City in the Boer wars when the total dead came to less than four hundred. Never having taken a real beating, English generals disregarded their adversaries. In their well-advertised wars among poorly armed savages, the losses had always been trifling, although the literature was always epic.

Gaunt was the son of a Scottish crofter. He had battled his way up from private soldier to general. He had never forgotten the power of the peasant, and so he was not dazzled by helping rule a third of the world's heathen. He knew someday there would be a bloody reckoning. If it happened here, he wondered how well many of his colleagues would handle it, generals like Ha-Ha Splendid Aitken, who was most at home with a bodyguard of turbaned Pathans, crimson-jacketed, with jackboots polished like glass and gold-mounted scimitars at their sides.

Quentin Pope was astonished when he caught up with the Kommandeur's staff to learn of the marching retreat. The American correspondent felt a brief stir of guilt when he heard that Tom von

Prinz was staying behind on the Kaiser Wilhelm Spitze. The trial of Major Truman was swept away by events. What lay ahead offered journalistic challenge of staggering proportions. Pope said as much in a dispatch to *The New York World* that he left in the German fort commander's office in an envelope clearly labeled To Be Tele-graphed Courtesy of Captain Myles Hagen. Many weeks later a version appeared in newspapers around the world.

By then, two hundred sixty German officers and almost three thousand askaris had retired to the Olduvai crater. Twenty thousand carriers and camp followers were with them. After blowing up the Moshi fort's magazines, Paul's rear guard had departed on light cavalry horses, hot-tempered hunters of limited stamina who would be quickly worn out and then hacked up for food and raw material. The cavalcade consumed itself, the bags of mealie flour on porters' heads deflating, the flocks of Abyssinian sheep dwindling. The curvetting hunters eventually would be rendered into soup paste, thongs, jelly, and anything Professor "Ersatz" Etrich could devise.

Kate shared the rigors of the march. She felt she was on trial before the askaris and their womenfolk, and she wanted to see things from their viewpoint. She was plagued by the leisurely bloodsucking of huge brown flies, by the sharp attention of *dudu* insects climbing her ankles, by the persistent whine of mosquitoes. Tall grasses and thick bush restricted her vision to the heels of the man in front. She seemed to march backward in time to a primitive existence when ears and nose were more important for sensing danger than eyes. The monotonous rhythm of the march induced a walking slumber from which she was aroused by sudden irritations: the treacherous wait-a-bit thorn tearing at her face, the scorching heat when sweat inexplicably and without warning poured down her back, and the choking dust when a horseman galloped by.

She was persuaded to mount a mule, to the evident relief of the askaris, who regarded their white comrades as entitled to such privileges. Black hands slapped black skins with the mindless regularity of a wildebeest's whisking tail, and black faces wrinkled with laughter at white officers less patient about the vexations of the bush, the *bundu*.

From the saddle Kate glimpsed distant vistas. The slight increase in height enormously increased her vision. She understood better Paul's purpose in keeping the lookout monkey, Bamboo, perched high to give warning of danger.

On the march Pope wrote almost daily reports that he kept for the next opportunity to pass them through the English to his New York office. He was fascinated by the German retreat into self-sufficiency. A chemist, dragged from his labs at Moshi, might spend an entire day trying to coax drinkable water from a water hole. One glass of liquid would be half filled with vegetable matter which had to be precipitated out with Eno's fruit salts, fizzing up hundreds of green bubbles and leaving a green slime floating in the upper half of the tumbler where it could be scooped out. The smell was no worse than that of exhausted bodies now reeking from ulcers for which nobody had yet found a natural cure.

Governor Schnee traveled with four hundred baggage carriers, two printing presses, and three tons of German paper currency. Paul went to pains to avoid a direct confrontation, hoping the Governor would set up a separate administration Paul could bypass. But Schnee demanded the protection of *Schutztruppe* guns, and in reply to Paul's polite inquiry about his extraordinary baggage the Governor wrote: "Civilized standards must be maintained! We must keep printing money, for which the presses are necessary, in order to pay the natives for whatever we take."

Paul had ordered his demolition experts to turn the Moshi garrison into *Ein Truemmerfeld*, a junkyard, but to leave buildings standing that might be recaptured later. He wanted Hagen to move in. The further he could suck the main English forces into his own territory, the better.

He had left raiding parties to operate from mobile bases beneath Tom von Prinz's position on the mountain. They worked with Cornelius's guerrillas and became bolder as they learned to fight as teams. *"Raus!"* *"Tuendeni!"* The whispered orders became so familiar they needed scarcely to be breathed. *"Feuer!"* They blew up Uganda Railway bridges, trapped enemy trains, blocked tracks, took English prisoners for interrogation, and then always pulled back into the black roots of the mountain. The English were forced to move their trains dead slow with mine detonators in front. Rail cars plated with six-inch steel became cremation chambers when troops were trapped inside by the raiders.

Cornelius spread the rumor that English telegraph lines were bad magic, "tying up" Africa with strings pulled by London. Native villagers stole them, finding that the copper wire made attractive bracelets, and were overjoyed that the wire was always hurriedly replaced and seemed to regenerate continuously from an unlimited source. It was wonderfully entertaining to watch, from behind the trees, the effect on English tempers.

Lanni moved into Moshi when the English took over. She was too striking a woman to remain undiscovered, so she gambled on the reputation of her royal family and English reluctance to offend the Sultan of Zanzibar, her kinsman. Among the new English faces were those of self-proclaimed experts on African politics, and they consulted Lanni with an eagerness that was not entirely innocent of sexual desire.

So Lanni discovered that Captain Hagen and General Gaunt had enemies in their rear. The worst were the senior staff officers of the new campaign headquarters. All were hostile to Hagen and his volunteers after the recent debacle. These critical officers clustered around a brother of Lord Kitchener, sent out to head a royal commission investigating the reasons why German East had not yet been conquered.

General Gaunt had trekked across the harsh *dursteppe* in Paul's wake. But Paul had carefully timed his withdrawal for the first weeks of 1915. The weather, pestilence, and the seasonal fevers brought down a barrier of natural disasters between the German forces and the English coming up behind. Nobody dared call Gaunt a coward when he turned back. Gaunt had saved the hide of his war minister, Lord Kitchener, in the campaign against the dervishes. Gaunt wore the blue and green ribbon of the Indian frontier, the blue and white of the Egyptian campaign, the yellow and black of the Matabele rebellion. When he described the route taken by the retreating Germans as "the hellscape of a soil so poisoned all vegetables are inedible and meat turns rotten within hours of being shot," nobody dared call him a liar.

"We blockade the German coast, command the inland lakes, hold the railroads, surround that blasted Kaiser's Mountain, bottle up the bloody *Koenigsberg*," complained Colonel Kitchener to Gaunt. "Explain why you need more troops."

"Not more troops," said General Gaunt. "More brains."

This observation quickly went the rounds at Moshi. Kitchener had brought a small posse of languid young gentlemen with his commission. They included the Duke of Napier and a multitude of pen pushers. They lingered over gargantuan meals in what had been the Kommandeur's mess; they consumed prophylactic gins with Bombay tonic water; and because they had come at their King's command to find out a few things, they kept up a desultory bombardment of questions in a tired drawl.

Hagen was first to lose patience. A lisping exquisite wanted to know why cavalry could not be dispatched to dispose of the German encampment now reported inside the crater at Olduvai. Hagen had just finished explaining how German officers had learned to dispense with horses. They fell easy victim to the tsetse fly, which the Germans had mobilized as yet another natural weapon. He turned on the lisping youth and snarled, "They the tsetse fly have got—and we have not!"

This offended the youth's uncle, the Duke, who tackled General Gaunt. "This is no time for ill-placed humor, sir. Precisely *why* are we in this mess?"

"Your Grace," said Gaunt, resolved to take a final shot at logical persuasion, "Your Grace, we had a bush-fighting unit that promised to get better with experience, the Uganda Railway Volunteers. But look what we're getting now." And he described the colonial regiments whose men wore an identifying twelve-inch patch exactly where a German sniper should sink a bullet; the patch was intended to make command easier. The King's African Rifles looked splendid on parade, their officers resplendent with scarlet jackets made from cashmere and royal Tudor blue collars and cuffs, but their uniforms were an invitation to disaster in battle. Said Gaunt: "Veterans of the Uganda operations of sixteen years ago wear medals of silver with a figure of Britannia rising before a lion. Very impressive, but a perfect target for marksmen." Too late, Gaunt noticed one of Kitchener's aides turning purple in the face; he was wearing the equally prominent, equally inviting Ashanti medal with a British lion on black and green.

Colonel Kitchener, who may have listened but obviously hadn't heard Gaunt, interrupted. "Wham! Bam! Over by Easter! That's the ticket when your opposition's no more than three hundred half-baked German officers."

"The Kaiser," muttered Hagen mutinously, "promised it would be over by last Christmas. For his side in Europe, of course. The rhetoric was the same."

Kitchener refused to be put off by vulgar sarcasm. He had just bought a swagger stick of rhino horn from the market. He twirled it appreciatively. It would look splendid beside those ostrich feathers for Lady Cunard. "Mow down a few niggers and the rest'll join us," he said, slicing the air.

"If we could trap even a round dozen of your—ah—*niggers*, there'd be another hundred volunteer Africans to take their place," retorted Hagen.

"Nonsense," protested the Duke's elegant male secretary. "Jigaboos go where the power is."

"If so, the power rests with the Lion of Africa," General Gaunt said flatly, tormented beyond discretion. He glanced apologetically at Hagen. "I'm advised we shouldn't give Lettow a gratuitous propaganda advantage—"

"Not to worry," replied Hagen. "Since I warned you, the London papers have got onto it. I don't know how."

The Duke pinched his lower lip. " 'Pon my soul!" he muttered to the secretary. "A general with forget-me-not badges and a common intelligence captain who talks to him like an equal—"

General Gaunt's patience was exhausted. Glaring at the Duke, Gaunt said in a surprisingly quiet and even voice, "I wouldn't call the finest of fighting tribes *jigaboos*. Not when they call this German by such a name as *Simba*. They're being trained by him in modern weapons to fight modern armies."

"Man's a traitor!" exploded the Duke.

"Hardly," said General Gaunt. "Not when he's already our enemy."

"A traitor, sir!" Colonel Kitchener took up the refrain. "He's a traitor to the white race!"

18

A SHARP-FEATURED man in the Kitchener commission had been watching Hagen and saying little. His name was Briggs. He wore a lightweight charcoal-gray suit for this job. Six months ago he reeked of Tibetan butter and sat astride a yak. Next summer he was liable to become a Russian muzhik in Samarkand. Today, the gray suit gave him a gray air of English respectability. He buttonholed Hagen.

"Winnie's angling to get out here, cobber." The Australian accent was the only feature about Briggs that was far from nondescript. "He wants to be commander-in-chief, and that means catching the Lion of Africa. That's the name *he* uses too, cobber."

"Thank God someone understands the threat," said Hagen.

"Winston Churchill surely does. But there are a hundred and fifty generals, at last count, trying to get here, too. They see the chance for glory and easy promotion. This new name for the German has captured the English newspaper public. *Simba* sounds romantic. The bloody fools don't understand that lions make ugly man-eaters. If someone like Smuts comes instead of Churchill, you're headed for the pickle jar."

Smuts! Hagen groaned. Jan Christian Smuts had won eminence fighting England. Now he was South Africa's soldier-statesman seeking a place in the British Imperial War Cabinet, whose chief had hailed Smuts as the hero of the hour: "He belongs among the Caesars and Cromwells and Napoleons." Of course, thought Hagen, it was all blarney to keep Smuts from joining the German side, where he belonged spiritually.

"What you need," continued Briggs, "is to infiltrate a couple of black characters into London to propagate your ideas among the Gladstone liberals."

"You'd better tell me what those ideas of mine are," said Hagen. "They're apt to change from day to day."

"To beat the German you need armed black guerrillas. The old guard in London won't hear of it." Briggs's blue eyes twinkled. "Send over some articulate token natives who'll spout off about black aspirations, preferably to Church of England types and their political friends who are all for liberating Africa. I've got the right man, too. The commission chaplain."

The Very Reverend Canon "Bunkers" Beane was a chubby free-lance chaplain under the Bishop of St. Albans-and-Gibraltar. He mystified Hagen, whose knowledge of church affairs was limited to military funerals. Over a few drinks in Briggs's tiny room, Bunkers Beane demystified him. "When an obstinate man of God gets over seventy, the Church Commissioners in their infinite wisdom have invented a role for the old codger. If he's fit and loyal to the monarch, he goes on a list for temporary foreign assignment to embassies and English communities abroad." Canon Beane came to a dead halt and sounded a last trump into his soiled handkerchief.

"You're an artful dodger," Hagen said flatly.

"Exactly," replied the Reverend with glowing cheeks. "A spy from the house of God."

Hagen had the professional's fear of the amateur's clumsiness. But Bunkers Beane had served as a chaplain to the King, which guaranteed discretion, and he had a key to the side door at Buckingham Palace, which was a privilege shared only with the chief of secret intelligence services. So Hagen, thinking it could do no harm, authorized Canon Beane to keep an eye open for likely recruits.

Beane had reservations about Hagen that might have surprised the younger man. The chaplain had glimpsed an obsessive mania that was driving Hagen to extremes. So, to be on the safe side, he decided to limit their meetings, preferring to work through Briggs. And since Hagen likewise had reservations about Canon Beane, they failed to consult fully when the chaplain met that beautiful octoroon, Princess Lanni Reute, among the worshipers at the garrison church. Everyone knew the romantic story of her mother, the estranged sister of the Iman of Oman and the Sultan of Zanzibar.

"She could be the right voice for black Africa," Canon Beane confided to Briggs. "She's got all the sophistication in the world, the right aristocratic connections, and nobody could refuse those gorgeous amber eyes."

"Have her talk with Hagen," suggested Briggs.

"No," said the chaplain. "We don't want to run risks by putting her in touch with more than one contact."

So Hagen never had a chance to associate the princess with the black girl who had helped Kate Truman pour the contents of a chamber pot on his head.

Briggs kept pushing for more African natives to beef up English forces. He motored around Moshi in a Siddely tourer with a compressed-air pneumatic movie camera, filming the King's African Riflemen, for whose black members he had certain ambitions. In conferences, however, he bumped up against Kitchener's deep-rooted prejudices.

"We could train black guerrillas and take a leaf from the German's notebook," Briggs proposed cautiously at one of the rare commission meetings when Hagen put in an appearance.

"We'd have to offer more than the privilege of fighting for England," suggested Hagen. "The German has outlined, for each tribe that cooperates, its future boundaries."

"As if they were nations?" spluttered Kitchener. "Next thing, there'll be black ambassadors trotting into Court. And black presidents! The mind boggles."

"We need black to fight black," Hagen argued back. "Our technology won't crush 'em. For example, Paul's guerrillas have learned to stop our new Willoughby armored cars by firing through the radiator louvers. One bullet halts all that steel and firepower."

But this observation only fired the Duke's crusade against Churchill. "I told Winston the things were death traps. Bloody fool's messing around now with what he calls tanks. Results'll be the same." He rose to leave. "Well, thank you, Captain—er."

"Hagen. Myles Hagen," said Hagen through clenched teeth. "Director of Intelligence, in case you'd forgotten."

The sudden impertinence provoked the Duke's bored secretary into a shrewish observation. "Do you secret service wallahs usually refer to the beastly Boche by his first name?"

Hagen knew he had slipped up. General Gaunt, at his side, said quickly, "Paul is our code name for the German commander."

"Ah!" The secretary swished at the empty air with his new fly whisk.

"Time for a quick one before tiffin," announced the Duke. "Join us for a wee dram, eh?" He was not a bad fellow and was famous at White's, his club on St. James's Street, as the chap who never bore a grudge.

"Thanks, Your Grace, no," said Hagen, who always bore grudges. "I haven't touched a drop since the Tanga fiasco."

The Kitchener commission finished its work, to Hagen's profound relief. Here in Africa he was a law unto himself, and he ran his artful dodgers any way he pleased. The London desk johnnies boosted their reputations on the carcasses of dead agents. They ran agents as if they were game little fillies, cursed if one fell when taking a jump, and pulled out the knacker's pistol to put her out of her misery.

Why was he thinking in terms of females? That octoroon princess! It was too late now to take a squint at her. She was boarding the steamer at Mombasa with the commissioners. He sent for Briggs, who was leaving to catch the same boat that night.

"She's got blood, even if it's the wrong side of the blanket," Briggs reassured him. "The old Duke's taken a fancy, which won't do any harm."

"How'd you plan to use her?"

"Like we agreed, cobber. You need money and some kind of legal mumbo jumbo to recruit black guerrillas. That little filly can speak for the blacks."

Hagen winced at the word filly. "The Duke?"

Briggs scratched his trim silver hair, thinking Hagen's reaction puritanical. We're men of the world; the girl is gorgeous in her translucent white bodice cupping tits the size of Cox's orange pippins. But Hagen hadn't seen her, Briggs reminded himself. He said, "The Duke can give the girl entry to the right circles. She'll chirrup away, the blasted liberals will agree the way to freedom for blacks is to arm 'em, and you'll get your budget. You can repudiate all promises later, naturally."

Paul groped for his pistol in the darkness of the tent. The gun was a token of dying dependence on the world outside. Ammunition his men stole from the enemy. Fuel was a local benzine brewed by Ersatz Etrich. Food was helped by substitutes: lard from elephant fat; salt leached from plants; and for the gourmet palate, bush rat pie, monkey's brains, and tongue of hippo.

Kate slept in the thatched hut nearby. Paul stepped outside, and an askari sergeant mumbled, "Jambo Bwana Simba Mkubwa General Kaiser." The muddled greeting was a poetic invention. Good-morning-great-lion-master-general-emperor.

He looked in at Kate, heard her stir. "Sleep in," he whispered, reaching through the mosquito net to brush her face. She filled his senses.

Kate shivered under the rough texture of his hand delicately sensing her. If only he could cast aside his armor forever, if only she could know he would never leave her again. She lay rigid, swearing yet again to match his control.

"I'm riding east," he whispered. "Cornelius will meet me tonight."

"Stay—" Her nails dug into his unyielding arm as she stifled the words. "No," she said. "Go!"

She listened to the muffled sounds of his departure.

During this past month of March 1915, Paul had brought into the Olduvai crater the bulk of his *Schutztruppe*, all dispossessed settlers, and the nomad warriors. Olduvai was a natural fortress. Within the volcanic crater his community settled into Laager-120 W, the first planned bastion, identified by its name as one hundred twenty kilometers west of the Kaiser's Mountain.

He met Cornelius among the flat-topped mimosa trees spread like sun umbrellas against the copper sky beyond the crater. The two withdrew into a *manyatta* Masai warrior's lodge.

"You've taken the brunt of the fighting," said Paul. "It's time you were relieved."

"Relief's not what we want. The men thrive on action." Cornelius opened a leather pouch and pulled out a copy of *The East African Standard*. "We get regular delivery now from agents in Moshi. Read this."

The newspaper had reprinted one of Quentin Pope's dispatches to *The New York World*. Some of Hagen's propaganda experts had stretched a pen into the editorial columns. The Germans, they said, were using ignorant black savages to do their fighting for them.

"What we want," said Cornelius grimly, "are a few dead Germans to disprove this. The word is spreading, the English will offer better terms to native Africans—land, guarantees of tribal independence, and real army uniforms."

"*Are* the English offering better terms?" asked Paul, looking Cornelius directly in the eye.

"They'll pretend. But everything has to be referred back to London. That's why they're sending Lanni—I'm now in regular contact with her. She's been told to play the game Hagen's way. You know Jacob will put her in touch with Zionists in London."

Paul nodded. "He sent me word. My biggest worry is ending the laager's isolation. We're cut off physically, but it doesn't mean we shouldn't find a way to keep in touch with Berlin. This psychological isolation could prove the worst of our enemies. I never thought I would say this, but our self-sufficiency is almost too great. We're preoccupied with beating the elements and neglect the war. Chuck Truman has found a tribe that has made steel for generations. Imagine! Steel! Yet the way I feel now, I'm almost afraid to touch it because men who should be fighting will start thinking of things to make with the damned stuff!"

"Perhaps it would restore your spirit to make a journey to this steel-making tribe?" asked Cornelius.

Paul rose from his seat on a *ngoma* drum. Six-foot warriors were planted like saplings around him, armed with long spears and two-foot swords. The chief *moran* carried a buffalo-hide shield quartered with clan signs. "The quickest path to martyrdom," a Masai expert had once told Paul, "is along their trails." Trails that ran two hundred miles deep into English territory, along which they could run all day without losing breath.

"Restore my spirit or my stomach for a fight?" Paul asked with a grimace. "Come on, spit it out!"

"The Masai have a saying: 'He lies with a woman too long and loses his manhood.'"

Paul began a response and then stopped. He was in danger of forgetting that not only was Cornelius denying himself the comfort of Lanni, his own woman, but also he was allowing her to go on the most hazardous of missions to England.

"*Karibu, Elmoran, mutakufa wote!*" said Paul, throwing one of their goatskin blankets over one shoulder. "Come on, warriors, you shall all die if I die."

19

Lanni was literally thrown into the Duke of Napier's arms by a torpedo that struck their ship ten days out of Mombasa. The Duke had been talking with her at the deck rail when there was a mild concussion followed by a deathly hush.

"My deah," said the Duke, "put on your life jacket, do. We seem to be sinking."

Lanni thought he was joking until the stricken liner took a sudden list. There were no other ships in sight except a Japanese destroyer acting as their escort. Japan was popular among the passengers because it had declared for the Allies, but there were one or two fingers of suspicion pointing now at the Rising Sun coming up on the starboard bow. The Japanese were exonerated when lookouts spotted a periscope on the opposite side.

"I must get to my cabin," said Lanni, her remarkable eyes wide with what the Duke took to be terror. When he saw her determination, though, he volunteered to go himself. He could have found her cabin blindfolded. Lanni followed because she had to be certain of rescuing her vanity case, where Jacob Kramer's uncut diamonds lay in a false bottom. The diamonds were her currency for the mission arranged by Cornelius on behalf of his Zionist allies. Knowing nothing about this, the Duke of Napier was awestruck. He would say for years afterward, "Plucky little minx, wasn't going to be yanked out of the briny looking like a drowned rat, what!"

They made their way back to the deck, the Duke popping into the bar to liberate some brandy. Then, with an arm around Lanni, he walked off the sloping deck into the sea. The lifeboats and rafts had pushed off by then. Over the calm sea floated the voices of some four thousand men and women, many singing ragtime and music hall songs. The Japanese destroyer began the task of rescue, and the U-boat surfaced to slide another pair of torpedoes into the crippled ship. About half the passengers and crew died in the subsequent explosions.

Lanni and her Duke had swum clear. The jackets kept them bobbing like corks in that buoyant salty sea. They opened one bottle of brandy and then another. They were both tiddly when the Japanese got around to them three hours later. The Duke was troubled when he saw "the little yellow sailor men" blaming themselves for the tragedy. "My deah," said the Duke to Lanni, "tell them, please do, they mushn't commit that Harry Karry stuff with their lovely swords. Too messy, dahling." He was under some alcoholic illusion that Lanni's less reputable side of the family was vaguely Asiatic.

She convinced him that she did not suffer from the female modesty said to afflict the Japanese. By the time they reached Tilbury Docks aboard a troopship, Lanni could make the Duke sit up and beg. She taught him delights he had never imagined. The Duke would have been stunned to learn they were the sexual secrets of a central African tribe.

Lanni had acquired a protector in the Duke. She was settled into a spacious private avenue whose mansions stood on what had been the kitchen garden of Kensington Palace, where Queen Victoria was born. The house was owned by John Egg, of the gun-making family on Pall Mall, and it breathed Victorian sanctimony. From the Duke's point of view, No. 10 Kensington Palace Gardens was a most discreet address.

It bothered Jacob Kramer's brother, however, and he delayed bringing Lanni to the Jewish quarter in Limehouse until the source of her sudden affluence was explained. Then, after she had handed over the diamonds, she was invited to speak to an audience of thickset Jewish street fighters in a dusty attic over a warehouse on the Commercial Road. She traced a smugglers' line for them on a Bartholomew school atlas: six thousand miles by sea to Cape Town, thence by rail to

Elizabethville, overland to the Lualaba River of Livingstone fame, and upriver to Lake Tanganyika.

"What's most needed," she said, "are wireless parts that can be concealed in English military stores. If you get them to South Africa, with the necessary technicians, we'll do the rest."

"Stealing the stuff's easy," said a gang leader. "Shoving it into the Aerated Bread Company's Christmas puddings ain't no problem. But if any of us gits shopped, we're fer the high jump. The rope, missus. Traitors is hanging fodder, see."

"Traitors to England—or Zion?" demanded Lanni.

"Ain't much bleedin' use to Zion if I'm swinging and me wife's a poor hempen widow!" He shrugged. "Orl right, you ain't even one of the Chosen, but yer've risked yer own neck. So just leave it to us, missus. Now orf you toddle to yer duke, dearie."

The mystery of Lanni's royal birth, her striking appearance, and her sophistication opened many doors. Young women of good family were in war work, and there was a shortage of bright and attractive companions just when the feminists had won new freedoms. Sex as a diversion was openly and daringly discussed, but the opportunities were much diminished. "Sex on approval" was advocated by Maud Braby's marriage manual, but the eligible young men were mostly dying in the trenches.

Soldiers home from the Western Front were outraged by the contrast between the filth of those trenches and the social whirl of London. The affluent still paraded in Hyde Park on Sunday mornings after church. Lanni noted the bitterness. She heard war songs reflecting the resentments. There was an undercurrent of rebellion, perhaps even a failure of national nerve. England, while being drained of its youthful vitality, was quite unconscious of the threat to its strength. In pubs Lanni watched men on leave squander their pitiful savings in the dice game of crown and anchor, the banker keeping up a stream of patter to lure the punters: " 'Ere we are again, then. The Sweaty Socks! Cox and Company, the Army bankers, badly bent but never broke, safe as the Bank of England, undefeated because they never fought, the rough and tough, the old and bold."

There was madness in the air. A boy bugler could have his photograph and that of his mother inserted into a forbidding pastiche. The postcard, with the boy wearing a halo and the mother clutching her head, against a background of shell-blasted trees and trenches, bore such verse as: "Farewell, Mother, you may never, you may never,

Mother / Press me to your heart again; / But O you'll not forget me, Mother, you will not forget me / If I'm numbered with the slain."

The same lad was likely to become a patron, shortly after mailing his postcard, of one of the numerous brothels where, noted the poet Robert Graves, "a queue of a hundred and fifty wait outside a door for his turn . . . each woman serving a battalion of men a week for as long as she lasted." A double standard prevailed and made many men feel there were now two quite separate Englands.

Lanni saw much of the other England. Champagne still flowed. Caviar cost a fortune at Fortnum & Mason's and was delivered by uniformed boys. For common folk there was rationing, whereas Lanni's Duke could get salmon from his Scottish estates, grouse in season, and the best cuts of meat.

There were military barracks at the bottom of Kensington Palace Gardens. Lanni walked past them each morning. It was no longer a social crime for a lady to walk on the public pavements, even unescorted. From the Queen's Row she could see the reservists called back to the colors and collecting their khaki. The remounts were being broken to cavalry drill. Purple-faced sergeants screamed incomprehensible orders: "Bah the reeight quick maaarsh! ABOUT TUN! HOOOOALT! Order ahhhms! Slope ahhhms! Preeesent ahhhms!"

Lanni, shrewd and quick, recognized the signs of shortages, the lowering age level of recruits. The English were, she believed, sick of the war in Europe. It had become a quagmire for "millions of the mouthless dead," in the words of the poet Charles Sorley. She heard the marching songs: "Nobody knows how tired we are, tired we are / Tired we are, tired we are, TIRED WE ARE / Nobody knows how tired we are / And nobody seems to care."

Then one day Lanni was taken by the Duke to a dinner party at the French Embassy. Without warning, the King-Emperor arrived. The ambassador had been asked to say nothing beforehand. Lanni curtsied, and as she rose, she was transfixed by the bright blue-eyed gaze of the fifty-year-old monarch. Her first thought was "How German." And, of course, his grandfather had been German. She was looking especially beautiful in an expensive gown, her lustrous black hair elaborately coiffed, her skin more gold than brown, her shoulders exquisitely bared. The King-Emperor planted himself before her, the bluff challenge of a naval man, legs braced apart, beard cocked.

"They tell me you know Africa, ma'am," he said.

"Yes, Your Majesty."

"We have a great admiration," said the sailor-king, "for the German Kommandeur out there, von Lettow."

Lanni felt her chest constrict with sudden fright. George V was watching her closely.

"We are interested in the future of black Africa," he continued. "There seems a dispute between some of my government advisers. A majority fear the training of Africans in the martial arts would work against our interests. What do you think, ma'am?"

Before Lanni could find her tongue, an equerry slid between them. King George set his mouth in a firm line. "We would be obliged, ma'am, to have your confidential views in writing." He gave her a brief nod and moved on.

A handsome young Frenchman introduced himself almost immediately. "Claude Dupuis, *aviateur.*" He was both frankly admiring and inquisitive. "I saw your small heart positively *flutter* when the King spoke. May one ask what he said?"

"It was," said Lanni, falling into her Parisian style, "extremely personal."

"Aha!" said Dupuis and at once brought her more champagne.

The sailor-king left before the dinner. In his wake the gossips' voices rose like gulls in pursuit of a battleship. The political significance of this seemingly casual visit was debated in undertones among the men, but the women agreed the only incident worth remembering was the quiet conversation with Lanni. None had overheard. All were dying to learn more. During the next few days Lanni was overwhelmed with callers and invitations.

Lanni had become more than a spy. She represented the unknown quantity in Africa. The armies of King George V might hack away at the armies of the Kaiser, but both sides were still in touch with one another. King and Kaiser still had a common interest in keeping Africa white. As Briggs pointed out to her, "The King is the greatest empire builder, and the Kaiser commands the most inventive nation in history. The King would like the inventive talents of Daimler, Diesel, and Siemens. The Kaiser would like the resources of India, Malaya, and Kenya. But neither has control over the movements you represent, so they're more likely to bed with you than fight you." Lanni was certain she could get as cordial a reception in Berlin as she had received in London.

"You've met, I believe, Claude Dupuis," said Briggs one morning. He watched with quiet amusement as Lanni lowered her eyes, for he knew of at least three secret meetings, each of a passionate nature, in a Mayfair flat.

"Monsieur Dupuis is a distinguished flier with the Lafayette Escadrille," continued Briggs. "He has been in England to demonstrate a new aeroplane and to work out tactics against a new German threat in the air—the long-range airship of Count Zeppelin."

Lanni went on studying her folded hands, a young woman caught in a compromising social indiscretion. She knew about Count Zeppelin's bomb-throwing airships that might appear over London any night. She knew about the new French bomber designed by Gaston Caudron. She and the young *aviateur* Claude Dupuis had shared more than physical delights in bed. Some of the most interesting items to Lanni seemed routine to him since they formed part of his daily chatter over drinks in Royal Flying Corps messes. What Lanni gambled upon was that Briggs did not know her whole story.

He said, "We can arrange that you return to Africa with Dupuis."

She looked up, astonished.

"He's testing the capabilities of the new Caudron R-11. More I can't explain. We'll bundle you into the third seat. You don't weigh much, so he won't have to sacrifice much fuel. If you agree, we've some errands for you."

The Australian disclosed only that she would fly to Nairobi in the trial model of an astonishing reconnaissance-fighter-bomber version of the Caudron stick-and-string aeroplane. There would be a lot of refueling stops in a flight of peculiar significance.

Lanni learned from Zionists inside the Court that her survival had not been a matter of sheer luck. Word had come from East Africa that she was involved with pro-German natives. Lanni guessed that the English intelligence director, Hagen, had caught on to her masquerade. So! The flight back to Nairobi was intended to deliver her into Hagen's waiting arms. She saw no way of avoiding this outcome. Still, there was some possibility of disarming Hagen, for she seemed to have won the patronage of George V. The King-Emperor had stopped an investigation into her background, and therefore it seemed likely that Hagen was under orders to make use of her rather than dispose of her. The King, said Lanni's informants, had written in a confidential memo: "We are not concerned with this lady's external alliances. She will shift naturally to whatever side stands to help her people the most. We wish to make use of her extraordinary knowledge of awakening Africa."

Lanni was missed by the Zionists of Golders Green. From Berlin, through roundabout commercial channels, came a warning from the Jewish patrician Walter Rathenau that the Kaiser was more racist than ever. The Kaiser spoke constantly of Anglo-Saxon influence as the original Germanic element in English culture. He made racist appeals to King George. Stop white fighting white in Africa! That, said the Kaiser, is *Rassen-Verrat*, race-treason!

"Rathenau's got it all wrong," said Jewish community leaders in London. The Kaiser couldn't slaughter the English in the trenches and simultaneously become partners with them in Africa.

"Berlin is the center of Zionism," they protested. "Racism's a thing of the past in Germany."

A dissenting voice was that of Chaim Weizmann, a chemist helping England make synthetics to replace the supplies sunk by U-boats. He said if the Kaiser could slaughter Anglo-Saxons in Europe and at the same time proclaim their blood brotherhood to preserve their racial purity in Africa, racism was far from gone in Germany, and such fanaticism boded ill for the future of the Jews.

Part Four

Cloud-Cuckoo-Land

20

From Paul von Lettow's war diary, Laager-120 W, Olduvai, May 1915:

The insult to the British of our holding the Kaiser's Mountain must be immense! More and more enemy forces hesitate on all flanks, waiting for the signal to destroy me. What stops them? Disease and heavy rains. When English cavalry chase me, their mounts drop at a terrifying rate from horse sickness. English troops die like flies from terrible afflictions. My own troops and the women seem hardened against such malignancies. Our bacteriologists have adapted Dr. Ehrlich's 606 to produce a cure for sleeping sickness. Professor Etrich has found synthetic quinine and now seeks other medicines with Kornatzki's witch doctors. I brought back from my Masai land safari the steel-making secrets of the Haya tribe; they burn charred swamp grass for carbon and blow hot air into the base of a furnace of slag and mud. They build up such high temperatures that their goatskin bellows are connected by long clay pipes to protect the smelters. So now we have steel!

Olduvai might be man's birthplace, so an ancient art of steel making is not so surprising! My old friend Dr. Hans Reck discovered fossils here that led him to believe man evolved from baboons by cooperative social effort and not by aggression. Suppose my companions should demonstrate that written into the human heredity is a predisposition to destroy ourselves? A victory for poor Reck's critics!

Laager-120 W has survived by cooperation. But I have to stage constant raids against the Uganda Railway to keep our tribal allies content. In so doing, we have evolved methods of causing large-scale destruction for a small outlay, which delights Cornelius's Thunderbolt guerrillas. Example: The English depend on that railway; they imported eight T-9 Greyhound locomotives, said to be the best in the world, to beat our saboteurs. But we have sent each one to the bottom of ravines with the application of a little dynamite and a few men—the equivalent of destroying an army in the field because of the disruption!

So we are hunters and killers. And we are also evolving by cooperation! What does this prove? Kate would say that we've created our own Cloud-Cuckoo-Land wherein sanity prevails only because there is an apparent order and routine to give normalcy to what is abnormal.

Dear Kate! She has given purpose to a community dwelling on shifting sands.

21

"TODAY I saw the ghosts of my ancestors," Kate wrote in the war diary after reading Paul's entry. "I looked at the footprints discovered by Dr. Reck. They are said to have been left three million years ago by two protohumans. I could actually follow them for half a city block! I walked in their footsteps, the impressions preserved in black lava. I followed these ghostly forebears until I could feel them watching me. I was stunned. Their senses became my senses. My mind opened to a strange range of stimulants. For the first time I experienced some faint echo of a primitive memory, a leap across distance and time. If only we can leave footprints in time, whatever happens to us will then seem worthwhile."

She locked the diary back in its box. Whenever Paul was on operations, she made entries in the diary; and by this method they conveyed messages that reminded her of secret love notes in school. Nights without Paul were hard to endure. She had awakened today with a powerful sense of danger and of her need for Paul. She had resolved to curb her passion, though loving Paul was incomplete if their bodies did not mingle. She had no right to complicate his life by competing with his sense of duty, she had decided, and so she threw herself into the daily life in Laager-120 W.

The laager was a rocky fortress, as it had been to the first manlike creatures that crept out of the central African forests. Here Paul's friends from the Berlin university had retrieved remnants of huge sheep bigger than oxen, giant crocodiles, baboons that must have stood twice as high as the tallest men, and even mammoth rabbits. Here the earth's skin had stretched until the skeleton of Africa showed through in the form of craggy *kopjes*, outcrops rising as the land settled. Here, etched into lava rock and burnished granite, were ancient scratch marks made by Stone Age men.

These were ancient rocks, island sanctuaries in the ocean of the plains buried in ash blown from the old volcanoes of the Great Rift. A seasonal river had long ago gouged through the ash deposits so that, from the bed, it was possible to gaze up at the fortress walls and see history stacked in neat layers. In those layers were fragments of bone, flakes of obsidian, and polished quartz used as tools by man's ancestors. The *kopjes* on the crater floor formed archipelagoes where life evolved in isolation. At the base of one giant fig tree there was a stone hearth where hominids had made fires and sharpened spears. Samples of prehistoric life had been laid bare by that enormous upheaval when the Great Rift split Africa open from the Red Sea to the distant south. The gorge at Olduvai was twenty kilometers long and three hundred feet deep.

Kate, lost in thought, was surprised to find Count Kornatzki beside her. She told him about the ghostly footprints and said, "You're a scientist—don't you think we might find the origins of man here?"

"I'd need an army to dig for evidence," replied Kornatzki.

"You have an army."

"To dig graves."

"Perhaps that answers the other question."

"What's that?"

Kate smiled sadly. "Is man a beast of destruction or a creature reaching for better things?"

She walked to the shore of the lake glittering under swollen silvered clouds. A machine gun chattered on the far shore, a faint stutter that ended abruptly. Then, from the inner rim of the crater, a gun boomed, its sound not so different from the thud of poles pounding mealie flour in the hardwood *kino* vessels where the women prepared the morning meal.

A pair of machine-gun bearers trotted past her. They were big, cheerful Wazukuma and very excited. Behind them ran a woman with an infant peering big-eyed over the cloth strapping it to the mother's back. An askari sergeant roared at his men.

Kate turned toward what she had learned to call the *kraal*, a portable village. The sky was swiftly brightening. She smelled the long overdue rain, a wonderful revitalizing earthiness carried on the morning breeze. The dry spell was ending. Soon they would have to move out of the security of the crater.

Life had become very comfortable here. The poor rations of cereal were supplemented by wild game, sugarcane, yamlike *muhogo* roots, freshwater fish, and other small luxuries. A few proved dangerous, like the *mbinji*, whose stones when roasted tasted like hazelnuts. Ever since Laager-120's chemists had discovered that *mbinji* also contained prussic acid, Kate had been ordered to check all food substitutes.

More gunners ran past her. They wore rainy-weather camouflage. They forecast the seasons like the leaves of a tree, she thought. Paul had to change and change again with the seasons: changing camouflage to suit the overnight eruption of green shoots and the red swirl of flash floods; changing the tactics of raiders to meet the alteration of the land when rivers revived and switched their courses. The scourge of dry heat would give way to humidity that rotted the skin. Man-eating lions that terrified the carriers would shift attention; in their place would come tiny creatures, multiplying in dark corners of damp clothes, whose bite could bring a lingering death. Somewhere on the Serengeti, as the heavy clouds burst, the relentless rains would smash the crops of maize, and springing up where once was desert would be fungi as edible as childhood mushrooms. The seasons turned and the struggle twisted with them.

A German officer appeared. His reddish matted hair matched the headdress of his askari, short ostrich feathers that made them hard to spot among the thorn trees. From this camouflage, it was evident the patrol had traveled a considerable distance in dry conditions. The officer halted his men and came to meet Kate. His voice was crisp and toneless. Paul had said the commandos were hardening to a mood of *Allgemeine Wurchtigkeit*, a kind of absolute callousness, not so much ruthless as indifferent to hardship and fatigue.

As he neared, Kate recognized Major Wolfe. She was shocked by his emaciated condition. How long since he slipped off on a mission? Perhaps ten days.

"Magdalene," he asked. "Where is she?"

"With the Governor's wife in the field hospital," Kate said. She put the palm of her hand against his burned face. "You're a skeleton. You look exhausted. Get some rest, and I'll fetch her."

She was careful to ask no questions, but Wolfe said, "Don't frighten her. Tom's done good work."

So that was it. Wolfe had come from Tom von Prinz on top of Kilimanjaro. And Tom's wife perhaps in bed with the American correspondent. Kate pointed toward the rest station. "Dismiss your men. Eat. There's some fresh-brewed sugarcane beer and an empty camp bed right in front of you."

"But I should see Magdalene," Wolfe said obstinately. "I've a letter—"

"Then let me have it."

Major Wolfe dropped his arms to his sides. He swayed in defeat. His eyes had that glazed look of total exhaustion.

"What is it?" asked Kate. Magdalene seemed unable to speak. Her hand shook uncontrollably each time she looked at Tom's letter.

Kate had found her alone in the dispensary on Quentin Pope's stretch of the lake's shoreline. The clinic cared for a small commando of askaris that used the lake as a fast route to the region where English patrols could be intercepted. Pope, recording the story of this strange war, was accompanying the raiders more and more. The proximity of the dispensary had made his meetings with Magdalene easy and unobserved.

Magdalene raised her head. "Tom accuses me of having an affair with Quentin."

"Well, aren't you?" asked Kate.

Magdalene leaned back, groping behind her, feeling the edge of the trestle table so that she could rest on it. Her bronzed features were not gaunt. "You remember old General Wahle's son?"

"How could I forget? Strutting and screaming. *And* slapping Lanni—"

"Remember he disappeared? Well, now he's with Tom!"

"And the boy knew?"

"He thought he knew," said Magdalene. She looked intently at Kate. "I've done nothing to be ashamed of. Young Wahle sensed the feeling between Quentin and me after the night we spent on the farm. We did nothing but talk, Kate—"

"I believe you," Kate said quickly.

"We've done nothing since." Magdalene's voice was abruptly edged in anger. "Why should I suffer this indignity? Why even deny something that hasn't happened?"

Kate stared helplessly at the stricken woman. "You love Quentin?"

"Yes." Magdalene shivered. "I suppose in my mind I've sinned. I expect that's what counts."

"Nonsense," Kate said briskly. "Let's see what needs to be done now."

"Nothing," replied the older woman. "It's a savage letter. Tom plays the outraged husband fighting in the jaws of death while his wife is bedding with a war-dodging foreigner. He's even dragged in the children. Here, look for yourself."

Kate took the letter reluctantly. She knew about Tom's infidelities. He was an Englishman disloyal to his native country and to his wife. And yet she'd felt sorry for him. She glanced quickly through the pages. Love was in every tortured, angry line. Love. Must it so often be doomed?

"Burn it," said Kate, handing it back. "Burn it now. Then forget it. They don't put women in the stocks for what you've done, not anymore." She slipped an arm around the older woman. "Don't let this damage whatever you've found with Quentin."

When Magdalene was alone again, she folded the letter and put it away. The cry of the water-bottle bird echoed through the rain forest: "My husband is gone / My lover is gone / And my heart goes *doom, doom, doom.*"

The last three notes fell like rocks. The bird's song repeated itself but this time on an ascending scale. Was this love? This sudden ascent and inevitable fall? It all seemed shameful when reduced to Tom's filthy denunciations.

She walked distractedly to her quarters. By another dreadful irony, the last supply column had brought in the salvaged remains of home, the contents of the farmhouse built by Tom and her. For days, with Quentin coloring her every thought, she had postponed the task of sifting through the debris.

Now she moved among the smashed crates and half-opened boxes from which spilled reminders of marriage and motherhood. No demon could have designed a more exquisite torture. Here was the bronze bell Tom used for summoning the children. There was a desk stuffed with receipts, notes, lists of household needs, the twigs two people used to bind a nest. She saw Tom bending over the table, struggling with homemade glue to rejoin joints swollen in the rainy season. Each inanimate object reproached her betrayal. But what had she betrayed? She turned from the wreckage. Tom had gone to his own true love—war. And Quentin? He had never raised a family whose members protected one another against all dangers.

She fingered a battered tea kettle that once was always on the stove. Reliable. Always on the boil. Each in her family had been steady, dependable. As one unit they moved across Africa, defying uncertainties, never doubting each other's loyalty.

Had she always known, in some poetic corner of her being, there would be a Quentin? She had never appreciated how huge was the gap in her life until he had come to fill it. And so she had dreamed of yielding. And now this. Her husband heroically defending the mountain, symbol of her Fatherland's will; the debris of their lives scattered by disinterested hands across a compound's earthen floor; her family relying on her to rejoin what was broken and replace what was missing.

She picked up a schoolbook damaged by termites. "This belongs to Ilse," her youngest child had written inside. Automatically she shook the leaves to see if the book could be saved. But it was too late to save, rejoin, replace. She must lock tight the compartment labeled *Family*. She had rediscovered what it was to be a woman, open and unafraid.

Magdalene was burning the letter when Kate stopped by.

"You didn't say Quentin had gone on Paul's safari."

"No." Magdalene considered the matter. "Habit, I suppose. 'Never give information unless necessary,'" she quoted from field regulations.

"It's the Governor who sent him," said Kate. "They're expecting trouble. Did you know your husband denounced Quentin to the Governor, even before that letter was written?"

"Are you sure?" Magdalene stared at the curling brown papers in her hand.

"Yes." Kate could not keep alarm from her voice. "Ada says the Governor wants to get rid of your lover—" Kate's eyes searched among the disordered books, then settled on the family Bible. She turned to the Second Book of Samuel, scanned it for a few moments, and quoted: "He wrote in the letter saying, 'Set ye Uriah in the forefront of the hottest battle . . . that he may be smitten and die.'"

Kate lifted horrified eyes. "He wants to get rid of Paul as well. And in the same way."

22

COMMISSIONER HACKMANN knelt upon the muscular buttocks of the black girl and made her scream again. A comfortable sound. What a treasure! Katrina. That was the closest he could get to her tribal name. He loved to wake her early when the wildlife kicked up all that racket, noisy enough to drown out even the Berlin traffic. Grunt of leopard. Scream of baboon. Hysteria of hyenas. Such a hullabaloo. It blanketed Hackmann's lovemaking and the girl's yelps, which were not always of pleasure.

Someone coughed loudly outside the wattle-and-daub walls of the hut. Hackmann tied a cloth around his waist and waddled out. The girl heard a policeman from her own tribe loudly declare that the Governor must see Hackmann at once.

She lay still while Hackmann grumbled and fumbled for his bits of uniform. Then, suddenly, she felt his stinking breath on her neck and his thick thumbs digging along her spine. She bit her lip until the blood flowed. He gave her a final jab and turned her over on the earthen floor, forcing her mouth open for a final indignity.

The moment he was gone, she was at Hackmann's folding army desk. She found what she wanted in the cunningly carpentered drawer that opened to Hackmann's secret touch, the touch she had learned from prolonged observation.

Hackmann returned when he was sure she would have removed the papers. Lord, how simple-minded these Ugandans were! They were tremendous beer drinkers and made mead from the honey they valued more than cattle. He glanced at Katrina curled on the floor, pretending she had never moved. He believed in letting her booze as much as she wanted so long as it was not honey mead. Honey mead made her people dangerously quarrelsome, as if the very bees got inside their woolly heads.

He chuckled. They said he was only a Berlin cop. What better? His police methods worked anywhere. Cultivate informers. Confuse with false rumor. Keep the most painstaking files on everyone of any importance. Exploit each unfolding event.

Governor Schnee had created this event by sending for Captain Looff of the *Koenigsberg*. Now the Kommandeur was off to "guide Looff into camp." Hogwash! Paul Lettow was heading off the warship's captain before he could become an ally of the Governor.

So! Hackmann cocked his head over Katrina's naked form. She had been allowed to steal a forged document purporting to show that the Kommandeur and Captain Looff were meeting secretly to make a joint proposal to the English for peace between the whites and combined operations against all black African rebels.

He stirred the girl with his foot. She would never guess the SK police report was meant for the eyes of her tribal leaders, not for the Governor.

She moved sleepily to the cot. She yawned and felt him inspect the blood still trickling down her thighs. Through half-closed lids she studied the coconut-shaped head with relish. She did not think the order would be long coming to hide the razor-sharp ring knife.

Katrina's tribe gave their loyalty to Chief Obwe, otherwise Big O, self-styled King of Uganda. There were many branches of the Uganda family, but to most Germans they were known as Ugandans. They were great storytellers. One night the learned men who had perused Hackmann's false report came to Katrina with honey grubs, which she recognized as the signal taken from the legend of the hyena and the cock, familiar to every Ugandan. She placed within her vagina the ring knife in its special sheath, and she went as usual to Hackmann. She poured him fermented palm juice, and she fed him the fish curry he craved, with spices smothering the taste of the sap taken from euphorbia for its soporific effect. When he told her to disrobe, slurring his words, she went as usual to the root store. When she returned, her slender body shone with the oils that made her even more desirable.

Hackmann was on his back, head hanging over the end of his cot. Katrina stood behind his head so that he could rub his face into her bushy triangle where the knife lay hidden. He reached his hands up and behind her buttocks. His throat presented itself, begging to be cut. So far the routine was unchanged. Hackmann began forcing her thighs open, and she wriggled to signify pain from the finger-nails he dug into the folds of soft flesh. Swiftly he shifted his attention, and she bent forward whimpering. Her open crotch slid over his mouth and chin. He caught her buttocks between his teeth. She relaxed her vaginal muscles to release the knife and tightened her powerful thighs around his head. Then, fast as a striking green mamba, she drew the suddenly naked blade across the stretched throat.

———

Hackmann's head was carried through the bush to where the Ugandan army waited. It was a pity the rest of Hackmann was missing—he would have appreciated Big O, a childlike giant who confirmed Hackmann's view that the tribe was simple-minded. The self-styled king had marched his best warriors south to seek an explanation for Paul's journey along Uganda borders. Suspicious, but not yet inflamed, Big O was reluctant to find himself at war with the Germans. He was not convinced that the Hackmann police report was true. His best contact inside the German camp was the Boer expert on the central tribes, Der Dicke, and in his simple-minded way, Big O felt it would improve Der Dicke's performance to see what happened to those Big O distrusted.

The first day out of Laager-120 W, Paul had to reprimand another returning patrol. Wounded men lay writhing in dog carts hauled by perspiring porters. There had been a skirmish with an English patrol. Some of the wounded were close to death. Nevertheless, the Kommandeur bawled out their leader for speeding things up by taking a well-worn trail.

One of the wounded men rolled out of a dog cart. Quentin Pope watched as the man dragged himself through the dust. Paul shouted at a corporal, who pounced on the injured soldier to restrain him. A struggle began in which others joined. The victim screamed that his child was dying, a *toto* abandoned on the trail. The men let him go, and the injured askari scuttled like a crippled lizard between boulders burnished by the wind. The corporal followed, and when they were out of sight, a pistol cracked. The corporal reappeared, and soon the column resumed marching.

Paul saw the anguish on Pope's face. "A military necessity," he said and looked at Pope's stubborn mouth. Either the American understood, or there was no point explaining. The men had been forced to abandon an outpost. When they had asked to withdraw and join the main German force, Paul warned that women and children came at their own peril. All would be regarded as soldiers if they were caught in battle. Well, they had been caught. The men had fought their way out of the enemy ambush but were unable to rescue the dependents without suffering heavy losses.

"One man's weakness undermines all," said Paul.

"He wanted to save the baby," protested Quentin Pope. "I heard him. He'd left his woman behind. But the baby was already out of the fighting zone—"

"That was hours ago, Mr. Pope. I would make the same decision if the child were my own." Then, annoyed at wasting words, Paul spurred forward again.

Der Dicke jogged alongside Quentin Pope and rolled his eyes skyward. He seemed to weigh down his Boer tripler pony, a short-coupled, tough steed, standing fifteen hands but bowed in the middle under the rider's great bulk. "Ruthless, eh?"

Pope nodded curtly and reined back so the man could pass. His macabre laughter had been unnerving Pope all morning. The man was grotesque. A medieval friar with colored ribbons in his hair.

Pope let the carriers trot ahead. He knew most of them. He had foraged for food with them, watched them cook spinach from foliage, fashion sandals from captured English saddles, make bandages from bark. They were commando carriers, able to cover forty kilometers in a day. They would fight if ambushed instead of dropping their loads to flee. They were a tight-knit team, free of the usual female and boy companions and good for this swift foray to meet Captain Looff and guide him in.

Pope was not sure why he was on this safari. Governor Schnee had suggested it, and Pope had jumped at the chance to talk with the legendary captain of the *Koenigsberg*. Nevertheless, he had misgivings about Schnee's motive. He knew there was a dangerous alliance between the Governor, Der Dicke, and that gross police chief, Hackmann. All three were clearly opposed to Paul. If they could sow seeds of suspicion and dissension among the tribes, they would do so, provided Paul was the victim. Pope had heard about Ugandan armies coming to seek reassurance. He was not an eavesdropper, but he had also overheard Hackmann speak of inflaming the Ugandans and the Governor observe that any conflict between a large tribe and German armed forces would be sufficient excuse to stop fighting the English and concentrate on the fundamentals of colonial rule.

Pope had wondered if he should say anything. The problem was Paul, who seemed increasingly autocratic. How could you discuss gossip with him? He kept everyone on their toes, including dear Magdalene, who had quoted Goethe in a moment of exasperation: " 'Given a choice between injustice and disorder, the German chooses injustice.' " Paul's passion for order seemed to leave no room for initiative.

———

Paul reminded himself to keep down the pace of his horse. The carriers mustn't tire. Not yet. He was sorry Quentin Pope was on this expedition. There wasn't time to explain the need to stop men from using the same trails because the English were spotting German bases from airplanes. It was said an aviator could pick out the trail of a single animal in the morning dew more easily than a native tracker could from the ground. Paul felt the bones of the buckskin between his knees. Poor devil! The rations were simply not enough. The horse had a few kilometers left in him before heading for the butcher, the candlestick maker, and others. Paul eased out of the saddle. The pain in his spine was worse when the buckskin jog-trotted. He'd have to work out a program for capturing English remounts. They were bringing up Basuto ponies from the south—small, thickset, and capable of carrying two hundred pounds long distances each day. He began to roll a cigarette, working opium and shreds of tobacco between fingers and thumbs. Thank God the opium was plentiful. But he must anticipate the time when there would be nothing else to numb the wounded.

A shout brought his head up. Skaramunga was running from the column's right flank. Paul turned his horse and rode to meet the old man. Without Kate around, Skaramunga returned to his role of bodyguard, gun bearer, adviser, chief cook and bottle washer. Now he led Paul to where two scouts, probing forward, had come across a cream-of-tartar tree with the head of a man trapped in its pulpy embrace.

"Take the column farther west," ordered Paul. No point in alarming the men. The head looked no bigger than an acorn in the forty-foot-thick base of the baobab. Eyes bulged from a face smoothed of wrinkles, tongue protruding from a mouth of prominent teeth. Paul approached gingerly, not out of squeamishness but from a healthy fear of booby traps. He fought down nausea, though, when he recognized the loose lips, the hairless cheeks, the small ears curling against the bony skull. The born sycophant. Commissioner Hackmann.

Paul drew back. Der Dicke came galloping like an enormous retriever, quivering with curiosity, his columnar legs curved around the pony, locks flying. He spun his horse around in a cloud of dust and forced it to face the severed head. He had not identified the object. His nose for trouble had brought him at the gallop, and now, suddenly, Der Dicke collapsed in something more than sheer horror. The body bent at the middle like a punctured sausage. Two ham-like fists beat against the bearded cheeks. The great head with its mass of greasy curls sagged forward. Paul slowly drew his revolver.

"God in heaven!" sobbed Der Dicke. He straightened slowly like a reinflated rubber clown. He had not yet seen Paul's gun. "Dreadful! Atrocious! What horror!" But there was an artificial ring to these cries of distress. "I must go back, prepare the Governor—"

"No!" Paul cocked the gun, and the click of metal made Der Dicke turn. Sweat glistened and ran down the sweep of his forehead into the bulbous eyes.

"Wrap it up," Paul said abruptly.

"What?" Der Dicke's head jerked nervously.

"Take the scarf from your neck and tie up what's left of Hackmann. We still bury our dead, don't we?"

The Boer nodded dumbly. Under the barrel of a gun, he had no option. The head was embedded in the soft bole of the tree. He wrenched it free and rolled it onto the spread scarf, finally knotting it.

"I'll ride with it full tilt back to the laager." Kneeling over the bundle, Der Dicke looked up hopefully.

"Thank you, no. Put it in your saddlebag."

"There must be the rest of the poor fellow around here."

"Possibly. We'll not waste time looking. Get back in the saddle and stay close."

Der Dicke stuffed the pongee scarf and its burden into a canvas bag and sprang astride his pony with an agility surprising for someone shocked by the violent death of a friend.

"Give me your rifle," Paul ordered.

"Have a heart," pleaded the Boer. His hands were shaking with a new fear. Paul took the weapon from Der Dicke, knowing he would not desert unarmed.

"You could save your skin now by telling me," Paul said, sliding the rifle under his own saddle.

"There's no trap," the Boer blurted out.

"I never said there was," said Paul.

The rendezvous with Looff's party was set for sundown near the southern tip of Lake Manyara. Paul made camp at about four o'clock and had the men sup on mealie porridge and acorn coffee. The trackers descended into a ravine to look for Looff, the foragers scoured the lake shore for food, and the carriers prepared shelters. Thunder rumbled in the hills.

"Pray the rain keeps off," Paul told Pope, "or the journey back will take twice as long."

Pope crouched beside him over a fire, Der Dicke standing a few feet away. Skaramunga was on the bank above with the monkey, Bamboo, watching the Boer with unblinking eyes. Paul had ordered all fires doused an hour after sunset. The pickets took up their positions. Despite the distant thunder, the skies overhead were clear. In the bright starlight Pope could see Der Dicke chewing on a strip of biltong.

The moon, three-quarters full, was slipping over the rim of the southerly hills when Paul's trackers returned with two of Looff's guides. They reported the main party, consisting of Captain Looff, twenty sailors, and two hundred porters, had been delayed.

"Delayed?" echoed Paul. He saw Der Dicke stir and remembered his incautious reference to a trap.

There was a sudden warning sound. Pope heard the soft movement of men rising to their feet around him. Rifle bolts clicked. From the direction they had come earlier, up the watercourse, he was aware of a subtle change in the noises of the night. A silence crept over the bush. The buzz-saw hum of insects ceased. The stir and mutter of night prowlers, usually an unnoticed accompaniment, died away.

A burst of rifle fire echoed down the gorge, followed by a rustle of wings and the blurred sound of bodies hurtling through the underbrush.

A shadow crossed the moonlit gravel in the bottom of the dry watercourse. A voice called out in German, hoarse with terror.

"Get him!" Paul dropped the words like pebbles.

Skaramunga slid into the riverbed. There was another cry, swiftly strangled, and a commotion in the long flat grass where Skaramunga had vanished. Then he was back with one of Paul's rear guard. The man's right arm dangled. The gaping wound in his shoulder glistened in the moonlight. Paul dropped beside him and cradled the head. The lips already foamed and the breath rattled in the wounded sentry's throat. Paul put his ear to the man's mouth until the final convulsion.

"We're trapped!" Paul rose from the corpse. His voice was low and conversational. He spoke in the same tone to the men around him, calling each by name, delivering each an order. One by one they melted into the bush. An askari, at Paul's bidding, prodded forward Der Dicke.

"You're the expert on tribal politics," said Paul. "What's gone wrong?"

"Wrong?" the Boer echoed foolishly.

"Mother of Jesus!" Paul advanced a step, and for a moment Pope thought he would strike Der Dicke. "Your task was to deliver us into enemy hands, no?"

"No. I'm no traitor, *jong!*"

The Kommandeur turned to Pope. "You handle guns?"

"Yes," Pope replied tersely. He saw no reason to recapitulate his U.S. army service on the Mexican border, nor his hours on the New York police range.

"Then take this." Paul offered a rifle. "It's English."

"I can't. Not as a civilian."

"The natives out there won't make the distinction! They'll cut off your balls and stuff them down your throat. Then try claiming your privilege as a civilian." Paul thrust the rifle into Pope's hands. It was a Mark II Lee-Metford, capable of rapid fire and more accurate than the Lee-Enfield. Automatically, Pope ran the palm of one hand over the worn stock.

"You're lucky," Paul told Der Dicke. "I was preparing to give you a fair trial and then shoot you, all inside thirty seconds."

The Boer forced a laugh. "The Kommandeur's humor is well known. A trial for what?"

"Treachery." Paul paused to listen to the returning sounds of the rain forest. "Well! Stay alive. I may need you warm and articulate. God knows you're both." He raised his voice slightly. "*Effendi!* Stick close to this man. If he bolts, put a bullet between his ears. If he turns on you, shoot him six o'clock for belly."

A black underofficer moved up on Der Dicke.

"We'll climb to the ridge," said Paul. For Der Dicke's benefit he added, "Move your carcass. This *effendi* has a nervous trigger finger."

Paul assembled a textbook picture of the situation, his mind clicking methodically with the rhythm of the climb. Max Looff's KLF troops were stuck at the other end of the narrow gorge, imprisoned by an unseen enemy content to kill anyone moving out of that area without launching a direct assault. Paul's men were similarly trapped. These tactics were the trademark of the Ugandans. Their warriors encircled a foe and then settled on their haunches, picking off any stranger who strayed from the circle. They would add to the tension by beating drums and uttering bloodcurdling nocturnal cries. Holding the initiative, they would strike only when their enemy's morale was at its lowest ebb.

Paul called Skaramunga. "Can we work our way through the

ravine tonight and make contact with Looff's *manowari* force?"

Skaramunga had reached the same conclusion as Paul. He did not need to ask whom Paul meant by "we." The trio had fought their way out of tight corners before: Skaramunga, the Kommandeur, and Bamboo the monkey. It would be like old times again to be alone in the *bundu* without the Kommandeur's woman.

Myles Hagen had received Der Dicke's clandestine message in Moshi. It claimed Governor Schnee would welcome English intervention to put down a Ugandan uprising on the basis of their original agreement for joint Anglo-German operations against black rebels. Hagen distrusted Der Dicke, but that was the cross you bore when handling double agents. There was confirmation of Der Dicke's claim that Max Looff was moving upcountry with the *Koenigsberg* Land Force, because Pieter Pretorius had also reported the KLF's departure with weapons.

Hagen's Kikuyu intelligence aide, Gideon, limped into the office looking as if he had been dragged through a hedge. "I tried to take the train on the new spur line," said Gideon, "but the coaches were full of white termites, and I was made to sit in the engine fuel box."

Hagen was on the point of burning Gideon's ears for employing a native expression for noncombatant English officers. But he was also disgusted by the behavior of these same termites, and so he said only that "the phrase white termites is impolite."

Gideon accepted the reprimand and eyed the billy can of tea Hagen always had on the hob. Gideon's boots stood on the floor. His feet were blistered. He had walked across the top of the Masai steppe rather than suffer the discomfort of the trains.

"Tannic acid's good for what ails you," said Hagen, dipping his handkerchief into the brewed tea. "Sore feet are a dead giveaway, laddie." Any bushwhacker would have known that Gideon in his ragged trousers and moth-eaten topcoat was no kaffir wandering home from the southern mines, even if he had fooled the Germans. "You," Hagen added, "have been desk-bound too long. You're getting out of practice."

"Desk-bound?" Gideon repeated the unfamiliar word.

"Glued here. Like me."

"Then get unstuck," said Gideon. He liked new words. He was proud of his English. Mission school had done that for him. "I get out more than you do."

Hagen nodded distractedly. London had said he must choose between directing the bulging African intelligence bureau and getting back into battle.

"They won't close the ambush yet on the German," said Gideon, examining his toes.

"What makes you speak of an ambush?"

The Kikuyu tapped his skull. "A picture forms."

Hagen retreated into respectful silence. He had known these men. From the Himalayas to the Mountains of the Moon, their nomadic life opened their senses to signs invisible to others. Whites scoffed at these visions or thought them magical.

"It's the Ugandans who have encircled the German Kommandeur," said Gideon, emerging from his private world. "It's their way, to surround their victims, exhaust them with many hours of fear, strike when the sun is high and enemy spirits low."

"We can't have the Germans massacred."

"You mean, you can't have whites massacred by blacks?" inquired Gideon, looking innocent.

"I could put you on charge for insolence."

"Why else rescue Germans?" Gideon had no fear; he knew how much Hagen relied on him. "England cannot afford an *independent* black rebellion against any white's rule."

"Blast your impudence. Our agreement with the German Governor—with the Governor, not the Kommandeur—is to support his pacification of unruly tribes. It's not a question of rescuing Germans."

"But of bashing a few black skulls," amended Gideon. He grinned knowingly. "It's many moons since you killed."

Hagen glanced at the knobkerrie, always near since he had killed to get it from Kornatzki. He must get back into battle.

23

LANNI WAS aware of Hagen before she dared open her eyes. No man had ever frightened her, but this one came close. This one came closer than any white, except Paul, to getting inside a black skin. The difference was Hagen meant to dominate.

"I'm off to save your blasted German," said Hagen. "It's time to pay your dues."

Lanni drew a thin cotton *kanga* tight around her naked body and sat up on the earthen floor. It was a month since Hagen had met the French experimental biplane from England on which she was a passenger. He had put her under detention at his personal pleasure, cunningly refusing to arrest her. This way there was no file, and no body to account for if he had to kill her. Two nights ago she had been moved to Moshi secretly by train, with Hagen as her only escort.

They had struck a bargain during the night journey. She had been curled up in the corner of an empty carriage. Even in the darkness she was aware of brand-new rolling stock—glass windows instead of wooden shutters, patterned upholstery covering the bench seats, an electric bulb glowing erratically with the changing speed of the train. She had said, "This railway's new."

"Demands of war. Someday it will serve your people."

She had distrusted his amiability, but it was worth exploiting. "In London they say African warfare costs more in six months than the whole empire produces in a year."

"Propaganda." Hagen leaned forward. "You will face a far worse catastrophe if your comrades continue to support the wrong side."

"My comrades seek freedom and justice."

"Quite so. Nevertheless, your Cornelius will die violently. The rebels you serve will be put down, their villages razed, their women and children scattered, their lands given to the tribes who fight loyally with the English."

Hagen regarded her face as it turned toward the naked bulb. *La fille aux yeux d'or.* The golden-eyed girl. Even in clumsy overalls she had a golden presence. The mannish clothing stirred him, and he loosened the thong around his thick wrist and laid aside the knobkerrie.

"That club's become part of you," observed Lanni. "Someday Count Kornatzki's going to take it back."

"Kornatzki's dead."

"Oh." Lanni considered a moment. "I'm sorry. He was a gentle, a good man. How did he die?"

"Come now. You were there."

Lanni concealed her excitement that Hagen would believe one of his most dangerous enemies dead.

"At Tanga hospital," Hagen continued. "I was sorry, too. But it was a fair fight."

"Kornatzki was the real Governor of German East," said Lanni. "He was a Western-trained doctor who respected our folkways. I suppose being a priest altered his view of us, made him less arrogant. His favorite hymn was 'Onward, Christian Soldiers, Marching as to War.' "

"And smite the enemy, hip and thigh?" Hagen knew those robust killer-Christians. "For your own sakes, Kornatzki's better dead."

Lanni decided she could afford to show anger. "The reason he loved that hymn was that it predicts the fall of crowns and imperial thrones. He was a more positive factor than men like you."

"Men like me want peace and prosperity for Africa. We can work with Governor Schnee. With your hero gone, there's hope your comrades will end German resistance."

She laughed softly. "We can do nothing."

"The proposal," said Hagen carefully, "is simple and legal. We are moving to uphold Governor Schnee's authority. I'm asking your tribal leaders to become allied with England in restoring law and order. Your people will get all you wish for them."

Lanni stiffened. "What exactly are you offering?" she asked.

"You mean, what's the price you have to pay?"

A sudden silence fell. The train sounds were muffled. Lanni saw reflected in the window a disconcerting image of the apostle of English enlightenment haloed against the primitive bush. The head was spotted and blurred, reminding her of a leopard. She knew the leopard's killing habits. She knew, in a flash of insight, that Hagen could be lured emotionally into the pagan world his body had savagely occupied so long.

"Yes," said Lanni. "What is the price I must pay? Why bring me to this carriage, just us alone?"

"You're desirable, God knows." Hagen, sitting opposite, was watching her in the window, too. They seemed to speak to each other through protective glass. "I'm a man of strange tastes. One is for privacy. Physical intercourse repels me. Intellectual intercourse is a challenge, steel against steel. Only a man provides it."

"You don't regard me as a woman?"

"Perhaps not. A female animal I can respect, admire, acknowledge as an opponent."

"Did you ever love a woman?"

"Love? It's not something one cares to discuss. Love of country?

Yes. Humility before God, respect for a good woman."

"Lust?"

"One elects to be the victim."

Tensely now, Lanni said, "You would be hard to hurt."

"One learns to handle pain. Like your own people."

"Is that why you tolerate me when you hate most women?"

Hagen turned his head and looked directly at her.

"You're very frank. Is that wise?"

Lanni considered. "I've nothing to lose. You could dispose of me and nobody need know. You're a killer."

"Then we're well matched," said Hagen. "I kill for king and country. You kill for a cause. It's a higher form of love."

"I'd rather die for love of a people than a king."

"What do you know of kings?"

Lanni stretched. "George the Fifth, His Gracious Majesty, spoke to me flatteringly about Paul."

Hagen pondered. The King's remarks had been a tribute to her skill as a spy.

"I could do better in the Kaiser's court," said Lanni, as if she read his thoughts.

Hagen burst into laughter.

"Your King and the Kaiser are in secret contact," she added quickly.

Hagen stopped laughing. She could smell the violence in him now.

"The Kaiser wants to merge the Second Reich and the English Empire," Lanni persisted. "A white union to dominate a nonwhite world."

"Man's a fool!" said Hagen. "We're destroying each other in Europe. Nobody'd take him seriously."

He was staring into the carriage window again. He saw her as a blur mirrored against the night. She was crossing to his side of the rocking carriage. In her swiftness she triggered Hagen's bush-wise reflexes. His hand tightened in a fierce defensive grip, and he forced her arm up and behind her body. His other hand dug into her opposite shoulder, pinning her against the seat.

"Harder," Lanni whispered. She was curled like a wildcat, her knees drawn up, one heel pressing into his groin.

Her whispered word penetrated him below the level of conscious thought. She was as light and tightly wound as a watch spring. Her body was curved like a steel bow, and she spat cobralike into his eyes. A red film distorted Hagen's vision. A familiar heat rose in his bowels. The girl's foot had insinuated itself between his thighs. By the same disgusting misuse of her body, she had insinuated herself into English society.

Then the film dissolved. He saw his own hand, the back of it bristling with red furry hair, squeezing the girl's windpipe. His other hand seemed like a dreadful claw, hooked into her hair, hauling it back until it must be torn from her scalp. He released her. Slowly she raised her head. For a moment pleasure or triumph gleamed in her gold-flecked eyes. They became calm but watchful as a cat's.

He moved back from her. The train must have stopped suddenly, catapulting her across the carriage. He had taken a risk being alone with her, but this was the way you broke in agents—conditioning them to your ways, winning their confidence by revealing a little of yourself, asserting your ascendancy. He would get her into harness.

"That was savage," said Lanni. She matched his composure, concealed her pain as he had concealed his own. Her eyes were smiling. "I learned to fight a leopard in that same way. The game was to play close to the edge of hate, wrestling, but never so hard that the leopard unsheathed its claws. Like holding death in your arms."

"Don't test me again," Hagen cautioned. "A leopard kills for fun."

"My word would be pleasure," said Lanni.

"Pleasure's for primitives." He stared into her cat's eyes and saw himself reflected. "Great causes flourish on taming primitive instincts. Then one plays the game for sheer fun."

"Translate that into my terms of action," Lanni whispered.

Hagen nodded approvingly. "You play the game for its own sake. Good. You would play it best of all in Germany, I'm thinking. For yourself. For me. You could wrestle with the greatest of all leopards, the Kaiser."

Lanni held her breath. The man looked insane. The proposal was madder. But Hagen had divined her unspoken, crazy, dangerous ambition, which was to prevent the alliance between the Kaiser and England that would end all hope of black African independence.

"I'll get you into the Kaiser's court," Hagen continued. "You will pay me for it, of course. One favor deserves another." He asked abruptly, "How good's your German?"

"*Der Potsdamer Postkutscher putzt den Potsdamer Postkutschkasten*," she said quickly, reciting a famous tongue twister. The rush of words underscored her eagerness, and Hagen grinned.

"I need to test your talent a little more," he said. "You blacks have one dedicated enemy, that renegade Englishman Tom von Prinz. He hates your lover, Cornelius. Bring me Prinz's head." Hagen's voice turned savage again. "Get the bastard off the bloody mountain, girl."

She moved back to her side of the window. She knew Hagen thought her a political prostitute, ready to work both sides of the street. She sensed the weakness in him and why it made her desirable. She would get more out of Hagen by destroying Prinz and pay no more, perhaps, than to serve Hagen's warped passions. His soldiers considered this flank of Kilimanjaro as German territory occupied now by Englishmen. They failed to understand that all African territory was hostile to German and English. This was the land of her people.

Smudges of firelight dotted the night, sentinels of the mountain, nothing more than cow-dung cooking fires glowing through layers of their own smoke, of no significance to the white imperial armies but speaking to Lanni of a black unity no white man could penetrate, signaling a black unity that would let the white gods destroy each other over the body of a black Africa none had ever possessed.

That journey had been two nights ago. Now, suddenly, Hagen was dragging her off again. Lanni repeated the words with which he had burst in upon her. "You said *rescue* Paul. Save your enemy?"

"Neither he nor I can afford to permit an independent African victory."

"At least you're candid."

Hagen tossed her the Royal Flying Corps dungarees she had worn for the long flight from London. "I don't want you recognized for a woman. Not here."

"What's my part in this insanity?"

"You'll see," said Hagen. She was left alone holding the dungarees. They had been taken from her in Nairobi. Now, mysteriously, efficiently, they had been restored to her. She glanced around her cell and realized how completely she was in Hagen's hands.

24

COUNT KORNATZKI studied Kate Truman's face. "These are serious accusations, child."

"Why do you call me 'child' when you don't want to treat me sensibly? It's a man's trick. You say 'dear' or 'little cabbage' when you want to put a woman in her place. You don't want to face up to what I'm telling you, so you dismiss it by diminishing me!"

Kornatzki rubbed his shock of white hair. "How can I justify a rescue operation?"

"You don't *justify* one. You *lead* it."

"Yes, yes. But we're limited in men and ammunition."

"Which was the Governor's excuse for calling the *Koenigsberg* crew in."

"How did you know that?" Kornatzki demanded.

"I questioned the Governor's wife."

Devil take the women! Kornatzki cursed under his breath and said aloud, "Thank God Ada's on our side. Stay here. Forget all that nonsense about Uriah the Hittite. If treachery's afoot, we'll see Paul doesn't get smitten."

Kate let him go. There was nothing more she could do. She had called Kornatzki to her tent, knowing his tribal network could swiftly investigate her fears. "Der Dicke's an English spy," she had told Kornatzki, "and he's leading Paul into a trap." She sank onto her cot and began to clean her rifle. She knew Paul was in danger. If Kornatzki trusted his witch doctors, why not trust her intuition? She worked on hunches, instincts, flashes. These were regarded as essential qualities in men at war. But Kate was not a man, and she was not locked in mutual hatred.

Or was she? The question disturbed her. She watched with a strange sense of detachment her own hands busy in the gun box, separating trigger guards, a revolver, a naked bayonet. She rubbed animal fat on the blade of her bush knife, burnished the bayonet. She knew how to wield all the weapons in Paul's armory. Her hands followed a drill imposed by Africa's violence. She corrected herself. Africa's violence, the violence of the *bundu,* was a natural part of the cycle of life and death. The drill she now followed was the violence created by man.

Kornatzki returned to find her grooming her horse. "You mustn't think of coming—"

"He's in trouble, isn't he?"

Kornatzki inclined his head. "You were right about a trap. I'm an idiot. Others found out. Why didn't I? These tribal agents! They're like cockroaches, into everything. They smelled treachery. They killed Hackmann to warn the conspirators without knowing exactly who was conspiring."

"If they killed Hackmann, they're enemies of Paul's enemy."

"That, my dear, is the message I plan to get through to them."

"Then you need me as evidence of good faith."

"The *bundu*'s crawling with treachery."

"I can handle a gun better than you, Count. Ride better, Count, much better than you!"

She stood with legs braced apart, her trousers tucked into calf-length boots fashioned from deerskin and elephant hide, a bayonet dangling from her belt in its scabbard, her double-barreled rifle slung across her shoulders, the webbing and belts of ammunition crisscrossing the faded shirt and emphasizing her breasts, her face so deeply tanned that under the helmet it was that of a beautiful but resolute boy. There was nothing posed or feminine in the picture she presented in an age when young women were supposed to be swathed in fourteen pounds of underwear.

Kornatzki surveyed her and sighed. He had celebrated his fifty-fourth birthday two nights ago. He had confronted his limitations. Still, he was big and powerful, and he knew an African trick or two. He sighed again.

"God knows I need what help I can get."

"That's a poor little grudging tribute," said Kate.

"I'm afraid to encourage you. If the Ugandans won't listen to reason, you'll have the choice of dodging long-bladed spears with a range of fifty yards, arrows deadly to a hundred and forty yards, a knobkerrie able to dash out your brains at seventy yards."

Kate smiled. "Don't try to make my flesh creep."

"You've never treated a boy with his entrails falling out between his legs," Kornatzki said somberly. "That's their idea of making eunuchs. You've not picked up girls raped, not a few times but again and again and again on the march."

"My thighs are nutcrackers, Count."

Kornatzki was forced to grin. "Smite me if you haven't turned into a real live African pagan," he declared.

"Me? A pagan? A partner in killing English soldiers and poisoning English wells! Isn't that Christian enough, your reverence?"

Kornatzki remembered his priestly functions. "A blessing on yourself and your weapons," he mumbled. "If you are taken alive, scratch yourself with this." He handed her a small gourd with a needle-tipped stopper. "You'll be dead before you know it."

She took in the palm of her hand the seamless sac that had once contained the testicles of a Cape buffalo. From it emerged a short bamboo shaft. The poison inside was brewed from a toxic nightshade. Pygmies had shown Kornatzki how to measure the strength by the way it turned fresh blood black. The pygmies lived by killing elephants with arrows smeared in the deadly tar. The gourd resembled a man's genitals. Kate slipped it into a saddlebag.

Captain Max Looff put on his mildewed jacket with traces of gold braid on the sleeves. He donned his gold-leafed cap, hoping his head would not poke through the frayed crown. He tied his tattered shorts with string and tried to squeeze his feet into homemade sandals. His feet were badly swollen, and he decided to face his unseen enemies in a last pair of navy socks. He had a reputation to keep up. He was still Bwana Unguja, Mister Zanzibar, to the natives impressed by his sinking of English ships at Zanzibar.

His *Koenigsberg* Land Force had poked into the overgrown ravine and found itself in a trap. Boulders and giant trees blocked their path forward or back. Invisible in the dense vegetation of the steep slopes on either side, natives armed with arrows, spears and clubs had killed any of Looff's men who strayed into the jungle. The KLF had formed a small laager on top of the hillock plugging the gorge. Dirt-filled crates blocked the gaps between carts on which a 4.1-inch naval gun and some quick-firing 47-mm guns had been mounted. Sailors had worked alongside porters for three nights to dig trenches. The position seemed impregnable against a conventional raid. But the enemy was not behaving conventionally. The nights echoed to drums and barbaric yelps. Men posted to outlying pickets disappeared.

Max Looff shook himself as if to destroy the eerie carapace forming itself around him. He was covered in sores. When he urinated, black fluid emerged. There was not much left of the dashing corsair except the jutting black beard, hollowed cheeks, piercing blue eyes, nose like an imperial eagle's beak, and the durable air of command.

He jumped with unaccustomed nervousness at the sudden chatter of a monkey. The sound was low pitched and came from the purple mist of a Judas tree. Looff looked more closely in disbelief. Skaramunga's vervet monkey! He lowered his rifle, calling softly, "Bamboo." An adjacent bush parted, and the monkey scampered toward him. "Come out," said Looff, feeling he was in a dream. "I'll not shoot."

Skaramunga crossed the open patch of ground, followed by Paul.

"It's not possible," said Looff. "You're supposed to be fifty, sixty kilometers away."

"You asked us to meet you here," Paul replied, looking closely at Looff. "My party's stuck at the other end of the gorge. I couldn't have got through if it hadn't been for these two." He jerked his head in the direction of Skaramunga and the monkey, moving toward the line of KLF sentries. "Last night was the rendezvous, remember?"

"No," said Looff. "There was no rendezvous. We were to march to Laager-120 W. Even got entry permits from one tribal territory to the next. All the paraphernalia of civilization." There was a sarcastic edge to his voice. "Let's get under cover."

Paul followed him, bewildered. Inside the laager, Looff held out a dirty scrap of paper. Paul saw, against the sunrise, a crude lightning flash worked into the paper with lemon juice. "Even a watermark, eh. I didn't know Cornelius was issuing passports."

"Nor the Governor, I suspect." Looff's expression warned of trouble.

"You do know," Paul began, "this—passport—this bit of paper isn't working right now?"

"As evidenced by the ambush? It seems strange you got through when my men cannot."

"What does that imply?"

"You control the tribes through Cornelius."

"My men are just as immobilized as yours." Paul took a clay cup from a bearer and gulped down the schnapps made from potato spirits. "Where's your report?"

"My report goes straight to the Governor."

"For the love of God!" exploded Paul. "I'm fighting this war, not the sodding Governor!"

"But who do you fight it for? The Fatherland? Or blacks and Jews?" Max Looff flicked an imaginary speck from the sleeve of his tattered jacket. The jacket was so long, it hid his torn shorts. His knees were raw. He was lowering himself onto a crate when he saw Paul's horrified expression. "Perhaps you think I'm crazy?"

"No, Max, but very sick."

"Cornelius has led me into this trap. Cornelius was condemned according to German law to hang. Cornelius was and is your ally. Am I crazy to conclude you're up to some trick?"

"Max—"

"It would be better if you'd refer to me by my correct title."

"Captain Looff, we're both victims of the same trick. The quicker you get medical attention, Max, the sooner we'll get out of this mess." Paul caught Looff by the arm. The man was swaying. Sweat poured down his face. "Get a doctor!" Paul called out.

A young lieutenant came forward. "Dr. Richter died two weeks ago, sir."

"You must have orderlies."

"Sir?"

"Run!" shouted Paul. "I want your stretcher bearers."

The youth cocked his head. His uniform was as mildewed and bizarre as his captain's. "Yessir," he said and shuffled into a lazy trot. Paul realized that every German in sight was functioning on the edge of collapse. One of the porters was kneeling beside Max Looff now, obviously accustomed to dealing with this crisis. Looff vomited and then slid to the ground, his back against a cart wheel.

"This is Seaman Diver Martin Innocence Mohammed." The lieutenant was back with a young light-colored African.

"What does a diver know about medicine?" asked Paul.

"Two years ago, sir, your medical director selected me. Count Kornatzki. I had worked with him in the bush. I finished one year of medicine in Berlin when your naval intelligence took over, sir."

Paul waited patiently while Innocence explained how he happened to have been diverted from an altruistic ambition to the unusual occupation of diving beneath the sea.

"So what's happened here?" Paul finally asked.

"Fever, sir. Lack of salt. And horse sickness, which took all our mounts, sir."

"How did you know it was horse sickness?"

"The staggers. The horse trembles, falls, cannot get up. The horse blows bubbles from his nostrils and drowns as the lungs fill with his own foaming discharge."

Paul nodded, satisfied that Innocence knew something. "What about these open sores?"

"Malnutrition. And the lack of salt. I did fear *ngonjwa tumba.*"

"Cholera!"

"But not all the symptoms were present, sir."

While they had been talking, a throb of drums had grown in volume, beginning almost unnoticed and then swelling to a monotonous roar. The drums crept upon the hearing like the rising scissor-grinding rasp of the giant cicadas. The sound was nerve-racking.

"The sickness strikes only whites," Paul observed. "Why?"

"Blacks stand more pain, sir," said Innocence. "Blacks go hungry, go thirsty longer. Blacks fight germs better."

"Can these blacks fight out of this trap?"

"I believe so, sir. But who will give orders?"

"I will. And you'll relay them. I want every white officer and man brought to me here."

Paul waited as Innocence came back across the clearing. Poor devil! Sent to Germany with a promise he'd return to his own people as a doctor. Now his people surrounded him, beating drums that gave Paul a dull headache. Innocence had run the English blockade in a cargo ship that had deliberately rammed a reef near the Rufiji. Deep-sea divers had gone to work, unobserved by English agents, under the hull of the submerged blockade runner. Innocence had directed the removal of the cargo and equipment, and now the diver had described to Paul the *Koenigsberg*'s crew as a community of all talents. "What better than a boiler man to rig a steam tractor?" he asked Paul. "What more handy than engine-room artificers, gunners, and sailors so clever with canvas that they run up a camouflage suit in seconds?"

Precious few were proving useful now, thought Paul, sourly contemplating a line of delirious crewmen shepherded by Innocence. Doubtless the diving helmets and pumps they had brought with them would help raise the German steamers sunk on the inland lakes. But how like German naval intelligence to interrupt the medical training of this young African and turn him instead into something so perfectly useless to his people as a deep-sea diver.

"Ship's company all present, sir," reported Innocence. His eyes turned away from Paul to Captain Max Looff, now standing again, all his willpower focused upon keeping some semblance of authority.

"Thank you, lad!" said Looff unexpectedly. He turned gravely to Paul. His mouth opened and closed several times. Finally came the traditional words to signify the handing over of command of a ship. "You have her, Kommandeur," said Looff, who was caught by the young lieutenant as he collapsed again into a dead faint.

———

The following dawn found Hagen and his volunteers some thirty kilometers west of Moshi and approaching the ambushed Germans.

A large Union Jack fluttered at the head of each column.

"Always show your true colors in a confusing situation," Hagen decreed.

"If we're rescuing Germans, shouldn't we fly truce flags?" asked a callow subaltern. "Otherwise the Jerries'll shoot us."

"We are white men rescuing white men," responded Hagen.

From ahead came a warning. "Scouts report contact."

Hagen called a halt and turned to Lanni. "Follow me."

The girl led her pony to where Hagen's carriers were making camp. A group of English regulars had discovered that inside the mechanic's uniform Lanni was all woman. "A pretty hot 'un, to judge from her golden optics. A classic buckskin, yellow with a black mane. A filly with guts." The speaker glanced up, saw Lanni, and sprang to attention. "Ma'am!"

"A remarkable horse you've just described," Lanny said mischievously. "May I see?"

"Yes, ma'am, I mean—" Blushing crimson, the young officer looked for help and found it in Hagen. The porters, moving like a circus team, were already hammering the last pegs around a tent newly erected. Hagen beckoned the girl. She smiled at the young Englishman, handed him her pony's reins, and joined Hagen.

"You're happy with our bargain?" asked Hagen.

"I can hardly afford not to be."

Hagen escorted her into the tent. His batman had already opened up the safari desk. Hagen straddled a camel seat and went through the brass-bound mahogany desk with practiced speed. "Here." He unfolded a linen-backed chart. "Tom von Prinz is here. Our fellows are dug in below the crests along these ridges."

Lanni asked in a whisper, "What can I possibly do?"

"He knows you. He connects you with Paul Lettow's black friends. He's seen you nursing alongside his own wife. He trusts you."

"I can't betray his wife."

"That's rich!" Hagen twisted on the wooden saddle to stare directly at her. "Surely the cause you serve admits of only one kind of betrayal, the betrayal of the revolution?"

She said softly, "What are you proposing?"

Hagen flashed her a pleased smile and turned back to the chart. "I can get you forward to this ridge. There's no great hardship or danger to eight thousand feet. But you'll need a good cover story for Prinz."

Lanni said quickly, "That's easy. I'll say Lettow sent me and that I slipped out of a Ugandan ambush."

"You're glib, I'll give you that," conceded Hagen. He stood up, hoisting a booted leg over the seat. He towered above Lanni, but she no longer feared him. She knew she would find a way to kill him, just as she would Tom von Prinz. In his own twisted way Hagen admired her, perhaps loved her as a man loves a pet leopard, loving the control over a creature capable of destructive fury. She wanted Hagen to see her as a woman, not entirely ruthless.

He said, nodding his head toward the entrance to the tent, "This is Elmer McCurdy. He'll be your—ah—bodyguard. He has the arrogance to call himself *The* Frontiersman."

She turned sharply to watch the agile white man treading softly behind her.

"Howdy, ma'am!" McCurdy lifted his face to hers. "The world's greatest train robber at your service. Raised to climb afore I walked, no finer mountain boy."

Lanny returned the smile through a mist of anger. Not bodyguard. Captor. Jailer. Warden. So much for Hagen's trust! And a cursed American white, at that. Well, it was better than a firing squad.

"I'm enchanted to meet you, Mr. McCurdy," she said.

25

KATE WAS riding hard when the new day swept in from the Indian Ocean and illuminated the plain. Around her were the dark shapes of Count Kornatzki's horsemen jogging in loose formation through the wait-a-bit thorn trees. They were crafty jungle fighters, swifter than marching columns, slicing through the long exhausting night like hawks.

Kate was at a pitch of heightened perceptions, lifted there, despite physical weariness, by excitement. She had learned to trust that extra bush sense, "the African blessing." She was aware that her spirits were falling and rising because of fatigue and that her body had become open to the subtle signals of the bush. She had a subconscious ability to collect the evidence of her senses and, after some mysterious process, to visualize a distant situation. She had marveled at this in the African trackers who could tell you where a pride of lions lay concealed, having made no visible contact with them. It seemed like witchcraft.

Count Kornatzki cut across her path, one arm raised. She reined in. "I'm calling a halt."

"I could ride forever," said Kate.

"That's the trouble." Kornatzki gently nudged his own horse against hers until they were facing back toward the rest of the halted riders. "You seemed carried away. Didn't you hear me shout?"

"Kate!" Magdalene von Prinz interrupted them. "You were going as if the devil possessed you." Her pony glistened with sweat. She was wearing against the dawn's cold a burnoose whose hood she threw back so the early light fell soft on her troubled face.

Kornatzki said dubiously, "I'm leaving you two here, with the rear guard." He held up a hand to stop their protests. "Sorry, but I can't afford needless risks."

Magdalene waited until he rejoined the detachment. Then she burst out, "Why, Kate? Why anger him with your recklessness?"

"I heard or saw someone."

"You're overtired."

"No." Kate drew back from the other woman's restraining hand. "Kornatzki's instincts are good. We'll be among the rebels in an hour." She pointed dead ahead. "Paul's down there, at the far end of the gorge. Don't ask how I know."

Magdalene shot her a startled look. A strange emerald light flickered across the eastern sky as the sun plunged over the earth's rim. A pastel flush of dawn dissolved the gloom in Kate's face. She said, "I'm going over to those trees. Tell Kornatzki—a call of nature— I won't be long." She spurred away, not in the direction of the gorge, but making for a lonely clump of flat-topped locust trees. Heavy dew sparkled on the flat, long grass, and the growing light revealed a fresh trail. She glanced back. Magdalene had returned to Kornatzki. The horsemen stood in their stirrups, motionless, watching Kate.

She walked her horse into the salt-rimmed bowl of a water hole. Two men stood like spears under a candelabra tree. One wore a

Masai's toga. The other was almost a dwarf and looked pixyish in a pillbox leather cap and bush-buck cape, rings glinting in his ears, and in his hands a longbow loosely held.

"Don't come closer!" The tall Masailike figure rapped out the words. He gestured at the gnome. "He's longing to kill."

"Cornelius!" Kate let out a sigh of relief.

The rebel chief watched her dismount. "You're lucky," he said and then added quickly, avoiding elaboration: "Tell me what's going on."

"Paul's trapped."

"That we know." Cornelius let his gaze stray, warning Kate of more pygmy hunters concealed around the water hole. "The Ugandan king was told by his spies of a meeting between Paul and Captain Looff to sell him out."

"Nonsense!" declared Kate. "Utter lies!"

"I can't control a powerful chief like Big O. You think of rebels as one big tribe. They're not. They rise against white domination, but they don't blindly follow me." Cornelius studied her carefully. "I can't stop the Ugandans attacking Paul unless you can prove what you say."

"Count Kornatzki's back up there."

Cornelius scratched his chin. "Kornatzki's respected. Would he come down and talk?"

"Of course, if I explain." Kate caught a quick movement in the encircling trees and suddenly Cornelius was hissing to her, "Get back." She remounted and saw near-naked bodies flit through the thin bars of light. She had an impression of dwarf tumblers in a circus, and Cornelius's tongue cracked like a whip with strangely worded orders. Then he slapped her horse, and as the horse jumped forward, she heard him shout, "Bring back Kornatzki!"

She cantered toward two German horsemen swishing forward through the dew-kissed grass, the same who had watched her departure. She sensed the hunters behind her, drawing their longbows. She shouted a warning. One of the riders stopped and raised his rifle. Kate pulled her horse into the line of fire. She recognized the skewbald mount of Major Wolfe as she closed the distance, watched as Wolfe slowly lowered his gun, then saw him rise in the stirrups and clutch his shoulder. She saw his companion reach to hold him upright in the saddle. Then she was there herself, reining up on Wolfe's free side and groping for the arrow caught loosely in his cape.

"Be careful," gasped Wolfe. "It's poisoned."

She tugged the arrow free. The head was a flattened nail covered in thick black tar. She slid the ugly vulture-feathered arrow gingerly into her saddlebag and looked at Wolfe. He was tearing at his clothes with a knife. She thought he was stabbing himself until she saw him cut into the flesh around the slight wound. It was in the thick upper arm muscle just beyond the reach of his tongue, which flickered oddly. She realized what he was trying to do, and she leaned sideways in the saddle, grasped the pommel with one hand, and with the other hand thrust away the knife. She put her mouth over the rapidly purpling area of the wound and bit hard into the flesh. She felt Wolfe jerk in renewed pain. She put both her hands on him and held her horse motionless with her leg while she sucked at the wound.

She heard Cornelius running and shouting. She continued to bite and suck, spitting out or swallowing the foulness in the wound. She knew she must be swift and she must not stop until other hands gently pried her loose.

Later, resting where Kornatzki had bivouacked, she was overcome by sudden nausea. She said to Magdalene, "It was my own stupid fault."

"Stop worrying." Magdalene put herbal tea leaves into a billy can over the fire she tended. "Major Wolfe's none the worse."

Kate lay back and closed her eyes. At once the image returned of Major Wolfe twisting his head, like a dog snapping at its own haunches, straining with his tongue as if the tongue were a red-hot poker to cauterize the wound.

"You're shivering," said Magdalene.

"Only with horror. At myself. I don't much like what I'm becoming."

Cornelius was blunt with Count Kornatzki. "If you were not making a deal with the English, why is there an English force making its way here?"

"I find that hard to believe."

"Nine hours' ride away. What's more, Lanni was seen departing from the English camp with an American." Even with his face masked in Masai markings, Cornelius betrayed his agony of spirit.

"Send your people after her," Kornatzki said quickly. "She'll confirm there's no conspiracy."

"I'll try." Cornelius hesitated. "Look, the Kommandeur is encircled by Ugandan warriors. But I'm just as trapped. Other tribes will take their lead from the *Kabaka*." He used the Ugandan term for a king. "You know the man's reputation."

Kornatzki nodded. He knew too well that Big O had as many personalities as he had names. He had been partially tamed by the English, who had issued him ten rules of guidance, forbidding the cutting out of his opponents' tongues, genitals, eyes. Among the forbidden barbarities was the confinement of young black girls in hutments until they turned a milky color from lack of sun. Big O believed a white-skinned woman had godly virtues. The thought no sooner crossed Kornatzki's mind than one of the twittering pygmies darted forward.

"The chief is demanding all of you pay him tribute," translated Cornelius.

The Ugandan king wore a lion's mane over his head, and when he turned ponderously, a breeze ruffled the gold and black pelt. Necklaces of lion's teeth cascaded down his massive chest like regimental medals. A belt of monkey tails girdled his shining belly. Garters of colored feathers were tied around his columnar legs.

Kate saw him first in the clearing to which they had been escorted, talking with Cornelius, who seemed to have shrunk in contrast. She waited at a distance, feeling that she had stumbled on a picnic, very civilized, almost carnival. The squadron of German horsemen was drawn up beside a watercourse. Behind them, in trees densely laced with vine, drums thrummed at a low, somnolent pitch. A soft wind moaned through the long grass in the meadow sloping up from the chief's *boma* encampment. Some of the gnomelike hunters had put on ceremonial headdresses that turned them into birds of brilliant plumage darting among the Ugandan spearmen, as still as naked clay statues. Major Wolfe, his recovery accelerated by Ugandan gin, sketched the scene, squatting on his shooting stick, his charcoal flying across his pad.

Only when he left Big O's shadow did Cornelius recover his own considerable stature. He walked slowly over to Kate, the purple knife scars standing out in his taut face. "He wants to speak with you."

Kate moved into the presence. A plump face peered down at her, seemingly disconnected from the black cliff of a chest. The voice was disconcertingly high. Kate found it difficult to see the villain in that small boy's quizzical stare over the parapet of a barrel chest. He spoke in dialect, and Cornelius translated.

"The *Kabaka* welcomes you to join his *haroun*." Cornelius corrected himself hastily because the word came out *harem*. "He means household."

Already Big O was swinging around with a jingle of decorations, his enormous buttocks gleaming between ribbons of fur. Kate could see no choice but to follow. She heard Cornelius mutter a protest, and glancing back, she saw two Ugandans close on either side of him with spears angled. Other guards fell in step. She became part of a procession, with Cornelius forced to bring up the rear.

Big O spoke as he walked into the shade of a *makuti* matting of coconut leaves. He swung around again, and with a womanly lifting of his monkey-tail skirt, he sat on a bench, spreading his legs. He gestured, and a spearman rummaged behind him and emerged with what appeared to be a hatbox.

"The *Kabaka* honors you," Cornelius said haltingly. "He wishes to show you a problem that has been on his mind. First he wishes to feel your skin."

Big O smiled encouragingly while Kate eyed the hatbox and remembered Count Kornatzki's stories of executed wives whose heads were kept in such receptacles. She stepped up to the glistening knees and looked again into the brown liquid eyes of an inquisitive schoolboy. But the powerful body odors were those of an excited man, and the huge hand stroking her arm was moist and trembling. She forced herself to remain still while Big O's hands moved over her shoulders and face. His touch was gentle, almost effeminate.

"The *Kabaka* wishes to know how you make your skin so white," said Cornelius in a tight voice. "He has tried with hundreds of his women, and the best he can do is the color of English chocolate."

Kate said, "I was born this way."

"The *Kabaka* wishes to know if the babies would be white that you bear him."

Kate felt the muscles in her stomach tighten into a knot. Cornelius added quickly, "Careful how you answer."

She debated with herself. She knew Big O would be quick to take offense. If she said the only guarantee of white babies was in the mating of two white persons, it would be a slur. She said, "For a king, all things are possible."

Big O cocked his head. "Making my hat white is not possible." He took the lid off the box, and Kate saw with a shudder that he was lifting something head-shaped into view. She stared in a mixture of horror and disbelief while he held up between his large hands a flesh-colored object and then extended it toward her. It looked the size of a head, and Kate shrank back. Big O began to laugh, and the rolls of fat around his belly rippled and gleamed.

"The *Kabaka* says it is only the hat given him by the wife of the English Governor of Uganda."

Kate resisted a mad impulse to ask what had happened to the wife. She began to laugh in wild relief and then caught herself. Big O's face was solemn again.

"The *Kabaka* wishes you would show his people how to make the hat white again."

She received it gingerly. The battered old felt hat must have been white once. Now mold and dust had darkened it to a fleshy hue. She remembered Professor Ersatz Etrich restoring Governor Schnee's uniforms to their pristine whiteness with a concoction of his own. She said, "Can I have some *posho?*" She thought quickly while Cornelius conveyed the question and the king conferred with his aides. Then she asked, "And may I have some privacy?"

Big O was watching her with widening eyes. His head rolled, his tongue flickered, and the reply came back, "No, we must see what the white woman does with our hat."

"Then it will take some time," warned Kate as a guard dragged in a bucket of *posho*—mealie flour. She called for water and cotton rags and set to work.

Major Wolfe sketched to keep his hands busy. He could not trust himself to remain impassive, like Kornatzki. It was an hour since they had seen Cornelius go into the shelter.

"Here they come!" Major Wolfe jumped up, almost knocking over the Ugandan who stood guard beside him.

Kate walked out first, smiling. Big O towered behind her, but his bearing now was protective.

Kornatzki scratched under his beard in a frenzy of impatience, his eyes popping. Fears of rape and worse evaporated in the sunshine of the faces advancing upon him. He had heard that Big O, growing old, turned now to the comfort of small boys. He knew, too, that the *Kabaka* was quixotic and could become as swiftly and deeply involved in trivia as he could in the massacre of his German hostages.

The Ugandan king stopped halfway across the meadow and before Kornatzki's astonished gaze raised aloft a gleaming white felt hat of the sort worn by European women in hot climates. He placed the hat carefully on his head and bathed in the glow of admiration from his warriors, the hat tight over his skull down to the ears, snug as a young girl's cloche.

"One thing led to another," said Kate later. "I dry-cleaned the blessed hat with the *posho*, rubbing the felt with a cloth and then getting the smoothness back with another sort of polishing cloth. The chief was pleased and asked me to solve another problem."

"Which was?" asked Wolfe adoringly.

"What should he do with the Germans!"

Kornatzki slapped his thigh, began to laugh, and then turned nervously away from the Ugandans silently observing them. Big O had withdrawn for an afternoon nap, and the two groups formed separate camps. Kornatzki said, "You told him to release Paul, of course."

"I told him to arrange a meeting between Paul and Hagen," Kate said defiantly. "Then he'll see there's no conspiracy between my husband and the English."

"Shouldn't we break the siege now?" asked Major Wolfe.

"No!" Kate's eyes gleamed angrily. "I want the Ugandans to wipe out Hagen."

Wolfe's face lengthened. "How?"

"Those pygmy scouts brought back intelligence about Hagen's volunteers that Big O can't analyze. So I told him. Hagen plans taking over all Big O's territory."

"Clever!" exclaimed Major Wolfe.

"Lies can backfire," muttered Kornatzki.

"Not these," flashed Kate. "Big O is considering a joint operation with Paul. He said I was right, he *should* stick to the treaties with Paul and Cornelius."

"You're a military genius," said Major Wolfe.

"Or a woman in love," mumbled Kornatzki, fingering his beard. "A cold-blooded murdering streak"—he caught himself and bowed ironically to Kate—"is a characteristic of the *Kabaka*."

She met Kornatzki's oyster eyes with a level gaze. "No, Count, you were right the first time. There's a cold-blooded murderous streak in me where Paul's survival is concerned."

26

INSIDE THE besieged camp Captain Max Looff squinted suspiciously at Paul.

"What time is it?"

"One hour after noon."

"You say this is when the Ugandans normally attack?" asked Looff, slurring the words.

"There's been no drumming for the past ten minutes."

"They've likely gone for siesta." Looff reached for the jar of fermented coconut juice and sat back helplessly when Innocence took it away. Looff's fever had subsided, but it left him weak and unadventurous.

Paul rose from his seat on the crossbar of a crude gun carriage built to carry the *Koenigsberg*'s dismantled gun, and picked his way among the sprawling sailors. It *was* curious that the drumming should stop so abruptly. He walked to a point where fine spray issued like steam from the soil.

The mist formed a rainbow above a waterfall. In the middle stood Myles Hagen beside an English rifleman bearing an enormous Union Jack with a white flag improvised beneath it.

Paul lifted his eye patch. He found his monocle and screwed it into place. He knew Hagen's spies mingled with native informers even this far from English encampments. But Hagen himself!

"Colonel! May we come forward?"

The familiar voice held a note of impatience. It was Hagen all right. He had turned and was addressing Ugandans pouring over the lip of the gorge. They formed a solid wall behind Hagen, their spears ready. Hagen strode forward. "They won't attack unless you cheat." His eyes darted under the shaggy red brows, noting weak points, weapons.

"Stay where you are!" commanded Paul. He moved toward Hagen. "Keep your head down. Wait for the blindfolds."

"Blindfolds? Damnation! We came at *your* request."

"You're lying." Paul raised and cocked his pistol and the Ugandans stirred, spear arms trembling. "Turn around!"

"These black sons of Satan said they were sent as negotiators." Hagen indicated the nearest Ugandan, then put his hands behind his back and with a resigned shrug slowly revolved on his heels.

Paul began to adjust the blindfold.

"I say, old chap," murmured Hagen, half turning his head, "are you saying you did *not* ask me here?"

"Precisely," said Paul. "Here, tie the blasted thing yourself."

"Then what the hell— Did you know my men were nearby?"

"No."

"Then not only have you been ambushed, but the bastards have taken me, too!" Hagen's huge frame began to shake with laughter. "That's rich, by Christ!"

Big O's translator was listening intently, his suspicions reviving. Hagen slapped his pockets and withdrew a folded form. "I would have sent you this under a white flag anyway. The War Office in London forwarded it. May I read it?"

The Ugandan intervened. "I read." There was no room for argument.

"A noble try," said Paul, knowing Hagen sought an excuse to remove the blindfold and steal another look at his defenses.

Hagen surrendered the telegram with a wry grin. The Ugandan intoned, "Lord Kitchener has the honor to advise the Kommandeur of German East Africa that the Kaiser has been graciously pleased to award him the Iron Cross, First Class."

Hagen said, "Congratulations, Paul."

Paul accepted the Englishman's blindly groping hand. "You'd better get back to your lines, Myles Hagen. The next time we meet, one of us will end up dead."

Hagen rejoined a troop of his volunteers waiting on the edge of the forest to take him to the main camp. Der Dicke was with them.

"Whose bloody side are you on?" demanded Hagen. "You fight us, join us, swing like a weather vane."

"I was brought here by one of your slippery Gurkha Kaffirs," grumbled the Boer spy.

"He'd guarded your carcass too long. I put you in the German camp to keep us informed, not stick your fat head out."

"*Ja!* That crazy headhunter tried for me, got Hackmann."

Hagen stared. "My *jemadar?* Not bloody likely. He knows I need Hackmann alive because Hackmann hates the Kommandeur."

Der Dicke had swapped his identity as court jester for that of an Afrikaaner. The locks of black hair tied to his beard were a bush fighter's camouflage now, not a fool's decoration. He said angrily, "My job's political intelligence. Not for England. Not for empire.

For Smuts and Pretoria. I saw what was coming when Hackmann's head was stuck in my path. I had every reason to suppose that whirling dervish of a kaffir mistook Hackmann for me." He plucked his beard. "But if you weren't after Hackmann, it could have been Kornatzki."

"Kornatzki?" Hagen lifted the knobkerrie strapped to his wrist. "Kornatzki's dead." Now he knew the blasted Boer was lying.

Count Kornatzki listened to Kate in glum silence.

"Big O wants you to chase Hagen, kill him. He says the meeting between Paul and Hagen gives rise to new doubts. They were too friendly." Kate broke off. "What's wrong?"

"Hagen has returned under a white flag."

"Oh, damn you lily-livered liberals with your Christian scruples!" exploded Kate. "Hagen didn't scruple to have one of his Gurkhas kill a sentry and make off with Der Dicke."

Kornatzki lowered his head. He was a doctor first and then a none-too-consistent priest and philosopher. But the tool of his trade was more than ever the gun. If he didn't get Hagen now, he supposed this war would go on and on. He hated what it was doing to Kate. Instead of the woman moderating Paul, she was catching his blood lust, his *Allgemeine Wurchtigkeit*, his absolute callousness.

Hagen halted his small party in a depression some miles short of his base. The cheapest and most humane way of disposing of the problems presented by the shifting loyalties of Der Dicke was to dispose of Der Dicke. Two white subalterns with Hagen would make up a field court-martial. One was enough to read the charge: treason against His Majesty. The other could utter words in defense. Hagen would deliver the verdict and a Gurkha the *coup de grâce*. It would serve Der Dicke right for calling the Gurkha a whirling dervish kaffir.

Der Dicke was never given time to declare his true loyalty again, although the two young English subalterns would have said Der Dicke was a bit of a hero for working inside the German camp. He looked heroic now with the shadow of death upon him, lifting his heavy, shaggy head and sniffing danger on the breeze, his beribboned black locks hanging over bloodshot eyes widening with the stare of a cornered beast. He shouted a warning and whirled to face Count Kornatzki bursting through the bush with a platoon of Ugandan spearmen.

Not yet seeing the German, Hagen cried, "Get him!" The Gurkha whipped out his *kukri* knife and sprang. The Boer was moving to meet the threat from Kornatzki and never knew that his last impulsive act on behalf of the English was hastening English vengeance. The scuffle on barren soil created a small dust storm. Kornatzki launched himself directly at Hagen, and the two men clawed at each other, half-blinded.

Less than a hundred yards away, an American machine-gun crew from Hagen's volunteers saw the dust rising lazily in the hot afternoon sunshine. The Vickers had just been set up on its tripod. The servers of the gun had been busy entrenching and were not especially aware of Hagen's movements. There had been much activity between the main base and the forest, and their instructions were to cover the route back to base. Now, hearing pistol shots and native war cries, the corporal in charge did as he had been told. He was a fifty-year-old Chicago millionaire who had first gone big-game hunting with Teddy Roosevelt and now had a taste for hunting the strangest of game, man. He raked the nearer ground with fire, gauged where the dry earth spurted, and slowly advanced the deadly stitching toward the scene of the fight. The hammering of the Vickers was terrifying and disconcerted the Ugandans; some ran out of the dust into a shower of hot bullets.

When Hagen emerged, the machine gun stopped firing. The dust dispersed. Seven men lay dead. The incident had lasted five minutes, the length of time Hagen had estimated he would need for the trial and execution of Der Dicke, now headless, his stomach ripped open.

Hagen was left minus his knobkerrie. He announced this profanely to the subalterns, but both were dead. He searched for the club and found nothing. A suspicion formed that he had glimpsed his old adversary, the medical director of German East, Count Kornatzki. It was impossible. Kornatzki had died at Tanga. Except . . . Hagen recalled what Der Dicke had told him. He searched again, this time for someone resembling Kornatzki, among the corpses. But there was no Kornatzki.

And then Hagen acted. He had the expedition's army photographer take pictures of the carnage. He would have the pictures dispatched to London for English newspapers to publish and distribute abroad. Der Dicke would become a patriotic South African, loyal to King George, treacherously beheaded by the Huns. The speared subalterns would be presented as English youths mutilated by Paul's lost army whose beleaguered troops were reduced to near cannibalism. Hagen had a London journalist among his volunteers, financed by "H.M. foreign and other secret services." The man's job was to write propaganda.

"Our truce team was treacherously murdered," Hagen told his tame correspondent. "I am launching an immediate offensive to punish the culprits."

"But doesn't the enemy outnumber us?"

"No—" Hagen corrected himself. "Numerically, yes. Man for man, the Ugandans and Germans don't stand a chance." Well, that was true, he thought. The German naval party had a 4.1-inch *Koenigsberg* gun he knew about, a battery of mountain guns, and five thousand shells delivered by a god-rotting gunrunner. But Captain Looff and his sailor-soldiers were sick, Paul was poorly armed, and the Ugandans—well, the only thing the Ugandans had was an ability to spear innocent men in the back. He added, suddenly inspired, "The German Kommandeur is resorting to barbaric methods. Write that down, my good man. Of the thirty innocent men killed by treachery here today, twenty-three bodies were dragged back to the German camps by black mercenaries. What is the purpose of stealing our dead, you ask? It is to feed the *Kadaververwertungsanstalt*, the corpse exploitation unit that boils down the corpses for soap and explosive glycerine."

Big O was delighted with Count Kornatzki's raid and escorted the German rescuers to Paul and Captain Looff, for whom the Ugandan siege was lifted. There was still a price to pay, though. The chief announced that Kate must advise his warriors when Hagen returned to the attack.

"What?" exclaimed Paul when he heard. "You, a military adviser?"

Kate told him of her success with Big O.

"What makes the *Kabaka* think Hagen will be back?"

"I told him Hagen came here to place you at a disadvantage. I also said Hagen didn't want Ugandans to kill you but planned to kill you himself once he got you free from Big O's grasp." Kate paused. "It wouldn't hurt to have Max Looff fire his guns. Let Hagen think we're still fighting the *Kabaka*."

Count Kornatzki, a participant in this council of war, looked in Captain Looff's direction. Casks of rum had been broken out, the last of the emergency rations, and Looff was issuing tots to his sick crew.

"Those men shouldn't be manning guns. They're delirious and drunk," said Kornatzki.

Paul gestured helplessly. "Looff's technically in command."

"I could declare him mentally unfit," grunted Kornatzki. He was still recovering from his narrow escape. It had yielded him back his knobkerrie, but not Hagen. His nerves were frayed. "As an acting governor, I must have some blasted rights."

"Ease off," advised Paul. "Have them pop off the guns during the night, but keep a close watch."

Count Kornatzki roamed the camp all through the dark hours. He was secretly overjoyed to see Paul restored to Kate, but he still smarted over her explosive criticism of his "lily-livered liberalism." It's not my sensitive conscience, he told himself, it's a cold recognition of facts. If the English don't win with one army, they send in three more armies. "They'll spend and spend, money and lives," he warned Paul.

"You never talked this way before," said Paul. It was dawn of the following day and Big O had just sent for Kate, adding that she could bring the Kommandeur if she wished. Paul continued, a trifle biliously, "We *want* more English armies here, Count!"

"We're doomed, then. Their empire's run by men with big reputations to protect, and it won't cost them their own lives or their own money. They squander from a bottomless purse."

"There's more in this than profit and loss," replied Paul. "Germany will be judged in future years by what we do here."

Kornatzki shook his head, baffled. "I'd hoped Kate might gentle you. Instead, you've made her as wild as you were ten years ago. There's a new violence in you both, something you produce together."

"A love child, bloodthirsty and unnatural?" asked Paul, lighting a cigarette. "You're wrong. It's Kate who changes me."

"A woman of passion in war," said Kornatzki, eyes flickering, "is bloody and unnatural."

Kate, coming up behind, overheard. "Dearest Count, a woman of passion is always a power to reckon with. You won't ever win a war against me, so why not call a truce? But hurry"—she gestured toward Cornelius, who had stolen up beside her—"his lookouts say Hagen's coming back in full battle order."

Hagen's volunteers attacked with an exquisite precision dictated by Colonel Daniel Patrick Fenchurch of the Fenchurch Fusiliers. Unluckily for Hagen, the Colonel led reinforcements whose help was vital to Hagen's design. It had seemed to the English commander, as Kate predicted, that the German barrage during the night meant Paul was still fighting the Ugandans. And, as Kate had guessed, this seemed to the English to be the best possible way to catch Paul, by slicing

through the Ugandan siege and falling upon an exhausted and encircled Kommandeur.

When this was explained to Big O, with suitable admonishments
by Kate, the chief could hardly believe his good fortune. The English
passage across the volcanic soil was marked by a telltale plume of dust.
Fenchurch marched the combined forces into the forest, and they
continued to move row on row. Big O thought it must be a trick.

"No," said Kate. "The English move in teams. If the teams never
break apart, they cannot be beaten."

"What keeps the teams together?"

"The man at the head of each group," said Kate. "The group leader
wears special tabs and colors. To break the teams, you simply aim at
the colored tabs."

His round face aglow with enlightenment, Big O whispered to his
scouts, who slipped away, swiftly, invisibly. He commanded two
thousand Uganda spearmen and four hundred pygmy bowmen.

Fenchurch led his first battalion in arrowhead formation. As they
penetrated deeper into the forested gorge, Hagen began to wonder
how long this regimented efficiency could last. The rotation of the
first battalion back to third place, while signal men unreeled wire from
inside the constantly changing arrowhead, was fine in theory. Now,
however, the signal men were getting lost in the dense jungle. Fresh
orders were carried instead by runners, who disappeared in their turn.
The porters had been organized to bring up the rear in groups of
diminishing importance, but the single simplifying feature was the use
of colored ribbons to mark priority loads. A shrewd enemy could thus
identify vital ammunition loads, as Hagen pointed out to Fenchurch,
adding, "This is suicide."

"My dear chap," said Fenchurch, "the Ugandans saw what your
machine guns could do, and they scampered, fled, vamoosed."

"Don't you believe it." Hagen came to a dead halt. "For God's sake,
tell your platoon commanders to tear off those damned badges." The
silence of the forest screamed to him now of invisible danger. No
creature stirred, no bird exploded through the trees because there were
men concealed behind them. The only sounds were the ringing of
axes, the whisper of orders.

Hagen stood stock still, mule stubborn. "Your young officers are
doomed if they don't tear off those bits of blasted ribbon and buttons." Behind enormous roots and twisted vines waited his enemies,
motionless like Hagen, wily like Hagen, hunters who, like Hagen, survived on courage and cunning.

Fenchurch turned an irate face and was caught in a shaft of sunlight. He saw Hagen stationary, and his mouth opened to shout annoyance. A gigantic splinter of wood bisected his chest. He fell all the way onto the shaft of the thrown spear. There was no cry, not even a murmur.

The slaughter was swift and almost silent. Machine gunners identified by their badges and attendant carriers had no chance to assemble their weapons. The three battalion commanders were killed simultaneously by bowmen.

Captain Looff and his KLF, heavily doped with the *Kabaka*'s native medicine, slept through the battle. At sundown Paul roused Max Looff and reported two hundred enemy dead. Or fatally wounded. All wounds were fatal when Ugandans took care of the wounded. The English field commander, Fenchurch, was dead. Hagen had escaped. The remainder of the English force was in retreat.

Looff heard this with grave attention. He shook Paul's hand and said with an unconscious irony that left Paul wordless, "I couldn't have done it without you, Colonel."

That night Paul's men buried the bodies and placed rocks over them to delay the jackal's hungry digging. The sound of flies besieging the dead was like a waterfall.

27

PAUL LAY with Kate under soft Jaeger blankets, prizes of war taken from the abandoned English camp.

"Big O thinks you're a warrior-goddess," said Paul, watching the smoke from his cigarette curl among the stars. "It might be worth encouraging the legend."

"Legend!" protested Kate. "It's nothing less than the truth."

Paul sighed. "It's hard on my Kassel-trained Prussian character to concede this, but you might be right."

"It's your Prussian character," replied Kate, relenting, "that brings sense to all this lunacy. Somehow the sense of order makes it all valid."

"Like any human activity," said Paul drily, "the ritual discourages us from questioning the central core of belief. I go through the ritual of fighting Hagen, but he really should be with me fighting Kitchener and the Kaiser."

"But Hagen's your equal. He wouldn't want to beat a lesser enemy and no more would you."

"*Kätchen*, it's true what Kornatzki says—you're getting more bloodthirsty than me."

"Kornatzki! What else does he say?"

"If every victory costs such a price, we'll lose the war."

"Count your gains." Kate raised herself on one elbow. Hagen's men had fled leaving vintage wines, double-roof ridge tents, canvas baths, sporting guns, tinned Scotch haggis, canned fruitcake, oceans of gin, and fancy safari kits. Some of the American white hunters had brought salt and moth killer to preserve whatever they shot. The Ugandans had cheerfully downed the moth killer with the gin. They had staggered home, firing colored emergency rockets, dressed in Newland and Tarlton safari hats, their thickly muscled limbs thrust into dazzling silken underwear. They had tottered in, balancing Fortnum & Mason picnic baskets and Nairobi Emporium chests containing Bird's custard powder and Lyon's Christmas puddings. "One of your gains," added Kate, "is the undying devotion of the Ugandans. They'll give you the Ugandan Railway next."

"I wish they hadn't killed Fenchurch," said Paul a moment later. "He lost his wife and took the whole continent for his love."

"Isn't that what you did?" asked Kate in a small voice. "Isn't that why you came here after Rachel Rathenau—well—died?"

But Paul was still not ready to talk of it. He said, "Fenchurch once walked with a crushed arm for six weeks through the bush. He suffered hardship for Africa."

"And so he walked into a trap," she warned.

"*Kätchen*, you're angry."

"Not anymore." Kate stretched luxuriously, recognizing the signal for lovemaking that released their minds from tension.

When daybreak came, Paul felt refreshed and carried forward on a crest of renewed confidence. He wondered about Fenchurch, who must have loved his wife very much. In ten years of solitude Fenchurch had transferred that love. It hadn't saved him from catastrophe; it hadn't made him more wary. By loving Africa, Fenchurch had squandered his emotional resources. Paul's critics would say there was something swinish in the way he let the Ugandans loot, in the way he made love after a massacre. But he needed this love. He needed Kate and these hours of communion.

Kornatzki aroused them. "Looff wants to see you."

"Why doesn't he turn in?" protested Paul. "He was to stand the night watch."

"He's insistent."

Paul found Max Looff near the hut of the *Kabaka*, whose warriors sprawled around in various stages of drunkenness or fatigue. The overnight huts, built with wattle and daub by alcohol-addled troops, looked tipsy in the cold light of dawn.

"You had a long night, Colonel," said Max Looff, standing at the center of an explosion of English boots and boxes, saddles, spears, guns, and bodies. "Why are we dawdling?"

"My men need another day to complete the recovery of enemy stores."

"You mean another day of looting?"

Paul took a deep breath. "The Ugandans looted, Max. It's the price I must pay to keep a foot in Uganda."

"Nevertheless, you must be getting rich at it. Banditry is no way to wage war."

"I must make the enemy's arsenals mine. It's hit, grab, and run."

Looff said, "These raids of yours have become a way of life. Highway robbery made legitimate by a state of war. You risk nothing and you gain gimcrackery!" Looff gestured around him. "Look at this fairground! No military value, but I'll wager your treasury is in excellent health!"

Paul clenched his fists. Kornatzki caught his arm. Looff cocked his head.

"What makes you so cautious? Is that woman of yours pregnant?"

Paul wrenched free from Kornatzki and would have struck Max Looff. A shout from the chief's hut arrested him. Big O's bodyguard struck their spears on the baked earth. Two of the warriors were suddenly at Looff's side. The *Kabaka* loomed in the hut's doorway.

"*Simba!*" Big O's schoolboyish head stared quizzically over the parapet of the barrel chest, the squeaky voice as penetrating as scratched slate on a blackboard. "*Kommen-Sie hier!*"

Paul jerked his mind away from Looff and walked at a furious pace into Big O's presence. Beside him stood Cornelius, his face tense.

"The *Kabaka* is pleased to report the capture of Lanni," said Cornelius, translating as the king reverted to dialect.

Magdalene von Prinz came running. "They've got Lanni—" She broke off. "You know?"

"Yes," said Cornelius quickly. His eyes conveyed a warning.

Unobtrusively, Count Kornatzki moved closer to Max Looff. On the far side of the Uganda camp came a squad of warriors walking the black girl between them. Lanni looked as if she had been beaten. Her English dungarees were ripped, and the vaguely military jacket was torn. Kate barely recognized the proud octoroon princess who once struck Kurt Wahle with his own riding crop.

Paul thrust his way through the girl's captors and faced her.

"Lanni, look at me!"

She raised her head. Her face was bruised and streaked with dried blood and mud. Her hair was shaved. Her eyes still had the flash of gold, but she avoided his stare.

"Lanni, it's all right. You're safe."

Paul was aware of the emotional crisis taking place behind the neutral expression in Cornelius's eyes. The black rebel, though Lanni's lover, could only stand helpless and silent beside Big O, who fired questions: What had the girl been doing in English ranks? Why had Hagen let her go on a separate safari? From a distance Max Looff made a noise of disgust in his throat. Lanni shifted her gaze. She dared not yet face the tortured Cornelius. Her eyes appealed to Paul for guidance. She twisted her body slightly. A short stick had been thrust across her back, her arms lashed to it at her elbows. When she lifted her chin, a thin cord was revealed, cutting into her neck. The cord was secured around the stick at her back and then passed down between her buttocks and legs. She was trussed in such a way that she could walk, but painfully.

"Release her!" Paul ordered when he saw this. He turned to Cornelius, his face suffused with anger.

Cornelius spoke directly to Big O. The high-pitched voice of the chief summoned the guards, who hastily slashed Lanni's bonds. She remained exactly as before, making no move to ease her distress.

Paul's head throbbed and his eyes misted. Only the Lord knew what had been done to her. "Tell the chief this is my woman."

Cornelius translated and Big O sighed noisily. Those other Ugandans within earshot seemed to lean back as if, not daring to shift their feet, they still sought escape. Then Paul turned and roared, "Kornatzki! Bring help! My woman is in great agony of mind and body."

Big O swayed in the gale of words, rattling his girdles and leg chains of ornaments, and swung his great belly while he twittered to the guards. Lanni's escort was suddenly flanked by the chief's own

spearmen, and Kornatzki was allowed to pass through with Magdalene and a Ugandan medicine man. They held Lanni until two of
Paul's men ran up with an improvised stretcher to carry the girl to
the German line.

Big O addressed Paul.

"He regrets the misbehavior of his men," translated Cornelius. "He
reminds you, the American woman suggested this."

"She did not propose rape, brutality—" Paul caught the warning
glint in Cornelius's eye and stopped himself. Cornelius spoke evenly
to the chief, who peered down at Paul with the same inquisitive
friendliness as before.

"He understands," reported Cornelius finally, "your other woman
is brave like the American and also fights for all Africa. He will be
honored if you would attend the punishment of her captors." Cornelius saw the fury flame up in Paul's face again and added hastily,
"No, don't interfere. He'll lose face if these men are not tortured and
dismembered."

"There will be no executions!" declared Max Looff, entering the
circle. "We've wasted enough time."

Big O peered down. "Who is this man?"

"He came across the water in the German man-of-war," replied
Cornelius. "He and his crew are sick."

"From eating cassava roots on the march," said the *Kabaka* unexpectedly. "They were not properly cooked."

Max Looff interrupted. "Tell this ape I have things to do!"

"Ease off!" Paul took a step forward. "I need his help, Max. Ease
off!"

"You may need him, but I'm in command," roared Looff, rocking
on his heels. "I'm putting you under arrest." He turned and shouted
to one of his gunnery officers.

Big O spoke again, rapidly. There was a rattle of staves, and in
front of Looff appeared a forest of spears.

Looff said, "Threatening a superior officer is punishable by death."
The only response was Paul's release of the safety catch on his pistol.
The metallic click sounded unnaturally loud. Cornelius jerked for-
ward, uncertain if Paul was threatening Looff or the Ugandans.
Blocking Paul's aim, he spoke urgently to the *Kabaka*, who hitched
the lion skin over one shoulder and replied in an undertone.

When Cornelius turned finally to Paul, the sweat was pouring
down his face. "The *Kabaka* would have disposed of Captain Looff
to save you the trouble. The sickness is well known. It affects the
head long after the body is cured."

"I'll worry about that!" growled Paul.

The *Kabaka* clicked his teeth when the reply reached him, and his eyes rolled knowingly.

Thunder exploded and great forks of lightning in silver veins pierced the darkening sky. A ghostly glow infused the air, and a strange electric smell rose from the dry earth. There was no rain, just flashes from horizon to horizon.

Lanni lay under shelter. Kornatzki had stripped her to tend the wounds. Thin beams of pink and lilac light fell intermittently across her torn body.

"Paul's coming," said Kate by the entrance. She looked down again at Lanni. *My woman*, Paul had called her.

"So!" Paul burst in and knelt to cradle Lanni's head, the inadequate words of consolation pouring out of him. Kate turned away, jealousy and guilt blinding her. The octoroon's beauty was a triumph of will. Kornatzki had bathed her, covering hips and breasts with a cotton sheet, lifting it only when necessary, unusually solicitous of her modesty, but still affording glimpses of long and strongly molded limbs and the taut gold patches of belly and thigh.

"Hagen dispatched you to kill von Prinz?" Paul took his eyes off Lanni for the first time and glanced at Magdalene.

"Speak freely," said Magdalene. "I must know."

"Hagen can get me to Berlin," said Lanni. "There I can get money and support for the movement."

"What does Hagen get?" asked Paul.

"Another agent for himself." Lanni coughed and sipped from the glass Paul held out for her.

Magdalene said, "With my Tom removed, you'd be sent to Berlin?"

Paul twisted around. "Tom's in no danger." Then, seeing Magdalene's face, he held Kate's gaze and gave her a slight nod.

"Let's talk outside." Kate put an arm around Magdalene's waist. The older woman offered no resistance. She seemed to move in a trance. Once beyond the men's hearing, she said, "If Lanni does get to Tom, they'll work out something?"

"Of course," said Kate, feeling sick inside.

General Forget-Me-Not Gaunt met Hagen on his return to the Kilimanjaro garrison. "It was the killing of Fenchurch that did it," said Gaunt. "London's furious. The papers are full of criticism—why endanger prominent men whose professional skills could be used in Europe? That sort of thing. American papers are shriller, squealing about their millionaires getting into a colonial war. War Office says your defeat proves we're stretching our lines too far, too thin. So we're to pull out of the Kaiser's Mountain, out of Moshi!"

Hagen groped for the knobkerrie, but the comforting feel of its thong around his wrist was gone. Damn and blast! He'd lost the kerrie, too. In this kind of war, that meant more than the surrender of a position. Try telling London that! The only poor, suffering bastards who understood the struggle between symbols, between Paul's jujus and Hagen's, were here in Africa. He was glad the black girl was still in action. Hagen wasn't off the mountain yet!

His mind still preoccupied with symbolism, Hagen was caught off-guard by Gaunt's sudden question: "What about this woman, Myles?"

"Woman?" There was only one woman in Hagen's head, Lanni. But she came under the heading of secret operations since he had taken her over.

"Yes, woman!" repeated Gaunt sharply, noting the other man's veiled expression. "Crazy stories are getting into the penny dreadfuls about some female Hun. The London press is full of it. Kitchener threw a tantrum!"

Hagen shook his head, now honestly perplexed.

"*The Daily Mail* says she's a Saint Walpurgis. Who the hell was she, Myles?"

"Walpurgis died twelve hundred years ago," said Hagen woodenly. "She was an English abbess who preached in Germany. On the feast day of Saint Walpurgis, witches fly to the highest German mountain. Or so they say. Now how the hell would a scandalmongering rag like *The Mail* get hold of a yarn like that?"

Part Five

Too Much Chocolate

28

From Myles Hagen's The Bird Watching Notes of an English Country Gentleman, *Nairobi, June 1915*:

The little yellow-throated bee eater has returned (see my sketch). . . . My long-range plan is to have Lanni taken back to Berlin by Prince Turvchenko. He came here to negotiate secretly with British East Africa settlers because the Kaiser's still convinced that Africa can be exempted from the general war. Stupid bloody idiot! Lanni has first to finish a small task I gave her. Even if she fails, I'll use her in Berlin directly she's back from Kilimanjaro and Tom von Prinz. Lanni must be the most superbly qualified recruit an intelligence director ever set eyes on. They loved her in London (fools!) for her elegant black aristocracy. In Berlin they remember her Prussian father and her royal Zanzibar connections. The Kaiser was always fascinated by her grandmother's domination of one-tenth of all Africa. It reminded him of his own English grandmother's immense dominions. My hopes now rest upon Lanni's work in Germany, and I know precisely how to get her there. . . . Secret power, such as I have accumulated despite setbacks, can be wielded without outside interference behind the shield SECURITY OF THE STATE! If I had daily to account to superiors, I could not maneuver the German Kommandeur, whose psychology I have gauged. He is priestlike in his dedication to the religion of war. My latest encounter with him was a renewal of vows. We need each other. It is amusing to read these tales of a superhuman female Hun! The last thing Paul wants around him is a woman. She would only come between him and me, his necessary Lucifer. He is now back in Laager-120 W, about which my agents have more to report. Cloud-Cuckoo Land they call it. Fools' Paradise! I want him to stay there while his followers get sick on too much chocolate, as in the German legend.

29

BACK IN Laager-120 W a few days later, Ada von Schnee laughed outright at Kornatzki's shy request.

"Seduce the commander of the *Koenigsberg?*" she asked.

"That's not precisely what I said," Kornatzki apologized.

"It's what you meant. The funny thing is, Count, I'm having second thoughts about morals in general and myself in particular. You're a doctor of the body and the soul. You should advise me."

"My dear woman—"

"*After* I've taken Max Looff in hand, is that it?" She ran experienced fingers through his mop of silver hair. They were standing outside what now served as the Governor's palace, a substantial creation of palm leaves and poles. "You're such a pillar of virtue, I wonder what you'd be like in bed. But you mustn't mind my nonsense. I say what's on my mind, and that's the only difference between me and the virtuous faces over there." She nodded across the compound at members of her women's corps working in the open-sided "factories."

Kornatzki kept his mournful eyes on the Governor's wife. "Ada, this is serious. If Max Looff and Paul keep up this feud, we might as well surrender right now."

"I fancied Max two years ago when I first saw him, so it won't be a painful duty, and I'll not pretend otherwise." Ada turned her periwinkle eyes full force on Kornatzki. "But I'm serious, too. I find myself unexpectedly in need of—lacking a better way to put it—spiritual guidance."

Kornatzki contained his astonishment. God would witness that Ada had every reason to rebel against a man as dull as the Governor. Could she, so late in life, feel guilt?

"Don't worry, I won't confess," said Ada. "I merely observe changes in outlook within this small world here. And I worry. I worry because good young women like Kate and Magdalene are becoming callous."

Kornatzki shot her a startled look. Ada always mystified him with what she knew. Of course, she saw and heard everything reported to her husband. Not for the first time, Kornatzki regretted it was Schnee, not his wife, who ran the colony. Taking his leave of Ada, he kissed her on each cheek. "Do what you can for Max," he said. "Afterward, we can have that little talk about morality and mortal sin."

Ada had watched Looff's KLF march into camp. She had studied Max, and her heart had gone out to the man. Why, he was hardly more than a shadow of the handsome young sea captain she remembered! In her new mood of spiritual zeal, Ada found no difficulty transferring her earthier talents to the task of restoring Max to health and vigor. She had been warned about the long-term effects of cassava root fever. There was nothing that a bit of loving would not cure!

Max Looff made straight for the Governor's quarters.

"We were informed you were ill," said Schnee. "You look fit enough to me."

"Thank you. I am."

"Sit, my boy—for heaven's sake, don't stand on ceremony." The Governor scuttled behind his desk and found a bottle, a humidor, two glasses, and a water flask. He shook out two cigars and handed one to Looff. "We've made ourselves comfortable, as you see. Surprising what German ingenuity will do."

Looff looked around the room. The walls of woven leaves and clay were covered in animal skins. The steeply pitched roof provided vents for the circulation of air. Behind the Governor were neatly stacked filing cabinets and shelves of reference books.

"You certainly put down roots," agreed Looff, lighting the cigar and accepting a tumbler of palm wine. He gagged on the cigar. "Forgive me, Excellency. The last few months have been, for me, spartan."

Schnee gulped his brandy and refilled the glass.

Looff leaned forward. "I'm having problems with Colonel von Lettow."

Schnee fell eagerly upon this subject. "The Colonel openly defies my policy of accommodating the English—"

But Looff was not listening. "He seems to think he's in charge of the entire war."

"—when we should be living peacefully beside our English neighbors," continued Schnee, still heading in another conversational direction.

"You must clarify my position as senior officer," Looff said. "The Kommandeur drew a gun on me. There's only one sentence on conviction of threatening a superior."

"Death?" questioned Schnee.

"Quite so. It would be simple justice if I pressed charges against him. But I'm not blind to his administrative skills. I shall put him in charge of transport."

Schnee squinted uneasily at the naval captain. "I am the supreme commander," ventured Schnee.

"A bureaucratic bungle," said Looff airily. "Berlin did not visualize war from Europe spreading here. I am, nonetheless, willing to keep you informed of my decisions."

The Governor, his vision blurred by rising panic, cast about for the bottle of brandy. "Try some. We blend it here from what our natives call liquid-fire grain." His hand trembled while he poured.

Looff shook his head. "One of my first actions will be to dismantle the means of producing such luxuries. Your settlement has become too complacent, too *settled*. Lazy from an overabundance of good and easy living. Too much chocolate, as they say! I shall order resumption of the march."

"Resumption of the march?" echoed Schnee. "What march?"

"Strategic. I shall call a meeting to discuss a general offensive." Looff stood up. "You have arranged quarters for me, of course—Excellency?"

Schnee groped for a firm hold on his desk and slowly rose. "General Wahle is on safari," he said, seized by an inspiration. "We could put you in his hut." Then, overcome again by panic, Schnee shook the bronze bell on his desk with unaccustomed violence. To the bearer who softly materialized, he said, "Ask Madame Schnee to be good enough—"

But Ada was already there.

"Hagen's been recalled to Nairobi," Cornelius reported to Paul. "He remains director of intelligence and secret operations. Lanni says we're better off with a devil we know. She says London wants to put an arch-imperialist in Africa. Winston Churchill."

"What else does Lanni say?"

"She wants to keep out of sight here."

"She understood why the Ugandans had to be told she was my woman?"

"*I* understood I don't always carry your authority with my fellow blacks," Cornelius replied sourly. "As your woman, Lanni would get the chief's protection." He shrugged. He had changed into the uniform of the white man's cheap labor: kaffir shorts, a shirt torn and stained, boots broken.

Paul watched him pace the tent, then said, "I want Lanni away from here the moment she's fit and ready. If Hagen is still operating, Lanni had better give him what he wants."

Cornelius winced. "Including Prinz's head?"

"You can't be squeamish," said Paul. "A lot of men are dying for your cause."

"But it's not your cause."

"You forget Israel."

"I sometimes wonder," muttered Cornelius, "if we won't pay too dearly for Jewish help."

"You make what allies you can get. If I were black, I'd consider Uganda a small price. A Jewish state, Jewish brains, Jewish sobriety and diligence and hard work. My God, Africa would be transformed."

"We might exchange one imperialism for another."

"Academic, these questions. More to the point, what do I do about the Governor? He tried to kill me through Big O."

Cornelius stopped pacing. "Why don't *you* stage an accident?"

"No, my friend. Rule of law must prevail. I can't *prove* the Governor's treachery. And I need him as the symbol of the Kaiser's authority. Like a totem pole."

"Your totems get less and less European," warned Cornelius. "It's your own kingdom you're creating, with its own code and its own morality and motives. Perhaps that's as well, because you may not have much of Europe left soon."

"Oh?" Paul cocked his head.

"Lanni says nobody knows the true dimensions of the slaughter in Europe. English and German censors hide the casualties. Only the high commands know the extent of the killing. They're overwhelmed and regard the African campaign here as a diplomatic bargaining counter."

"All the more important that Lanni should get to Berlin soon."

"But surely there's a simpler way?"

"No," said Paul, closing the conversation. "We can get nothing out of German East. Our wireless operators tried to contact the West African station with news of the Ugandan victory. But the Boer general, Botha, has conquered German West for the English. They've sealed us in. Now they're tightening the screws."

Ada was pleasantly surprised by Max Looff, who had insisted on inspecting the work of the women's corps. It was a typical Monday morning. The women, black and white, were at benches under the grass rooftops of the wall-less factories.

"We make chocolate and cocoa here," said Ada and wondered why Looff scowled. "Five thousand pounds in the past four months." She guided her guest to the next shelter. "This is the explosives factory. We're repairing the ammunition you brought us. Each round has to be opened, cleaned, and dried in the sun after all that soaking in the sea. These girls are making fuses for shells." One of the black girls handling the fuses looked up and flashed Looff a dazzling smile.

"Best set of teeth I've laid eyes on these past months," said Looff, recovering his amiability. "We rotted, teeth and all, in the Rufiji."

It was his first reference to the *Koenigsberg*. Ada concealed her eagerness to hear more. She said instead, "We've put up three thousand packages of tooth powder since we came here. Health is a priority. We found ways to make castor oil and soap. Come, let me show you the refinery."

Ada led him hastily past the distillery where palm wine and grain alcohol were produced. "One of our settlers discovered a form of ersatz gasoline called trepol. We make it from copra."

Ersatz Etrich made his jealous entry. His affair with Ada had been a stormy one. The black-bearded Austrian sensed Ada's rapport with the newcomer. Overhearing Ada's last remark, he said belligerently, "Not a settler. I—*I* perfected what was a concept."

Ada smiled. "Professor Etrich is a great inventor. He flew his airplane to Africa, but it was stolen."

Looff was all attention again. "Who stole it?"

Etrich told him in full detail, including a colorful description of Chuck Truman's escape in the Taube monoplane and an even more lurid account of Kate's influence on Paul.

"You mean this American girl has a brother in league with a Zionist?" asked Looff.

"Don't jump to wrong conclusions!" warned Ada, who silently cursed Professor Etrich.

The rest of the tour was accomplished in a tense silence until Ada steered the fatigued captain into General Wahle's quarters, now prepared for their new resident. "You're exhausted," she said when they were alone under the rustling palm-fronded roof. "Lie down and I'll tell the bearers not to disturb you."

"No," said Looff. There were a lot of questions still to be answered. "No," he repeated. "You stay here."

His demand fired her enthusiasm, transformed him into the handsome man she remembered. The beard and black curly hair were already regaining their vigor. The mildewed and eccentric clothes did not diminish the piratical panache.

Nor was Ada the middle-aged frump Max Looff had last seen presiding over a dull prewar banquet in Dar es Salaam. The harsh diet and the physical dangers had refined her figure and added character to her face. She felt the sexual tension growing between them. The heat inside the hut enclosed them in a sensual embrace.

"What," asked Ada in a thick voice, "do you want?"

"I feel an absolute bitch in heat!" declared Magdalene. She was greasing a revolver before putting it away in her gun box under the camp bed. "But the more I hate myself, the more I know it's all play-acting. I want Tom out of the way. There, I've said it! You see, Kate, I want the luxury of a conscience *and* freedom to fornicate."

"Stop condemning yourself and stop using such language."

"Fornicate!" repeated Magdalene. "There's no nicer word. I lust for Quentin. Oh God! Kate. What's happening to me? I lie in bed indulging the most lascivious dreams."

"You're not alone. Don't you think I need Paul in the same way?"

"And you do have him, you do know him in the biblical sense. I can't make love when I'm conspiring against—"

Kate pulled the other woman around to face her squarely. "You goose! Lanni will find Tom. You can't stop that, you mustn't stop it. So much else hangs on it. There must be a way that Tom will survive and still give Hagen an impression Lanni did what she was told."

Magdalene seemed to shrink. "Why, though?"

"Because Lanni can do a lot for us later." Kate spoke hurriedly. "You told me you married Tom as an act of rebellion. Perhaps all you really married was the symbol of rebellion."

Kate walked back alone to her own quarters. She caught sight of Paul before he had time to see her and was engulfed by waves of desire. Months of bush fighting had honed him until he was lean and graceful and quick. He put away the chunk of wood he had been carving and looked up, smiling.

"You've become notorious, *Kätchen!*" He waved some papers. "Hagen's back to the poison pen as a weapon."

She scanned the handwritten report and felt her anger rise. The *Koenigsberg* wireless operator had rigged a receiver to monitor

English radio signals. They provided Paul with some insight into enemy thinking. One message from Nairobi, destined for a London newspaper, reported the inhuman German exploitation of women.

"I don't find this amusing," said Kate.

"When the enemy makes up lies like this, he's losing heart. Propaganda's two-edged."

"You don't mind being called a barbarian?"

"Not if it makes them all the keener to catch me."

Kate heard the shrillness in her voice, but she was powerless to mute it. "I must say, you do your damnedest to help the barbaric reputation."

"What does that mean?" asked Paul, turning suddenly cold.

"Tom Prinz! You tossed *him* to the wolves fast enough when it suited you."

"He knew he was on a suicidal mission."

"There's a difference between dying heroically and being sacrificed by your commander."

Paul stiffened. "A commander stands by his men."

"I know all about your strict code of honor! Pompous, self-deceiving drivel. You would deliver Tom, your old friend, into the slaughtering hands of a Marxist woman agent and justify it on grounds of military necessity when it's your own personal aggrandizement you seek."

"Kate!"

"Don't Kate me! You, Magdalene, Ada—what's happening to you? Prinz was right—you'll sink as low as your alley cat allies. Look at Cornelius. Look at Lanni. No more loyalty—"

"Kate!" Paul seemed to tower above her. "Nobody knows Tom's thoughts about native rebels. If Lanni caught a hint—" Kate began another angry response, and he clamped a hand over her mouth and wrenched her into his tent. "You'll sign Tom's death warrant if you don't close your mouth."

He had never treated, never spoken to her like that before. She saw the muscles in his face twitch, felt his hands trembling in their grip upon her. Then he drew back as if the touch of her delivered an electric shock. She turned. Cornelius! The rebel leader's face was blank—or was there cold hatred set in those narrow, almost Chinese eyes?

"The Ugandans will give you free passage," Cornelius said.

"Quicker than I thought." Paul was all brisk goodwill again. "Kate, you've days and nights of paper work ahead. We're breaking camp."

"That order," said Cornelius, "has been given already."

"The Governor has no right—"

"Not the Governor." Was there a special note of satisfaction in Cornelius's voice? "Captain Looff is calling a conference of company commanders."

"Nobody calls my commanders except me," said Paul. "No conference takes place without the full participation of the community."

Cornelius looked down at the palm-strewn floor of the tent.

Kate said quickly, "It's a challenge. Max is throwing down a challenge in front of everyone." She turned to Cornelius. "I suppose you back whoever wins?"

The rebel frowned. "I don't have the morals of an alley cat, Missus." The final word was almost a hiss.

"Oh God!" Kate covered her mouth.

"Don't worry," interrupted Cornelius. "I still think of you as the missus who saved a plantation nigra from hanging. We all have our stereotypes."

Kate confronted the paper work, most of it useless bureaucratic nonsense from Governor Schnee's staff. She would burn as much as she dared. Even so, there were detailed orders to be issued that would ensure the reassembly of the huge community at the end of the long march ahead. Where it was heading, how soon they would leave, was still secret. She was glad of the secrecy and of the necessity for activity. She was uncertain about how to approach Paul. She was too proud to apologize and not yet sure that she should. But her views on Lanni were altered when she came across the black girl's intelligence reports from England.

Lanni's shrewd account of the flight back to Africa held Kate's attention. The black girl had squeezed out of the French aviator an enormous amount of technical detail about the new air route. It was an impressive study. Kate now understood why Paul wanted to get Lanni to Berlin.

Magdalene had gone to find Quentin Pope in the quiet sanctuary of his tent. Going to him seemed like another stab at her husband. Yet what harm could she do Tom? The last few days had been torment; her fear for Quentin's life after the ambush had not been followed by any consummation of their love. She was victim of too many conflicting emotions, and he was patient and understanding enough to wait.

She walked along the shore of the nearby soda lake, gleaming like frost in the early moonlight, claret hued in parts. Salt, more valuable than ivory, was piled in the grass between here and the bigger lake. The sudden challenge of an askari made her jump. She was puzzled and then angry, for she was accustomed to go unchallenged at any hour. She glimpsed a small knot of men beyond the sentry.

"Let her through." It was Cornelius.

Magdalene approached him, and her blood turned to ice when she saw Lanni wearing the same mechanic's dungarees, torn and muddied, in which she was captured.

"Yes," said Lanni, recognizing Magdalene's sudden apprehension, "I'm leaving for the mountain. Have no fear for Tom."

Have no fear? The words echoed mockingly in Magdalene's ears. Guilt, she thought, not fear. I'm his executioner.

Lanni's next words removed all possible hope of escaping that guilt. "Have you a message for your husband?"

"No! It's too dangerous for you, carrying messages." Magdalene felt another rush of shame, recalling Tom's last lovemaking, the copy of *Faust* in the ruins of the farmhouse, her refusal to plead with him to stop these adventures.

"The dangerous part is only convincing Tom," said Lanni. She glanced at Cornelius. "Some small sign from his wife—"

"*N'dyo!*" Cornelius nodded quickly. "Something he'll recognize. He'll be full of suspicion when Lanni first makes contact."

Magdalene realized what Cornelius felt for Lanni in the way he touched her shoulder. "Can you wait?" Without listening for an answer, Magdalene ran back to her quarters.

Cornelius and Lanni stood motionless, welcoming these extra moments, though their bodies scarcely touched and had not mingled since the long-ago parting that had taken them into separate dangers. Now there was no hope of drawing strength in that way. Lanni was stoical beside the man who had seized the core of her being. His ideology lifted any burden of guilt for the way she served the cause.

Her Ugandan escorts stirred impatiently. Ahead lay a journey none relished, to restore the girl to the English as if she had never been in Ugandan hands.

Magdalene returned and gave Cornelius a sheet torn from a book. There was not enough moonlight to show the marked passage from the scene when Mephistopheles is speaking to Faust about physical love: "to lie on mountains in the dew and night, embracing earth and sky in raptured reeling, to swell into a god."

The lines from *Faust* were among the most sensual in German literature. Walking away, Magdalene found it hard to imagine a

black-bone-and-muscle man like Cornelius understanding such romantic fancies. She felt sorry for savages. The poor creatures must
lie mute in each other's arms. She supposed there must be genetic
reasons why passion between simpler members of the human race
could never rise to divine heights of language. Magdalene drew comfort and acquittal from her reflections, and she ran to Quentin with a
sense of positive virtue.

Cornelius said goodbye to Lanni at the edge of the camp. "I doubt
there's any code in it," he said, indicating Magdalene's torn sheet.
"But examine it in daylight. Get rid of it if there's the slightest
chance of discovery by—what *is* the man's name?"
"McCurdy."
He touched her hand briefly. "You've no qualms?"
"None."
He looked into her golden eyes. "Take care."
Cornelius walked back to the army lines. He tried to shake off
depression. Once, when Lanni and he had been very young, they
had lived together for a week as if they were the only humans in
creation. They had made love in the manner of the lions, hours at
a stretch, sweetly, restlessly, naked in the sun. They had talked and
loved and talked and loved and heightened the intensity of their
lovemaking by the intensity of their language. It had been truer, he
had told Lanni, than any words printed in a book.

Safe in Quentin's arms, Magdalene felt the tides of passion rise.
She was frightened by her own body's demands. Still hesitating,
playing for time, she said, "Someone was leaving your tent. I had
to wait until he'd gone. Who was it?"
"A Uganda runner." Quentin spoke carelessly. "He's taking copies
of my reports. A party of scouts are going through English lines;
there's always a chance of leaving the stuff where they're bivouacked.
I wrote a covering note—"
Magdalene tried to conceal her alarm. "How did you know—"
She stopped before Lanni's name escaped her lips.
"It's my job," said Quentin, unconscious of the havoc he was
creating. "First thing you learn as a correspondent is that you're
no damned use if you can't communicate. News is perishable. I've
let too much perish already." But Magdalene was only half listening. She prayed she had stopped soon enough, had not aroused
suspicion, had done no harm.

"Everything is ersatz except this," Ada was telling Max Looff. Her words and movements slowly relaxed him. "This is a resource you don't have to worry about depleting. You worry too much—shortages here, stores running out there, boilers cracking up, inferior coal—"

Extraordinary, thought Max. This woman understands war. And love. She dulled the sharper edges of his Lutheran mind. Sins of the flesh? She made them a celebration. She presented herself in ways that flattered the male ego and recalled the advice of his brother, Hector, albeit in regard to a matter hardly akin to love: When attacked by the male leader of a pack or herd, turn and bend over in submission. It was an act of trust. Max had known seamen make their women bend over the rail and take them from behind. Ada offered him a gentle encompassing love that made her as vulnerable emotionally as symbolically. She moved from one position of surrender to another, overcoming his suspicion, his shyness, his scruples. Max Looff talked and planned with the excitement of a schoolboy, for he had discovered that the physical pleasure released his mind to float free. He had never felt so sure of himself. And Ada blessed Count Kornatzki for imploring her to seek Max's rehabilitation.

"How will you deal with Max?" Kate whispered, lying unnaturally stiff beside Paul.

"Follow Shakespeare's advice: 'Shut up! Thou art but a soldier.' "

She let the words hang between them in the darkness. They lay on a bed under stolen English blankets that on other nights had been snug and reassuring. Her body ached for Paul, but her mind continued to rebel against his decision to use Lanni. She groped for a way into the subject he had declared to be closed.

"Ever since the Africans began calling you Simba," she said, "I've seen you as 'Lion.' I don't ever want to know you as less than a lion."

"But I'm less a lion now than I was before!" Paul was suddenly wide awake. "Is that it?"

"Yes," said Kate in a tiny voice.

Paul sat up, groaning inwardly. Dare he tell Kate the whole truth? That Lanni never would reach Tom von Prinz? The knowledge would then become a burden on Kate, as it was now on himself.

"I know the arithmetic in your mind," Kate said. "If Tom is to fulfill his task, he'll be killed anyway. Meanwhile, there's much more to be won if Lanni gains greater credibility with Hagen. So let Tom be killed—"

"No! *Kätchen*, stop torturing yourself. You must accept my word. Tom is safe."

Kate felt the anger in him. "I'm sorry, Simba."

"Don't add to my agonies," he pleaded.

"I would rather die."

He took her back into his arms and knew that it was true; she would die for him. Sometimes, he thought, the love she gave him was almost too much to bear. Before Kate, he had disciplined himself to find escape within his own mind. Since his marriage to Kate, his nights were voyages of discovery into her realm. He found in her soft cries, in the whisperings of her mind, and in her body an inexhaustible source of delight. Words merged into movement, and it became difficult to recall what was said aloud and what had been stated through the variety of other senses.

In this way, mysteriously, almost mystically, Kate learned Paul's reasons for dispatching Lanni back to Hagen. The relationship between Lanni and Hagen seemed to tie them all together. It was as if Lanni had come to Paul with a message from Hagen: "I, your sworn enemy, desire you to keep on fighting because without you my reason for existence ceases. We are partners in death. Send me back Lanni to serve us both."

Paul had entered inside Hagen's mind through the agency of Lanni. So Kate, in these moments of heightened perception, believed. Paul could predict in some real measure the Englishman's course of action. But Kate did not think Hagen had the same insight. Hagen viewed his enemy single-mindedly, whereas Paul lived a double life now and was not blinded by obsessions that made Hagen fanatical. Kate was glad Hagen knew nothing about her presence, her place beside Paul. Yet this oversight was mysterious, too, as if Hagen refused to know and jealously blocked her out.

She felt Paul deep inside her. She was foolish ever to have doubted him! She felt him dissolve and the quick upsurge of life dissolving her in its turn, and all she could think of now was what a magnificent warrior he was and how indestructible they were together.

Near dawn Paul stirred. His eyes were open, and he chuckled involuntarily. She was accustomed to his muffled laughter punctuating his slumber. This time there was a mocking note. She held him, questioning him gently, herself amused.

"Sun-Tzu. I remembered Sun-Tzu. He dreamed he was a lion.

Then he woke up and wondered if he was a lion dreaming he was a man." Paul was silent for a moment. "I studied Sun-Tzu for his military philosophy. Now all I remember is his dream. It's hard, it's very hard, to wake up and find you're only a man."

She stroked his head, waiting for him to doze off. "You'll recover from the dream," she murmured. "You'll still be my lion."

30

THE COMMUNE was aroused at daybreak by what seemed to be an unbroken roll of thunder reverberating around the crater walls. Paul was on his feet and calling out the morning guard while a cloud of pink flamingos still rose from the water of the big lake.

"*Mungu! Mungu!*" An askari came running, one hand waving at the sky.

"Over there," said Kate at Paul's elbow. "A biplane, there at nine o'clock." She was using Major Wolfe's field glasses and handed them to Paul. He squinted into the east. The glare of early light hurt more than usual.

One of Max Looff's guns, a 47-mm, barked. Machine guns picked up the chorus. The lake shore came alive with the crackle of rifle fire.

"Stop firing!" Paul had to bellow the order to be heard above the uproar. Major Wolfe passed the instruction and added warningly, "Kommandeur, it *is* an enemy machine, sir."

One of the naval guns exploded once more. "God blast their eyes, stop firing!" was Paul's response to the Major's caution.

A seaplane with awkward-looking pontoons lumbered out into the lake, and the firing came to a ragged halt. Max Looff came running, cursing. He pulled up short when he saw Paul. "You let an English machine escape!"

"Right, an English machine," snapped Paul. "Didn't anyone see the white streamers?"

"White smoke, by God, and you let him go," declared Looff,

shading his eyes and searching the mist that covered the center of the lake.

"Not smoke," said Paul stubbornly. "Streamers. Torn sheets. A signal of neutrality. You're the naval expert—get out boats and find the poor devil. Oh, for God's sake!" he added in disgusted anger. "Wolfe, organize a rescue party!"

Major Wolfe hesitated a fraction. He had caught Kate's eye and was asking, in sign language, if Paul's vision was reliable. Everyone knew his sight was worsening.

"It wasn't smoke," said Kate. "The pilot was flying long white streamers."

Max Looff turned upon her an expression of such hostility that she felt an almost physical shock. At the same moment a conviction came over her that the machine was being piloted by her brother. She was afraid to voice this intuition until she had Paul alone. He was arguing fiercely with Looff, and she waited, her eyes fixed on the middle of the lake.

"Then we'll settle this question of command once and for all!" she heard Looff mutter before he stormed away.

"I'm sure that was Chuck," she said when Looff was out of hearing.

Paul saw the blood draining from her face. "It was a hydroplane," he said gently, "for landing on water."

"Could I go with the rescue boats?"

Paul hesitated. She rarely asked favors. Her intuitions were seldom wrong. But Looff's conference of commanders was to start in an hour.

She saw his indecision, although she was unaware of the cause. "If you need me here—"

"Yes," said Paul. "I need you."

Max Looff strode into the dim coolness of the church, accompanied by his *Koenigsberg* officers. The altar had been partly covered with the German flag. The cross behind the altar was flanked by maps. The body of the church was filled with men and women, not immediately visible to Looff because the windows of stained glass admitted only the most feeble light in contrast with the brilliant sunshine outside. The pews and hymnals had been removed. The Holy Ghost fathers had designed it for virgin Africa and gave priority to simplicity. But one among them with a need to preserve some memory of home had carved a fair imitation of the Blood Altar by the greatest of German woodcarvers, Riemenschneider.

Other copies of medieval religious art decorated the white walls. A theme common to all was the torture of Christ and the pain and cruelty of everyday life.

Most of the commune squatted on the cool stone floor, leaving two aisles along which the military commanders could pass. At the altar with Looff were the Governor and Count Kornatzki. The doctor had donned his priestly robes.

Looff climbed into the simple pulpit. He kept his cap on his curly head, the peak with its bits of gold braid set at a jaunty angle. He was about to speak when the doors were flung open again and Paul entered with a group of his unit commanders in torn khaki shirts and ragged shorts, moving with the muscular grace of men conditioned to survive in the wild. Each made his way to the altar, walking with the heel-and-toe action of bushmen. The last was old General Wahle, who had marched into Laager-120 W that very morning. He moved like a cavalryman, legs bowed, feet angled as if he wore spurs.

Looff waited for the commotion to subside. He saw Ada leaning against a wall, dressed in riding breeches and holding a short whip, and in that split second he marveled again at her energy.

"The appearance of an enemy plane this morning emphasizes what I have to say," he began, then paused, weighing the effect of his voice in this shell of a church. "This camp presents too large a target. Worse, the psychology of *permanence* has taken hold. You are not building Cuckoo-Land here."

There was some polite laughter tinged with uneasiness. Everyone was now familiar with the legend.

"You are dying of too much chocolate."

This time nobody even smiled. Paul stood with his hands behind his back, frowning at his feet.

"The campaign in Africa is a sideshow," continued Looff. "It has small bearing on the outcome of the war in Europe."

Paul looked up, his face dark. Count Kornatzki intercepted the glance and began to finger his beard.

"There must be an end to this putting down roots as if you were pioneers in the American West." Looff paused, expecting more laughter, but there was none. "You will want to know how the *Koenigsberg* has fared in the delta. Our sailors have hurt the English fleet, but *not by digging in and making ourselves comfortable*. Our defiance is not a story to be told here—" Looff was seized by a fit of coughing.

Paul's face had hardened in intense anger. Count Kornatzki shot a look of despairing appeal at Ada.

Ada pushed herself away from the wall and said in a ringing voice, "Captain, you are wrong! We're all dying to hear your adventures in gallantly resisting such a powerful enemy."

A keener ear than Looff's would have recognized that the subsequent applause was ironic. Nobody there needed to be lectured about self-sacrifice. Paul, taking his cue from Ada, walked slowly to the altar rail and said, "Captain Looff, please go ahead. We need to boost morale."

Looff nodded. He was ordinarily a reticent man. But as he plunged into his account, he was carried away by his own enthusiasm for setting these landlubbers an example. For more than half an hour he held forth on the war at sea. He started with the *Koenigsberg's* bold action at Zanzibar; he concluded with the saga of the German East Asia Squadron trapping and destroying a task force of Royal Navy cruisers.

After the cheering stopped, Looff continued. "I have reported to you our own successes. Now I must tell you that the *Koenigsberg* is out of action." He sketched the situation in the Rufiji delta. "Our first job was to dismantle the boilers from the engine room and transfer them by sled and trolleys to the foundry in Dar es Salaam. If plans have not been interrupted, the repaired boilers are being reinstalled now by a skeleton crew."

General Wahle called out, "Well done, my boy!" Looff's two nieces, Celeste and Elsa, jumped up and down and threw their arms around Alex Hammerstein. The army Captain turned red and in self-defense shouted, "Three cheers for the *Koenigsberg!*" The Governor, in an attempt to retain some semblance of authority, felt he must lead the huzzahs.

"Hip-hip—" cried Heinrich von Schnee.

"Hooray!" responded the congregation.

Ada smiled sardonically at the spectacle of her husband forced to make the church rafters ring with applause for a policy opposed to his own. Her eyes danced when she looked again at Max Looff. There was a man!

Looff raised a hand for silence. "You will wonder why I am here and not with my ship. While she's under repair, and having to bring stores and weapons to you here, I wished for this opportunity to make sure the war ashore in Africa is being waged as offensively as we hope to wage it in African waters."

General Wahle interrupted. "Captain Looff, you do the Kommandeur an injustice, sir! At this very moment, sir, General Botha, fresh from his victory over us in German West, is marching to join imperial English forces marshaled against us here. No, let me correct myself!" boomed the old General. "He is marching against Colonel von Lettow, sir!"

Max Looff tightened his hold on the pulpit and glanced at his brother, Hector. "General Botha is a Boer. What does his intervention do to the loyalty of Boer settlers among us?"

"My husband is a Boer from South Africa," spoke out Hanna Rasche. "He is with the Bismarckburg Detachment on Lake Tanganyika. A risky assignment. He would not appreciate having doubts cast upon his devotion to our cause."

There were cries of "Hear! Hear!" Then the door to the sacristy opened, and Elsa Looff emerged with a tray of mugs. A black girl took one of the mugs and placed it beside the lectern. An aroma of well-brewed coffee followed her from the improvised canteen behind the screen. Looff stared down at the mug.

"Please don't misunderstand me, madame." Looff looked up again. "A threatened community must guard against treachery. Security here is lax. I shall continue the expansion of the security police begun by the late Commissioner Hackmann. A gentleman, I might add, who was himself killed through treachery."

Count Kornatzki said in an ominous voice, "Nobody here needs to be policed, Captain Looff."

There was a general sigh of assent.

Looff sipped the coffee with an expression of surprise. "My dear Count, I'm not suggesting there's a question of *German* loyalties. Pure-bred German stock I will trust. The political police would have powers to investigate other members—"

Paul cut in. "A civil guard, Max? Nothing more! And glad I am to know you feel like all of us. There are dangers in stagnating in one place." He spoke hurriedly, distracting the audience from Looff's insulting implications. "Our detachments are engaging the enemy in the Congo, Rhodesia, Nyasa, and on the Portuguese borders." He walked to the side of the pulpit and addressed himself to the English-speaking askaris, hoping to divert them before Looff's words sank in. "Our commandos are mixed forces, white and black—"

General Wahle picked up the theme. "This is people's warfare, Captain."

"*Women's* warfare!" retorted Looff.

Hector Looff shouted hastily, "Max, we've heard your side, but do you really know ours?"

His brother nodded. "I know your ingenuity. It comes from the women. Women have no place in battle. Women concoct luxuries, certainly! But to what end? To unman us, sap our fighting spirit, feed us too much chocolate." He prodded the empty mug. "Coffee *and* cream!"

A groan of protest went up. "Cream!" exclaimed one housewife. "The crushed kernel of coconuts is our cream!"

A settler shouted, "You haven't seen our children dying of dysentery. If the Lord leads us to green pastures, we have an obligation to graze until the next calamity!"

Angry shouts filled the church. Kate thought, Oh God, this could smash the fragile tolerance Paul's achieved. She thought of Looff's strange ideas: secret police to patrol the people's minds, guns before butter, purification of the race. She heard Magdalene urging her to speak. The appeal was taken up by the women's corps. Ada called out, "Set him right, Kate. We women have something to say—"

General Wahle took Kate by the elbow and steered her to the pulpit. He had learned in the past hour that Looff had been moved into his quarters. "Come down off that blasted pulpit," roared General Wahle, "and let a lady speak!"

Looff descended the steps, forced by his own sense of discipline to defer to Wahle's rank. The hubbub in the church seemed out of proportion to what he had been saying. He was gripped by agonizing pains in the head. At the bottom stair he mustered strength enough to say in a hoarse voice to Wahle, "Above all, General, we must beware the Zionist hooligans."

Kate did not fully absorb the remark. She knew only that order had to be restored by some exercise of sanity. Her appearance in the pulpit drew shouts of approval. She spoke in good colloquial German and her voice grew confident as the murmuring died away. "Let me tell you some of the things we women do, Captain Looff. If you judge the effects to be debilitating, then I suggest you are waging war against womanhood—not the English!"

There was a roar of laughter. Looff looked up briefly and then resumed a whispered altercation with Count Kornatzki, who had prudently stationed himself at Looff's side.

"Our women superintend the expansion of rice fields on the shores of Lake Victoria," Kate resumed. "Every month the wives of askaris make up a column of six hundred carriers, each bearing a load of fifty-five pounds of rice on a thirty-day march from the rice fields to here.

"Our women hunt and cook—hare, dwarf antelope, guinea fowl, partridge, duck, bush buck, even jackal—whatever gives protein for the men who fight.

"When we move on, Herr Captain, the women will dismantle those defense works of thorn and bush made by the wives of as- karis and porters. Your own nieces, Captain, last week stole *ninety kilometers* of telephone wire erected by the English. Your nieces, sir, have considerable experience in this direction. And we now have several telegraph and telephone systems by courtesy of the English general post office."

Paul, leaning by the altar, felt a tug at his elbow. His orderly indicated a side door, and Paul followed him, slipping quickly into the blinding sunlight outside.

Major Wolfe was waiting. "We found the hydroplane. The pilot and a passenger have been taken to your quarters to avoid attention."

"Who are they?" demanded Paul.

"Charles Truman and Jacob. You should see them right away." Wolfe's voice was urgent. "Before the Governor hears their story."

Kate was winding up, astonished by her own loquacity. "We women do the donkey work that keeps information moving by drum, helio, and signal lines to detachments striking the enemy hundreds of miles away. Women are mapmakers, wireless monitors. It was Frau Feilke whose patience makes it possible now for us to pick up broadcasts from the Mauen transmitter in Germany itself when conditions are good. I suggest," she concluded, "we deserve our coffee wtih cream, Herr Captain."

Looff ducked his head while applause showered Kate. Several of the women surged around the pulpit as Kate tried to leave it. Count Kornatzki rescued her. Sensing his agitation, she went with him to the sacristy.

"Two bulls contending for leadership of the herd." Kornatzki shook his shaggy head. "Damn fool nonsense! If they fight, the only winner will be the Governor." He bent upon her a look of such severity that she had to ask what was troubling him.

"Max declares your brother and you are Jewish," said Kornatzki heavily. "His head's full of nonsense. What can you expect, months at sea, then stuck in the Rufiji quagmire? Still, it's dangerous talk."

"And what's dangerous about being Jewish?" asked Kate coldly.

Kornatzki tugged his beard. "Nothing, child. Nothing at all. But when the sentence used is 'Zionist hooligans plotting to destroy the Teutonic race!'—well, fanatic it may be, but troublesome, too."

"Who put such ideas in Captain Looff's head?"

"The Governor. Who got them from Hackmann, who was a police spy in Berlin and wrote a report on your family." Kornatzki raised troubled eyes. "These people are mad—"

"Who are *these* people?" blazed Kate, but before she could get an answer, the door flew open, and Major Wolfe burst in.

"I thought you'd vanished! Your brother's here. Hang it all, I wasn't supposed to let anyone else know." Wolfe grinned at Kornatzki. "Still, isn't this a kind of confessional, Count? And you a priest." He spun Kate around. "Come, don't keep him waiting. You look positively—" He caught Kate, who seemed about to faint.

Kornatzki began to shake out his cassock, embarrassed by the unnecessary warmth of Wolfe's embrace. The Major had both arms around Kate. Her color had returned, and her eyes were suddenly bright with excitement.

"You make my heart dance," murmured Major Wolfe. "I don't care if you are the Kommandeur's wife, my heart dances to see you happy."

"Even if I'm Jewish?" Kate asked, her face turning grave as a child's.

Wolfe blinked. "Yes, even if I'm king of Bavaria." He hugged her again as he rushed her through sacristy.

Kornatzki, watching them go, thought, Whatever they may be, she is a woman, he is a man, and he is in love with her.

Kate mistook Chuck's immobility for coldness. She came to him slowly, spirits dampened, a little afraid. He stooped like an old man, oddly still. There had been no communication between them since her marriage. Perhaps he was still angry? She reached out, and he took a stumbling step forward.

"Your leg!" She held him by the shoulders.

"Sis." He buried his face in her hair. "My little sister, married! I'm so glad for you both." He was laughing, tumbling her hair, kissing her, but always in that strangely rooted fashion and with one hand clutching a cane. "Kate, you look *stupendous!*"

"And you're—oh God, what is it, Brer Fox?" She felt the tears coming.

"It might be worse. It might have been the whole leg. Only the foot deserted," said Chuck, forcing a laugh. "Gangrene."

Kate clung to him, her eyes drawn to the wooden peg protruding from the bottom of his cotton trousers.

"How could you fly?" she whispered.

"Easy." Chuck laughed and turned his head. "Jacob did the foot-work."

"Jacob Kramer!" She held out one hand to grasp that of the figure beside Paul. Still clutching her brother, she held tight to the older man and, laughing through her tears, said, "You haven't changed, anyway."

"No," replied Jacob solemnly. "At my age why be a slave to fashion?" The black cotton suit, the mildewed *kupa*, the open shirt were all taken in by the sweeping gesture he made with one hand.

Chuck disentangled himself from Kate. "Any second the Governor will want to see me. Paul, we had better act fast. Before the Guv has time to think."

"Think about what?" asked Kate.

"President Wilson has sent his own man to Nairobi. Winston Churchill's on his way, too. They want total surrender of German forces in Africa. America will come into the war if the demands are not met. And if the demands are not met, there are armies on every side waiting to march."

Count Kornatzki slapped his thigh. "You've done it, Paul! *Sakrament nochmal!*"

"There's more," said Chuck. "Max Looff has accomplished at sea what you've done on land—a gigantic diversion. The hydroplane I brought here was one of several Sopwith machines sent out to search for the *Koenigsberg*. I stole it—I'll explain later. The point is, the most powerful fleet ever seen in African waters has been assembled by the English to block the *Koenigsberg*'s escape. At least one battleship, several armed merchantmen from South Africa, high-speed gunboats from the Med. I've even got the names— *Salamander*, *Fly*, and *Pickle* are three. There's a seaplane tender and a merchant cruiser escort, four special big-gun monitors diverted from the Brazilian navy, for God's sake. Seven steam trawlers and some ocean-going armed tugs and aerial observation balloons fixed to some very odd-looking torpedo boats. Curtiss of New York is sending out new flying boats ordered especially by the Admiralty. And, of course, there's still," Chuck concluded, running out of breath, "the Cape Squadron with King-Hall flying his flag on the *Hyacinth*."

"Good!" said Paul with quiet satisfaction. "If Max can divide up their forces, the Grand Fleet and our U-boats have a better chance to cut off their empire."

"But if America comes into the war?" demanded Kate.

"That's mostly a threat," Chuck replied. "A kind of blackmail. The real danger is an African carve-up between America and England."

"Leaving no Israel," said Paul.

They all looked at Jacob, who said softly, "Leaving no place for any of the oppressed—including Africans."

31

"You call this a white man's war. But it is your path to freedom. Do not let your white comrades down." Cornelius was addressing the porters who would bear the biggest loads when Laager-120 W disbanded and the *communards* moved along. Chuck Truman, standing beside him, thought the French word for the supporters of the 1871 Commune was appropriate here forty-four years later. He remembered suddenly that Kate's birthday was this very Sunday, June 20, 1915. Back at the Trumans' summer home on Cape Cod, with the summer solstice now upon them, the air would be vibrant with butterflies similar to these brimstones and meadowbrowns drifting like confetti in the wake of the last of the heavy rains.

Chuck turned to the new black commandos who had followed the porters into the compound. "Don't be overawed by the English," he advised them through Cornelius. "The English you call *wadoga kabisa*. Very small." He put his hand ten inches above the ground. Then he jumped high in the air, stretching the same hand as far above his head as he could reach. "You are *mkubwa sana*—that big!" There was a roar of proud laughter. "But only if you face the new English weapons. The bigger the weapon, the more bits will break. Look for these weak bits! This flying machine you call a god, it comes in wooden boxes. That is the time to hit it, not when it flies."

He pointed to the hydroplane floating sedately on the lake. "That one came in an English ship. We stole it while it was still in boxes and helplessly floating onto a beach. . . ."

Later Chuck showed them over the hydroplane. The first youngster he took up, when asked to identify a "weak bit," pointed unhesitatingly at the fuel tank. "Damn right," muttered Chuck, contemplating the havoc caused by Ersatz Etrich's homemade benzine.

When Cornelius translated these lectures by Chuck, he slipped in references to *maji*, magic water, and its power against bullets. The Maji-Maji rebels were notorious for having set Africa aflame a few years earlier. Chuck recalled that they had suffered heavy defeats when white colonialists demonstrated the emptiness of the *maji* magic. "What will happen," Chuck asked Cornelius, "when lead bullets kill these chaps stone dead? Won't they lose faith like the Maji-Maji did?"

Cornelius shrugged. "I preach that if anyone falls in battle, he failed his faith, not that the faith failed him."

Chuck confided his other misgivings to Kate. "If America comes into the war in Europe, what's our position?"

"You're workng for the rebels and an ideal. For that matter, the Germans out here are rebels, too. They're defending a way of life that's in conflict with Germany's established ways."

Count Kornatzki joined the discussion. "You're arguing that your chosen ideals have a greater priority than blind patriotism. But look what happens to Jews who put their faith above local loyalties. They get in trouble for showing devotion to something higher than the state. Each nation is nothing more than a big tribe. And if you cross your tribe's borders, you're in danger of being condemned as a traitor."

"But if the Jews get Uganda, won't the new Israel become just another tribe, too?" asked Chuck.

"If their neighbors attack, they'll be forced to react like every other nation in history." Count Kornatzki fingered his beads. "Prussia swung from culture to militancy for that reason. Incidentally, you both know *you're* under attack for being Jewish?"

Kate tossed her head. "That's Max Looff. He's a member of the Society Against Presumptuousness of the Jewry. Some lunatic priest, begging your pardon, *Father* Kornatzki, started it with pamphlets stamped with some symbol—a crooked cross, I think."

"A swastika," said Kornatzki.

Captain Looff was in a hurry to get back to his ship. He claimed he could hear the whine and crump of the new English biplanes bombing Kilimanjaro for practice. He became edgier with each fresh report from the mountain that told of a city-size staging area for the big English offensive to be led by General Botha, who was tasting blood after his conquests in German West Africa. The English ports were said to be choked with imperial reinforcements, and a steel carpet of trolley lines linked their base camps with the English-controlled sectors of the German colony.

Ada came to see Paul. "Don't judge Max too harshly," she said. "He put himself in a false position and now he doesn't know how to retreat."

"You know how he can make his peace with me?" Paul fumbled for his monocle. "I loathe this bit of glass. Some day a shell will blow it right back into my brain. But the poor old optics are failing, Ada. I can't see the end of my rifle sometimes."

"Max has given you all the medical stores except what's absolutely essential for the *Koenigsberg*."

"Drugs won't fix things. What I'd really like is a pair of binoculars."

"My God, don't you have any?"

Paul looked embarrassed. "Vanity will be the death of me."

Ada kissed him impulsively. "I love you. Stubborn, arrogant, rigid in your wretched army discipline, and yet you won't admit your frailties. I'll get your binoculars, provided you let me go with Max."

Paul held her at arm's length. "So! I suggested your Pumpernickel take his blessed administration to the *Koenigsberg*. And instead he sends you!"

"No, it was my own idea. From the *Koenigsberg* I'll provide a direct line to you. Max trusts me. He's still sick, and the sickness warps his judgment. I'll iron out the misunderstandings and stop any more fights between you even before they can start."

"You realize there's no hope Max will ever leave the Rufiji?"

"There are worse places."

"The English will take pot shots night and day. The *Koenigsberg* will become a fortress sunk in a river stinking of disease and crawling with death in a thousand forms."

"Dear Paul! Love's made you poetic. If I had to share a rotting hammock with Max for the rest of our natural lives, it would be better than another night with my Pumpernickel, your Governor."

"Ludicrous," muttered Paul, "that he still has the power to divide us."

"He no longer matters," said Ada. "It's Max who counts. I love the corsair in him more, I think, than I love you."

Kate walked into the tail end of the sentence. "Good grief, Ada! Haven't you taken enough scalps already?"

Ada gave her a quick hug. "What can I do to guarantee your man is safe?"

Kate was still smiling but her eyes had grown cold. "You can get the secret police file, the SK file started by Commissioner Hackmann. The top label reads ISRAEL, and the Truman family is inside. You'll find it in your husband's safe."

Ada's mouth opened, but she bit back the questions on her tongue. She returned within the hour. "Heinrich is stewed to the gills. He won't miss this if I can keep him busy." She gave Kate a brown folder. Then she took from her haversack a folded telescope. "For you, Paul. Max will send you another for the good eye when he gets to sea again." She caught Paul's faint grimace. "I know. It will never happen. But the possibility buoys Max, and it's my job to keep him afloat, fair means or foul."

But there was one more task, she told herself as she went back to the Governor's quarters. A task she preferred nobody should know about. She had found Heinrich maudlin and amorous in his private hut. She prayed for stamina now to survive the pawings ahead, the wet kisses. Here he was, naked on his bed, crying in self-pity. She dared not betray the nausea that would wound his pride. He was limp and Ada groaned. She knew a trick that might help, and in the meantime she bolstered his confidence with words.

"You're still Governor," she whispered. "You were clever to make me your eyes and ears in the delta. Together we'll keep Looff and the Kommandeur in their places."

She hated herself for what she was saying, she who lied so cheerfully before. She forced her body through motions that were purely mechanical. She swallowed bile while he jerked inside her, and when it was done she waited cowlike for him to roll off her wet body. She could not have invented a situation more ironic. For the first time in her life, she loved someone more than herself, and it was not this mewling jelly.

Footsteps sounded in the outer vestibule. Because Ada had her own quarters, servants and officers were accustomed to move freely through the Governor's residential hut. The footsteps were too heavy for a servant. Ada panicked. Her self-contempt and the strain reduced her control. She tried to push Heinrich off. His body weighed a ton.

He seemed to turn quite cold. She whispered urgently, but he showed no response. The erection for which she had worked was now refusing to deflate. Her vaginal muscles convulsed in sheer horror as the dear familiar voice of Max Looff sounded in the doorway.

In matters of sex, the commander of the *Koenigsberg* was not sophisticated. He'd been to sea since he was a boy, and his experience was sharply divided between waterfront whores and a forlorn love affair. He had been led to believe Ada was the Governor's wife in name only. What he saw resembled a pair of dogs trapped in copulation, the commonest dockside spectacle, the butt of seamen's jokes, to be sprayed with ice cold water until the soldered creatures jerked apart. He turned on his heels and fled.

"I'm sorry, Paul. I was told the record concerned only myself." Kate closed the stolen file.

"Does this change your feelings? Should I have told you the whole story about Rachel?"

"No to both questions. Was she—would you have married her?"

"Yes."

Kate nodded. She had known that would be the reply. It was typical of Paul, the real Paul, not the Paul in this filthy file assembled by Commissioner Hackmann using gossip and guesswork to prove the Kommandeur was part of a Zionist conspiracy. No wonder he labeled it ISRAEL, though it touched on American diplomats in Berlin, a legitimate target for Hackmann while he was still in the German capital. What Hackmann set out to prove to the Governor was that Paul's stubborn refusal to make peace with the English here was a logical consequence of the scandal surrounding his secret liaison with the niece of Walter Rathenau, the Jewish industrialist. Rachel Rathenau had been sent to Austria by her family. She had killed herself the day in the summer of 1913 it was announced Paul would return to Africa. But according to Hackmann, there was more to the scandal than that—Jacob Kramer had blackmailed Paul into his Zionist role.

"I think I should tell you more," said Paul. "I was sent to look at the fortifications in the Crimea by the Russian Section of the German Foreign Office—it's some years ago. I was eating with the German consul in Sevastopol when we heard shouting. Russians were breaking down the doors of Jewish homes and shops, raping Jewish girls. Some slobbering brute with a club chased a child just as I ran into the street. I got into a fight. Suffered a few broken bones but gave more than I got—and a lot of Jews died horribly, including that sad child. More horrible was the sense I had for the first time of what it was like to be a Jew in such conditions. I resolved whenever and wherever I could to help the Jews."

Kate felt her heart shrink. "I really do believe I'll go back to the faith of my people."

"Good! I'll support you, even if I am fearful of the vulnerability of Jews, particularly children."

"Don't say that!" Kate hugged her waist and crimsoned at Paul's startled look. She dropped her hands. "Darling Simba, I wasn't going to tell you. If you want, I can abort. The *bibis* abort all the time."

Suddenly he was clasping her tight. "A gift from Africa! Remember? *Bibis* are not you, *Kätzchen*. A battlefield *toto* will grow to be a real man."

Man? She let the slip pass. But later that night, delirious after her solitary nursing of anxiety, she wondered how he would feel about a girl born in the cannon's mouth. She was ashamed of her earlier panic, her entertainment of thoughts about abortion. Of course, the pregnancy was a gift, a message from savage African ancestors that the future of man was the triumph of love over brutal instincts. Fantasizing now, in her giddy relief from the burden of her lonely secret, she decided she would show the cynics they were wrong to believe man's fate was by way of bloody carnage to the breeding of supermen. Baby Paul would show them otherwise. Like Paul, she already thought of the child in her womb as a boy.

Max Looff walked blindly away from the Governor's quarters and found himself standing in the church of the Holy Ghost fathers, staring at a crude attempt by some lonely long-forgotten missionary to reproduce the religious art of home. A medieval spirit of self-punishment matched Looff's bitterness. He felt guilt and he sought the torments of the flesh. His memory of Ada, spread like a cross under her husband, became blurred. Pain was the proper condition of human existence. Christ on the cross was before him. There was the evidence in frame after maggot-ridden frame, the colors faded and seeping, the eyes accusatory and the paint sliding into gaunt cheeks. Ada was a whore, the Governor her pimp. What she gave Looff was corruption disguised as love. Love was to suffer as Christ had suffered for the sins of men. Love was to crusade against the enemies of Christ. Love was to be stretched upon the rack for Christ. Looff fell to his knees before the altar where, in arrogance and under the spell of Ada's sinfulness, he had so recently presumed to preach to the commune. He shuddered. There was no true joy save the flagellation of flesh depicted in this procession of religious ghosts haunting a savage continent. Man was born evil.

He heard footsteps, then saw Ada pass through beams of sunlight piercing the damaged fabric of the church. Her arms were stretched out to him. He groaned. Wicked, shameless, abandoned woman offering lips of lechery. The flesh of the fornicator beckoned between the folds of the gown she had wrapped hastily around herself.

"Jezebel!" He tore the garment from her body, still warm from the husband's bed. "Harlot!" He beat her to the floor as if each blow tamped down his own devilish desires. The passion with which he hit her was his own punishment. She sprawled naked, submissive to the blows of the transgressor in torment. His fury began to exhaust itself. He sank to his knees. He had been guilty of loving Ada in a sinful way. Now he must love her to salvage her future everlasting. He prayed.

" 'For the lips of a strange woman drop as an honeycomb, and her mouth is smoother than oil: but her end is bitter as wormwood, sharp as a two-edged sword.' " The Bible was his familiar. " 'Joy shall be in heaven over one sinner that repenteth.' "

Ada shifted under him. The fury of the attack had stunned her. He was in an attitude of prayer, but with his knees gripping her waist and his weight on her buttocks. She lay face down, the red packed-earth floor grinding one cheekbone. She dared not move. She had known too many men whose lovemaking was akin to sudden violence. His hands were at her neck. How easy it would be to kill or be killed in the intimacies of sex.

"There is no repentance beyond the grave," intoned a voice.

Ada felt the hands tensing around her neck and then relaxing. She twisted her head. Behind Looff, holding a gun against his temple, was Jacob.

Motionless, only his eyes shifting, Looff shouted, "You desecrate the House of the Lord, Jew!"

"No," replied Jacob calmly. "*You* trespass on army property! I could call the guards. They might be less restrained, Captain Looff, than I. Please stand up."

The weight lifted from Ada. She groped for her robe. Jacob took her by the arm, his gun still aimed at Looff. She leaned unsteadily against the flag-draped altar. If she was to bring Looff back from the edge of lunacy, now was the time. "I love you, Max." She tried to keep the panic from her voice. "This is hard to say. Despite what you saw, despite what you've just done, I love you."

Looff only gave a harsh laugh.

"Heinrich never made such demands before," she said desperately. "I had to—to divert him. Other lives were at stake!" She saw the loathing in Looff's eyes, but a spark of doubt, too. "Max, I would walk across Africa for you, share any hardship, die for you. Don't, for God's sake, destroy what we have!"

"We have nothing."

"I had to detain Heinrich because of the police file. Ask Jacob—" She looked to Jacob for help and was frightened by his darkening expression. The truth involved Jacob's whole reason for living, she realized with a shock. To keep Max, she must tell the story of the ISRAEL file. But if she disclosed that, she would destroy Jacob.

The choice is yours. The words were in Jacob's unwavering eyes. You fornicate freely, you can have any man within reason, you've never before shown such delicacy of feeling, there must be lots of wives who loved the husbands you so carelessly took to bed. Why such a fuss now? If you win exoneration from Max by revealing that file, you will do irreparable harm. For what? Another man in an endless series of men?

She pulled the robe tighter across her breasts. "Please, Jacob, walk me back to my quarters."

Toward evening Paul went in search of Max Looff amid the signs of imminent departure. Looff's KLF was taking only enough to sustain and defend the journey back to the Rufiji.

"I'm grateful, Max." Paul indicated the arsenal being left behind. "Sorry you changed your mind about taking Ada."

Max Looff continued strapping his kit in the circle of dead grass where his tent once stood. He looked away, then said, "You've worked out the new liaison—our new lines of communication?"

"Frankly," Paul persisted, "Ada would be ideal."

"Please!" Looff flashed him an agonized look. "I never want to hear the name again."

Paul concentrated on rolling a cigarette. "You wouldn't care to tell me what went wrong?"

"The sea's my element. On land I'm a sick man. That's no excuse, Paul. I apologize for my behavior." Looff stuck out his hand and looked relieved when Paul took it. "What the devil are we doing here in this dark place? We got along fine together at Wilhelmshaven, remember? That's where we should be, fighting a real war."

Paul licked the cigarette paper. "If we get just a trickle of support from the Fatherland, you'll see all the fighting you want—but not at sea."

For a moment it looked as if Looff was returning to his former belligerency. Instead he gulped down a powder wrapped in paper-thin bark. Paul recognized Ada's handiwork, a substitute for aspirin made from willow bark and leaves. Concealing a smile, Paul added, "You need to know what I've done to bring this about."

He had Looff's undivided attention now. In words more specific than anything he had confided to Kate, he told Looff how Quentin Pope's regular reports were doctored for Hagen's eyes. The impression had been conveyed in these newspaper dispatches that the rebel tribes were still distrustful of the Kommandeur and the German Governor, that Cornelius would like to reach an agreement directly with Berlin. The purpose of this misrepresentation was to persuade Hagen and his political intelligence advisers to speed up their plans for Lanni, who, because of her connections, would seem a first-class agent in an English maneuver to separate the black independence movement from its German allies.

"Once I get Lanni to Berlin, she can speak for a very different cause," Paul concluded. "She's possibly the only person in the whole of Africa who can persuade the Kaiser to break the blockade."

"Even the Kaiser can't do that where I've failed," objected Looff proudly.

"Not a conventional blockade runner," said Paul. "A Zeppelin."

"And I thought I was mad!"

"The biggest Zeppelin ever made," continued Paul. "Every single part designed for a different use when it gets here. Gas bags for tents, for example. Even the rubber treads on the gangways will be converted for African campaigning. Every crew member trained to become a bushwhacker. You can say I'm mad, Max, but not Chuck Truman and Ersatz Etrich *and* not Lanni, who has witnessed what our enemies are doing in the air."

Paul was relieved to see Looff's expression change. After all, they had trained with the naval airship service when Paul commanded the marine unit at Wilhelmshaven, and they had both agreed then on the Zeppelin's potential.

"In a way," Looff said slowly, "the Zeppelin was designed for such a mission. But where would you get the biggest?"

Paul hesitated and then decided it was too early to disclose Jacob Kramer's part. It was bad enough that an American and an Austrian aircraft designer had participated. A Jew would be too much for Max

Looff, especially because Jacob had got his information on just such a Zeppelin from another Jew, Walther Rathenau in Berlin. Instead, Paul punched the other man's arm in a final gesture of goodwill and said, "I'm sure you understand the need for secrecy."

Ada had never believed in the possibility of love so powerful that nothing else had significance. Rather than brood about whether she might have kept Max by betraying Jacob, she plunged back into work, dispatching units of the women's corps along the southerly lines of retreat. Ten thousand families had to be escorted on foot to the new defense line cutting across the middle of German East. It was a movement of humanity rivaling the huge migrations of wild animals, and it looked like a massive withdrawal.

32

"THIS HER?" asked Myles Hagen, pulling out a creased photograph of Lanni.

"You are a magician," said the Baluchi *havildar* sergeant.

"Tell me more," ordered Hagen, immune to the flattery.

"Dark skinned like a Pathan, with narrow smile and eyes tilted." He hooked up a corner of each eye and managed to look lascivious.

"I know what she looks like, idiot," Hagen said amiably. "Tell me about the papers."

"Left in a tree by enemy scouts who had been trailing her to within a night's march of the American cowboy."

"He is not a cowboy," Hagen said mechanically. "You must learn these things. He is a Uganda Volunteer." He lapsed into silence. So Ace McCurdy had been rejoined by Lanni, who had been reported lost. Where the bloody hell had she been?

"Did you wish the enemy scouts killed?" the *havildar* asked politely.

"No! How often must I tell you. Gather information, *not* heads."

The *havildar* concealed his frustration. "And the woman?"

"Bring her in!" grunted Hagen. He had just learned that his quarry on top of Kilimanjaro, Tom von Prinz, had daughters in an English boarding school. It would be easier to have Ace McCurdy deliver an ultimatum and pull Lanni off the mountain. She was needed.

Hagen examined the papers again, with their covering note from Quentin Pope of *The New York World*. Hagen waved the *havildar* away and then followed him out onto Government Road. Nairobi spread dustily around him. Horsemen swarmed in the personal uniforms of volunteer cavalry raised by patriotic settlers: Lord Delamere's Masai, Bowker's Horse, Cole's Somalis, Wessell's Scouts, the Gishu Boers. Some wore patched riding britches and frayed Norfolk jackets or stained regimental ties around soiled wing collars. The bizarre atmosphere intensified near the "Japanese Consulate," the brothel on Victoria Street where "Kill-or-Cure" Burkitt, the town's first private physician, clung to the back of the only zebra broken to saddle.

Hagen moved through this circus in a two-seater driven by Paymaster Badger, who, like Hagen, had urgent business with the English Governor here in the capital of British East Africa. Like Hagen, Badger was an intelligence officer whose Royal Navy rank was a blind. "Damn fool!" growled Badger, honking his bulb horn at an American white hunter known as Buffalo Jones. "He's turning the place into a Wild West show."

Hagen never looked up from Quentin Pope's reports, which had suddenly started to exercise a peculiar fascination. "Eh? Come again—" He cupped an ear to catch Badger's last observation.

"I said the *Koenigsberg*'s readying for sea."

This time he had Hagen's full attention.

"Boilers fixed up good as new in Dar were being installed yesterday afternoon." Badger spoke with the authority of a man who had flown over the German battleship in one of the new long-range Henri Farmans powered by Canton Unne motors for extra height.

"Bless you, Badger. Are you going to stick this dynamite up His Excellency's rear end, or shall I?"

"You're seeing him first," responded Badger cheerily. "Had a feeling you'd need some ammo."

Hagen watched him disappear in a cloud of red dust. The Governor, Sir Henry Belfield, had accused Hagen of trying to push British East into full-scale war by any means—a strange accusation, thought Hagen, seeing as how half the settlers were already fighting the

Germans. But Governor Belfield wanted peace as much as the German Governor. Now Hagen had extra ammunition to add to the explosive stuff from Quentin Pope about Cornelius and the rebel tribes.

Two nights after Lanni was recalled and Hagen's new instructions were delivered, Ace McCurdy summoned the sergeant whose Baluchis were now his sole companions for the long toil up the steady slope of Kilimanjaro. The sepoys were mountain fighters. Like the American, they found the climb a bore.

"I'd like to force the pace," said McCurdy, glancing at the light snow covering the tents. "Too many nights up here and your boys will catch pneumonia."

The nut-brown face of the sergeant squinted in the light of the paraffin lamp. He wore two heavy British army sweaters and a balaclava plus a scarf wrapped around his head. "We came to Africa," he said with a condescending smile, "prepared for sunstroke, not frostbite."

"Could you scout around, then, figure where the Jerries are, get back here by morning?"

By morning he was back. Ace McCurdy listened to his report with growing skepticism. No bunch of kaffirs stumbling around in the dark could assemble so much information. Their notes were written in the fractured English of the *babu* Indian clerks they despised. They had mapped a *boma*, or fortress, where Tom von Prinz and Kurt Wahle held the steep-sided spur that alone gave access to the very summit of the Kaiser's Mountain. The *boma* was a mile from where McCurdy had camped for the night and two thousand feet above him.

"I don't believe it," said McCurdy, scrutinizing the alleged German position. "Tell your coolies to do the job properly. No more pulling the wool over my eyes." He watched the sergeant pick his way over the rock-studded scree. "Lazy bastards." It was obvious the Baluchis were exaggerating the enemy's strength to dodge a fight.

McCurdy did not blame them altogther. It had taken very special reasons to bring him up the mountain. He decided to do some scouting on his own, up narrow ravines that ended in unscalable chimneys, working his way around what he thought was the granite spur below Prinz's *boma*. He returned toward noon, having seen no sign of the enemy. He sat on his bedroll and eased off his boots. Then he looked up and saw the sergeant carrying a gunnysack. "What's that?"

The sergeant reached into the sack and took out a series of objects that he dropped in front of McCurdy. "This is the revolver of the commander of the enemy picket to the west. This is the German corporal's stripes. Here, the German sentry's rifle. This, the German bugler's bugle. Now do you believe us 'coolies,' sir?"

McCurdy looked at the ancient Mauser without touching it. He regarded the dented bugle with its German markings. He stared up into the sergeant's eyes watching him steadily from between slitted lids. "Sergeant," said McCurdy, getting to his feet, "I do believe you have just made me look like Senator Windbag his very self." His face broke into a smile. The smile became a roar of laughter. The laughter spread to the sergeant. The Baluchis watching from a distance began to laugh, too. Soon the little camp pitched on a steep mountain slope along the snow line echoed to the deep-throated rumble of men's laughter. The sound was the only cheerful feature of that bleak day in the high mountain valley where a merciless sleet and a bitter wind now started to freeze the sepoys' wet clothes into boards.

Darkness fell early. McCurdy made himself as snug as he could and drifted into sleep. He dreamed that a misbegotten hyena, huge jaws and skinny body on genetically crippled hind legs, nuzzled under the tent and shoved its snout into his armpit to chew on him. He had been warned of this hyena custom. He woke himself up with his own yells. The next man awoke with a shout that awoke another. McCurdy, shamefaced, clamped his mouth shut while the shouts spread like a plague until the whole camp was aroused. Men seized their guns. Night sentries came running. The time was three o'clock. Typically the weather on Kilimanjaro had suddenly changed. The night was clear, crisp, and cold. The sky crackled with stars. The noise of the false alarm reverberated in the valley, and it was another hour before the men finished blaming one another and settled back into silence. The only man to escape accusation was the culprit, who pretended to sleep through the uproar he had started.

He was disturbed again at daybreak by the sergeant gently shaking his arm. "The enemy is all around us," said the sergeant bitterly.

McCurdy crawled out of his tent. The sun sent long slanting rays across the scree, throwing into sharp relief walls of stone that had not been there before. The walls were chest high and further protected by spiny branches. The camp was threatened from every direction by the barrels of the unseen enemy's guns.

It was too late for recriminations. Besides, thought McCurdy, he might himself have alerted the damned *Pickelhaubes* with his em-

barrassing shrieks. The Huns had slipped into position like eels. Mc-
Curdy was aware of the sergeant awaiting orders. He said, "Tell the
men to throw down their arms."

The sergeant looked at him in stunned silence.

"Surrender!" said McCurdy. "We've no choice."

The slant-eyed sergeant shifted uncomfortably. "It is contrary to
our tradition—"

"I don't give a damn what you call tradition," snapped McCurdy.
"Surrender before we all get killed." He fumbled through his kit
bag for the dirty white sheet he'd planned to use as a flag of truce.
There was no chance of meeting Prinz on an equal basis now, he
thought bitterly. It was the last thought McCurdy would have for
some time. Something struck the back of his head, and he toppled
onto his face, out cold. The sergeant examined the calloused edge
of his rigid hand, guilty of a terrible offense. He rolled McCurdy
over and assured himself the Frontiersman didn't count as a superior
officer. Then he turned to the nearest *naik* corporal and ordered his
men to open fire.

Tom von Prinz was enormously cheered by the skirmish. The
sepoys never had a chance. Young Kurt Wahle, who was in command of the ambuscade, had been told to avoid a fight because of
the shortage of ammunition. At first Prinz suspected Kurt of forcing
a fight anyway. The General's son was a true bushwhacker, dedicated to bloodletting as other youngsters his age were devoted to
the pursuit of women. But it was clear the Baluchis had made a
suicidal bid to break out. None had been taken prisoner. The only
walking, talking prisoner was not a sepoy but an American. Prinz
told the cooks to prepare supper and rescue the wine he had stored.
Then he debated if he should receive the prisoner in his command
post, a cave linked to other caves in the side of the cliff by tunnels
that were being extended daily. Prinz's ambitions had gone beyond
merely holding the heights of Kilimanjaro for symbolic reasons. At
least three caves were ready to house the big guns from the *Koenigsberg*.

Prinz went through the personal possessions of the dead. The sepoys were well trained. Nothing identified them or their unit. He
turned to McCurdy's papers. Train robber. Another criminal seeking legitimate adventure. Still only twenty-seven years old despite
what seemed a long record, to judge by the wallet of newspaper
clippings. About the same age his own son would have been.

He was startled by the sheet torn from *Faust* that Lanni had passed on to McCurdy. His hand began to shake. This was Magdalene's: her favorite quotation, her penciled marks. What on earth could it mean? That she loved him still? He sat staring at the lines and tried to control the tide of anguish that pulsed through his veins. He'd been through all this already, when young Kurt Wahle first arrived with that incoherent account of Magdalene's infidelity. Prinz had wanted to leave then and there to kill Quentin Pope. It was lucky Major Wolfe had soothed him, reminded him of his duty here.

He stared dully at the pages. Magdalene! Perhaps he'd loved her too much. Only Magdalene ever aroused him to such passion that he was frightened of what might happen if he should lose her. War had become a means of loosening his dependence on her. Perhaps, unconsciously, he'd driven her into the arms of Quentin Pope, who didn't find it necessary to court violent death every second week.

The torn page had a more recently penciled line. He reread the erotic passage: "A supernatural delight! To lie on mountains . . . to probe earth's marrow . . . then overflow into all things with love so hot. . . ."

He was positive now that Magdalene, by means that baffled him, was conveying some message. To lie on mountains. Was she asking to join him here on Kilimanjaro? He wondered if he could forgive her. A man got soft-hearted, alone in this wilderness. A man clung to sanity by sticking to a rigid timetable. Which included dinner at seven. Sharp! He called for his orderly.

Young Kurt Wahle watched McCurdy with veiled curiosity during the meal. Kurt had been under siege with Prinz long enough to know his mannerisms. One was to eat in the English way with knife and fork. McCurdy had the same habit, and his other unconscious gestures mirrored Prinz's. It was not some convulsive imitation by a junior nervous of his senior. By the end of the meal, McCurdy had given nothing else away at all, and yet Kurt Wahle knew everything.

When, over Kilimanjaro-grown coffee and ersatz brandy, Prinz warned McCurdy the rest of his imprisonment would be less comfortable, McCurdy broke silence. "My original assignment was to gain entry here and then—uh, kill you. That's changed. Hagen wants you back, alive."

Prinz spat an oath.

McCurdy said calmly, 'Hagen says you've got two girls in English schools." He held up both hands protestingly. "Now he ain't sayin' harm'll come to those girls."

"Blackmail!" snarled Prinz.

Watching both men get to their feet, Wahle thought, They're dif-

ferent in size, different in everything except—God save us!—Mc-
Curdy's the ghost of Prinz.

"What," asked Prinz, dangerously calm, "is Hagen threatening?"

"To send your girls out of Africa." McCurdy stared through
Prinz. "Same as me."

Wahle, crouched on a crate serving as a chair, watched incredulously his bearded commander stuffing dry grass and tobacco leaf
into his clay pipe. Surely the truth no longer escaped him?

"You were sent out of Africa as a child?" demanded Prinz.

"Yeah, but Hagen doesn't know that." McCurdy chewed his lower
lip. "Parents dumped me some place with a German name, back of
Johannesburg, when I was eleven. The limeys shipped us out near
the American coast. People called McCurdy adopted me so's I
wouldn't have to stay in prison."

"Prison at eleven?"

"Sort of. Some island around Bermuda."

Prinz's face vanished in a cloud of tobacco smoke. "You remember
your family? In Africa, I mean?"

"Not to recognize. Just my ma, a bit, maybe. Guess she died in
one of the limey concentration camps."

"Your parents never dumped you," Prinz said quietly.

"They let me go just as surely as you turning down Hagen's offer
would be abandoning your girls."

Prinz bent and stirred the fire. When he rose again, his voice was
gruff. "What really brought you to Africa? I know you've had contact with our German forces."

"No, sir. Nothin' like that."

"You carried a message from my wife."

McCurdy looked puzzled. Then his face cleared as Tom held out
the page torn from *Faust*. "*That!* The black girl had it in her possession."

Prinz stared at him for a long time and then reached for one of
the bottles on the rocky ledge above the fire. "I hope you're not
tired," he said grimly, "because we've a lot of talking to do."

Much later Kurt Wahle escorted McCurdy to the prisoner's billet.
Wahle was perplexed and filled with hate for McCurdy. The American had disclosed only what he seemed ready to reveal, though he
had been interrogated skillfully by Prinz in every matter except the
one that alarmed Wahle—the certain fact that his freak prisoner was
the son of the man who had become Wahle's hero.

The cell was formerly a dugout for storing roots, dry, comfortable, and easily guarded. Wahle was tempted to shoot the prisoner and then claim he'd tried to escape. But Wahle had matured a lot in the past campaign. He decided to bide his time.

Tom von Prinz spent the rest of that terrible night writing and then tearing up what he had written. But in the cruel light of dawn he had a letter that met his needs:

My darling Puppi. I read your lines from *Faust*. That same book we kept all those years! Your pencil marks speak through my fingertips of your love renewed. I forgive you with a love so great I tremble as I write in joy and sadness. Joy when I touch the page that touched your hand. Sadness because I face a most terrible choice.

You know of the son of mine, victim of English atrocity. You have never asked what happened in those years before we met. When I was sent to support the Boers against the English, I thought myself in love with a Boer girl, Louisa. She became pregnant. The parents hid the girl and refused to let me marry her. When civilians were moved into the English concentration camps, my poor Louisa was taken too. She died of the plague. Our little boy was sent out of Africa. None of this I knew until so much later, my subsequent inquiries were fruitless.

Now comes a tragic irony. A strange young American leads an attack on me here, is captured, and is found to be—my son! How he came here and why, I cannot truly comprehend. That he came back to Africa seeking revenge is, I think, clear. He seems blind and deaf to what stares him in the face, unless the ultimatum he brings is his diabolical method of vengeance, for it repeats the pattern of his boyhood. He presents me with an English threat to send away from Africa our two darling daughters if I do not surrender this position!

Puppi, my love! You alone know how this would destroy me. I cannot betray my adopted country. But neither can I betray my daughters!

And you? A woman bears children, protects them, and then is required to give them up as cannon fodder? No!

My solution, arrived at after hours of despair, may horrify you. However, it is essential to my plan that you know all of this. This American stranger of my flesh and blood is in his own country a criminal. He does not recommend himself to me in any way. It can be arranged that this *stranger* is reported killed in the skirmish that destroyed all his comrades. The English must then assume I never received this ultimatum. They will leave our girls alone.

The son I lost I never saw. Upon that son I lavished a love entirely romantic. I must weigh the *stranger* against yourself, my darling girls, and Germany.

Eventually there will come another ultimatum. Therefore, you must confide this to the Kommandeur and to your American newspaper friend. When the threat is repeated, I shall let you know, and then it must be widely publicized. There will be sufficient outcry to stop English machinations.

I am sending this by safe hand, double sealed, protected by fire makers that explode if unauthorized hands attempt to open this letter.

Prinz sealed the letter and turned to the Kaiser Wilhelm Spitze war diary, where he recorded the massacre of the Baluchis and hesitated only a fraction before entering the last name: *McCurdy, killed in action.*

Kurt Wahle had been expecting the order to carry dispatches to Paul. "But suppose the Kommandeur requires me to stay?" he asked Prinz. "I still face a court-martial."

"Any charges against you were destroyed with other documents when the fort at Moshi was evacuated. And I'm recommending we mark your twentieth birthday," added Prinz with a sudden smile, "by confirming you deputy commander of this detachment."

Wahle blessed his good fortune. He was getting experience normally denied an officer of less than ten years' seniority and a chance to redeem himself in the eyes of his father, General Wahle. He wrapped Prinz's packages with Promethean fire makers—sulfuric acid in glass capsules coated in sugar and gum. If there was a danger of the papers falling into enemy hands, he need only bite a capsule to ignite the chlorate and engulf everything, including himself, in flame.

He traveled by night and on foot and finally reached the trek pad of Paul's migrating settlement, strewn with carcasses of pack mules, horses, and oxen. Heavy rains had churned the flatlands into black cotton, a clay into which men and animals sank to their knees. The main column had progressed only fifty kilometers toward Tabora on the Central Railroad, and behind it straggled the wagons of the settlers. When Wahle reached the tail of Paul's column, he had survived for five days on biltong and rainwater.

Guides took him to a Masai *manyatta* camp where Paul was stopping overnight. While he waited, the Masai women made him drink curdled milk from a gourd. The milk was mixed with blood, and he was reminded of the official pageants sponsored by the Kaiser and filled with a monumental patriotism in which Germania drank blood from the skulls of warriors. But what had been sentimental nationalism in Berlin last year was excruciatingly repugnant now: the bloody mixture tasted of ammonia because the gourd was customarily washed out with urine.

The Kommandeur received Wahle in a covered wagon. Paul went swiftly through the papers, separating the envelope for Magdalene. His manner was brusque. "Get a good night's rest," he advised Wahle. "I'll want to question you before you go back."

Magdalene was sheltering with Quentin Pope from the downpour. The envelope was delivered by Paul's orderly. Rain pelted against the canvas like buckshot and made conversation difficult. Pope had spread a rubber ground sheet on layers of branches. Their sleeping bags were still drying out, and he was folding coarse blankets when he saw her face turn gray in the light of a spirit lamp. She was reading Tom's letter with trembling hands, kneeling in the lamp's dismal glow. "It's all too late," she said. "He forgives me and he cannot see how late it is."

She turned and unthinkingly thrust the letter into Pope's hands. There were tears running down her cheeks. "What am I to do?" The words were scarcely audible. Pope took the letter to the light and looked at her inquiringly. "Yes, read it!" she said, almost angrily. "Whatever I do must be for the children. No, please, don't touch me. Read it."

A thunderstorm broke during the night: African thunder, which sometimes reverberates without ceasing. Old General Wahle, struggling up the line, timed one roll of thunder for thirty minutes without a single pause between the peals. Vivid, almost continuous lightning revealed an ocean of mud from which protruded the bare upflung arms and broken arches of devastated trees. He sat astride a heavy gray cavalry horse, one of the few remaining of the bigger, colder-blooded, hairy-heeled charges. On this strange night it seemed to come plunging out of a primordial ooze.

Kurt Wahle, unable to sleep, left his shelter to watch the storm. He saw his father as a vast figure, with bulging eyes like some giant warrior descended from an ancient race, spawned by Wotan in the Prussian plains. The racked sky illumined his father's face, daubing it tawny beyond mere sunburn. The square shoulders twisted in the saddle, and the square head bent in young Wahle's direction. For a moment they stared at each other with a fixity of expression matching in latent physical fury the steady hammering of the gods above. The old soldier's horse leaped from a rearing position, sprang sideways, and snorting in sudden fear, descended to its chest in mud before plunging on.

Toward morning the rain stopped, and the stars came out. Magdalene crept from Pope's side and emerged into the freshened air. A huge globe of light appeared on the horizon to her right and soared majestically across the plain with an eerie crackling sound that lingered after the sphere vanished behind the northern hills. She recognized the ancient omen of evil portent, a fireball.

Others had seen the phenomenon and were discussing it when Paul sent for Kurt Wahle after breakfast. "Call it an ill omen for the English," Paul was advising another occupant of the operations tent. "Spread the word among your people. Call it a thunderbolt, a sign of heaven's approval for your cause." He stopped abruptly as Wahle entered.

"Lieutenant Wahle, describe everything about Kilimanjaro and your journey here," said Paul. "This man knows what I know, but we both need to know more."

Wahle glanced distrustfully at the stranger, not recognizing Cornelius. He saw a Masai standing storklike with a leg hooked behind the other unbent knee, leaning on a spear. The lieutenant plunged into his summary of events. When he finished, Paul said, "You've done well. Return immediately. You will have Masai escorts. Our future depends on your brave conduct."

Wahle felt a surge of affection. Emboldened, he said, "Captain Prinz will find the sacrifice worthwhile, sir." He caught a glint in Paul's eye and added, "I mean the daughters."

Paul cut in sharply: "Nobody, Lieutenant, is required to make impossible sacrifices within my command. The wife of Captain Prinz will travel with you, to join him and share his ordeal."

After a bewildered Wahle took his leave, Cornelius said, "The harder sacrifice is Magdalene's, surely? She gives up the American?"

"It's her decision," muttered Paul. "It must tear her heart out, but she knows her duty. And she's worth a battalion to Tom right now."

Part Six

Timeless Night Descends

33

From the war diary of Colonel von Lettow, while on the march, July 1915:

We are waked by *streptopelia semitorquata* species of dove cooing delightfully the deeper we plunge into central regions. My purpose is to set up Laager-500 WSW (that is, 500 kilometers west-southwest of Kilimanjaro). Desperately short of everything, we shall make use of Central Railroad upon reaching that immense ironway opened in the last days of peace a year ago. Cornelius and his guerrillas work closely with our attack squads to keep enemy guessing. . . . Lanni's mission supremely important now we are totally cut off. . . . Chuck Truman remains with his hydroplane at the crater. Before we left, I omitted recording the gorgeous spectacle of the lake waters covered in pink flamingos.

From Myles Hagen's The Bird Watching Notes of an English Country Gentleman, *Nairobi, July 1915:*

Blasted maribou storks covered fever trees like shitting frock-coated secretaries when I took Prince Turvchenko sightseeing with the half-caste Zanzibar so-called princess, Lanni. Spotted unusual species of weaver bird. . . . Seems that the prince is getting off with the princess, no matter how phony their titles, which is according to plan. Lanni confirms, in her increasing indiscretion, that Cornelius and rebel tribes are tiring of Paul's dictatorial attitude. She says with smirk Paul needs moderating influence of a woman. Hah!

Letter from Jacob Kramer to Dr. Bodenheimer, former president of the German Zionist Federation, by safe hand of Lanni:

The bearer has performed noble work among our brothers in England. She places her faith in the promise voiced by the official German Zionist weekly, *Jüdische Rundschau*, that "Germany will liberate the oppressed." She works ostensibly for England. Her true loyalties are with us. . . . Despite Walther Rathenau's hostility, imperative he share with Lanni his prewar plan for airship route to Africa.

Letter from the Secretary of State for India, Edwin Montagu, to Myles Hagen of the English Secret Intelligence Service in Africa, Summer 1915:

All Zionists are German agents. Their objective is to promote German imperialism and to weaken English influence. Please note enthusiastic support by German Zionists for Kaiser's war on the grounds Germany "fights for truth, law, freedom, and world civilization against Russian tsarist despotism" (extract from editorial in *Jüdische Rundschau*). . . . "England accessory to crimes against Jews by allying herself with Russia," etc.

The Indian Empire cannot afford to tolerate machinations of Jewish organizations within our imperial territories, especially Africa. I regard with perfect equanimity whatever treatment Jews receive in Russia.

I caution you, Myles, against the probability Zionist agents are masquerading as sympathizers and peacemakers. Reports to hand indicate Prince Turvchenko, using false Russian papers, represents Jewish interests close to Kaiser. Turvchenko is kinsman of Kaiser . . . and took part in financing Berlin-to-Baghdad Railroad (Imperial Ottoman Baghdad Railway Corporation) intended to threaten our imperial route via Suez to Asia.

God Save the King!

34

PRINCE TURVCHENKO was openly referred to as the Kaiser's spy soon after he reached Nairobi. White settlers in British East Africa were not all in support of a local war.

"Well, it's no secret!" said the Prince, dining in the regimental mess of the 130th Baluchis. "The Kaiser thinks a direct appeal to the colonists might work, and you can't arrest me for espionage, can you?"

Hagen shrugged good-humoredly. "We could but we wouldn't. You're too well connected."

"My head to my shoulders? But I forgot"—Turvchenko wiped his fingers on the loose Russian-style smock he wore—"you don't cut off heads here. You stretch our necks, right? You're correct about family relations, absolutely. Kaiser Bill and I share the same great-grandfather, Paul the First, Tsar of Russia. Dotty, poor chap."

"Which one's dotty?" asked Lanni. "Kaiser or Tsar?"

"Both, come to think of it," said the Prince, quaffing wine from a pewter mug. He knew all the scandals.

Hagen watched the interplay between the Prince and Lanni. The dinner had been designed to bring them in intimate contact. She looked, as she always did on such occasions, ravishing in Hagen's eyes. The Prince would have been an outlandish figure anywhere except here in the English colonial capital, which was now attracting flamboyant adventurers from all over the world.

"I've pressed the Kaiser's views on everyone, and you're the brightest in a dull lot, Hagen," said Turvchenko. He turned heavily to Lanni. "Present company excluded, Maharani."

Lanni smiled. She guessed that Turvchenko's interest in her as a Moslem princess was heightened by the Kaiser's campaign to dilute Christianity with some outside religious influences. If Turvchenko wanted to take her to Berlin, he would seek as many ways as possible to make her presence effective. She said, "This so-called campaign, this war for civilization between Protestants and Catholics, this *Kulturkampf*, does it continue even now?"

"A toy war. I can suggest a better one, in which, if you give the Kaiser a small victory, you will win a greater one." Turvchenko sneezed into a large red handkerchief.

Hagen signaled the mess waiter to retire. The man was the Kikuyu agent Gideon, and his concept of an appropriate disguise was a blue frock coat with lacings of gold braid, cherry-colored trousers of calico, and a bright green waistcoat with yellow buttons. Hagen had still not fully recovered from his astonishment. He was grateful that Gideon was outshone by Lanni in a simple white cotton *kanga* robe.

"The Kaiser plays with real soldiers," continued the Prince, "as he plays with toy soldiers on toy battlefields. He much admires how you rescued his Kommandeur in German East because this appealed to his chessboard mind and he saw what your next move would be."

"Then he's more clever than I," muttered Hagen.

"Dear boy!" Turvchenko laid a hand on Hagen's sleeve. "Give my emperor a mock war. Allow him to win back his mountain. Honor satisfied, he will then join you in the struggle against—*the Bolsheviks.*"

Hagen flicked a glance in Lanni's direction. So far she had played her role perfectly as an aristocrat opposed to the peasant uprisings she secretly supported.

Turvchenko misinterpreted the look, and leaning toward Lanni, his full lips wetly shining through his beard, he said, "Your own interests are at stake here! You are shocked, but you will not think so when the Bolshevik devil strikes. Vladimir Ilyich Ulyanov waits now in Switzerland, tempting Berlin to give him safe passage to Russia with his promises to corrupt Holy Mother Russia and wipe out the generals leading the Russian armies against Germany. A Jewish devil—"

"Ah, Lenin!" Hagen sat upright. He began to talk, slowly at first but with a convincing passion, then with a growing extravagance. He recalled the warnings of other Jews who, fearing Lenin, tried to persuade King Edward that England should have united with Germany against this subtle threat. The Jewish banker Sir Ernest Cassel had argued with the King on his deathbed that the greatest mistake England made was to stifle the popular German revolt against social discrimination and militarism. The King's greatest error had been to frighten Germany into believing in an English plot to encircle the Kaiser's empire, for in the end it pitted England against Germany. "But a victory over Germany won't be the end," Hagen quoted the the banker as saying. "It will deepen the German sense of injustice and feed political extremes. There will be polarities—dictator against Zionism, Lenin against capitalism. To rise above the rivalry between England and Germany would be to lift mankind to a higher plateau."

When Hagen finished his account of the deathbed scene, Turvchenko's face was red with excitement. "Yes, yes, the sentiment is precisely correct. So give the Kaiser his toy victory in order to end our fratricidal struggle. Then we can concentrate on destroying these alliances between black Bolsheviks and black Zionists!"

Lanni returned to Berlin as a double agent. She simplified her real mission for Paul in a few sentences: *Persuade the Kaiser that if Germany is defeated, a German government can continue in East Africa. Dispatch a Zeppelin on a proving run to the colony to test the feasibility of moving Berlin leaders to Africa. Make the airship convertible so cargo, crew, and structural materials all benefit Paul's campaign.*

She traveled with Turvchenko, who coached her in court etiquette. He had once conducted the *Schleppencour* ceremonial for presenting guests to the Kaiser. "I had to walk up to trees during my training," he said. "To each tree I addressed a few pleasant words. In this way I learned one of the principal duties of royalty."

Under his patronage Lanni was greeted as a royal highness. She provoked the curiosity of those who remembered "Emin Pasha," the German Jewish physician Edward Schnitzer, who had become a Moslem under the influence of Lanni's grandfather and then converted back to Zionism in the cause of a national home in Uganda. Her manners being impeccable, her royal blood undisputed, she was allowed to cast an exotic glow upon a capital too long cut off from glamorous foreigners. The slaughter on the Western and Russian fronts had imposed terrible hardships, and the privileged classes in Berlin needed excitement to distract them from the rapid drain of young men and the sense of impending disaster. Lanni's romantic beauty captured a city hungry for proof of another world, or oriental mysteries. She made little attempt to correct their geography or enlighten them on the realities of Cloud-Cuckoo-Land. The most popular Yiddish writer of the day, Morris Rosenfeld, wrote a poem about her that ended with "Long live the Kaiser and the Maharani!" The schmaltz eased her entry into all sections of society.

She was established in the handsome house built as a palace for the Princess Hatzfeld on the Wilhelm Platz in the center of Berlin. Her protector remained a mystery before Turvchenko took her to a *Schrippenfest* held in the summer palace at Potsdam. He pointed out a silver cigar-shaped Zeppelin hovering about the courtyard. "It follows the Kaiser like a toy balloon," he said mischievously. Lanni found that to be true. It looked to her like a phallic symbol, trailing the Kaiser, whom she saw for the first time inside the palace. He was standing on a dais above the princes and princesses, and the royal persons were in turn separated from the commoners by the Empress Choir from Berlin.

"You are acquainting yourself with our customs." She turned and saw a blond Prussian in his mid-thirties who was introduced as Major Walter Nicolai of Department IIIb, the General Staff intelligence bureau. "I look forward to seeing more of you," said Nicolai, joining guests trooping back into the courtyard for a military review. The Zeppelin still maneuvered above. Lanni felt that she, like the airship, was at the mercy of the winds. Paul had warned her she must let Department IIIb take the initiative. Major Nicolai made his move a week later, calling without warning at Lanni's home. He told the parlormaid, a square-faced Wendish type from the forests outside Berlin, to take the day off, confirming just who paid the rent.

"Let me come straight to the point," said Nicolai, dropping his kid gloves on a side table and planting himself firmly in the middle of the drawing room. "You are now under our instruction."

Lanni returned the stern gaze with an expression of wide-eyed frankness. She found Nicolai more like a bush baby than the striped jackal she had taken him to be. She had no doubt this was the man leading directly to the powerful heart of the Second Reich. She said, "I was sent by Colonel von Lettow. We took the opportunity of using the Kommandeur's enemy. You know who I mean—?"

"Myles Hagen. He put you here to win favor with black revolutionaries." Nicolai's crisp voice belied his effeminate features. "Your masquerade is dangerous to yourself. We shall require proof you're not spying for the English."

"Here's the proof." Lanni went directly to the pigskin holdall made for her in Nairobi. She slit the lining and took out thin sheets of minutely scrawled notes. "This material was handed me by Hagen. I'm supposed to tell you I stole it, ingratiate myself with the highest personages, and return to Hagen with useful intelligence."

Nicolai nodded. "Let me worry about Hagen. You concentrate on the Kaiser."

Major Nicolai had just returned from a rewarding interview with a dancer at the Domhotel in Cologne. Her name was Mata Hari. She had volunteered to spy for Germany in France. The woman who had acted as intermediary was Liesbeth, Countess de Tallyrand, who was now assigned to Lanni as a lady-companion. She was a long-limbed youngish woman who was brutally frank while wasting few words. "You were respected in London as black royalty," she told Lanni. "Here you will be adored. Here everyone is Count This or Baron That. All the sons of a count can claim to be counts, so we get, for example, seventy-one Counts Wolffen. You can swim, little savage, in this sea of snobbery."

Liesbeth produced the *Pocketbook of Counts* and the *Almanach de Gotha*. "These contain all you need know about German politics. In a sentence, a scramble for titles," Liesbeth said drily. "You lived among Germans who went to Africa rebelling against the system. Here you must accustom yourself to Germans who will disclose their caste upon meeting you. Herr Snob will say he is a *Kaufmann*, a merchant. Frau Manufactory-Proprietor Schulze might own a steam yacht, a tiara, a box at the opera, and a husband honored for scientific achievement, but she still takes second place to Frau Second-Lieutenant von Bing. . . ." The mumbo-jumbo of black Africa, thought Lanni, was nothing compared with this ritualized society. She could imagine the shocked disbelief of the King of Uganda confronted by such pagan values. The black monarch might brain his opponents. Was it worse than softening their brains to this state of complex caste?

Liesbeth, in her sarcastic way, explained the *Rat* or councillor honorifics, awarded for blind obedience. A lawyer could become a justice *Rat*; a doctor, a sanitation *Rat*. A man might graduate by his unquestioning loyalty to become a secret *Rat*, or privy councillor; then to become a court secret *Rat* to which might be added the title Excellency, whereupon he was absolutely at the top of the *Rat* councillors.

"Titles of nobility by themselves don't count," explained Liesbeth. "The wife of a successful builder is Mrs. Really Truly Secret Court Building *Rat* and her social position depends on it. A wife whose husband in middle years isn't a *Rat* of some sort becomes a nag. He may have opposed the government at some time. This will be recorded in the police registers that cover every German citizen. So you see, by this system we keep tighter control of the population than by torture and the stake."

When Liesbeth made these dry pronouncements, she would turn her enormous blue eyes on Lanni and give a gentle mocking smile. "The plain people struggle to be given a piece of ribbon instead of the right to vote," she said one morning. "The decorations go all the way from the Order of the Black Eagle down to the Prussian Order of the Crown. There are subdivisions of the same order, so a man might earn the Red Eagle order of the fourth class. Even a faithful butler will receive some sort of order, provided he says nothing against the government that gets into the police register."

Liesbeth concluded: "Little savage, be sure to impress upon your African relatives the benefits they gain from associating with us Germans. We have the most perfect system for keeping everyone in his place."

Lanni went to a court ball. The guests assembled at eight-twenty precisely. Prince Turvchenko escorted Lanni and Major Nicolai took Liesbeth. "The dukes and dignitaries stand to the left of the throne," she whispered, poker-faced, to Lanni. "Foreign guests sit in order of rank to the right." Trumpeters in medieval costume sounded a fanfare from the musicians' gallery, and the Kaiser entered with his Empress and the ladies and gentlemen of the household, all brilliantly costumed. Giant officers of the court regiment paraded in silver helmets surmounted by eagles, steel breast plates, white breeches, and wide-topped boots rising halfway up the thigh. The Kaiser, one arm stiffly bent, began a leisurely march along one side of the room while his Empress reviewed the other. He jingled with decorations pinned to his ornate uniform. Lanni was reminded again of the Uganda king, who certainly looked more splendid in leopard skins and lions-teeth necklaces.

When the Kaiser stopped abruptly before her, she thought, This one can't boil me for breakfast. She remembered to bob and curtsy. He placed a gloved hand upon her arm, a touch brief and light, but it told Lanni more than any number of lessons from Liesbeth. This was a muddled, self-tortured man, forced to disguise his physical weaknesses so that his face twitched and his body quivered with angry frustrations.

Prince Turvchenko was eagerly answering an aide's inquiries. The Kaiser murmured words in the same way he'd learned to address a tree. Lanni whispered some idiotic reply. The little moment was over. The All Highest moved on, leaving a trembling wake among those courtiers flanking Lanni. Even Major Nicolai was flushed with excitement. "You made a good impression," he kept repeating.

By the time the Kaiser and the Empress were enthroned, several Vortänzer officers had summoned the young nobilities. Nobody else might dance, said Liesbeth. Nothing "demoralizing" was permitted in the nature of the turkey trot, the bunny hug, and the tango, all of which had filtered into Germany just before the outbreak of war.

Lanni thought the long lines of dancers radiating from the throne and moving through a sort of lancers looked painfully joyless. The rituals among these savages were quite pathetic. If the circumcision of black girls was a brutal assertion of the African male's denial of woman's joy in sex, the removal of joy in the imperial court seemed more subtly degenerate to Lanni.

She was starved for news from Africa when Major Nicolai gave a report she would have preferred not to hear. The *Koenigsberg* had been sunk. Captain Looff was badly wounded. "You will read an account, suitably censored, in the newspapers," said Nicolai. "I shall give you the facts as wirelessed by the *Koenigsberg* some time ago, because I need your advice, based on reality, not propaganda." A powerful English fleet, using spotter aircraft for the first time in naval warfare, had pummeled the corsair while she lay in the Rufiji. Lanni knew what this meant: injured men struggling against gangrene in the corrupt swamp airs; shortages of morphine and dressings; the dead buried hastily where neither crocodiles nor hyenas could reach the outraged flesh. For the living the greatest ordeal would lie ahead: the salvage of scrap from the abattoir and a dreadful trek out of the delta's watery compost.

Lanni stood by a window overlooking the Wilhelm Platz and saw not the paved road, the elegant motor carriages and petrol-driven berlins, but a ghostly column of skeletons straggling across a wilderness of demons.

Nicolai was studying her expression. He said, "Is this the beginning of the end?"

She turned in fury. "What end? A beginning, yes! A warship is lost. But the guns and seamen are released to strengthen Paul." She gazed disgustedly toward the Chancellor's palace. "If your people have the will, my people have the strength."

Nicolai consulted his notes. "There are ten-dozen German survivors to add to the Kommandeur's few hundred armed men. What hope could they possibly have?"

"*My* people," Lanni repeated. "My *people*, not black figures carved in wood. Black Africans."

Nicolai rolled his eyes and fluttered his long blond lashes. "The English fight with modern weapons. This isn't some tribal war."

Rage seemed to swell Lanni's bosom. "Haven't you learned *what* Paul is doing out there, *why* he survives, *how* the power of the peasants is the most terrible of weapons?"

"I'm willing to learn," Nicolai replied quietly. "Tell me about your people, not about the Kommandeur or the English or all those things you've been pretending to be loyal to. Talk to me about the naked savages you've been too arrogant to explain. Voice the thoughts you nursed when you compared our emperor with your warrior chiefs. I won't," he added with a half-smile, "eat you!"

Lanni was given three hours' warning of her first private audience with the Kaiser. A portfolio showed him in a variety of poses, photographed in Scottish kilts, Roman togas, Russian military tunics. Hastily reviewing all she knew, Lanni recalled the French general who, seeing the Kaiser in a Napoleonic stance, grunted, "That's not a portrait, it's a declaration of war!"

She was prepared to confront an operatic braggart, but Liesbeth emphasized his need for feminine sympathy. "He once discussed with the Duchess of Hohenburg—whose husband started this wretched war by getting assassinated—a costume he rather liked. A silver eagle perched on his head. Thigh boots for a giant encased his legs. Gold braid and medals dangled from neck to waist. The Kaiser grumbled, 'I look like a Parsifal-de-Passage.' The Duchess said, 'No, Lohengrin.' 'They're both the same,' said the Kaiser, but the Duchess insisted that one was a knight and the other a fool. 'Well,' said the Kaiser, 'I look like both.'"

Lanni was not entirely taken by surprise when she finally curtsied before the little man mounted upon a wooden gymnastics "horse" and dressed in a gold-trimmed Hussar's uniform. The Kaiser stayed in the saddle, swinging his polished boots in the stirrups, while the flunkies withdrew and left Lanni sitting on a stiff-backed chair.

"We have followed your career with interest," said this singular figure. "Your reputation for beauty is not exaggerated. Our misguided cousin, the King of England, found you wise and exotic, we are informed." He bent his head to examine Lanni more closely. "We have always said that in the matter of the colored races there is a need to show proper appreciation of the aesthetic qualities inherent in a darker skin. Our father, Emperor Frederick, was loyally served by mulattoes. Are you mulatto?"

Lanni began to reply but found this unnecessary. The Kaiser answered his own questions. "We ourselves like a bit of the mongrel, as Mr. Shaw has written, because they're the best for every day. You have heard of the sad loss of the *Koenigsberg?* We are deeply distressed. Did you know her captain? We have dispatched to him fresh honors and an Iron Cross second class for each survivor. Will you forgive such a bombardment of questions? Of course you will"—patting her head—"for we see you are a child of sensibility."

Fifteen minutes later the Kaiser was still speaking, and he had so moved himself by an account of his military misfortunes that a tear fell on the tip of his unlit cigar. Lanni wondered idly how his barber contrived to gum his upturned mustache to his upper lip each morning. The court gossip was that the Kaiser would entertain a mistress by planting it on delicate portions of her anatomy. Lanni found herself feeling sorry for this lachrymose man who was known to practice severity of expression before the mirror each morning to compete with those not handicapped from birth, as he was, by a crippled arm and damaged eyesight and hearing. She melted into a mood bordering upon affection for his childlike personality. But she was aware of the danger. If she aroused the Kaiser's sexuality, she could not afford to refuse him. If she permitted intimacies, she might be prevented from leaving the circle of police agents who protected his privacy. A vain emperor who calls himself the adjutant of Providence cannot afford to have his bedroom secrets escape.

A gong had been sounding significantly in the corridor outside when the Kaiser said that he would be obliged if she would assist him from his saddle. He laid upon her shoulder his right hand. This belonged to the withered arm and from constant exercise the hand was unusually powerful. The rings on the fingers were worn with the gems inside so they might dig into the hand of anyone grasping that of the Kaiser. She felt their sharp outlines mark her flesh. His hand remained like a claw on her shoulder after he had cocked a leg over the wooden horse and was standing upright beside her. Even with the raised heels on his thigh boots, she noticed he was not much taller than she. He rested briefly against her before moving to a bell rope and jerking it. He would arrange for her to see him again quite soon, he promised, for what she had to say was enchanting. She had said practically nothing.

Her next audience with the All Highest took place in the summer palace at Potsdam. The Berlin papers had reprinted *The New York World* reports of an English attempt to dislodge Tom von Prinz from Kilimanjaro by threatening his children. Suddenly the honor of the German Officer Corps was at stake in Africa, a forgotten theater until now. Kilimanjaro was fixed in the public mind by the popularization of Paul's name for it. The Mountain of the Kaiser became the dramatic symbol of the mighty Second Reich.

This time the Kaiser sat in a loveseat and wore an evening shirt under a green coat dripping in gold braid to facilitate the hanging of the Black Eagle, the Garter, and the Golden Fleece. He smiled roguishly and asked if she would take tea, then answered for her that teatime had gone and she should have sherry and biscuits. He made room for her on the loveseat and invited her to describe his mountain. Then he settled back, still as a waxwork, eyes fixed un-blinkingly upon her face. It was time, Lanni decided, to produce the great Zeppelin plan.

When she finished, the Kaiser patted his mouth delicately. "We were informed of your strong views. War is not a suitable topic for pretty young women." The rest of the words reached Lanni through a fog of anger. He became in turn serious, when his speech was staccato with a hint of a snarl, and good-humored, whereupon he roared at his own jokes and stamped his foot. Lanni recovered herself. She could have written a textbook on guerrilla warfare, and instead she had to pander to this royal buffoon. She laughed at his jokes and exhibited concern when he professed doubts about his adequacy as an instrument of God's will.

She was not surprised to be told it was the dinner hour and she must stay. She knew that the Kaiserin, Dona, was not in Potsdam. It was that amiable but dull woman who had painted on their lampshades the terse instruction: "He who prevails over himself conquers." Lanni had no plans to let the Kaiser conquer her and then blame her for his failure to prevail over his animal instincts. Her seduction of the Kaiser needed to go no further than enchant-ments, looks of adoration, smiles of understanding, flutterings of moist eyes. The roost was ruled by the Kaiserin, who had once banned Strauss's *Salome* as blasphemous. Lanni was certain the Kaiser liked to be teased, not propelled into a domestic quarrel with such a dragon.

Lanni left chastely at ten and was rewarded by an invitation a few days later for another tête-à-tête. She detected in the Kaiser a strong feminine streak, disguised by a desire to seem the most masculine of men. So she fed his vanity with questions that led him in the direction she desired. Their meetings became regular. A month after the atrocity report the Kaiser told her that Kilimanjaro and his reputation were inseparable. He had instructed the German Admiralty to take action on a big and dramatic scale.

The Kaiser's notion was to send the largest dirigible in the German Naval Airship Service. This Zeppelin would be remodeled, he ex-plained, for conversion into safari equipment. Lanni blinked, for he showed no sign that he knew he was following the plan she had brought him. The gas bags could be unstitched and turned into tents, sleeping bags, ground sheets, and rainproof shelters. The Duralumin framework would break down into portable hutments and signal towers. The muslin lining for the balloon envelopes was to be stamped with cutout diagrams for scissoring into hospital clothing, mosquito nets, bandages. The catwalks would be treaded with leather to make boots.

This new toy had served to amuse the Kaiser in what Lanni thought of as his nursery. He called it his War Room and showed her photographs of himself playing Supreme Warlord and bending portentously over toy battlefields, surrounded by his admiring toy generals. She could imagine their boyish chuckles, planning this Zeppelin, whose crew would convert into bush fighters when it came down. Nothing and nobody would be wasted when it collapsed in the *bundu*. Even the final belch of hydrogen would become fuel in gas-converter bags to drive automobile engines.

On the Sunday morning after this disclosure, Lanni attended divine service at the Potsdam palace. She realized with a shock that this was Thanksgiving in the German Christian calendar. Harvest and time to thank the Lord. The autumn of the year. She saw the Kaiserin in a black chiffon dress with a long train and an ugly hat covered in ostrich feathers. The Kaiser strutted in the new field gray that would make him one with the men in the mud-colored trenches. The choir sang:

> *Deutschland, Deutschland, über alles* . . .
> German folk above all others,
> All others in the world . . .

So many months had passed. What had she accomplished besides secret contacts with Zionism? She had amused a toy emperor and been rewarded with a toy airship. It was time she returned to the Kaiser's sandbox.

> *Wenn es stet zu Schutze und Trutze* . . .
> Joined as one for our protection,
> Standing firm in unity . . .

Funny, the music was that of an old English hymn. She'd last heard it in Westminster Abbey, near the tomb of Livingstone, whose heart was buried in Africa, where Cornelius had ignited their black **rebellion.**

35

THE VOICES of black askaris joined with those of German women and officers standing in the sun-baked court of Fort Tabora, renamed Laager-500 WSW, to sing the German national hymn:

> Now thank we all our God
> With heart, and hands, and voices,
> Who wondrous things hath done,
> In Whom His world rejoices. . . .

Paul glanced at Kate singing away. Gently he removed from between her clasped hands a tattered hymnal published by the Church of England. It was opened to the section marked Thanksgiving and hymn 379. He leaned closer and frowned. No wonder her voice sounded different. She was singing the English version!

> For thus it was, is now
> And shall be evermore.

She smiled at him as the hymn ended.

"That wasn't funny," he reprimanded her at lunch.

"But it's what I sing on American Thanksgiving," she retorted. She served him from a large plate of crisply fried sheat fish, the sardines of Lake Tanganyika. "We've been awfully lucky, Paul. I really did want to give thanks. We're not yet starving. Our powder's dry. There's ammunition in the lockers."

Count Kornatzki shared their table in the fort commander's mud-walled house. He shook his head. "Today we eat fish because a train got through. But when does the next train make it? Your askaris fight with shrunken bellies."

Kate listened to the lamentation. It was true. Kornatzki shriveled inside his old clothes. Paul's skin had a yellowish tinge. Even Fort Tabora was nothing but a square clay building with a flat roof and a crumbling wall that enclosed a few Dutch-barn offices. Some tin-roofed shacks radiated outward until they were swallowed up in shaggy yellow grass and thorn trees. The railroad tracks stretched into infinity, and you never knew when they might be struck by the enemy. The rivers were dry gullies. The air was filled with a fine red dust whenever the hot wind blew. The world was a coppery shell, the top a blazing sky, the bottom streaked and tatted like the skin of an old lion.

Yet Kate had never been happier. She felt the young life stirring in her belly. Her mood was one of irrepressible optimism, as if the unborn child guaranteed survival. She shuddered whenever she recalled her attitude of three months ago—the panic, the conviction that she must kill the baby in her womb in harmony with the killing around her. Now she welcomed each day's challenges, even the dust and flies that got into every bodily crevice. The jigger fleas burrowed into fingers and toes and caused glandular fever. Her brother, fitted with an artificial foot carved by Paul, boasted, "That's one advantage of a wooden foot," until she retorted, "Wait until the termites get it." The termites lived on wood, and furniture might be reduced overnight to hollow shells that collapsed suddenly. Tinned food was proof against them, but there was precious little of that remaining.

Kate had brightened the canteen menus with exotica: curried locusts, fried grasshoppers, blancmange made from packets of cosmetic rice powder stolen from English camps. The supply of forage oats outstripped the consumption of horses and donkeys, so the cooks benefited by an increasing surplus. If the oats were soaked two days and the scum removed for chicken feed, the residue could be boiled to a paste made edible by salt. Hardly anything was wasted when a horse gave up the ghost. Sausage skins were made from the bowels and stuffed with minced horsemeat; the mane and tail went to the hospitals to fill pillows and mattresses; bones were boiled for soup and pounded into powder to mix with flour; the skin and head and feet were boiled for hours and then chopped up small to jellify into "brawn." If the horse had shoes, these went to a simple foundry along with bent nails and other bits of metal for conversion into shell cases.

When Chuck Truman had rejoined them, he tethered the stolen hydroplane to a railroad flatcar. He hoped to find a way to launch it regularly from a carrier pulled at top speed by a locomotive. The hydroplane would extend Paul's ability to guard and repair the six-hundred-mile system of railway and trolley lines still under his control. Baghwash Singh employed several thousand Africans solely to repair bridges, remove boulders, drive off elephants, and replace the railroad ties destroyed by termites.

The Governor's Palace was now what had been the stationmaster's house, a single-story one-roomed shack whose roof was scarcely bigger than Governor Schnee's flag flying above the corrugated iron. He ran the tax office, the treasury, the registration of births, deaths, and wheeled transport, the licensing of liquor and tobacco, and a dozen new bureaus inspired by the need for more controls. There was a lunatic quality to these enterprises because almost none had any substance. The tax on native huts, for example, could not be applied. The Governor's tax collectors simply repossessed the money paid out by the army for goods and services, while the money itself was made with a rubber stamp and oblongs of recycled paper. To break this idiotic circle, Paul quietly produced his own currency of metal *Heller* pieces stamped out of Mauser cartridge cases, which, being substantial and ornamental, soon drove the Governor's paper bills out of meaningful circulation.

Governor Schnee issued edicts. Daily there was heard from his news crier a litany of minor disasters. Schnee saw the military situation in such terms that the defenses based on the Central Railway seemed like a cobweb with a few strands tied to distant and insubstantial posts, including the submerged *Koenigsberg*, shot full of holes, its crew missing.

Paul countered this diet of gloom and doom by circulating reports taken from captured English documents. A military appreciation prepared for the new commander-in-chief of English imperial forces, Jan Christian Smuts, reported:

The natural strength of German positions is formidable, starting at Kilimanjaro and running down a series of high mountains and big rivers . . . a land of dense bush, of mosquito, jigger flea, horse-sickness fly, and every human pestilence under the sun. Opposing us, a very large army, well trained and formidably equipped with artillery and machine guns, immune against most tropical diseases, very mobile and able to live off the country, untroubled by transport difficulties and with morale higher than that of our troops. . . . Physical and climatic difficulties add vastly to German power. From the coast to Kilimanjaro, enemy territory is protected by high mountains. The only useful gap is four miles wide at Taveta where the enemy has been entrenching and fortifying these past fourteen months. This is the gateway—very much closed—to German East.

"So long as they think we're strong, we *are* strong" was Paul's comment. General Smuts's advance guard was exaggerating the odds so that the South African war minister, now suddenly commanding all imperial forces, would either win an impossible victory or suffer an unavoidable defeat, in either case emerging without blame.

The more Paul analyzed the enemy, the more he sympathized with his personal adversary, Hagen, whose new masters suffered from the shortsightedness of the South African Boer, whose world was flat and who believed in a real Garden of Eden where the black children of Ham must forever toil at simple labor. A Boer general like Smuts had to overcome the South African contempt for blacks, which made it impossible to take native soldiers seriously. Thus self-deceived, Smuts's armies, when they entered German East, would flounder in an ocean of hostile peasants. Paul's forces swam like fish in that same sea.

Hagen was overridden both by the South African refusal to see blacks as human and by England's faith in technology. Aerial bombing, mechanized guns, motorcycles mounting quick-firing machine guns, new kinds of Carcass and Hell shells, and fire weapons to scorch the earth and wipe out life were what England, the most powerful nation on earth, relied on to finish this irritating little war.

By Christmas the preparations for Smuts's arrival were in full swing. English biplanes, mostly mosquitolike BE2's, scattered fifty-pound bombs and incendiary darts all over the landscape. Big new guns were hauled over steel tracks to pump shells into the empty mountainsides. The Carcass and Hell shells were iron cases packed with explosives, gasoline, and giant fishhooks to grab German askaris and hold them while they roasted alive. Armored machine-gun carriers snorted along the Kilimanjaro slopes, searching vainly to mow down massed armies, for the machine gun was the effective way to riddle the walls of men in Europe. If such guns moved at high speed, it followed they must kill more men.

But Paul would not cooperate. His men did not form solid walls. They bicycled silently through the bush when in a hurry. Otherwise they walked singly. They would capture an English post, occupy it long enough to rest and recuperate, and then make the English prisoners sign a document promising that if they were released they would not participate any further in the fighting. This seemed chivalrous to the English, but it actually saved Paul dragging large numbers of prisoners around the countryside.

On the Kaiser's fifty-sixth birthday, January 27, 1916, the Governor celebrated with a speech at Fort Tabora. He declared: "We who know the waterless areas and the trackless zones will prevail over an enemy weighed down by mechanical contrivances."

Count Kornatzki was indignant. "What the deuce does Schnee know about the blasted *bundu*?" he snarled.

"Don't complain," advised Paul. "At least he's admitting we're at war."

The Imperial War Cabinet in London hailed the arrival in the African battlefield of General Smuts. "He has warred against us—well we know it!" proclaimed Winston Churchill. "He comes from the outer marches of the Empire. He has led raids at desperate odds and conquered provinces by scientific strategy. He has quelled rebellion against our own flag, and now he travels a new and hazardous road in our common cause . . . astonishing . . . versatile."

On Sunday, March 5, 1916, a new general offensive began under this commander whose appearance at the front had been heralded by a publicity campaign unique in history. Smuts brought a South African expeditionary corps to swell his command of men drawn from the Gold Coast, the West Indies, Kashmir, Jhind, Bhurtpur and Kaparthalu, Rhodesia, Uganda, Singapore, the Cameroons, Nigeria, Belgium, France, England, and Canada. "They are being sucked into a game of hide-and-seek," predicted Hagen, "while Paul will still be cuckoo-ing somewhere in Africa long after the ceasefire sounds."

Kate gave birth to a nine-pound boy on that same Sunday. Like the askari *bibis*, she delivered during a normal day's work. Count Kornatzki was secretly impressed, although he complained she could have given him some warning.

"My stomach muscles have been so toughened," she said, "I really felt nothing until the last moment."

Paul wept silently when he lifted the child from her arms. She had never seen him cry.

The child had Paul's piercing blue eyes and Kate's silky black hair. His arrival had a more profound influence on the native troops than any amount of inspirational talks. Every soldier found time and opportunity to come and marvel at the infant. Every woman wanted to help nurse him. The parents were not allowed to debate his name. The askaris called him the "*toto*" Paul, and Kate and Paul slipped into the habit of calling him Baby Paul. Baby Paul was proof that Kate and the Kommandeur were part of Africa. He *was* African, so the askaris said.

When Baby Paul was carried in a sling on Kate's back, he wore a palm leaf hat from under which his sharp eyes scrutinized the brilliant world outside. If he woke during the night, he made singing sounds like an African chanting, instead of squalling. Skaramunga guarded him. The soldier of God took care the monkey, Bamboo, never came near. But Baby Paul and Bamboo eyed each other with an affection that bridged distance. Oddly enough, Kate's only real fear was not of enemy action but of the danger to the child from wild animals.

She waited for one of those infrequent occasions when she and Paul walked alone together to voice her worries. They came upon a giant fig tree that must have been old when King Solomon was a boy. A maribou stork with raw skull and rattling limbs rose like a lifting shroud. Hooded vultures loped into leafless branches with a dry thrash of wings. The rustle of departing carrion was ancient as the bulging tree, inspiring thoughts of man's mortality.

"Suppose the baby dies?" she asked abruptly.

Paul tightened his arm around her waist. "The child is a gift, remember? He belongs here, to Africa."

She was grateful that he avoided empty phrases of reassurance. She said, "I shouldn't speak of death, but I'm realistic. The baby's prospects are not the brightest."

They stood in a stillness that belonged to some early morning before man was born. Birds of the night lifted up like souls departing, African owls and pale stone curlews swirling toward the light creeping across lion-colored plains unchanged by the centuries. The hungry-headed hyenas skulked like werewolves through bushes astir with mousebirds and beet eaters.

"*So ist das halt*," said Paul. "That's the way it is. Or as Africa would say, God's will." He kissed her gently.

The soft wing snap of a flappet lark brought her head back up. The vultures were mounting the morning air, and she saw why. A pride of lions snaked out of a *korongo*, away from the night's kill. The cubs tumbled like thistledown in front of their indifferent parents, reminding her that every living thing needed this freedom in order, paradoxically, to survive. Even the newly born, she thought, must be let go.

Inside an airship hangar near Berlin, Lanni gazed raptly as two hundred overalled men, tethered like Lilliputians to a giant Gulliver, "walked out" the biggest and most powerful Zeppelin ever built.

"The Kaiser's toy, did you say?" Major Nicolai nudged her. "Some toy! She's seven hundred forty-three feet long, and there's nearly three million cubic feet of hydrogen in her."

The walk-out of LZ-57 was an awesome procedure: the massive machine looked like an airborne battleship with tremendous tail fins forming a cross several stories high. It slid silently out of the cavernous hangar, its six massive engines quiet, the paddlelike propellers still. At some date unspecified lay a twenty-eight-hour flight to Yanboli in Bulgaria, the southernmost point in Europe still held by Germany and her allies. From there the distance to Kilimanjaro was 3,600 miles, which required in the airship a still-air range of 4,350 miles. The final journey into German East would last at least five days of continuous flight. LZ-57 had been lengthened to take two more gas cells to help lift the record fuel load of 48,000 pounds of gasoline.

Lanni knew the details because she was to fly with the Zeppelin and thus avoid contact with Germany's enemies. "Unless," Nicolai had said, "you're shot down, in which case you'll be burned to a crisp and rendered incapable of giving away secrets."

Kapitänleutnant Ludwig Bockholt welcomed the idea of having Lanni as a guide. He was a Naval Airship Service captain, supremely confident of his navigation. In night raids on London, he had perfected a technique of joining the North Sea winds and drifting with engines stopped until he was over the target. He had shadowed English warships through the worst Bay of Biscay weather. But he got palpitations when he thought of trekking through the jungle in search of a German colonial army.

Today he was making a test flight. He was one of the oldest Zeppelin captains still alive: all of twenty-three years old, prematurely gray at the temples, his thin face sallow from lack of rest, a nervous tic afflicting the muscles around one dark eye. He presented himself before Lanni with a stiff bow.

"Do you feel ready for a familiarization flight?"

Major Nicolai intervened. "Our weather people say a low-pressure area is moving this way. Shouldn't you cancel?"

The little Zeppelin captain shrugged. "The test program's behind schedule. What's a storm more or less? We'll run into every kind of filthy weather on the final journey."

"Then I must exercise my prerogative and ban this lady from a needlessly risky flight," said Nicolai.

"As you wish!" Bockholt saluted and hurried away.

Lanni cursed the Major for being a stuffed shirt. Two hours later she was grateful. LZ-57 ran into a bad storm, was forced down near Berlin, and caught fire. The hydrogen bags exploded one after another. Most of the crew were killed. Bockholt walked away unscathed. He began to prepare a successor, LZ-59. Something told him the world would honor LZ-59 someday. So, to celebrate in advance, Bockholt invited Lanni to join him for dinner. He had decided to teach her all he knew about Zeppelins. He was in love with the leviathans. He was also falling in love with Lanni, though he mistook this for infatuation with the romantic nature of her cause.

"I shall have to leave you soon," said Paul.

"I shall miss you" was all Kate could reply. The days when she might have ridden out on commando with him were over. Baby Paul could survive a long march, but not a violent skirmish. She knew that this time more than a skirmish was involved. General Smuts's big offensive was reported in almost embarrassing detail by *ruga-ruga* messengers trotting in from the outposts on and around Kilimanjaro. Paul's blood was racing. At night she felt him tremble like the warrior horses of her girlhood. The words of Goethe repeated themselves over and over to the rhythm of her heart: "Tis I for whom the bells shall toll, and timeless night descend upon my soul."

She tried to put a distance between herself and Paul, as if to protect herself against any calamity to come. She watched covertly while he went about the business of Laager-500 WSW. Another laager had been set up, two hundred and sixty kilometers due south of the mountain, where General Wahle ran a communications center with extra help from the *Koenigsberg*'s wireless operator. She waited for Paul to go forward to this Laager-260 S, knowing what the move would signal. From there he could only dash north for the inevitable encounter with Smuts, a battle of giants.

She could still help him prepare. She studied all the reports from Tom von Prinz on the Kaiser Wilhelm Spitze, from Cornelius observing through the eyes of his guerrillas, from Major Wolfe, who was linking up with the remnants of Max Looff's *Koenigsberg* crew. She knew Smuts carried in his saddlebags the *Complete Works of Schiller*, Kant's *Critique of Pure Reason*, a German history of philosophy, and a German edition of *Anabasis*.

"Smuts seems more German than you," she said to Paul. "What is the language of the South African whites?"

"Flemish-German and biblical Dutch, with a dash of Portuguese from the East Indies. The true Afrikaaner speaks a language of the bush best of all."

Which was too complicated a reply for Kate, looking for weaknesses in her husband's new enemy. "Slim Jamie" Smuts, he was called, using Slim in the Afrikaans sense of "sly." He didn't want to become known as "Butcher" Smuts. This, it seemed to Kate, showed a gap in his armor. He was too political. He wanted big victories to win himself a seat in the Imperial War Cabinet, a fantastic ambition for a Boer. He knew England needed smashing victories here in Africa, needed a colonial hero to rally the empire, needed a colonial leader to placate the colonies tiring of English patronage and sick of bleeding in England's wars.

Kate coaxed a profile of Smuts out of unlikely materials: bits of gossip, stolen enemy papers, and the regular intelligence bulletins. Smuts half-groveled and half-bullied when he was at ease. Timid about breaking out of the imperial grip, he halved the world between whites and coloreds. "He's half-assed except in the saddle," an American general had reported. "But in battle Smuts fears neither God nor man, particularly the former." Smuts was a proud, spare martinet with burning coals for eyes and a red beard Mephistophelean in its horn-like trimness. His single consuming ambition was to vault into the forefront of power by destroying the darling of the English penny press, the Lion of Africa.

This lyrical analysis, Kate thought, would offend or amuse Paul. To her relief, he took it seriously. "What's the weakness in him to exploit, *Kätzchen?*"

"His pride," she answered promptly.

Smuts's armies were streaming under Kilimanjaro, kicking up clouds of finely powdered lava. A permanent line of chalk-white dust marked, for the watchers on the mountain, the passage of five thousand fresh front-line troops preceded by biplanes and automobiles, followed by carriers and supply carts drawn by slow-gaited oxen, and gun carriages and supply wagons each hauled by eight spans of mules. The noise of airplanes, the boom of English thirteen-pounders, and the sullen roar of motorized artillery gave the English security but robbed them of surprise.

Hector Looff was lecturing before the platoon commanders who perched on ridgepoles in the Fort Tabora courtyard. A drowsy nod of the head would mean slipping off the perch.

"We should utilize animal instincts," said the game park pioneer. "Herds with poor eyesight but keen smell mingle with herds lacking smell but with excellent vision. The quick impala warns the cumbersome rhinoceros. Soldiers should do likewise." He quoted the example of Bamboo, the monkey that served as Paul's eyes on patrol.

Thank God, thought Alex Hammerstein, for Celeste and Elsa. The two Looff girls stood behind their father, demure but tough as saplings, a delight to Hammerstein's eyes, which thus remained open.

"The camouflage of the zebra is the most effective of any wild animal," Hector Looff was saying, "The black-and-white striping seems to us to make them prominent. In practice they tone into the landscape no matter where—"

There was a loud crash as a sleepy young askari sergeant tumbled from his perch.

Celeste said, forcibly enough to distract her father, "There should be some way to domesticate zebras. They run like ponies, they look like ponies, why can't we ride them? It would solve our transport problems in a flash!"

Hector swung his head back toward the audience while the sergeant pretended to pick up a dropped satchel. "If we had the time, and under the pressure of necessity, doubtless we could utilize many wild animals. Why, for instance, do men use elephants in India but not here?"

There was another interruption. This time it came from Kate. "Sorry to interrupt you, Hector. Mind if I borrow one of the girls?" Then, seeing Celeste and Elsa dismayed by the prospect of only one making an escape, she added, "Well, truth to tell, I need both."

Hector waved his daughters away. "The usefulness of zebras or elephants is in the mass. This is the time of great migrations. If we had the means to stampede the big herds of elephants, we could stop an army—"

Kate paused, listening to Hector, who sometimes unconsciously inspired schemes from his wildlife lore. Then she guided the girls to an office that doubled nowadays as Baby Paul's day nursery.

"You're to give Jacob Kramer a crash course in riding a horse."

"Crash?" giggled Celeste. "Jacob crashed when I tried teaching him to ride a simple bicycle! My Lor'—"

Someone coughed discreetly.

"I'm sorry, Herr Kramer!"

"No apology needed." Jacob moved out of the shadows. "The Kommandeur's wife has turned me into a chameleon."

"She has indeed!" exclaimed Elsa, seeing Jacob's safari outfit, made from grain bags taken as war booty. He was no longer a Talmudic scholar from the ghetto. His features were tanned, the eyes quick, the body sprightly. His gray locks were vigorously silky and flowed abundantly from under his slouch hat.

"Jacob's joining your Uncle Max," said Kate. "Along with my husband. Jacob picked up a wireless signal."

The girls' eyes turned in Jacob's direction again. He was such a mystery! "Can we go, too?" they both asked.

"Too dangerous!" said Paul, who had just joined them.

"It's not!" said Celeste. "The English offensive is stalled by heavy rains. They're so dependent on wheeled transport and livestock, they're bogged down."

"Where do you girls learn these things?" asked Paul, not expecting a truthful answer. "Security here is like a sieve, full of holes. I suppose you knew about your Uncle Max, too, that he's safe—"

"And taking one of the *Koenigsberg* big guns up the mountain!" said Elsa.

"Enough!" warned Paul. "I'm riding forward tonight. Now, the both of you, put Jacob on a horse, give him sufficient instruction to cope. You will board a train with horses at dawn tomorrow, get off at Morogoro, and ride over to Laager-260 S. We've laid a trolley line to connect with the Northern Railroad section that's back in our hands. Then you'll see your uncle."

When the girls had gone to collect their mounts, Kate said, "You must have been listening to Hector, too."

Paul looked puzzled. "No."

"You couldn't have two more useful young women to execute an idea. Hector suggested it—by accident."

Jacob watched Kate talking to her husband. What a fine woman she was, like a young boy, casually dressed in shirt and jodhpurs. How it must break her heart to send those two girls with Paul when her place was at his side. But she was right. She dared not risk leaving Baby Paul, though—Lord preserve us! Jacob glanced into the corner where Skaramunga cradled the child. The soldier of God was grinning from ear to ear. Only the cunning monkey, Bamboo, sat on the floor scowling and striking a discordant note.

"To me, Jacob used to be the rabbi," Paul said later in the privacy of their quarters. "The bush has changed him, *Kätzchen*. He still has a phenomenal memory. Amuses himself on nights in the bush by recalling whole works of Jewish scholarship. But the discovery of muscles he never knew existed! Suddenly he's a warrior. He lost his spectacles and his eyesight *improved!* He's never talked much about his personal life, but I'd guess his world of business was cutthroat. His rivals lacked the challenges of the wild and substituted conflicts of the city, brittle, neurotic, artificial."

"War's better than peace?" Kate sighed. "*You* don't change much, at least. Only the warrior is noble."

"No!" Paul said sharply. "But war brings out the essence of a man's character—decency more often than not."

"But not in women?" The moment she spoke, Kate regretted it. She was becoming shrewish in her effort to prepare for the separation.

Paul ignored her ill humor. "Skaramunga guided Jacob in from his latest journey. Jacob had hurt his leg, and Skaramunga bound the wounds with his own dirty sock. It wasn't hygienic, but the gesture touched Jacob's heart and he protested it wasn't necessary. Skaramunga replied: *'Ni dasturi ya mvita. Hufanya kwa rafiki tu.'* "

Kate's eyes moistened. She translated: "Custom of war. One does it only for one's friends." Suddenly she felt the barriers between them dissolve. "Darling Simba, how long will it be?"

"As long as it takes to humiliate Smuts."

"Damn Smuts!"

"It's your own idea—"

"I have too many ideas," snapped Kate. "I'm sick of playing games in which women get trampled, exploited, left behind." The words trailed away as she pressed her face into his chest. "Please comfort me."

"The baby—"

"Damn the baby, too!" Kate pulled him to the bed. "Damn the Kaiser! Damn the war!"

He left her just before the abrupt return of night. She felt strangely guilty of blasphemy and stolen pleasures. She had a superstitious dread of some penalty to pay. She went outside to look for Baby Paul and found the regular nurse squatting on the hut's makeshift veranda. The baby, said the nurse a trifle jealously, was with Skaramunga.

Incredible, thought Jacob, the way night descended in the tropics with a single great crash! He was bouncing in the saddle while Celeste led his horse on a rope in the training ring, and the word *crash* was on his mind. Prompted by Celeste's cracking whip, the horse jogged and trotted and cantered despite the gathering darkness. Jacob regretted his earlier frankness with Paul, who had confided that a *Koenigsberg* gun had somehow to be moved through the enemy columns for delivery to Tom von Prinz.

"What can a navy gun do up there that mortars won't?" Jacob had asked.

"Humble the proud Smuts!" Paul had answered. "The *Koenigsberg*'s standard flying from the top of the Kaiser's Mountain and a four-oh-one popgun adding to Smuts's miseries below. Though I'm stumped by how I'll do it."

Jacob had stroked his chin. "Is there military merit to the scheme? Yes. Then do it on the basis it can be done. Approach it mathematically. Then follow each step."

"Good doctrine, rabbi. Where do I begin?"

Jacob had rolled his eyes heavenward. "I have the vision. Common folk work out the details." He'd had to dodge a friendly cuff from Paul.

"Here's detail number one." Paul had laughed, but his face was serious. "Go share your vision with Max Looff."

And that, thought Jacob, is how I come to be joggling on the back of a horse, bullied by a child. "Eh? What's that?"

"I said, what's the Kommandeur's wife doing?" repeated Celeste.

They both peered toward the phantom emerging from the bushes. Jacob slid down from the horse and felt his knees buckle. He saw Kate as a white figure in the sudden dark. "What is it?"

"Skaramunga! Have you seen Skaramunga?"

"No," said Jacob, puzzled.

"Baby Paul's vanished and so has Skaramunga."

Celeste caught the other woman as she stumbled. "Shall I get the Kommandeur?"

"The Kommandeur?" Kate recovered her composure. "He's left already." Her face hardened. "He must not be distracted. He must not be told. You understand?"

This was her own private crisis. She could not inflict pain on Paul when so many lives and such huge stakes depended on him. She had seen him cry at Baby Paul's birth, and she knew the volcano of passion waiting to erupt. He might do anything in his agony: move heaven and earth, throw away the war. She must bear the blame for that greed for her husband that blinded her for a spasm of time to her responsibilities. She was saddled with them now. With a vengeance!

"We'll organize a search," Jacob said. Hesitantly, almost angrily, she said he must do what he could now but she warned him to leave when the time came. Like Paul, he had a greater responsibility to many.

She drew strength from the askaris. She was a soldier's wife, too. You squatted in the midst of battle to deliver your sons. You died by your own hand if your man was killed. You fed him on the battlefield and comforted him under fire if he was in pain. You bore and carried the *totos*, and the other *bibis* took care of your own *totos* if the hazards of war took your man and yourself away.

Jacob and his group left at dawn, astonished by her stoicism, satisfied that everything was being done to discover Baby Paul's fate. She swore Jacob and the Looff girls to secrecy. There were so many reassuring possibilities. Perhaps Skaramunga had fallen asleep in the bush with the infant. She would not admit she was clutching at straws. She wanted Paul to do what he had to do. She would do what a soldier's wife should do. She felt utterly lost, but outwardly she was cool and composed. She did not fool the *bibis*, though, who closed their ranks about her and never left her alone.

36

A NAVAL GUN poked its muzzle out of the thick vines of the rain forest. The gun was a long way from the *Koenigsberg*, whose captain, Max Looff, had nursed it up the recaptured Northern Railway to this unlikely place called Store, below Kilimanjaro. The gun could fire 31-pound shells from a 40-caliber barrel, twice as long as a man is tall, with a caliber of 105 mm, or 4.1 inches. From the top of the mountain, the gun would bring Smuts's armies within German firing range. But Max Looff was damned if he knew how to lug the gun up there.

He had come to Store because it appeared, from captured English orders, to be an important position. What Max did not know was that the English were going by an old map left by Theodore Roosevelt years earlier. Roosevelt on safari had scratched his head over an empty place on his generally blank map and recalled that the single feature in this region was an abandoned Arab store. His English hosts printed copies, and it became the only map for military purposes offering any detailed information, including the cross over which Roosevelt had painstakingly lettered STORE.

To this desolate spot came Paul. With him was Skaramunga.

"Your gun bearer," said Max, "didn't he carry a monkey around with him? Your eyes and ears—?"

"The monkey was left behind," said Paul carelessly. "I decided to bring Skaramunga at the last minute, and he was afraid the monkey would get sick from the change in altitude and sudden damp." He turned quickly to the military situation.

"It looks like a split between Smuts and Hagen could help us." Paul unfolded English military dispatches decoded by the new wireless unit at Laager-300 S. "You haven't seen our ABC operation, of course. Short for Aerated Bread Company. They make Christmas puddings for English soldiers."

Max Looff stared at Paul, who laughed.

"We've been getting wireless valves smuggled out from England inside the puddings. Thanks to Lanni. She made the Zionist contacts. I know what you think, Max, but nevertheless I've got three Jewish boys from the London slums who are experts in the wireless field. It's not as crazy as it sounds. We took ABC as the code name for patching field intelligence into monitored English wireless traffic."

"How can Jews get in here when we can't get out?" demanded Max Looff, glowering.

"Ship to South Africa, no problem, then underground to Handeni. That's where I located Laager-260 S, on the coastal plain opposite the big English army transmitters on Zanzibar." To get the sea captain's mind off Zionism, Paul plunged into a review of his plans. "Your nieces are coming by train," he concluded. "With them will be Chuck Truman and the hydroplane. Ersatz Etrich has modified it for launching from a flatcar. What's the matter, Max?"

"Just a small prayer of thanks. I couldn't bear to think of that dreadful little professor pawing Ada."

"Ah—"

Max Looff grinned sheepishly. "I must have been sick in mind as well as body, the way I chastised the poor girl. She wrote me a remarkable letter. Took the blame."

"Have you replied?"

Max shook his head. "I'm no great shakes as a letter writer. And how in hell do you write to the Governor's wife asking forgiveness and—and—"

"Saying you love her?"

"Well, you know—" Max ran a finger around the inside of his mildewed cap. "I can't get her out of my mind. I've asked everyone who ever knew her to tell me snippets, good or bad. It's an obsession. She's been a wild one, but what's a woman of spirit to do, married to that oaf?"

"Write her," Paul said decisively. "I'll see she gets it, and no nonsense with messengers either."

Skaramunga interrupted them. "Our people have seen the Mzungu Mkubwa general they call Buffalo Prick."

"Smuts!"

"Riding alone," said Skaramunga.

———

Smuts spurred his pony forward and vanished into the sodden blanket of cloud rolling off Kilimanjaro. He knew Paul had taken up a position behind Store, and he wanted to scout the enemy's forward posts by himself. His aim was to finish the trolley line between the Uganda Railway and German Northern railroads by the time his First Division completed the pincer movement around the mountain. He had been alarmed to see the kaffirs sheltering where fresh earth had been thrown back for the new rail cuttings. The kaffirs feared landslides. Smuts had ordered a resumption of work and waited until he heard again the crack of the overseers' *sjamboks* before he rode on.

Ten minutes later he was below the cloud line. He slipped out of the saddle and tethered the pony in a dip. The rain fell in buckets, with intervals when he could see magnified in the rain-washed air the German-occupied plantation above the shining tracks of their own railroad. He was on a rise, his drab khaki uniform melting into the background of the mountain. The thorn trees and bush provided cover, but he had seen how the troops suffered from this malevolent vegetation, their uniforms slashed to ribbons, cuts festering. A scratch could make a man's arm swell like a balloon. He knew. He'd walked and ridden over more of Africa than any other man.

With the colossal fortress of Kilimanjaro behind him, he could better picture the trap he had prepared. General Jacobus "Japie" Van Deventer was driving down from the dead volcano of Longido, clearing the western flank of the mountain, while Smuts's men swept the eastern side. Smuts meant to attack Paul head on at Store while Van Deventer thundered across the German's path of retreat.

A lot of English officers hated Van Deventer, who spoke to them in Afrikaans and in a muffled croak because of a terrible wound inflicted by English guns in the Boer War. He'd been Smuts's strong right arm against the English that time. Thanks be to God, it was old General Botha, writing as the South African Union's first premier, who'd said, "Make sure Van Deventer keeps a captaincy with you when you fight alongside the English, just in case they turn again!"

Another curtain of rain swept the valley. Slim Jamie Smuts put away the binoculars and turned to find himself staring into the twin barrels of an elephant gun balanced on the shoulder of a black and handled by a scrawny figure who was presumably white under the leathered skin of a face partly concealed by green shades hanging down from a rusty brown helmet.

"*Wie's daar?*"

"Von Lettow. Kommandeur. German East."

"*Magtig!*" Smuts stood as steady as a lump of rock.

Paul studied his man: same age, same build, the mouth hard, eyes of black coal, the beard Mephistophelean. It was said that Smuts had a supernatural effect on his troops and could drive them to superhuman efforts requiring more stamina than the suicidal dash of a brief skirmish.

"You were with me under Botha," said Smuts.

"That is so."

"A sensible fellow, I remember. You've performed well here."

"Thank you," said Paul.

"Why keep up a senseless resistance?"

Paul smiled. It was difficult to believe the man was speaking into both barrels of a gun. "You, sir, are the one who must surrender."

Smuts allowed himself a bleak smile. "You know what I am now?"

"The new commander-in-chief of my enemies," said Paul.

"And very shortly to be your conqueror," retorted Smuts. "Unless you see sense."

Paul spoke softly to Skaramunga, noting as he did so the stiffening of Smuts's features at the spectacle of a kaffir taking a white man's gun.

"Smoke?" asked Paul while Skaramunga took over the elephant gun.

Smuts shook his head.

Paul make himself a cigarette. In total silence he handed it to Skaramunga and rolled himself another. He put away the flat tobacco tin and lit the second cigarette in the manner of a bush-wacker, protecting the flame inside the mouth of the matchbox, cupping it against the rain that had diminished again to a drizzle, hunching his back to the muggy wind. He was glad the peak of his helmet shaded his scarred eyes. He must betray only those in-firmities that might encourage Smuts to blunder: infirmities of spirit rather than of physique. His first instinct had been to take Smuts prisoner. Now, absorbing the man's personality, he remembered things Kate had said about Smuts that would make the Boer more useful if he went free. It was a bit of luck that he'd made Skaramunga bring the elephant gun. It was a twin-barreled Charles Lancaster .475, purchased in England originally by Selous, the big-game hunter, and just recently captured. It lent Paul a sporting air. It suggested an unprofessional game-playing approach to war. He puffed on his cigarette and then held it up so Skaramunga could light his own from the glowing tip. Smuts's disapproval was tangible.

"I suppose," said Paul conversationally, "I should take you prisoner. It's very careless behavior, roaming unprotected ahead of your men."

"I wouldn't count on it," said Smuts. "God sees all."

"I'm sure you're unprotected in every mortal sense. This territory's well covered by *my* men because it's theirs." Paul glanced at Skaramunga. "He'd know if you came accompanied."

"A dangerous game." Smuts made a gesture of impatience. "Now, if you'll excuse me—"

At once Skaramunga threw down the cigarette and raised the gun.

"Is this"—Smuts choked on the next word—"threatening me?" He moved forward as if Skaramunga had ceased to exist.

Paul drew his revolver. "You'll stay a while, General."

Smuts walked so that his chest came up hard against the gun. Paul had to admire the man while despising both his arrogance and his foolhardiness. Skaramunga could blow the idiot into a thousand pieces.

Smuts examined the revolver in Paul's hand and evidently decided it had a validity denied the gun in a black man's arms.

"I trust," said Smuts, "this is all a joke?"

"No, sir!" Paul's face hardened.

"There must be chivalry, even in war, man."

"Chivalry between commanders is called cowardice at the level of the askari," said Paul.

"Chivalry's not for kaffirs."

Paul clamped his mouth shut.

"I had," said Smuts, "an admiration for your skill in battle. I was not prepared to meet a scoundrel. This is a white man's war. Have you no concern for the future of Africa? God will punish you for arming the kaffirs. Think, man."

Paul thought and watched and listened. Then he said, "You are free to go on condition—"

"I never accept conditions!" Smuts pressed uselessly against the elephant gun. "You'll pay for this."

"No doubt. Now, your word, please, General Smuts, as an officer and gentleman, you won't report this encounter in any way. I make no other condition."

"My word as an officer and a gentleman?" Smuts's face darkened, but there was an undertone of flattered ego, for Paul had injected a touch of Prussian hauteur. "You have it."

But when Paul held out his hand, Smuts ignored it.

Max Looff was thunderstruck when Paul reported this meeting. "But why, Paul? Why let the devil go?"

"Because he's not the devil. He's a fool. Too proud to learn. Careless of his own life, so he'll squander the lives of others. Contemptuous of blacks, so he's doomed to be defeated by them. If I'd kept him prisoner, Max, the English might have put in his place a wiser man. Smuts thinks I'm a nigger-loving nuisance, a freebooter, a landlubber version of you, the pirate, easily wiped out. Now how on God's earth could I make a better enemy?"

This exchange was overheard by the seaman-diver Innocence, whose face darkened with emotion. Innocence had included a Chagga girl in the operation, a strong fine-featured young woman who was breastfeeding an infant. Paul guessed the father was Innocence. She came from the flourishing Kilimanjaro world of petty chiefdoms dating from Ptolemy and the second century B.C. The girl had gone with Innocence on one of his long patrols up the mountain into Chaggaland. Her father was the former Chief of Moshi, and at this season he would be conducting a ritual sacrifice to the spirits of the dead in accordance with Chagga belief. Word must have been carried back to the enemy. The patrol had been ambushed on its way home, only a few hours' march from Store.

Innocence and some of his men had broken out and had this morning marched into camp for help. Emboldened by what he had just heard, Innocence pleaded to go back with more men to rescue his *bibi* and child. Paul felt trapped by his own earlier words to Looff and said, "I'll go back with you. But don't hope for much."

The scene of ambush was a small crater formed when the molten core of a volcano subsided into the earth and the steep sides fell inward. They stood on the lip of the bowl, in a forest of African olives with silver gray-green shimmering leaves. Through Looff's telescope Paul saw five askaris sheltering in shallow trenches around a patch of dense bush where the woman must be lying with the child. He shut the telescope with a snap. "There's nothing we can do."

Innocence swallowed. "Then let me go—"

"No!" Paul drew back from a shaft of sunlight that penetrated the forest and painted the hoary twisted tree trunks a soft gold. He was never more conscious of the life around him and the life soon to be ended in the trenches below. "The child and your *bibi* are being used as bait."

Innocence leaned for support against a broad-backed boulder where leaves of wild cucumber rambled flat across granite. He was aware of cool shadows and deep humus smells, the ring of unseen birds, the movement of richly cloaked colobus monkeys in thick foliage. Gold-backed weavers swayed from long stalks of purple amaranth. The rank grass at his feet was inset with blue spiderwort and crimson hibiscus. Life never tasted so sweet or promised such hope. He stared again into the crater. No matter how hard he looked, he saw no sign of the enemy and death.

Paul, watching him, said angrily, "My men are worthless to me, trapped down there for the sake of your woman."

"All are wounded," said Innocence. He moved away. Paul's hand spun him around to face a drawn revolver.

"Any other man I would shoot on the spot for this," said Paul. "You're lucky I have a child of my own—"

A burst of gunfire echoed around the crater. Bushbucks raised their carved heads. An elephant trumpeted. Paul relaxed his grip on Innocence and pointed silently to where the English rose out of hiding behind another fusillade directed at the ambushed force. "They were there all the time," said Paul.

Innocence stared. His patrol had been encircled so well that he could have walked into the trap without knowing. Along the wooded edge of the crater, the buffalo began to run. Soon hundreds thundered under the walls, raising immense clouds of red dust that mercifully obscured the slaughter inside.

Max Looff had waited impatiently for the strange freight train toiling up to Store. He had seen his ship methodically destroyed. He had fashioned a cross from a *Koenigsberg* steampipe, and on a steelplate plaque he had recorded the names of his thirty-two dead crew members with the legend "*Beim Untergang S.M.S.* Koenigsberg *am 11.7.15 gefallen.*" He had arranged for a hundred badly injured seamen to be carried into Dar es Salaam, and finally he had wrapped up the *Koenigsberg* standard with the resolve that someday he would get his revenge under that battle-scarred flag. He was a long way from the sea now, but for the first time in a long while he was enjoying himself. At last he had some prospect of hitting back.

His dislike of Ersatz Etrich was forgotten in his admiration for what the Austrian designer had done with the hydroplane. It made an odd sight when the train finally arrived. The 720-pound biplane was tethered to a freight car, its wings folded like a bat. The propeller blades were sheathed in buffalo hide, regularly splashed with water to keep the blades rigid in a climate where propellers became dangerously warped. Homemade skis replaced the floats. Etrich had designed a simple booster for the hundred-horsepower engine that was normally cooled by the pilot manipulating a valve, the pressure of air being sufficient only at sea level. The scorching heat shriveled the rubber tubing, melted the horse glue, and peeled away the fabric, and Etrich had trained a black maintenance crew to protect and repair the frame under constantly replaced sun mats of woven palm leaf.

Max Looff was disappointed by the muted greetings of his nieces. He questioned them about Ada. They answered mechanically, not understanding his concern for the Governor's wife, and then Celeste burst out, "Did we just see the Kommandeur's gun bearer?"

"Skaramunga? Yes." It was Paul who answered.

The girls looked at each other doubtfully. Then Elsa made up her mind. "Your wife made us swear to say nothing, but this alters things."

Jacob, supervising the camouflage of the wagons before the morning sun rose much higher, was out of earshot. He saw Paul turn and beckon. He knew from Paul's face that the girls had told him, and he came running.

"Don't blame the girls!" said Paul when Jacob turned to them in fury. "They did right. Look, Skaramunga's here. He's said nothing about the child—"

With an almost nauseating sense of unreality, Jacob recognized Skaramunga for the first time, standing at a distance. Then he felt Paul shaking him by the shoulders. "Before I call him, what was Skaramunga's part in this?"

"Nothing we know for sure. The baby's nurse thought he had the child, that was all."

"That was all!" echoed Paul. "You could have learned, just by asking, that Skaramunga was with me."

They questioned Skaramunga. He could only say, over and over, "*Toto* was given to the new *bibi*." Nobody knew who this new black nurse could be. Skaramunga's innocence was clear from the devastation in his face.

The rain that morning fell with dreadful monotony. Paul took counsel under the camouflage nets spread over the hydroplane. "The baby's been lost five days," he said to Jacob. "Kate was in charge, you say, with the calm competence I would expect. By now she must know one way or another if the child is safe. By now there's nothing I can do."

"You could comfort Kate," said Jacob.

"She would hate me for throwing away this mission. It was her idea to humble Smuts, infuriate him into committing more armies. I've got him by the tail, and I'd be a fool to let him go."

The cold decision disappointed Jacob, though he knew it was irrational to react this way. They'd all faced harsh choices, resolving each dilemma in favor of prosecuting the war. Jacob, watching Max Looff, recalled how he himself had virtually forced Ada to give up her lover to preserve the secret of the ISRAEL file. He wondered, however, if any victory was worth this price.

Nobody commented when Skaramunga left to trek back to Laager-500 WSW. Nobody knew if Paul had sent him or if the gun bearer had different priorities from his Kommandeur.

Celeste and Elsa stood politely in schoolgirl postures while Chuck Truman interrogated them. His remodeled hydroplane spread its wings over them so that the trio seemed to stand inside shower curtains while the rain fell around them.

"Nobody knows why elephants migrate," Celeste repeated. "They go an awfully long way, but I don't think it's only for food. They come up the slopes of the mountain here for the berries of the *mukaita* tree in February but move down again after the rains start and when the mosquitoes and flies get so bad. The elephant flies are the worst, like bees, only dark gray. They give awful stings in fleshy parts and up the poor dears' trunks. When the grass gets really wet and the rains have flooded everything, the elephant fly makes them migrate downhill again."

"And always the same route?" inquired Chuck.

"Always."

Chuck held up a map, folded in the new fashion adopted by aviators for use in the windblown cockpit. "Here's the projected advance of the English. Can you see where the migration path lies?"

Celeste gazed helplessly at an oblong of almost blank chart. "There's not much to go by, is there? I suppose this is us." She traced a doubtful finger over the area. "These red arrows are the English, then? My guess is you'd find elephants moving across these lower hills."

Elsa, peering over her shoulder, made small noises of agreement. Then she asked Chuck, "Can you see much on the ground when you're flying?"

"A great deal when you know what to look for."

"Then look for mangled timber. When elephants have been feeding it looks like a battlefield."

"Wouldn't elephants themselves stand out?" asked Chuck.

"Elephants are impossible to pick out sometimes," said Elsa.

"But they'll be moving in hundreds," put in Celeste.

Chuck regarded her thoughtfully. He started to say something and then thought better of it as Jacob ducked out of the rain.

"A mad scheme," said Jacob.

"What is?" Celeste asked swiftly, almost protectively. "Elephants?"

Jacob looked blank. "No." He shifted his gaze to Chuck. "We're not into some other lunatic plan as well, I hope."

"Just chattering," said Chuck. "Where's the *Koenigsberg* standard?"

"Max was sending it up with a flag bearer. You're surely not going to try, in this weather?"

Chuck laughed, partly because the two girls were quivering with curiosity. He said to them, "Your Uncle Max is putting his warship's flag on top of Kilimanjaro for the Kaiser. I'm flying it up." He hesitated and looked again at Celeste.

"You're wondering about flying *me* up there, too, aren't you?" asked Celeste.

"Not with the flag. I'll need someone to drop it—could be dangerous. No, I had another idea for later. It'll keep."

Elsa said, "It will be a great honor to have the flag flying for the Emperor, but poor Tom up there would much rather have Uncle Max's gun, I'm sure."

"Which is another crazy enterprise," grumbled Jacob. "It took four hundred porters to haul one of those four-inchers on a gun carriage from the railway up to the ridge."

"Elephants!" explained Elsa. She was excited. "Daddy brought in work elephants from the Congo."

"I didn't think African elephants could be tamed," said Chuck.

"Lots of people think that. It's not entirely true. They're more trouble than Indian elephants. King Leopold started experiments with them in the Congo. We bought one pair. Later the Congo station sent us another pair because we'd done so well with them. They're probably still on our land. Old Juma and the hands would be still working them, I'm certain."

Once the idea took root, Elsa was impatient to get Paul's approval. Hector Looff's land was still under cultivation. His experimental game park continued to run itself; the passage of armies had created surprisingly little disturbance in the routine. It would take Elsa a day to ride through English lines, check, and return. It might require a week to move the Looff elephants, if they were still tractable, to where they could be harnessed to the naval gun.

Benedict was one of the African elephants captured and trained. He was eighteen years old now and stood eleven feet six inches at the shoulder. He weighed seven tons. He was what is called a "one-hundred-pounder," the weight of just one of his wicked tusks, now blunted. With his three sisters, he had spent a third of his life on the Looff plantation. He was tolerant of most humans, friendly to the Turkanas brought down from the north to work with him, and he had been devoted to Elsa.

Weeks ago he had sensed the approaching rains, heralded by the descending clouds of locusts, storks flapping across the foothills, and the early ripening of fruit on the *umganu* tree. Elephants would travel great distances to eat the fruit and became mildly drunk on it. This season there was nothing to stop Benedict from following the herds of wild elephants toward the lower plains in search of fresh maize, sugarcane, and mangos, salt pans, and fresh young coconuts that an elephant could open by delicate pressure of the forefeet. This past winter had made few demands upon his skills. His stomach made a deep rumbling sound that his original Belgian keepers called by the picturesque word *borborygmus*, signifying the healthy bubbling of digestive juices.

Benedict brought his large ears forward when Siam, the eldest of the three females, rapped the ground with the tip of her trunk. Each rap released a bubble of air from the trunk. The noise was like a sheet of tin rapidly doubled back and forth. Benedict recognized the signal as one of pleased excitement and he moved in her direction. From the surrounding forest, the sisters, Tomasina and Marlene, advanced with the same confident dignity.

They were all restless. Once the rains had broken, their instinct was to join the migrations across central and east Africa. They were held in check by Juma Gitan, the head driver who had first put the elephants to work. Juma had continued to work the beasts at hauling fresh-cut timber, but this was a joyless occupation on an estate deprived of its sense of direction. Juma had hung on, loyal to his master's final instructions. Today he had been rewarded by the sight of Looff's daughter Elsa riding into the plantation's cluster of buildings. When she told him what was wanted, Juma laughed and rapped his narrow skull with his fist. He had always been a merry little man.

Siam was first to reach out her trunk and sense Elsa's being. The gesture was more than one of affection. The trunk had orifices at the tip for smell. Delicate hairs reported the texture and shape and tem-

perature of anything the trunk touched. The trunk told Siam more
than her eyes; like all elephants, she had severely limited vision. But
to Elsa, fondling the great beast's "hand," those eyes appeared full of
gentle wisdom, an impression accentuated by the presence of the
elephant's third eyelid that moves across the eyeball from side to side
between the long curling lashes of the upper and lower lids. For Elsa,
these eye movements by her old friend seemed to communicate great
thoughts. It was a relief to find the four elephants in a friendly, indeed
a loving, mood. They stood in an admiring circle, each in turn extending a trunk and squeaking happily.

The English advance had again been thwarted by the weather. Using
faulty maps, ignoring Hagen's advice, the commanders moved along
a narrow strip of land between two foaming rivers. When the maps
were drawn, the rivers had been dried gullies. Now they were raging
torrents and the land between was a quagmire. Troops dug in wherever they were, using bayonets and knives and hands in lieu of the
trenching tools nobody had thought would be needed. The reports
of scouts and native agents were sifted by Hagen and the sum-
maries passed on to his single loyal supporter, General Forget-Me-
Not Gaunt.

Gaunt was studying a telegram from General Van Deventer: " . . .
seven hundred in hospital, three hundred in convalescent camp with
little hope of recovery. . . . Empty lorries only way of evacuating
our sick but ground impassable. . . . Lack of strengthening foods
such as bacon, jam, cheese, milk, oatmeal, et cetera causing great
debilitation. . . . Infantry arriving without blankets. . . . Shortages
of boots, soap, clothing because of interrupted supply lines. If no transport can come forward, if immediate steps not taken, situation will
become worse . . . animals weak . . . arrangements will collapse."

So the great western sweep around Kilimanjaro by mountain man
Van Deventer had bogged down, too. Gaunt turned to Hagen's reports.

"Who is this Bwana Unguja?"

Hagen said hastily, "The natives call him that. Mr. Zanzibar. Captain of the *Koenigsberg*. They've a word for that, too—*manowari*.
They remember the *Pegasus* was sunk at Zanzibar by Captain Looff."

"So the man who destroyed the *Pegasus* is here, eh? We're bringing
up the *Pegasus*'s guns, I suppose you know; salvaged 'em, got 'em as
far as the railhead here."

"I didn't know," said Hagen slowly. "It's precisely what an intelligence chief is expected to know, but those bloody South African

bastards, forgive the expression, hold back this kind of information. Since Smuts took charge, you'd think I was the enemy."

"You were, not long ago," said Gaunt.

The first gleam of sun brought Chuck Truman down to the railway siding where the hydroplane waited with wings folded. The Looff girls had nicknamed it the Stinkpot because of the fumes released when the pot-shaped engine was tested. The name had stuck.

"Is Jacob going with you in the Stinkpot?" asked Max Looff. "I've grown fond of the old man despite his Zionist mania. Don't you have someone more expendable?"

"No," said Jacob, ducking around the tail. He had been fussing with the hydroplane since just before dawn, when he could no longer hear rain. "With that wooden foot"—he nodded at Chuck—"it's as well to have me handy. We play on the rudder pedals like a piano duet."

Max shook his head in bafflement. "If your Zionist cause rests on your shoulders, how can you jeopardize it for this trivial gesture?"

"It's not trivial. You lost your ship. Now its standard will fly from the top of Africa, proclaiming the name of the *Koenigsberg* where the first King of Prussia was crowned. The Kaiser is cocking a snoot when that flag flies up there. I wouldn't call that trivial!"

"Empty symbols," said Max Looff, but he was secretly flattered. After all, it was his flag.

The hydroplane's flatcar had been shunted onto the main line. Chuck checked the wind. There would be less crosswind if the locomotive pulled in a southerly direction. Since this was downhill, there was a good chance of gaining flying speed before the porters chopped the ropes holding down the Stinkpot. "The most important thing," he told Etrich, "is to cut those ropes at exactly the same moment. I don't want to cartwheel."

"Yes, yes!" The little designer scurried around the flatcar, adjusting here, loosening there. History was being made. Flight from a moving platform. Nothing must mar a page with his name on it.

A distant rumble of guns reminded them that a lift in the weather was benefiting the enemy, too.

At 0720 hours on Monday, April 3, 1916, a diminutive locomotive hurtled along a straight stretch of the German Northern Railway between two points just south of Moshi and after attaining a speed of fifty miles an hour released a Sopwith hydroplane that seemed to bound into the sky and was quickly lost to sight in shrouds of mist and cloud blowing off Kilimanjaro.

"Imagine, a little old Jewish rabbi planting the German eagle on that mountain," Max Looff said to Paul. "I still can't fathom his reasons."

"Jacob's always had a premonition he'd be killed campaigning with me," replied Paul. "He talked it over with Chuck Truman. Should he save himself for the larger task? He concluded it was arrogant to suppose Israel couldn't be born without him. And there'd always be a nagging doubt about his personal courage. It's not easy to be a Jew, Max, and hear yourself labeled a coward. You know the things we said as kids."

"I never really thought about it."

"Perhaps I wouldn't have either if it hadn't been for Rachel."

"And Kate?"

"Yes, and Kate. Cross your fingers for her brother, Max, and for Jacob."

Where the new English railroad petered out, English soldiers hauled themselves wearily out of waterlogged trenches. Smuts discoursed upon the inadequacies of his opponent, who treated the war as a game. It was not an image Smuts would project back to England, where Paul's reputation as a military magician, a superman, would enhance Smuts's expected victory.

Hagen, all but ignored, made mental notes. The First Division was making no headway. The Second Division under Van Deventer seemed to be lost in the bogs. He seemed dense and slow to many of the English commanders, but when he made a decision, it was final and then he moved like lightning. The trouble was Smuts wanted Van Deventer to complete the pincer movement around Kilimanjaro but begrudged him any touch of fame. Smuts would never admit it, but so long as his own troops were stuck, he wouldn't want Van Deventer to advance.

Hagen had his binoculars focused upon a long-tailed bird of prey circling on motionless wings above the crags. He recognized the white head enriched by distinct black stripes that continued forward into black beardlike tufts under a fierce bill. This was the lammergeier, very large, soaring on great wings, sharp-eyed and tireless.

Hagen shifted to a spiral of vultures, each bird stacked at a different level, floating on thermals rising from the mountain floor. They seemed to communicate in some unknown fashion, for he had seen them rise from a carcass and soar effortlessly into a flight pattern designed to mislead an intruder and draw a rival predator away from the carrion. Sometimes a vulture, invisible to the naked eye, would plummet on a new kill and then the rest would appear out of nowhere and take up their station.

Hagen froze. Between patches of cloud, an airplane was unmistakably laboring up the side of the mountain. There was a brief glimpse of shining wet wings, sun bouncing off a whirring prop, and then Hagen spotted an ornate black cross painted on the large tail, though the machine was most certainly an English Sopwith.

He turned expectantly to Smuts and his gaggle of generals. They were still deep in contemplation of the unfolding of their universe, and Hagen knew before he spoke what little chance he had of disturbing their meditations.

"German aeroplane, sir." Hagen lifted an arm dramatically. "The Hun, sir, is flying overhead."

Smuts turned, his pointed red beard jutting angrily. "Why aren't you with your Bromo kaffirs, Hagen?"

The generals chuckled. Bromo was the brand name of the English army's toilet paper. Smuts had poured scorn on Hagen's intelligence operations, "the Dirty Paper Method" of recovering latrine paper taken from official orders.

Hagen said in a deadly voice, "General, an enemy machine is flying over our lines."

"The enemy is not in possession of aerial weapons," said Smuts.

"Except the navy's stolen hydroplane!" declared Hagen with sudden realization. He appealed to Smuts's companions. "Did nobody see that machine?" He looked for some sign of intelligence in their faces, but they were as empty as the sky where the sound of the engine had merged with the sigh of the wind.

"Probably a common crane," said Smuts, dismissing his intelligence chief for the bird watcher he really was. The generals resumed their weighty murmurations.

Hagen retreated to a wagon up to its axles in mud. He took out his diary. Under a note on the Kilimanjaro long-tailed sunbird, he wrote savagely: "I thought I saw an aeroplane / Above the Taveta plain / I looked again and saw it was / A red-knobbed Smutsian crane." A man had to keep his sanity somehow.

The big German Maltese crosses were sighted by Tom von Prinz before anyone had a chance to fire. His post was dug into the cliff face like an eagle's nest. The caves betrayed no sign of occupation. His position was impregnable except from the air, and his men were under standing orders to hold their fire rather than give themselves away.

"It's the American!" shouted Prinz, watching through binoculars.

Magdalene, who had taken over the duties of a quartermaster since joining her husband on the mountain peak, took the glasses from him. "Kate's brother! And the old Jew is with him. What if they try to land?"

"Impossible," said Kurt Wahle, standing on the lip of the cave. "No, they're trying to drop something."

Wahle craned his neck to watch the lowest cave, whose mouth was covered with slashed undergrowth. Down there, the American Frontiersman was still kept alive. Why Prinz had not killed him, after declaring the man officially dead, Wahle could not imagine. Ace McCurdy was a menace. Each day now he was permitted to share the evening meal with Prinz. That was Magdalene's doing. Trust a woman! She'd mellowed Prinz to the point of idiocy. But that wasn't the half of it. For some reason Prinz refused to acknowledge that this was indeed his illegitimate son, and McCurdy had never uttered a word to suggest that he was aware who Prinz was. Yet Wahle was sure McCurdy knew and planned some terrible act of revenge. It would have been so much easier, and militarily justifiable, to shoot McCurdy out of hand.

The hydroplane crept parallel with the cliff face, heading into the wind. Its relative speed was not more than that of a cantering horse. Jacob was hanging perilously over the side, balancing what looked like a cavalry lance.

Behind goggles Chuck stared directly at Tom von Prinz and nodded vigorously when Prinz gestured. The hydroplane made a wide, flat turn, crabbing into thick mist and out again. Prinz was shouting to the pickets on the adjoining ridge where the bush had been cleared to give a wide arc of fire. It was a bare patch of black lava with a sheer drop on either side. An askari unrolled a light gray blanket and weighed it down with rocks. It made a sharply defined marker in the dense mass of detritus scattered down the mountainside. The plane came hiccuping out of the mist again, but Chuck had misjudged and had to bank away sharply. The watchers could almost touch the wing tips. He was flying close to the point of stall, and the sudden steep turn required him to pick up speed quickly by dropping the nose. As the machine fell away, they all saw the pilot pointing to the marker and Jacob leaning dangerously across a wing root to get a good look.

The underbrush covering the lower cave parted and Ace McCurdy's old-young face squinted out. An armed guard was posted nearby, but supervision had become progressively lax. McCurdy, every askari knew, was on friendly terms with the commander. McCurdy felt the wind against his cheek. At this time of day, the wind picked up along the eastern ridge from the north. His pulse quickened. He was a train robber who had learned to be nimble on the tops of rushing carriages, who had learned to leap from coach to coach by judging the pressure of wind and the relative motion of flat moving surfaces. He saw how the Sopwith's homemade skids scraped the rock wall each time the pilot made a pass, and he decided to jump and hang on to one skid on the next pass.

It had taken Chuck a long time to climb to this height, consuming extra fuel and surely alerting the English. He would not get a second chance to fly up here. He was afraid of losing sight of Prinz in the flying mist and rain. When the marker caught his eye, he tightened his turn and judged by the shudder of the machine how far he dared push it. If he nosed into the wind, his speed dropped to nearly zero relative to the mountain face.

The noise of the straining engine made speech impossible for the watching garrison. Magdalene glanced down and saw the back of McCurdy's head protruding. She wanted to shout that he would be wiser to stand flat against the rock. Ever since she had arrived, she had hoped to bring him openly to recognize his father. Tom had declared him dead, and she shuddered to think that he might have put the word into action. Instead, Tom had kept the young man confined like an animal to the cave until she had persuaded him to get to know McCurdy better. The barriers first had to be broken down between the commander and the prisoner; eventually, Magdalene hoped, they would acknowledge each other as father and son.

The marker vanished out of Chuck's vision again, and he banked steeply into the boiling mist. When he found the ridge again, he was approaching the marker at a bad angle. Beyond was another outcrop, higher, razor-backed. He dared not take his eyes from the sheer wall of rock. He shouted "Now!" and punched Jacob in the arm, then flew over the marker at a crawl. In the next instant, with the rock face suddenly rushing up to meet him, he wrenched the plane into a tight turn. He felt the craft dip and lift, and he supposed this was Jacob dropping the *Koenigsberg* standard. He felt the skids bump against rock, and he hauled on the control yoke as if physically holding the machine back from mushing into the mountain. The air striking the side of his face told him he was in a sideslip, and he let the nose drop and maneuvered into a shallow dive away from the Kaiser Wilhelm Spitze and into the swirling dark mists below.

Prinz stood with an arm around Magdalene as the Sopwith turned away. They saw the lance fall and the slipstream tear away the wrappings so the flag unfurled and the imperial eagle lay there, a strange design in the harsh patterns of nature. The two sentries on the ledge ran forward and pinned the standard down. But a second bundle hurtled among them.

Magdalene was first to realize it was Jacob, a scarecrow figure, rags fluttering. He struck the side of the ledge, balanced there briefly, and then cascaded into the invisible depths of the mist-shrouded ravine.

McCurdy had jumped to grab one of the hydroplane skids as it sailed slowly by. He glimpsed Jacob's body plunging past him. From the way the machine and he were dropping, he thought it must have been the pilot. McCurdy dangled, his entire weight suspended from the one hand firmly clawed to the creaking skid. The other hand was jammed between a brace and the place on the skid where it had jarred loose from its lashings. Each time his body swayed under the pressure of rushing air, the gap widened, but before he could pull his fingers clear, his weight swung like a pendulum back again and closed the broken joint.

McCurdy's knowledge of aviation was nonexistent. All he knew was that the machine seemed to be out of control. If he squinted to his left, he saw jagged shards of rock rush in and out of the mountain vapors. Then, just as the sharp descent seemed as hopeless as a hangman's drop, he sensed a reprieve. The Sopwith flattened out and the mist thinned. He looked down and saw the top of a rain forest sloping under his feet. The broken spar escaped from part of the leather lashings and freed the trapped hand. Without a second thought, McCurdy let go and plummeted, eyes tight shut, into the topmost branches of a tree thickly laced with vines to break his fall.

"It was tremendously bumpy," Chuck reported to Paul. "There was a lot of negative gravity. Jacob must have undone the safety harness to make sure of hitting the marker. The way Prinz's men were running, I reckon Jacob bounced off the ledge and down another five hundred feet. He couldn't have had much chance."

"Well," Paul spoke the single word with flat finality, "you'd better record the details as best you can for his family. The machine's all right?"

"Broke a skid landing. Nothing that can't be fixed."

"Observe anything?"

"English troops, still bogged down. The Looff girls were right. There must be hundreds of elephants moving through the valleys." Chuck glanced at Elsa, who was making herself useful in the plantation office Paul had taken over.

"I'll help you with the reports, Mr. Truman," she said quickly.

After Paul had left, she said, "He's awfully cold-blooded at times like this."

"Paul? Can't afford to be anything else."

"But Jacob was very close to him."

"And to me," Chuck said. He stopped and put a hand on the young girl's shoulder. "I was always telling him not to take chances, he was too important. Now I've killed him—"

Chuck was aware of Elsa's hand creeping into his, and he turned his head away to hide his tears. English pilots were said to go on a drunken binge whenever one of their number was killed. No wonder. You had to be callous to carry on. He knew so much about Jacob's plans, his organization, his hopes. And as for family, Jacob's family was the whole Jewish world, past, present, and future. It really is my family now, thought Chuck Truman.

37

MYLES HAGEN broke all the standards of decency that silenced his fellow officers when he read Smuts's fresh claims of nonexistent victories. He wrote in fury to Winston Churchill: "Our generals and staff planners are gutless, rotting buffoons who sacrifice good soldiers for their own greater glory. One German schoolgirl and some elephants have hauled a naval cannon to the top of the Kaiser's Mountain, scoring in this single act of heroism a mighty psychological victory while Smuts struts and brags."

But Churchill was out of favor. The Germans in Europe had captured Vimy Ridge again. The loss shattered confidence in England's government. Smuts was under pressure to produce a triumph, so he boasted of plans to break out of the Kilimanjaro quagmire at the end of the long spring rains. He spoke in a language understood in London, where the big red arrows on wall maps carried greater authority than Hagen's wild prophecies of doom.

Hagen turned to two men who still believed in him, the cavalry general, Forget-Me-Not Gaunt, and the white hunter, Frederick Courtenay Selous. "In a land where men are not saints," Teddy Roosevelt had written, "Selous is a moral antiseptic." Now sixty-four, he had the hide of a rhinoceros and the stamina of an elephant. When he saw Hagen's blazing eyes and clamped teeth, Selous sent for that other legendary hunter, Pieter Pretorius.

Only another hunter of equal repute among Africans could have reached Pretorius through the grapevine. He had gone to ground after the sinking of the *Koenigsberg*, knowing the Germans were after his blood. Word reached him on May 1, 1916, and within three weeks Pretorius came back to Hagen.

The old elephant hunter lumbered out of the *bundu* without warning and headed straight for Nazareth's, run by a Goanese who had followed the armies of the English empire since time began. Each day for a week, Hagen and Selous had sipped Nazareth's foul coffee and chomped on his rock-hard buns, knowing Pretorius would show up there eventually. His first words were "What's all this about elephants?"

"Elephants aren't the problem," sighed Hagen.

"My information is they buggered up the almighty Smuts's time-table. Some bright spark stampeded 'em with his airyplane."

"A nonexistent aeroplane," said Hagen and described his argument with Smuts. "Aye, but it's true."

"You start a stampede when them animals is migrating," rumbled Pretorius, "you got trouble. They'll run ten miles 'n' more. Bazaar rumors are old man Looff's tame elephants hauled a *Koenigsberg* gun up the mountain."

"True again," confirmed Hagen. "Only Smuts says you can't tame African elephants. Therefore it didn't happen. Same as the aeroplane."

"Hum!" said Pretorius. He was forty-three years old, but he looked eighty after stumbling through the German East bush with two *Koenigsberg* bullets in each leg and shrapnel in shoulder and arm. He was not a large man but he gave that impression. His features were all bunched up in the middle of his face. He had big ears and he wore long baggy trousers. With his small bloodshot eyes and the clothlike loose skin around his odd little legs, he looked like an elephant. On the whole he preferred elephants to humans. He made two exceptions. He respected Selous as a grand master of bush craft, and he thought Hagen a promising young fellow. If Paul hadn't been German, he'd have added Paul von Lettow to the humans who were almost decent enough to be elephants.

"Lettow is making fools of you," said Pretorius after Hagen and Selous had herded him to a corner table. "He's never going to stand and fight. Can't those bloody fools in London see it?"

"They see names on the map," said Selous with exasperation. "They're virgins who squeeze their knees in ecstasy when a termite hill is captured, the honor of the empire saved."

"Paul knows the importance of symbols to those pea brains," said Hagen, watching Pretorius, shrewdly fishing for his interest. "He put the *Koenigsberg* standard on Kilimanjaro."

Pretorius fiddled with a damp match, trying to light his pipe. Nothing indicated his quickening interest except the way his eyes narrowed under the beetle brows. Hagen waited. He knew the real reason Pretorius had gone after the *Koenigsberg*. Years earlier the hunter owned a farm on the edge of the Rufiji. Some fool German official confiscated the land after Pretorius refused to sell it. When the *Koenigsberg* penetrated his private empire, he'd gone after her the way he would pursue a rogue elephant.

"The *Koenigsberg*'s flag, hey?" Pretorius emptied his pockets, full of old pipes. It was said he carried more smoking materials than cartridges. Today was the first time in months he's got his hands on real tobacco again. He tested one battered pipe after another, and he took his time setting the shreds of tobacco alight when he found the cherry-wood bowl he wanted. He puffed a while in tranquil dignity. Then he said courteously, "How did the friggin' flag of that effing battleship get on that bludgering blasted mountain?"

Hagen told him, further describing the mayhem inflicted by hundreds of elephants panicked by the stolen Sopwith.

"And Slim Jamie Smuts thinks he's going to sweep across German East?" said Pretorius. "He should know better."

"He does," said Hagen. "He knows what impresses London. He's sending Van Deventer charging at the head of the South African cavalry to take Buttermilk Hill. You've never heard of it? They have in London. Smuts made sure of that. Magnified a one-horse dump into the caravan crossroads of Arab slave routes. The capture of Buttermilk Hill will be heroic, though Paul won't be there. The London press will elect Smuts the winner before year's end. He'll take his seat in the War Cabinet, and to cover his arse, he'll keep on dispatching troops here. We'll be left in the quicksand, cursed for incompetence, losing good men by the thousands."

"What you need are a couple of white hunters," said Pretorius, his nose poking out of a cloud of tobacco smoke.

"If we hunt, we hunt for big game!" snapped Selous.

"That," said Pretorius, "is what I mean."

Hagen had been shifting the coffee mugs around the table. Nazareth's was empty. The proprietor had been told to make himself scarce. Hagen's men stood guard outside the shack. Inside, the heat was building up. Strips of sticky flypaper hung limp from the soft bark used to tie the crossed poles in the temporary roof. There was a smell of charcoal and animal fat and hot baked earth. Soon the terrible heat would descend, and men who now cursed the rain would fight over the juice in a coconut. Soon men and animals would start to fall again by the hundreds on another wild-goose chase.

"Paul," said Hagen, "is your target, Freddie. And your man, Pieter, is that frigging turncoat Englishman waving the German flag from the top of the mountain."

Pretorius considered. He had seen Selous go after a lion that had broken its back. While the vultures perched in the fever trees and the hyenas crept closer, the lion raised its maned head. In its tortured eyes, Selous had read an appeal to put a bullet in its ear. Death with dignity. No killing for the mere fun of it.

Pretorius himself shot elephants for gain, but he never wasted his powder. He went after elephants who squashed flat the native *shambas* in their search for maize and plantain stems and mangoes. Like Selous, he refused to surrender the animals he shot to the souvenir hunters who wanted the elephant's feet for umbrella stands and the lion's testicles to cure syphilis.

Paul the Kommandeur and Prinz in his fortress were worthy targets. A bullet between Paul's eyes would save the manpower and wealth of a failing empire. A slug in Prinz's brain would accomplish what a dozen violent assaults could never do. Paul and Prinz were doomed anyway, like the broken-backed lion and the toothless elephant. And Pretorius would be rid of the curse of the *Koenigsberg* once he'd torn down its flag.

"I'm worried about Kate," said Major Wolfe to Ada.

The Governor's wife took the remark as one more sign of poor Wolfe's infatuation. They were all concerned about Kate's mental state since the baby had disappeared, of course. The poor girl went about her duties like an automaton. She would listen dully to each new report of another search ending in failure. Ada was aware of Wolfe's anger with Paul for having left his wife to cope with the tragedy alone. In other circumstances Wolfe would have applauded the cold-hearted decision, for he certainly believed a soldier must put duty first. But, thought Ada, the girl has unwittingly turned the poor man's head until he doesn't know he thinks with his heart.

"We're all worried," she said. "My prescription is, keep her busy. Bring her with you to the bicycle 'factory.'"

Wolfe knew better than to ask questions. He had returned to Laager-500 WSW after escorting two more *Koenigsberg* guns from the coast. He was startled to find a remarkable number of askaris on bicycles. It was then Ada told him about the "factory" where Ersatz Etrich was assembling pedal carts, cycles, and bicycle wagons for the next long march ahead. It would have to be destroyed when the laager disbanded. Glad of an excuse to talk with Kate, and knowing she was now qualified as demolitions officer, Major Wolfe told her to join their inspection tour.

They pedaled along a hard-packed clay track. Metallic-blue guinea fowl scampered ahead, doves rose to avoid their spinning wheels. The air was cool under the leopard-mottled fever trees with their frothy umbrellas. The aerial roots of giant fig trees formed cool arches. Gold impalas leaped in graceful arcs across a green meadow.

"Do you want to bring me up to date?" asked Wolfe.

"Why not?" Kate wobbled around an obstruction. "We've put together several hundred pedal vehicles because the livestock's dead or dying. It gives us greater mobility. And if a bicycle's knocked out of action, you just throw it down and walk away. Not like putting a gun to a surplus porter, so badly hurt he's become a burden. Not like shooting a horse."

Her voice was savage and Wolfe put out a hand and lightly touched her arm. "Hold it, Kate. That's not what I mean."

She braked to a stop. "The baby's dead."

"Are you sure what happened?"

She was straddling her cycle. Ada had pedaled on. "I know the baby's dead." She stared through him with eyes that once matched the sky and now seemed slate gray and flat. "Bamboo was always jealous of the baby. While Skaramunga was looking after Baby Paul, the monkey snatched it away and went off into the bush."

"Do you have proof?" insisted Wolfe.

"A mother knows these things" was all she would answer before pushing off again.

They came to an old planter's house of gray stone with a red tin roof. Surrounding it were brilliant flame trees, yellow thorn acacia trees, and lavender-blue jacarandas with skirts of pastel petals. In the center of what had been a lawn was an enormous pile of bicycles.

"Such a pretty industrial site," said Ada when the other two caught up with her. "A pity we can't—"

Kate interrupted sharply, "Is that what you want dynamited? The old shed there and the house?"

"Yes." Ada glanced quickly at Wolfe, who shook his head in warning. "No need to blow up the house."

"Why not?" Kate swung a haversack from her shoulder. "Why not scorch the earth from here to the horizon?"

"She's right," murmured Wolfe. "There's no sense leaving anything to the English."

Kate tested the wind. Beyond the house and the barn, the tinder-dry land stretched to the horizon where the sky was heavy with the rains that had yet to reach here. "Fire this lot," said Kate unemotionally. "The wind's just right."

"For destroying the native *shambas* all the way north," amended Ada.

Kate ignored the protest. She was already laying out her demolition tools—explosives and improvised fuses, some small cans of grease, and packets of wire.

"Are you firing the underbrush?" asked Wolfe. "Now?"

Kate looked up with an expression of contempt. "I said the wind is right. There's no danger to the laager. So why not?"

An hour later a spreading column of black smoke rose above the plain. Major Wolfe, retreating across the shallow river between the condemned house and their camp, had to confess Kate was right. In a few days the river might have dried up, and nobody knew when such an advantageous wind might blow again. He shivered, though, when he saw the leaping flames reflected in Kate's eyes.

NORFORCE! thought Kate. She seemed to be somewhere else. PAMFORCE and GRIMCOL and LINFORCE and SHORTCOL! Musical notes in a symphony of war. Each was an acronym for an enemy force marching from different borders into German East. She had analyzed the ABC intercepts. ROSECOL was the Gold Coast Regiment under Colonel Rose. NIGORG was the Nigerian organization of trackers. PORTCOL was a Portuguese column in training to the south, where England's oldest ally prepared to move out of Portuguese Africa. These armies were little more than names in intelligence reports as yet, but they were coming just as surely as flood and drought.

"Let's go!" shouted Major Wolfe.

She roused herself. Then, in a voice that stunned Wolfe with its bitterness, she said, "I've got the resources to know where the enemy is and what he's planning. The enemy does what Paul wants. But where my baby is concerned—no, for something so tiny, we've no intelligence resources of any kind. So why not, Major Wolfe? Why not let Africa burn?"

Wolfe took her by the shoulders and forced her to face him. Ada, standing on the river bank, watched from a distance.

"Please, Kate. Hold yourself together until Paul gets back."

She gave a small laugh. "Paul's not coming back. Not before we resume the march. Maybe never." Then she sank her face into his shoulder and began to sob.

Skaramunga emerged from the tall elephant grass as the bush fire began to spread. He had been running and walking night and day since leaving Paul, his mind focused on the single necessity of finding Bamboo. The monkey had been left with one of Kornatzki's medicine men, a wizened gnome wearing a necklace of bones and daubs of white lime on his face and naked body.

Near the burning house Skaramunga hesitated, feeling the presence of other humans before he saw the Kommandeur's wife embracing Major Wolfe. There had been a time when Skaramunga resented Kate for usurping his position with Paul, but he had long since forgiven her. The coming of Baby Paul had won him over completely. It was because he feared Bamboo was involved in the baby's disappearance that he had deserted Paul.

He moved along the yellow clay river bank, naked except for a loincloth, his body emaciated, his limbs covered in sores, his hair matted and red with dust. "*Memsabu—*"

Before she had heard him call, Kate was already drawing her pistol. She twisted away from Major Wolfe and had an unobstructed view of the gun bearer. She fired once, hitting Skaramunga in the shoulder so that he spun and fell down the crumbling bank.

On June 18 Smuts marched at the head of his troops into the abandoned laager. There was not a German in sight. Typhoid spread rapidly among Smuts's men, forced to bivouac in the dusty streets because the houses were rat-infested, charred shells.

Smuts blamed the Germans for poisoning the wells and ordered the doctors to simplify their work by classifying the sick under simple labels. Blacks were known as prussic acids, whites as black pissers. The blacks were susceptible to poisoning from poorly cooked maize. Whites got black water fever, which was evident in thick black spurts of urine. Smuts had assumed Africans would be more resistant to disease, and the doctors did not try to tell him he was wrong. Black porters were actually dying from bacillary dysentery at the rate of one man in two.

Smuts's tent was identifiable by the moldy Union Jack hanging limp outside. He was reading Walter Lippmann's *Drift and Mastery* and wrote his wife in South Africa that Lippmann was a remarkable young American of great promise. Smuts did a lot of writing—letters to his family in the belief they would be published in due course, and glowing reports to the War Office. He based the Royal Flying Corps BE2Cs of No. 26 Squadron in nearby fields and wrote enthusiastically of the havoc caused by bombs dropped by hand from these mothlike machines. BE stood for Bleriot Experimental. Smuts omitted to mention the danger to pilots flying planes that had underpowered engines and were unsuited to the climate because their fabric and wood frames were susceptible to termites. He neglected to say Paul had improvised the first 360-degree-turn antiaircraft guns by mounting ancient 1873 Hotchkiss cannons on railway turntables to keep the bombers at bay.

Hagen fired off his own counterpropaganda to London. The South African generals were incompetent gas bags, their official reports amounting to mere flatulence. "Discipline does not exist, bush warfare is not understood, looting is rife, hospitals overflow with men suffering nothing but cold feet. Our English troops are running short of rations, live on wild game they shoot for themselves, and chew sugarcane to assuage their hunger."

Max Looff had moved back to the coast to defend Dar es Salaam. He rolled out an old naval cannon that for years stood outside the cathedral, its breechblock used by a local blacksmith as an anvil. Coconut palms were cut down and the long trunks mounted on wagon wheels to look like artillery pieces. Max had ninety *Koenigsberg* seamen to protect the capital. They sank the dry dock. They opened the taps in the beer kegs at the Schulz-Brauerei. At night they swung searchlights around the sky, bicycled up and down the front with lanterns, and lit dozens of small bonfires in the hillsides. Observing this activity, Rear Admiral Edward Benedict, commanding the English offshore squadron, decided to soften up the defenses with a prolonged bombardment. For hitting the cathedral, the Admiral was excommunicated by the Catholic bishop, who was the only German left in residence.

Major Wolfe and Count Kornatzki led the withdrawal from Fort Tabora, terminating Laager-500 WSW when a force of Congolese under Belgian command came within a day's march. The Congolese were known among the German askaris as yum-yums because of their alleged cannibalism. For this reason no wounded were left behind. Skaramunga was taken out on a litter, attended by Ada, who had supervised his care. Ada had failed to shake Kate out of her murderous trance and supposed Kate would remain in this state until Paul rejoined the main force. According to Wolfe's official version of how Kate wounded Skaramunga, she had mistaken him for an enemy askari.

By mid-September Paul had yielded the Central Railroad. He had lost the whole German coast from British Africa down to Dar es Salaam. But although the English searched diligently, nobody seemed to know where Paul was from one day to another—except Hagen, who got occasional information from Freddie Selous, stalking the biggest quarry of his career as a hunter.

Selous heard that Paul had been walking barefoot to see how well European feet managed without boots. One of the Kommandeur's feet had been badly infected, and he had experimented with papaya wrappings after slicing away the corrupt flesh. The foot, said the reports, was as good as new. "It would need to be," said Selous. "He's heading for the death trap Rufiji."

As the chief of British imperial forces, General Smuts did not relish chasing the Germans through the Rufiji. He wrote his son: "Papa is now going to fight the terrible monster Rufiji who drank so much water his snout is terribly big and his belly full of crocs and hippos."

On hearing that Paul was still separated from his main force, however, Smuts smuggled a seductive offer to Governor Schnee: "Your Excellency must see the end is not far off. The conspicuous bravery and skill of German defense cannot withstand the superior forces under my command. . . . On Colonel von Lettow rests responsibility for imposing terrible ordeals on the noncombatant populations. . . . Please consider if this useless resistance should not cease in a manner honorable to all." He signed in the outrageously insincere style of the period, "Your Excellency's most humble and obedient servant, J. C. Smuts."

Intercepted messages of this nature were now submitted to Kate as a matter of routine, since she was best able to judge their value to intelligence. She burned the letter and spoke of it to nobody. Governor Schnee was at the head of a twelve-kilometer column of civilians trekking steadily south. Behind him came Kate with Major Wolfe's main fighting force, another ten kilometers long. Smuts's latest letter was dated September 30, 1916; Kate calculated it would be two more months before they reached the Rufiji delta. It was already two months since she had last seen Paul.

Wherever Selous fell across Paul's trail, the old white hunter caught new glimpses of his quarry's character. Frau Ilse Engelmann, a planter's wife who had taken refuge at a mission in the central plain, told Selous: "Yes, the Kommandeur took supper with us some weeks ago. He talked about the revolutionary war in China, not this one. After the main course, we got news the English were nearby. We said he'd better leave at once. He laughed and said he'd better finish the meal like a good guest. Then he sent one of his officers forward with a white flag to request the English protect us."

Paul had been conducting a series of raids to delay Smuts's advance. His men helped themselves to English food and ammunition, but in the late autumn a blockade runner, the *Maria von Stettin*, managed to land him a battery of mountain guns, five million rounds of ammunition, and nine thousand four-inch shells for the naval guns.

Selous cursed when he heard this, then laughed at the news of a bag full of Iron Crosses included in the smuggled supplies. He missed the most important news of all, though. The Kaiser had also sent Paul the promise of the Zeppelin.

Early in December, Paul caught up with what had now become Laager-325 SSE, backed up against the treacherous Rufiji, seemingly trapped.

"You've become a buccaneer!" Governor Schnee accused, he being the first dignitary to see Paul entering the camp with his ragged followers. "You've signed no requisition chits in months. You're reported to have forced a district commissioner at gunpoint to ferry you across a river. You steal, burn—"

"Major Wolfe! Where's the Treasury today?" shouted Paul, spotting Wolfe in the gathering crowd.

Wolfe tugged his ear in embarrassment. The Treasury was the

Governor's baby: four tons of meaningless paper currency. "Four hundred porters carried it in," he said finally. "It's been sent down the hoists at Fort Kibata, into cellars we'd earmarked for ammunition lockers."

"Burn it!" ordered Paul.

"Burn it?" Wolfe's jaw dropped.

"Every damn rupee. Eliminate whatever cannot be justified in the Rufiji. Including," added Paul, swinging on the Governor, "fools who get in the way of the war!"

The hour was late, the sky smudged with pinkish mare's tails. A sound like a schoolboy running a stick aimlessly along a park railing disturbed the silence that followed Paul's harsh attack. Everyone recognized the rattle of machine guns, followed by the short-tempered bark of heavy guns.

"Ada!" Again Paul singled someone out from the crowd. "The women's units will go forward immediately."

Ada von Schnee moved away from the Governor's side. "So soon?"

"You heard the guns."

Count Kornatzki said softly, "Max is coming up with his own guns tomorrow. Ada's desperate to see him—"

"I want your group gone by daylight." Paul hesitated. "My wife goes, too."

Kornatzki looked at him as if Paul had gone mad. The missionary-doctor was a skeleton compared with the bearlike figure once familiar to German East's tribal medicine men. His gray beard reached to his waist, and his hair was a red mop of dusty locks. "Kate's ill," he whispered.

"Rations will be six hundred grams of cereal a day, which is more than I can spare. You'll get the commune safe across the Rufiji, Count, while I hold Smuts back until the river floods."

"Your wife is ill!" stated Kornatzki.

"She looks perfectly fit to me," said Paul as Kate walked into sight. "I've heard nothing to the contrary."

"She needs you," said Kornatzki. "Understand, for God's sake, man."

Paul ignored him. He had marched into the laager, ramrod stiff, but clad only in shorts and a shirt. The black eye patch was missing, and the damaged eye was encrusted in red dust matching the color of his matted hair. Behind him were a hundred men so tanned and weathered that they were scarcely distinguishable from black porters.

Paul watched Kate move across the square like a sleepwalker. She

stopped at a distance of some fifty paces, near the edge of the assembled settlers.

"She's not physically sick," said Ada. "But she's never cried since
she shot Skaramunga."

Paul's face tightened. "Divide the laager into three groups, Major
Wolfe. The first group will cross the Rufiji with guides from the
Koenigsberg. Combat troops will prepare to fight at Fort Kibata. The
third lot are to be handed over to the English. When you're done,
I'll call a meeting of unit commanders for later tonight. Now, if you'll
excuse me."

The eyes of everyone there were drawn to Paul's bare feet. He
moved with a fluid heel-and-toe action. He was more like a lean
animal of prey than a middle-aged Prussian soldier.

Wolfe shook himself. There was an appeal on the faces of those
around him, not for Kate and not for the Kommandeur, but for themselves. The deliverance of sick and wounded to the English in emergency was routine. But all knew that Paul this time was getting rid
of useless mouths. There was not an able-bodied man or woman
there who would have exchanged the safety of a prison camp for the
privilege of following the man whose iron self-control seemed to
border on the superhuman.

"He's so blasted indifferent," said Major Wolfe, standing later with
Kornatzki on the sandy shore of the river.

"Or stoical?"

"Indifferent to Kate, I mean."

Kornatzki responded slowly, searching for words: "Paul's afraid for
her. She's more vulnerable to danger with her baby gone. Over a long
period her mental balance could be disturbed to a point of careless-
ness."

"She might kill herself simply by not keeping up her guard?"

Kornatzki looked down. "She can handle a quick blow better, Paul
feels—"

"He feels! How can you know what feelings lie behind that mask?"

"Because he's spoken to me already."

"Ridiculous," muttered Wolfe. "It's ridiculous they don't talk to
each other about a tragedy so personal. Kate, you know, spoke to
me!"

"Oh?"

"She has strange notions. The child's African, belongs to Africa,
doesn't need European-style coddling. I listened to this, and then I

said, 'You don't believe all that stuff.' And she said, 'No, but it's what I have to pretend to believe for Paul's peace of mind. He's vulnerable. An error of judgment could cost him the war, and prolonged brooding will affect his judgment. So let the child become part of the rush of events, over and done quickly.'"

"She said this?" demanded Kornatzki. "To you?"

"It's not different from Paul confiding in you," said Wolfe defensively.

"My boy, there's a wealth of difference."

"What matters is that each behaves like a spartan to spare the other one's feelings."

"Life, to spare the other's life," corrected Kornatzki. "Those two share intensities of emotion denied you and me. Paul could forget the war and become a dedicated lunatic searching for a dead child. If either one gave way, we might as well surrender."

"Perhaps we should. What are we fighting to defend if we reject our best instincts?" Wolfe turned away in disgust and watched the hippos trotting down a grassy slope to the river, their tuba voices honking, cavernous mouths agape, tiny ears twitching, eyes bulging until the great water pigs splashed from sight under the scream of a fish eagle.

Watching the same scene from farther along the river, Paul said to Kate, "Don't consider how to explain our decision. Nobody will understand except perhaps the askaris. They, too, keep their wives and children on condition they're all treated as soldiers and share the risks. No dependent lost on the battlefield is to be saved at the risk of losing a single fighting man. That's the law."

"I've never thought you should break it," said Kate.

"Kornatzki will think you're inhuman." Paul's gaze followed the hippos rising from the water, their flayed skin the same red as the boulders, stained red by the laterite silt. On land hippos sweated bloody-looking secretions for protection from the sun. Red was a defensive device, the martial color of war gods. Paul thought, I have to hide behind the scarlet of the soldier's profession, to protect myself and Kate, too, or I'll turn soft, and not just the child but all of us will be lost.

Later, in the privacy of a patched tent, he said, "Let it all out, *Kätzchen*," and held Kate at last in his arms.

She looked up, dry-eyed. "I've no tears left."

He nodded.

"I want you to win." Her eyes were large and luminous in the gathering twilight.

"We will."

"Tell me why."

He broke away from her and sank onto a rough charpoy bed. "There's hardly a single South African soldier left in the theater. They've been invalided home, *unfit for service!* That means fifty thousand fewer troops killing Germans in Europe. Twenty thousand English troops poleaxed by disease. Sixty thousand enemy mules and horses died during the past three months trying to chase us through tsetse fly country. Hundreds of new Ford box trucks destroyed in our traps. Multitudes of cattle dead when they're supposed to be providing fresh meat for the new armies pouring in, killed because they were driven into diseased territory where we led them."

She sat opposite him, her thin face supported by her hands. "Are you sure of those figures?"

"I memorized them from a letter, reported back. London demanded the recall of the author, a professional writer named Francis Brett Young. He wrote to *The Times*." Paul fumbled inside a shirt pocket. "Here, this is what ABC recovered." He quoted: " 'The ghost of Kilimanjaro, which utterly and unexpectedly dominates the landscape, is now sinking below the horizon as we stumble deeper into Hell. We fight through scrub drawn tight as a fishnet while German rear guards pour shells from the *Koenigsberg*'s guns down from the hills.' The writer is accused of a breach of military security for publishing casualty figures. We're winning, *Kätzchen*, when a man takes the risk of being called a traitor because he knows the authorities are concealing the grim truth."

"What about our own Quentin Pope? He discloses too much information about us," Kate said coldly. "We can no longer afford an American reporter."

"If you believe so, then I'll have Wolfe turn him over with the third group. But you can't accuse Pope of revealing facts embarrassing to Berlin. Berlin's forgotten we exist." Paul reached over and picked up the large unfinished carving on her bed. "You managed to keep this?"

"It managed to keep me sane," replied Kate. Her voice for the first time lost its iciness. "When I thought I must scream in frustration, I held it between my hands and tried to guess what you mean it to become. No, Simba, don't tell me! I'm going to need it a long time yet."

"You understand, I must send you ahead tomorrow?"

"To set an example? Our Kommandeur plays fair, never asks for anything he wouldn't do himself."

"No," said Paul. "Because your Kommandeur might not have the courage by tomorrow to issue such an order again. It was easier an hour ago to commit myself to sending you ahead than it is even now."

They clung to each other all through that night. Neither the name of Baby Paul nor that of Skaramunga crossed their lips.

Celeste Looff arrived in time to join the departure of the first group into the Rufiji.

"I left Uncle Max with the guns a few miles back," she told Kate. "He's got about two thousand porters with him. It's been a long business, pulling those big cannons. We'd have been better off with the elephants."

"Where are the elephants?" Kate asked. What she really wanted to know was the fate of her brother.

"One got hurt after hauling the *Koenigsberg* gun up the Kilimanjaro slope. Juma Gitan, the trainer, stayed with him while Elsa took the other three back to our game farm." Celeste watched the Kommandeur's wife, so self-contained. Had the woman no feelings? "Your brother," she said, trying to shock Kate into some display of emotion, "is in love with Elsa, I think."

"And where is my brother?"

"Chuck was going to fly Elsa out, but the English engulfed our estate. He flew back to the Olduvai lake. Elsa'll be safe. She's self-sufficient and happy among her animals."

"She's only a child!"

"Listen to who's talking!" said Celeste. "You're only three years older."

And, thought Kate sadly, a hundred years older in experience. It had required all her self-control to say goodbye to Paul only a few minutes earlier. There was a limit to the amount of emotion she could exhibit.

Paul dreaded the inevitable question when Max Looff came over the last ridge a few hours after Ada left with the first group. It was difficult to distinguish Max from his crewmen and porters. They had replaced clothing during a five-hundred-kilometer retreat until the only piece of personal kit still hanging on Max's gaunt frame was his tarnished captain's cap with the gold braid turning a horrid green.

Behind him the hump-backed hills resounded to the chant of porters, their dark torsos almost horizontal against the cables hauling the last naval gun, several howitzers, and pieces of mountain artillery. "Are you there?" they called to one another. "We are here! Great is the safari!"

Max was losing no time. "Ada? Where is she?"

"Left already with the Governor."

"God's truth! You knew I was coming in."

"I couldn't delay, Max. If we move fast, we might just trap a substantial number of the enemy."

"Trap them? Trap *them?*" Max Looff threw back his head and laughed. "It's we who are trapped."

"Not so. I'm letting the enemy occupy the fort there. They won't expect us to have heavy guns. I'll allow three weeks for the first group under Major Wolfe to get to the other side of the Rufiji. Then we join them. And like the Israelites, if we're lucky we'll see the waters close behind us."

"And what the devil's on the other side of the Rufiji?"

"The worst of Africa," said Paul.

Part Seven

Beyond the Juju Huts

38

From the war diary of Colonel von Lettow, in the Rufiji, New Year's Day 1917:

We have commenced the retreat into the sewers where the *Koenigsberg* lies rotting. Kate and the first group must be near the other side. The siege of Kibata lasted the three weeks I had predicted. When we broke off the action, the rains fell, and we scurried into the Rufiji delta while the waters rose between us and the enemy. How Captain Looff cursed to find himself back in these pestilential swamps! And how useful his knowledge of them! I regret returning the American newsman, Quentin Pope, to the English. He was sent with other excess human baggage under a white flag to the command headquarters of General Henry de Courcy O'Grady, whose troops I had allowed to occupy the old German fort of Kibata. This was early in December when O'Grady knew nothing about my disposition of men and guns in the surrounding hills. Apparently O'Grady kept Pope and my other voluntary prisoners inside the fort, having assured my truce officers he would dispatch them forthwith to the coast. In consequence, when I began the bombardment of Fort Kibata, I was unknowingly killing some of our own people. I found this out during the Christmas truce, by which time our small force had reduced O'Grady's troops from ten thousand active front-line soldiers and support personnel to two thousand. They still outnumbered us. The day after Christmas, Gold Coasters and Nigerians reinforced the English garrison, and we could not prevent them breaking through. They brought a new weapon, the Mills Bomb, which is thrown by hand and kills and stuns by its blast. Thus the battle became one in which it was better to be killed than wounded. I was resorting to lion pits with stakes, man traps, and even native poisoned arrows. Cornelius sent in guerrillas and himself arrived in time to cover my withdrawal. Lions took three of my askaris and ten guerrillas. Black cotton soil swallowed up the English wagon trains. Huge rats destroyed the rations of both sides and gnawed at the dead and wounded indiscriminately. I can still hear the terrible cry of *Piga! Piga!* from both our own and enemy askaris as they charged in waves with bayonets flashing. This last pitched battle, fifteen days' forced march from the Kaiser's Mountain, will remind Myles Hagen that his generals still do not understand my tactics. As to my strategy? It is to hold out another ten months until the Kaiser's Zeppelins bring reinforcements. I am down to two hundred German officers, seventeen hundred askaris, and a couple of thousand carriers in all. This includes the first group. All the better to move swiftly in any direction, gradually working our way back to the mountain. All the better to be small and mobile for the invasion of northern Rhodesia or Portuguese Africa (Mozambique) or Nyasaland or all three neighborhood territories. . . . For in my situation, the best defense now is to attack!

Cable from King George V to General Smuts:

Heartiest congratulations on purging the Hun from Africa! We look forward to welcoming you to the Imperial Defense Conference.

From Myles Hagen's The Bird Watching Notes of an English Country Gentleman:

Smuts kicked upstairs to London! After ten months! He says *he's* kicked Paul out of German East. Wait 'til next year when London starts wondering what the devil we're still doing here—all thirty generals and fifty expeditionary forces of us. There's not a soldier left in the Indian Empire, and every fighting man from the Cape to Cairo is either here, or coming, or going belly up!

From a speech by Smuts at the Savoy, London:

The problem in Africa is like the one in America between black and white. With us there are certain axioms and the principle is *"no intermixture of blood between the two colors."* Earlier civilizations failed because of the intermixture of blood. . . . This war has been an eye opener. The German Kommandeur has broken faith with white Africa by making great use of natives and making natives aware of their capacity to wage war. It will be a serious question for world statesmen to undo this German's harm. He is defeated but the menace persists. We must stop the training of natives in Africa or black armies will endanger civilization itself!

39

KATE HAD never felt so lost and alone. The Rufiji landscape depressed the spirits. Tall trees without branches or foliage rose vertically, like petrified giant fingers, their twisted roots sucking little nourishment from salty estuarine waters the color of chocolate. Crocodiles rippled between the eroded tawny river banks, and their wide-angled eyes kept insistent watch on the marching columns. Piglike hippos trotted across the narrow sand banks, their manure supporting a rich growth of blue-green algae along the water's edge. Kate shot one whose gleaming tusks had grown into half moons. This deep in the delta, you shot anything that moved. The flayed hide was red from silt. The meat was cut in strips and smoked until a black crust formed to prevent the huge flies laying their eggs and rotting the flesh.

On Christmas day the noxious fog of the delta was so thick that Kate awoke from a nightmare, convinced she was strangling. She was astonished to see Skaramunga standing in the tent doorway. Since the gun bearer's recovery, he had stayed beside Paul. She asked in Swahili what he wanted.

In answer he held out a package. She sat up, drawing a bark-cloth cape around her shoulders.

"Bwana Simba sends it," said Skaramunga, squatting on his heels and watching her with unwavering eyes.

She unwound the palm-leaf wrappings and discovered a lump of partly carved wood. She took from beside her pillow the other unfinished carving and found that the contours fitted if she held the two pieces in a certain position. They reminded her of Major Wolfe's trick drawings: disconnected lines that made sense only when the artist sketched in the crucial segments.

The note from Paul read: "Hold this in your hands, *Kätzchen*. If I can keep you guessing, I can keep us both—" He had evidently been interrupted.

She smiled up at Skaramunga. "I'm sorry about the shooting. I know what happened to Baby Paul was none of your doing." It was the first time Kate had spoken to him about the child.

"I understand." He was watching her intently, looking for signs of emotional excess. "The Ugandan king"—he paused—"he once asked, Would you give him a white baby?"

Kate's hands closed convulsively around the carvings. "That is correct. What are you suggesting?"

"Only a possibility, *memsabu*. The possibility his witch doctors sent one of their number to join us, unbeknownst."

Kate had a sudden vision of a wizened old man daubed with white lime. "The man who doctored Bamboo?"

Skaramunga inclined his head. "The same, known as Mboya. His female disciple was the girl who pretended to be Baby Paul's new nurse. She would have delivered the *toto* to Mboya. What cannot be known is whether the baby was carried off to the Ugandans—"

"Or?"

"Or snatched up by Bamboo, who disappeared into the same night."

Kate asked in an even tone, her face expressionless, "Can you find out more?"

"It has taken all this time, *memsabu*, for me to learn even these few facts. Mboya vanished during the search for the child. The other medicine men would tell me nothing until I caught up with the first group here last night."

"Then bring me whoever spoke to you, now!"

Skaramunga shook his head slowly.

"All turned back during the hours of darkness. The first group has passed beyond the last juju hut. You are in a land of demons, beyond the magic of the witch doctors, beyond all help."

The first day of the New Year was spent on a gruesome march through misty quagmires where the bones of dead animals gleamed whitely and some huge mired beast would occasionally groan in desolation. Kate had to move between the military escorts and the

Governor's caravan. She seemed the only person Schnee permitted to conduct a regular liaison between army and civilian administration. Usually she found him festooned in mosquito netting like a deity. His porters had improvised a sedan chair, and he slumped in this with four men shouldering the poles. At eventide he would disengage from the floating gauze and creep stealthily up and down the columns, eavesdropping.

Every night since that dreadful Christmas revelation, Kate had suffered nightmares. Knowing Baby Paul might be alive was worse than having definite news of his death. She wondered what she should tell Paul and decided this was a burden she must carry alone. Sometimes, when she heard a baboon scream in the night and then the digestive rumble of its leopard killer, she would grip Paul's carvings until she thought they would break.

The scouts sent back word that an end was in sight. They were almost across. That night Kate was obliged to remain on a swampy island while a footbridge was restored. It had been constructed by General Wahle's engineers only two days earlier. The lashings were made of buffalo hide so the askaris could chew the protein out of the leatherish straps when the bridge was dismantled. But some ravenous, razor-toothed beast had torn the lashings apart.

Kate made camp with Ada and Major Wolfe. Skaramunga was now always at her elbow. He seemed resentful or suspicious of any attention Wolfe paid her. The Major said their island was near the wreck of the *Koenigsberg*. Baboons had made their home in the tiny oasis, for most of the land around was dying from the sea's salty inroads. Bush babies scampered through the camp and leopards kept silent watch.

Kate lay awake, listening to each brief squall of screaming and the heavy feeding grunts that followed. She finally dropped off toward dawn, only to wake in sudden terror, the echo of her own scream still in her ears. Paul! Something was threatening Paul!

Skaramunga heard the cry. He sprang from his lean-to. A leopard was spread on the limb of a tree and gathered itself when Skaramunga met its burning gaze, then charged. The jaws locked on Skaramunga's throat, and the hind legs raked with gutting claws. Major Wolfe reached him first and found his face ripped beyond recognition. The soldier of God was dead. When they tried to dig a grave in the morning light, they hit oozing mud before they had gone down more than two feet.

Skaramunga's body was finally thrown to the crocodiles, and for a long time afterward Ada remained rooted to the spot. "What a horrid way that would be to die," she said to Kate. They had both seen how the huge seawater crocs flayed and tore at the corpse.

That was on the morning of the fourth day of January 1917.

Captain Frederick Courtenay Selous was stalking Paul on January 4. In his meticulous way he knew not only the date but also the day of the week: Thursday. He had learned to keep to a civilized routine as a means of staying sane. He carried no diaries, no notebooks, nothing that might identify him. The calendars, the poetry, the maps, the hymns for eventide were all in his head.

Working alone with Ramazan, his gun bearer, he had no means of telling General O'Grady that the Germans were far from a beaten rabble. He had found Paul's trail and he stuck with it, living on wild honey and a native porridge. He doubted if the English would want to pursue Paul into what Smuts condemned as "an impassable jungle of dreadful menace." Selous the white hunter knew that Smuts the statesman-general had long ago concluded a secret deal with London so that he would not be required to chase the Germans once they sank into this land without hope.

The Rufiji held no great terrors for Selous, who knew how to travel without water or food. He utilized the acidic juice from a cactuslike plant to clear muddy water and make it drinkable. The fleshy catfish living in the water holes provided protein. Selous was moving along the cracked gray-brown banks of the Beho Beho river where it leaves the Rufiji near hot springs falling in translucent pools through a brilliant green jungle. It is a primeval landscape. When the dank vegetation permits a glimpse of distant horizons, the western sky is somber with the shadows of brooding blue mountains.

Selous had soaked his aching bones in the middle pool where the water boiled up from the bowels of the earth at a sulfuric 150 degrees Fahrenheit. Ramazan, tougher-skinned and only fifty to Selous's sixty-five years, refreshed himself in the upper pool, where few men could remain for more than a few seconds, the heat was so great.

So close to nature was old Selous that he was psychic in his apprehension of anything he hunted. To Ramazan he would sometimes say, "Go there and you will find buffalo," or "Try in those bushes for the leopard, in that tree perhaps." Now, rising like a god from the jade-green bubbling waters, he knew he was within range of his quarry.

He dressed carefully while Ramazan prepared his guns. He drew on tattered khaki shorts with an unlined crotch to prevent heat rash. He slipped on the earth-colored shirt. On his head went the knotted kerchief and the gray slouch hat. He never wore puttees. On the stalk he walked barefoot. He came down from the secret sheltered pools and he ghosted through the vine-hung hardwoods whose leafy branches shaded the trail over which the German advance parties had long before passed. He hoisted himself into a pulpy baobab and considered the killing ground.

He was unemotional about the task of execution. He had made the decision after working out the morality of it. The rest was no less mechanical than opening the bolt of his rifle, sliding the cartridge into the breech, guiding it into the hole where the bolt crept forward, and locking it home. His remaining action would come the moment he had the quarry's head between the sights and his finger squeezed.

He turned to signal to Ramazan and pushed his head into a small shaft of sunlight striking through the forest roof. Ramazan looked up. He saw the old hunter's mouth open, and then suddenly it was spouting some black-looking liquid and there was a single crack like a rotten branch breaking. Selous toppled forward out of his sniper's position and dropped onto the trail, stone dead.

Ramazan crouched back in the undergrowth and saw the enemy sniper dart away. Moments later a company of German askaris came running with Captain Alex Hammerstein in the lead. He ran straight into Ramazan's first shot. His askaris scattered as Selous's gun bearer broke cover, screaming now in tears and anger. There was a sudden fury of rifles, bayonets, whining bullets, fists, and hard-heeled feet. Ramazan died beside his master, but he had taken with him Hammerstein and four askaris.

"He ran amok," Paul said later, seeing the gun bearer's body. He bent over Selous, recognizing him at once. "What the hell was he doing here alone? There's not a German won't mourn this enemy."

Count Kornatzki hid his doubts. He said nothing while Selous was sewn up in a blanket that could be ill spared and the body thrust under the deep roots of the baobab where he had been shot. Kornatzki read a burial service. He did not voice his belief that a man of Selous's caliber must have been in the tree for one purpose only—to assassinate Paul.

Paul's remaining forces met him at a loop in the Rufiji where Major Wolfe's detachment had constructed a floating bridge built from the "wool tree," *Lannea alata*, whose tufted trunks gave buoyancy, so that Paul's men could cut directly into the swampland and pick up the trail blazed by General Wahle.

Late on the night of January 19, Kate waited at the far end of this raft bridge as Paul's askaris came swinging across under a rising moon magnified by the marsh mists. They carried their rifles reversed and chanted the *Schutztruppe* marching song: *"Askari wana-endesha / Tuna-kwenda, tuna shinda /* The soldiers drive on. . . ."

In Kate's hands was a block of wood, made up of the two incomplete carvings containing whatever inner vision guided Paul's whittling knife. When she had found they could be locked together, she decided Paul's secret was a representation of things living, molded together, inseparable. A great weight lifted from her mind when she felt herself reunited with Paul, as if they were safe together inside the wooden block.

"I spent Christmas drinking champagne," Paul said that night. "The English general sent me the second of two bottles he still had inside the besieged fort."

"My Christmas was a nightmare," she responded, suddenly sure she must tell him, after all. Skaramunga was dead and she could let the secret of Baby Paul die with him. But she could see now that it was wrong to hold anything back.

He was silent a long time after she finished. "I wasn't sure I should tell you this," he said finally. "There have been rumors among the Ugandans that you slept with the king and bore him a child. Of course, it would give him immense prestige among a tribe notoriously fickle in their loyalties. Especially because Cornelius says a white child has been seen in the king's company."

Kate stifled a cry of renewed agony. She slipped a hand under her pillow and drew comfort from the cold steel of her pistol there. She visualized her position, trapped in this sewer. She seemed to see a map of German East. Between herself and Baby Paul stretched "great mountain systems alternating with huge plains; wide unbridgeable rivers alternating with dry country lacking water to supply the nomads; trackless *bundu* and primeval forest; the malaria mosquito everywhere and everywhere belts infested with the deadly tsetse fly that make an end to all animal transport; the ground almost everywhere a rich black or red cotton soil that any transport converts into mud in the rain or suffocating dust in the drought."

She remembered these words from an ABC report of what General Smuts was telling the War Office in London. She was consumed with hate for the man. She wanted to see Paul shatter his arrogant prediction that no man, no rabble, could endure these conditions.

She heard Paul say, "After what happened at Ford Kibata, I want you to take machine-gun training, *Kätzchen*. Promise me."

"Don't worry, I will!" she whispered, tightening her grip on the pistol.

40

"THERE'S THE bullet killed Hammerstein," said Kornatzki wearily. He tossed a lump of metal into the ashes of a fire near his makeshift hospital where the sawing of bones could be heard through the walls of sacking. The last troops had withdrawn into the Rufiji. Kate and Celeste Looff were receiving casualties. An evening breeze swept away the sour smell of festering flesh and urine.

Kate watched in astonishment as Celeste sank to her knees, murmuring Hammerstein's name. A soldier's death was not exactly surprising, thought Kate, although she understood Kornatzki's disgusted gesture. The missionary-doctor was weary and disenchanted.

He moved between operating tables. They were covered in canvas painted blood red to conceal the carnage from the freshly wounded. The walls of the operating tent and the wooden floor were painted red, too. It was one luxury Paul allowed: a field hospital bloodily camouflaged. Years ago Paul had walked unaided from a West African skirmish, his arm dangling, a main artery severed. "The quicker the arm's off, the better!" he had growled to Kornatzki. A lesser surgeon would have amputated. Kornatzki decided the arm could be saved, though pain would persist. Much later, grateful for the arm while complaining of chronic discomfort, Paul promised the priest whatever was in his power to give. "Red paint," responded Kornatzki. "I can't stand those graying faces when they see blood."

Kornatzki lumbered back into the crimson aura where his "surgeons," mostly medical orderlies, had been taught to wield knives with the speed of butchers to reduce time on the tables.

Celeste had recovered the bullet and looked as if she were about to faint. "My poor child," Kate gasped. "I'd no idea." But the young girl's next words stunned her.

"Alex *dead!* And I'm carrying his baby."

Celeste rose to her feet and braced herself against a tamarind tree. The concentrated light of lanterns escaped through a crack in the big operating tent and reflected in her tearless eyes. She was clutching the spent bullet, and her mouth was open as if she had difficulty breathing.

"Don't speak to anyone of this"—Celeste straightened up—"or I'll be handed over to the English with the next batch of useless mouths."

"I promise," Kate said.

There was a terrible irony in the way Kornatzki could patch up men doomed to die but was forbidden to abort Celeste's pregnancy. The poor child would doubtless console herself that "something of Alex survives in me." Kate retired to the tent and lay sleepless until she heard Paul slip inside. She saw the glow of his cigarette and recognized his tension.

"Want to talk?"

"Yes." He ground out the cigarette. "If I cut down porters and *bibis* yet again, we've a fighting chance to reach the high ground Wahle's preparing."

Kate put aside any further thought of mentioning Celeste's pregnancy. As if he picked up some hint, Paul said, "I'm worried about the Looff girls. Their father's not long for this world, but he's one man I can't unload. Elsa's lost to us. Your brother has collected fuel for one last flight, but he wants to go to Zanzibar."

"He can't!"

"Chuck says America will be in the war soon. He's on the wrong side. When you married me, you became a German citizen. Chuck's in a different position."

Kate pushed aside the abstract complications. After all, it wasn't so long ago that the Governor was going to shoot Chuck for being on the wrong side here. She asked instead, "But Elsa? Wasn't he planning to try to fly her out?"

"Elsa's safer where she is." Something in Paul's voice jarred. There was an uncharacteristic note of caution.

"Safe or not, the poor girl loves Chuck."

"That's another thing," groaned Paul. "I hate to lie to Hector. But he won't like to think one of his daughters is marrying a potential enemy. It's bad enough—" He broke off and sat up with his chin resting on his knees, his despairing figure silhouetted against the brightening sky.

"What's bad enough?" asked Kate.

"His other daughter wanting to marry Hammerstein."

"So you knew?"

"Yes. I advised them against it," Paul said bitterly. "They looked at me as if I were the Lord High Executioner. If they'd dared, they'd have said, What about you and Kate? But dear God, the girl's a child, and what if she got pregnant while we're in this mess?"

What indeed? thought Kate, feeling deceitful.

"You might as well know the rest," said Paul. "I'm going to have to break the news to the Governor in a few hours. Ada's dead."

"She can't be. She's *with* the Governor."

"He left her to come back here with new complaints. Lord knows what I'll do. It's her Pumpernickel's fault that Ada was killed."

It had happened among General Wahle's trail breakers. They were moving through treacherous country, keeping to soggy soil between brackish waters where the sea crept inland through the arthritic roots of the mangroves far from the coast line. General Wahle, despite age, set a cracking pace. The old cavalry officer was no longer monolithic on an immense hairy-heeled Prussian-bred horse, but was bent over the handlebars of a laager-made bicycle. The women's corps were similarly mounted. Only the Governor still kept his retinue of porters and bowlegged, swaybacked mules, and during one rest period the General tackled the Governor about reducing his comforts.

Old Wahle was resolved to be diplomatic. "Us oldsters stand up to the strain better," he began. "My theory is, we've survived the lesser diseases and we're toughened. Survival of the fittest means you and I became tough as old boots." This was not at all to the Governor's liking, the General saw at once, and so he added, "Heinrich, old man, you're ten years younger than me, but let's face it, age creeps on." This made matters worse. General Wahle, his brief fling at diplomacy over, said, "How many of your loads are really necessary? You don't need all that paper and those files. Dump the stuff, and I can put the porters to better use."

Governor Schnee, deeply offended now, said irritably, "Jettison the women if you want to dispose of luxuries."

"Thunder and lightning!" rasped the General. "If it were not for the women, we would none of us be alive! What blasted use is all your wretched form-filling?"

Ada had tried to smooth things over. Her husband had been without grog—even the palm toddy had run out—and she decided from his mottled skin and pursed mouth that all this enforced abstinence was stinging back into life the ugly little brain cells that made him choleric in discussion. She had kept a few flasks of brandy for just such crises. She had also some jars labeled Women's Corps Riesling. She suggested the Riesling while Wahle and her husband were still eyeing each other. The wine was in reality a ciderlike liquid fermented from the fronds of a multiheaded palm.

Schnee tossed back the fizzy stuff and grumbled that she was trying to poison him. Wahle pressed his argument for cutting down the Governor's excess baggage and porters rather than unloading the women. "The women," said Wahle, "not only cook, they hunt, or don't you keep your eyes open?"

The Governor's eyes were sleepy from the women's corps fizz. It was time he had another talk with the Kommandeur, he burbled, because, while on the subject of paper, what had happened to his Treasury?

Ada said, "You know very well it was burned at Kibata."

"Oho!" cried the Governor, rousing himself. "So the Kommandeur *said*. But what proof have I got? What receipts and canceled orders? Man's a bandit. He probably stuffed away the currency notes for his own use later. I must go and check at once!"

The moment Governor Schnee said this, Ada acted. Before he had time to reconsider, she had him cushioned in a litter, already half-drunk and provisioned with the precious brandy, trekking back to Paul. The last she saw of him, he was proclaiming his intention to have General Wahle put into an old folks' home.

Next day Ada had gone off to hunt hippos. She was being unreasonable, she knew, but Heinrich's taunts about useless women made her reckless. He was fond of the tasty and delicate hippo tongue, and she wanted to stick a dish of it under his nose when he returned. The trick was to get a beast with a single shot as the head rose from the water.

Ada had taken with her Ali Hassan, who had spied for Paul among the English by cutting grass for their horses. Ali was quick and clever. She told him to stay on a farther bank while she stepped onto a spit of yellowish crumbling soil. On three sides stretched the metallic water broken by small islands. Some harbored crocodiles and some were indeed crocodiles lying motionless on the surface.

Like everyone on this exhausting march, Ada had grown careless. The swamps were infested with deadly predators. You couldn't keep your guard up all the time without collapsing from nervous exhaustion. Ada stood at the water's edge and studied a dark swirl just below the surface. Behind her an estuarine crocodile cruised along the opposite side of the narrow bank. It was well over twenty feet long. The pale green eyes swiveled in their deep sockets. The thousand-pound saw-toothed tail swung and caught Ada behind and below the knees, and she stumbled face down into the water, where another croc opened its massive jaws and locked its teeth into her pelvis, piercing a femoral artery. The water exploded into foaming blood and bubbles as the monster fought against the woman's struggles. She seemed to be dragged along the surface for an eternity while Ali scrambled for her rifle and took aim at the croc's blazing eyes. His first shot ricocheted off the carapace. The croc sank from view and then came up again with Ada flailing between the clamped jaws. Ali pumped a bullet into the nearside eye.

The Rufiji estuarine crocodile is one of the rarest and most vicious of the species, often swimming miles out into the Indian Ocean. Its teeth are like steel blades in a high-speed saw. The croc with Ada in its teeth was stunned by the rifle shots and for a split second relaxed its grip. Ada, with one leg broken by the lashing tail, many blood vessels torn, her lower spine crushed, still in her desperate fight tore free with such strength that she left only chunks of flesh in the croc's jaws. At once the first croc was upon her and, wasting no time, dived twenty feet to the muddy bottom. The drowning woman left on the surface a thick trail of blood. Still she struggled while the croc attempted to shove her into the mud. Then, using the ancestral experience of millions of years, the croc deliberately let her go. Ada felt herself float toward the surface and at once struck out. Her lungs bursting, she had no resistance left when the croc lazily tightened his jaws again and with incredible speed and agility went into a neck-breaking spiral dive that snapped bone after bone in Ada's body, tearing one leg out of its socket and forcing the stirred-up bottom mud into her waterlogged lungs.

Ali Hassan believed crocs would not chew. They would store Ada's body in a hole below the water level until she rotted sufficiently for them to tear pieces from what remained of her. The thought convulsed him. He fired again and again into the swirling waters. Then Ali Hassan himself tried to follow Ada, but the gunshots had attracted others who stopped him.

Paul had the details before the Governor was carried into camp that night. Schnee had drunkenly announced his intention of getting a good night's sleep before confronting Paul, who came shortly after the customary breakfast of watery porridge.

"Where are the accounts?" Schnee meant to drop the question like a bomb and then enjoy Paul's discomfiture. The Governor was nursing a monumental hangover, and in Paul's camp there was no hair of the dog. Temper and rage forced the Governor to his feet. He had dressed in ceremonial uniform—costing, thought Paul, the full-time services of two porters and their *bibis*—the trousers repeatedly restitched but still gaping in the seat, the jacket plugged with holes, the rotting cocked hat no longer feathered though still plumed.

"You mock my 'bits of paper,'" squeaked the Governor. "Let me remind you, Colonel, the honor of the empire is at stake. How can we pursue the Enthronement of Culture if we do not keep the accounts?"

"The accounts," said Paul, "were burned along with the rest of the Treasury."

Schnee's mouth worked open and shut.

"All your paper is worthless." Paul took a deep breath. "Excellency, I must prepare you for bad news."

"*Bad* news! What could be worse than undermining our colonial fiscal system?" The Governor took another turn around the table, one hand resting upon the broken weave of the uneven top, causing it to wobble. "There is nothing, sir, more dastardly than this desecration of the imperial accounting system."

The tirade was interrupted by the arrival of Max Looff.

"What's this about Ada?"

"You've heard?" asked Paul, trying desperately to delay the blow.

"That she drowned. Is it true?" Max ignored Schnee, who stood with one finger uplifted and one hand poised above the table.

"I'm sorry, nothing's been said officially, Max. Yes," Paul murmured reluctantly.

The Governor, unhearing, puffed up. "How dare you, Captain Looff, break in like this!"

Max stared him up and down. The Governor's featherless plumes drooped over his shiny forehead, the buttoned neck of his shrunken tunic dug into his scrawny neck. The Captain of the *Koenigsberg* looked no less ludicrous, his formal nauticals ending with the bottom of his mildewed jacket, whereupon he deteriorated into very short shorts and bare feet.

"I don't think you heard," said Max bitterly. "Your wife is dead."

41

SOUTH OF the Rufiji, Kate was taking weapons training with a fresh batch of black recruits under Major Wolfe. There was no shortage of machine guns, captured in surprise attacks on enemy posts.

"How do you smuggle the recruits here?" asked Kate.

"Every man buys his way into this army with a piece of stolen equipment."

"But aren't they frightened to come beyond the juju huts?"

"They learn the gun's a more powerful god," said Major Wolfe, unthinkingly adding, "This gun's your baby." He remembered for long afterward the anguish in Kate's eyes.

Kate thought the gun weighed as much as her baby, Toto Paul. It was more demanding, more temperamental, more in need of feeding and watering. Six men nursed it.

She took part in exercises as each of the men in turn gave his place to her. She advanced finally to the number-one position. Her fingers bled from the constant repetition of assembling and firing the gun. Her heart pounded long after the percussion stopped. She showed such devotion to the gun that the rest of the team put their lives in her hands and promoted her to captain.

As number one, she learned to dash forward and set up the heavy tripod, release the ratchet-held front legs and secure them rigidly. Then, squatting, she snatched away the metal pins in the tripod's head to let number two secure the gun on top. Her fingers were quick and deft. She laughed scornfully to herself when the men complimented her on such dexterity, for it was a simpler routine than pinning up the baby's diapers.

To sight the gun, she flicked up the stem of the rear sight and spun a spring-loaded wheel to select the range. Number three dragged up an ammunition box with canvas belts of ammunition pocketed to hold 250 rounds. Number two inserted the brass tag on the first belt into the feed block and Kate jerked the tag out the other side, pulling back the crank handle twice to load the breech.

She loved opening fire. The hot gun's barrel ejaculated death at six hundred rounds a minute, heating the metal so critically that water had to be circulated around it and through a tube into a bucket. Number two controlled the entry of the ammunition belts, and number three kept up the supply of ammunition boxes. The rest of the team fetched and carried until called on to replace any member of the firing crew who was hurt or killed. It seemed to Kate like a complete life cycle.

She became a servant to the guns, obedient to the guns' dictatorship. The *bibis* regarded her skill as a tribute to their sex. She saw how the guns gave the women pride and united the different tribes supplying the guns with those who stripped, serviced, and waited upon the guns.

The flooded Rufiji had halted the English. Units were marooned on islands created by the swelling of the river, which burst its banks with such ferocity that a tidal bore was measured rushing at twenty miles an hour across the plain. The sixth general to serve as commander-in-chief against Paul was the inarticulate "Japie" Van Deventer, who began infiltrating the land around the Rufiji. Japie built up new armies secretly, landing troops along the coast to the south. The secrecy was aimed at the English public, who could not be told the African mess was worse than ever.

The Rufiji covered an area as large as England, and the rains that year continued far beyond the end of April. The main English force, spread along the four-hundred-mile northern edge of the floods, began to rot.

German couriers sped around these obstacles, and by May there was a stream of information reaching Paul from the ABC wireless unit now stationed at the first laager's site in Olduvai. In this way Kate learned that America had entered the war on April 6. She had to work out on her fingers the year 1917 and could not believe it was already four years since her first meeting with Paul. She wondered what Americans could do to change history. According to ABC, the U-boats threatened to bring England to her knees. Russian armies were in retreat and ready to defect. Litvinoff was spouting his Bolshevik propaganda in London, and the Tsar and his family were reported in danger of their lives from revolutionaries.

The couriers brought word of a new breed of young Englishmen moving among the tribes. They were Hagen's breed: tough, solitary, wise in African lore. They bribed village headmen to recruit anti-German guerrillas. These English guerrillas wore potato sacks, with holes cut for arms and legs. Cornelius was forced to order all his guerrillas now to mark themselves with the white lime thunderbolt flash to avoid any catastrophic mistakes in identification.

Paul could scent the presence of Myles Hagen and his converted general, Forget-Me-Not Gaunt. Their askaris had cousins among Paul's askaris, and they told of confusion as new English expeditions landed south of the Rufiji and blundered into the interior. Turbaned Kashmiris dragged their guns into the hills. Riflemen in red tarbooshes marched to the Swahili version of "Rule Britannia," which was about the only patriotic English song without a German counterpart. There were two hundred Uganda Railway Volunteers reported near Mahiwa; they were the two hundred left alive out of the fifteen hundred eccentrics who first rallied to Hagen's side.

Mahiwa drew them. Here Paul had settled Laager-550 SSE. It seemed a sad echo of previous laagers. A few hutments were dispersed in the forested valleys, but there was none of the bustle of farming families now. A *boma*, an old mud-walled fort, stood on Mahiwa Hill. Paul refused to occupy it because the new English long-range aircraft would spot the activity. The long period of waiting approached an end.

Count Kornatzki decided to bring some romance back into the lives of the two people he loved. Kate was more steel than butterfly now and so thin she seemed to have grown taller. Paul had grown a short white beard that emphasized his hollow cheeks, and the sight in his good eye had been impaired by a bullet grazing the brow. The Count insisted they spend a night in the fort alone, and for breakfast he created a miracle from his private hoard of captured English supplies: a tin of bully beef, condensed milk, tea made from acacia tree bark, and a packet of King Stork cigarettes. They sat in lonely splendor with a view toward the Indian Ocean through a gap in the crumbling wall. The sun shot a first long ray of light through the gap, illuminating the red-roofed quarters where they had slept. A cloud of Urania moths sparkled like emerald drops.

"You were asking some hard questions during the night," said Paul. "What's the point of fighting on? I've never heard you ask this, not since the baby— Yes, I know—you were letting off steam! *Kätzchen*, we created this society with its own rules. Don't look outside it. Perhaps the Zeppelins won't ever come. The signals from Kilimanjaro grow fainter. Our Jewish friends are tuned into transmissions from the future. Everything begins with courage. Nothing is possible if that fails."

Kate went back to work in the hospital. She overheard a black orderly use the phrase *Aliyefanya saanda*, referring to Paul. Maker of funeral shrouds. She felt a stab of almost physical pain and had to walk outside for fresh air. Patients littered the hospital grounds. There was a man with an open wound in his head where a bullet had gouged away part of his skull. Incredible that a man could live with his brain exposed! Yet they were treating worse cases. Maker of funeral shrouds? Paul fought for life, not death. He had brought together whites and blacks to pool their medical resources, and as a result the incidence of tetanus and gangrene was low. Terrible injuries were treated with native medicines, and native surgeons operated on seemingly hopeless cases. The catalog of plants yielding disinfectants, purifiers, anesthetics, and heart stimulants kept growing. Deadly scourges like diarrhea had been stopped. Kate watched black girls beating bark and palm leaves into a fibrous material that would make bandages and protective hospital sheets. They were producing lifesaving materials, not funeral shrouds.

Yet the approach of another bloody battle was clearly visible, slow but inexorable. She wondered how many battles more before Paul was hung with the funeral-maker label.

She found herself thrown into the company of Major Wolfe while the enemy tightened the noose around Mahiwa Hill. Day and night it was vital to keep the English under observation. She rode out on patrol with Wolfe, and danger and hard exercise made their intimacy predictable. She told him of her worry that the black Africans were suffering from too much bloodshed and might blame Paul.

"It's a doubtful compliment," said Wolfe. "The askaris respect him for his indifference to death."

"A doubtful compliment?"

"Yes. Indifference to human emotions is not something I'd boast about."

"You think him callous?" asked Kate, adding quickly, "Then I must plead guilty, too. I could never have predicted our acceptance of the way Baby Paul simply—disappeared. A year ago I would have expected Paul to give priority to such a calamity. Now I'd be appalled if he jeopardized the campaign for personal reasons."

Major Wolfe looked at her strangely, compressed his lips, and finally commented, "War alters our perspectives. If you rule by the gun, the gun will govern you."

"Without courage, all fails." She had unconsciously repeated Paul's words to herself.

"But where does true courage lie?" Wolfe moved ahead before she could reply.

She had forgotten this response by nightfall. Paul had recalled all reserve companies manning the farthest outposts. He told her, "General Gaunt is leading the English attack. His style is to throw men in, regardless of cost. Only Hagen ever made him change, and now I think Hagen's encouraging a frontal assault. This could be my last chance to wipe out a substantial army." Kate thought the sentiment sounded ominously familiar, but it was too late now to challenge him.

Kate was range taker to a machine-gun company once the English assault began. The number one, the firer, was Baghwash Singh. As officer commanding railways, he had complained of having no railways and gladly turned to the lesser task. The gun commanded a shallow valley, with machine guns sited on either side at intervals of seventy feet.

An English mortar barrage opened the assault on October 14, 1917, and the effect was terrifying for those unused to shells falling vertically without a warning scream. Mountain guns laid a barrage in advance of enemy troops who launched bayonet charges the moment the shelling ceased.

Baghwash Singh fired bursts of thirty and forty rounds, as he had been instructed, and Kate called out ranges. She saw the enemy run up the valley, saw legs collapse as the gun traversed the ground. She had difficulty not correcting Baghwash Singh's errors, and she longed to take over the gun. She knew he had been made firer because Major Wolfe, commanding the machine-gun companies, balked at putting her fingers to the trigger. Nevertheless, in the next four days of confusion, she prayed for a chance.

Forget-Me-Not Gaunt dispatched men into the machine-gun fire as if they had been condemned to death and were merely surrendering to the execution squads. Kate was deaf to the noise of explosives, but she heard the low-pitched cries and hoarse commands. There were moments when she heard them in one language and other times when she seemed only to pick out the words of alien dialects. The faces were dark with fear or hate or lust for battle. She could not tell if they were white or black or if the natives were English or German allies. The voices and the faces merged and, always by her side, the turbaned Indian railroadman muttered to himself in his *babu* English a phrase or two of self-reassurance: "Here we go, then, *la!* Oh, such silly fellows. Where, then, is Jemadar Hira Lal?"

The gun crews changed, the relief parties brought up food and water, but Baghwash Singh stuck with the gun and Kate stayed with him. The trenches below were deep in blood, the leaves of the trees were hung with flesh, and the voices ebbed and flowed: "Fix bayonets!"—"*Piga! Piga! Piga!*"—"*Gefechtschiessen!*" Then silence as Singh's turbaned head sagged forward and Kate stared into an empty face and lips drawn back from betel-stained teeth. She took over the gun without a pause and was dimly conscious of the late commander of railways being dragged away by his heels.

She gripped the machine-gun handles as she had been taught, minimizing the vibration. She waited for a carrier to cool the barrel, and she sighted on a group of men bunched together as they climbed up through the drifting smoke. She felt nothing when the gun stuttered. Her eyes were fastened on the enemy, jerking and tumbling under her fire as if they were pulled by strings. She was excited by the smell of cordite, the trembling of the gun, the dancing men. She opened fire again, and the gun bucked and the vibrations transmitted themselves through her arms into her body and down into her groin. She thrust her hips against the dry powdered earth, and she sighed as she released the gun triggers and waited for another delivery of ammunition belts while the fear and frustration poured out of her.

The slaughter after four days was too much for Gaunt. In bayonet attacks alone, half of his white officers and a third of the English askaris had been wiped out. The Kommandeur had erected a wall against which Gaunt had flung his men until they bled. It had seemed the quickest way to crush the Kommandeur, and Myles Hagen had for once made no protest except to plead for more attention at his intelligence briefings: "I specified the baobab trees as targets," Hagen told General Gaunt, "because each tree holds two hundred gallons of water, and those baobabs were Paul's only source of water. So you shouldn't give our men hell for aiming too high; they were trying to knock hell out of the trees."

Gaunt meekly accepted the reprimand and listened when Hagen offered an alternative plan. Then Gaunt ordered the retreat, and soon the sad notes floated over the hills. Hagen hung his head and paid silent tribute to Paul, quoting Kipling to himself:

> He rushes at the smoke when we let drive
> And before we know, he's hacking at our head.
> He's all hot sand and ginger when alive
> And he's generally shamming when he's "dead."
> He's a daisy, he's a ducky, he's a lamb!

He's a injia-rubber idiot on the spree!
He's the only thing that doesn't give a damn
For a Regiment of English Infantree.

Such an enemy, said Hagen, had almost exhausted his repertoire. Assassination had failed. Encirclement had failed. Shelling, aerial bombing, hot pursuit, mass onslaught had failed. "Give me complete independence of action, like the German gives his unit commanders," suggested Hagen. "I need a flying column of fifty horsemen, and nobody to account to."

But Gaunt only scratched his head and pursed his lips.

The Governor was shell-shocked and thought Ada was back beside him. General Wahle was a stretcher case with part of his throat torn away. Celeste Looff had miscarried. Kate was beyond shocking, though sometimes she saw again Baghwash Singh's blood-red turban. She heard Paul tell Cornelius, "I'm going to have to fight on without carriers. I'm out of men and food. I'll have to invade Portuguese Africa."

Cornelius regarded the Kommandeur with that noncommittal expression that allowed him to prepare for any surprise. The mahogany face was caked in dried blood. His shoulder was purple with recoil bruises from his rifle. "Invade?" He slowly turned his head. The hillside was covered in bodies. The branches of acacias and baobabs bent under the weight of bodies blown into the trees. The hillside would drip blood for days. "Invade with what?"

Paul sidestepped the question. "The Governor should cease to exercise any authority when we leave German East. You'll replace him. A symbolic gesture. But important. The first step to black independence. A black Governor."

"And what will Captain Looff say?" scoffed Cornelius.

"Max? He took shrapnel in the spine. He might recover if the English surgeons work on him in time."

The *Koenigsberg*'s commander's last captaincy was a fleet of gun carriages bearing the sick and wounded. The two-wheeled limbers were dragged up and down the hills by porters and the sole surviving horse. The horse had been ridden by General Wahle, who had been written off, erroneously, by an English diarist: "I took my hat off to this old man who rode at the head of his company into an assault before he disappeared, never, I should think, to lead his troops on earth again, for not less than two machine guns and two score of rifles were aimed at him." General Wahle was among the Germans who now insisted on following Paul into Portuguese Africa. The old General argued that Paul needed his brains, not his legs. By the time Paul's streamlined forces had slipped away unnoticed, Max Looff had supervised the erection of international red cross signs all over Mahiwa Hill and calmly awaited capture.

On the English side Hagen was consulted. Were the red cross signs a trick? "No," replied Hagen. "The General doesn't abuse the weak and helpless, whatever our propaganda says."

"General?" echoed Forget-Me-Not Gaunt. "Let's not give the man more credit than he deserves."

"He's earned it," said Hagen in an odd voice. "He wore full regimentals during the battle for the first time in three months and three years. That's how long I've had to think about him, hunt him, curse him."

Three years and three months. Had it really been so long? Hagen tugged at the full beard and sideburns, once naturally red and now red only from the all-pervasive dust, but mostly white at the roots. Hagen had done three extra tours of duty to continue the chase of Von Lettow. The skin was tight on Hagen's frame now. His weight had dropped forty pounds from recurrent fevers. His hawk's-bill nose had prodded through the bush, searching for ways to outwit Paul, and in this process he had forgone promotions and postings.

He glanced slyly at General Gaunt and then made a decision. "Perhaps you should read this, sir?"

The telegram read: "SECRET from War Office Director of Intelligence to Hagen: His Majesty King George is canvassing opinion on proposed appointment Colonel von Lettow to head interim German government in event of Germany's defeat in Europe. Lettow acceptable to political experts here predicting shambles in Germany and need for strong leader of character and courage. In event of Germany's surrender and if Lettow still alive, you are authorized broach this highly confidential matter with him."

General Gaunt shoved his helmet back on his head and said, "Lumme. You had the right instinct, long ago, when you set out to rescue Lettow from the Ugandans. Keep him alive, eh?"

"*But do not strive,*" quoted Hagen with sudden fury, "*officiously to keep alive!* He lives by the gun and so does his wife."

"Wife? I don't think I can take so many surprises in one day, Hagen."

"I'm a fool, sir. I should have found this out long ago. I was so con-

vinced Lettow was a dedicated soldier, I couldn't let the evidence
speak for itself." Hagen told the cavalry general what he knew about
Kate. "She's Saint Walpurgis, not that black Zanzibari princess!
What's more, she had a baby by the Colonel."

This conversation took place in a campaign caravan. After General
Gaunt left, Hagen went through the interrogation reports again. It
seemed incredible that he could have missed these details. Already a
plan was forming in his mind. If he could start rumors among the
natives that the Lettow child was alive in the Kilimanjaro region . . .

An eager young Loyal Lancashire regiment lieutenant interrupted
him. Hagen stared at him belligerently and thought the boy must
have been in knickers when the fight with Lettow began. The lieutenant stared back, reflecting the man must be a paper pusher to be
this old and still only a captain.

"I think we've cornered the German commander!"

"Then get him, lad!" muttered Hagen and followed the boy into
the compound where litters of German wounded were being laid out.

"The General!" shouted the young Lieutenant. "Where's the
General?"

Well, Hagen mumbled into his beard, he's got that bit right.

"The General?" croaked a German in an English stretcher, leaning
on his elbows.

The Lieutenant whirled, catching the suggestion of gold braid on
the German's mildewed cap. Hagen recognized in the skeleton another ghost from the past: Captain Looff.

"Your so-called General's gone to hell!" croaked Captain Max
Looff and laughed and laughed.

That night Hagen drafted his reply: "SECRET to DIRINTEL:
Tophole idea. With all due respect, suggest our royal connection with
Berlin advise that Lettow be promoted to full general. If Kaiser flees
to his African possessions in attempt salvage part of Second Reich,
he will naturally respond better to general than colonel. Furthermore,
Lettow will need social eminence as well as status as war hero to deal
with nuts and rabble-rousers likely to emerge in postwar Germany
chaos."

The whole proposition was remote, though not ridiculous. Hagen
remembered again the eerie moment when he had glimpsed Kate at
the machine gun like a terrible vision of revenge come true. He should
have known! Ah, Paul, my sweet enemy. I rescue you and then I
try to kill you once more. And now, if I cannot kill you soon, I shall
have to promote you!

42

SOMEHOW THE story spread of the Kaiser's plan to move to his German colony in Africa. It circulated among the askaris on both sides. It changed shape and acquired some odd embellishments. The King-Emperor of the Second Reich was arriving by airship. He would land on his mountain, Kilimanjaro. By the time the story got back to Hagen, it bore no resemblance to his original top-secret telegram to DIRINTEL.

The report reached Paul on November 25, 1917, when he was invading Portuguese Africa at the Rovuma River where it entered the mountains some hundred kilometers from the sea. He dismissed it as just another tribesman's invention.

"I'm leaving a military squad behind," he told Kate. "I've got to cut numbers. You'll be safe with them—"

"If you're testing me, the answer's no. I refuse to stay behind."

"It will be government by the gun now," warned Paul.

"I surrendered to the gun's dictatorship long ago," she replied.

Bayonets and rifle barrels glinted in the moonlight. Shadows moved over wet banks. A black irregular returned from across the river to report that the new enemy was fast asleep.

"Only take guns and ammunition," Paul instructed Cornelius, who replied coldly that his guerrillas wanted nothing else.

"They've already rejected English promises of gold and *pombe* beer," Cornelius added. "Their loyalty is truly remarkable. They seem to expect gifts from heaven." He pulled out a wad of paper from under his cloak, and his teeth gleamed in the darkness. "If this could be true?" He uncreased the message. "It says LZ-59 left the Zeppelin base in Bulgaria."

"Where did this come from?" asked Paul.

"ABC," replied Cornelius. "Time of transmission was five days ago. What I cannot understand is the last part of the signal. 'Failing any response from you, German airship headquarters directed the Zeppelin to Kilima Njaro.'"

"Don't make any false assumptions," Paul said quickly.

"I'm not. However, the tribal chiefs might." Cornelius was motionless against the long spikes of bamboo behind him. "They are not fighting in order to give sanctuary to a beaten Kaiser."

"No, of course theyre not," Paul said briskly. "These rumors must be stopped." He rubbed his chin. Cornelius must know Lanni was on LZ-59. Perhaps he needed some military or political justification to be there when—if—it landed. "Perhaps you should go?"

"You're thinking of Lanni," Cornelius accused him. "No, sentiment cannot come into this. There are plenty of other rebel leaders who can verify the Kaiser is not aboard."

After Cornelius had left, Kate said, "This Kaiser business is getting beyond a joke. Cornelius is suspicious, however much he pretends. He's fighting for independence, not for a white emperor in his midst. I thought you were making him a kind of honorary governor once we left German East?"

Paul sighed. His spirits had been buoyed for days by the approaching prospect of dumping Governor Schnee at the border. But the Governor had forestalled him: "My duty lies with you wherever you go, for I'm still supreme commander."

The Governor was not without courage. Some of his old qualities had reappeared since Ada's hideous death. Paul could not forcibly restrain him from crossing the border. Now, as he broke the dismal news to Kate, another day dawned. The sun's early beams lanced the plains below. Long, towering shadows fell across the biscuit-colored grasses to the east, and there was the same inexhaustible change of light that never failed to excite Kate and must forever haunt her. The river forest shadowed their camp and wove a pattern of vivid green as far as the foothills climbing into the Livingstone Mountains.

With each day's birth came the smell of another Africa, essences carried by a fresh wind out of the grape-blue hills and bearing a touch of twisted olive and flat-topped acacia—nose-tickling, feathery, tingling aromas containing the bone-dry, penetrating, chocolaty, red dust with the hint of moisture in the sandy riverbeds or of distant rain splashing as if from a sprinkler on an early morning lawn.

"It would break my heart to leave all this," said Kate. "It would kill me to let you cross over without me."

In that same week, the Zeppelin LZ-59 was walked out of its shed on Yanboli base in Bulgaria. Her captain, Ludwig Buckholt, went through the routine yet again of inspecting the ship and crew. She carried 20,200 pounds of ballast, 48,000 pounds of gasoline, two helmsman, a sailmaker, two wireless operators, a dozen engineers, and five deck hands for general duties on ballast and fuel. His observer worked with Buckholt and nine officers in the forward car. Five men stayed amidships in the main engine pod. Eight were stationed in the larger power gondola aft. These were all the participants in what Major Nicolai of German Intelligence code-named "The China Matter."

Ludwig Buckholt had explained the dangers many times to Lanni, standing in the girdered control car that was so like the glassed-in bridge of a ship. LZ-59 was one of the new "sky climbers," with a planned ceiling for the Africa adventure of 15,000 feet. The crew would suffer dizzy spells, high pulse rates, and severe headaches from remaining aloft four or five days at that height and in freezing temperatures. Lanni's presence was felt to be vital when it became known Paul's small army was cornered in unmapped regions. She was one of the few who knew the precise location of Tom von Prinz's mountain aerie.

Twice they had voyaged out of Bulgaria. Twice they were forced back. On November 21, 1917, the two-dozen ground crew released the giant airship for the last time. She was embarking on a historic flight, covering unheard-of distances into an unknown continent. In peace such a story would have monopolized newspapers around the world. But this was the week when English armies were losing a quarter of a million men to capture an insignificant village in Europe named Passchendaele.

This time the weather was kind. LZ-59 flew a dogleg over Turkey and picked up the German-built railway in Asia minor, then swung onto a course for Crete. Buckholt's observer logged each detail, checked navigation charts, rang changes on the telegraph system to engineers and elevator trimmers and ballast shifters, and advised Buckholt of thunderstorms ahead. There was even a rudimentary wireless guidance system, but electric storms were not popular with the crews of highly combustible airships trailing long aerial wires. An order was recorded to wind in the aerial. This order became controversial later when Berlin claimed to have wirelessed LZ-59 to abandon the mission because news had been received of Paul's defeat. The message was transmitted before the German naval staff, responsible for LZ-59, heard of Paul's invasion of Portuguese Africa. Buckholt later claimed he never got the message. His aerial was streaming again by the time he crossed the African coast with the vast golden desert of Libya dead ahead.

A young settler-lieutenant in the East African Mounted Rifles, Lord Bertram Francis Gordon Cranworth—Lord Bertie—had been absorbed into the bloated intelligence establishment in Nairobi now handling coded wireless trafic. Lord Bertie was stuck with decoding London's verbiage and deciphering whatever was recovered of German wireless signals. A powerful transmitter at Nauen in eastern Germany was trying to reach LZ-59, and Lord Bertie matched the signals against London's wild guesses about LZ-59's intentions. London was unaware of Nauen's orders to LZ-59 to turn back and the fact that LZ-59 was ignoring the orders or couldn't hear them. Lord Bertie reviewed the German file. After a night of skull-cracking cogitation, he figured LZ-59 was making for Kilimanjaro. A signal to this effect was sent to Van Deventer, chasing Paul seven hundred kilometers to the south.

The German ABC wireless monitors had sited their equipment near Olduvai to pick up these weak local English transmissions. The sprightly seventeen-year-old Zionist who had come out from London with the ABC equipment and whose job was essentially to brew tea for his five companions ran along the shore of the lake to Chuck Truman's hut. " 'Ere y'are, guv. Don't make no sense to me, but it's sumfink to do wiv flying and that's yore department, 'n' it?"

Chuck had been living in a grass hut where Laager-200 W was formed three years before. He had planned to fly the Stinkpot to Zanzibar, but always some more pressing business delayed him. He had sworn to replace Jacob in the Zionist cause, and the ABC team and Jacob's contacts were always producing sudden emergencies. He spent hours at work on the Stinkpot, jealously guarding the 66-pound drums of fuel left him by Professor Ersatz Etrich. He could manage one long final flight. All this seemed increasingly nebulous against the day-to-day problems. Chuck was the junction box for information passing through tribal territories. He settled squabbles among the displaced Londoners. He lavished care on his goddess of cotton skin and wooden bone, the Stinkpot.

She had been refitted with floats. She sat sedately on a mud bank by Chuck's hut. He hobbled around her, polishing, fixing, dismantling, and rebuilding. His artificial foot hampered him, and the Londoners considered he had "gone bush" and ought to be weaned away from his machine. They worried when he talked to her. They tried to keep from him the news of casualties because he took it all so personally.

He had collected what he called his "flying uniform," which was kept inside the hut and never seen by the ABC team. They supposed he would wear it on his courier voyage to Zanzibar. Meanwhile, he went about with nothing more than a kind of loincloth, his body burned black, his once-blond hair now dark and greasy and reaching to his waist. He smelled of animal fat and charcoal. Yet he was unfailingly polite and he kept his charming smile. Still, the Londoners suspected the wild wandering of his eyes and the savage way he drove off anyone who strayed near the Stinkpot.

He might have continued in this state of suspended animation if the challenge of LZ-59 had not come along. Lord Bertie's opinion that the Zeppelin would be near Kilimanjaro around November 25 rekindled a flame. It was the day Paul would invade Portuguese Africa. The Zeppelins were a mystery to Chuck, but he was sure of one thing. They went up like bonfires at the slightest excuse. He supposed LZ-59 was using Kilimanjaro for a guidepost. He knew where Paul was. Why not guide the ship in and guard her against English fighters? This, after all, was what the Stinkpot had been waiting for and why she had resisted the flight to Zanzibar. Chuck tested the engine one more time, called out his eleven-man native team that had been drilled to perfection in the launching of the hydroplane, and informed the ABC group of his intentions. Then he went back inside his hut to dress properly for the occasion, while his mystified assistants stuffed into the cockpit the rolls of yellowish bark cloth whose use he would not explain.

Kapitänleutnant Ludwig Bockholt stood in the control car, weighing his chances. Luck had been with him all the way. His body protested against almost eighty hours of sleepless anxiety. When he did climb into his hammock, he remained conscious of each small change in the noises around him: the pitch of the four high-altitude Maybach MB IVA motors, the beat of the propellers, the deep boom created by the rush of air along the airship's outer skin, the creak of iron girders, the echoing bangs of stays inside the gloomy belly where the huge balloons of gas sighed and moaned. He worried about the engines and shut each one down in turn while his engineers made running repairs and checks. When he could get away from the bridge, he scurried through the interior to see that nothing had been overlooked, balancing on catwalks while he contemplated the innards of what he called his whale.

Airmen in this dawn of the age of flight were like fledglings, obsessed with the will to fly, mindless of the possibility of failure. Bockholt was certain he could complete the mission, though some of the crew were not in good shape. Staggering along narrow catwalks in semidarkness, clinging to greasy handrails in temperatures swinging wildly from a hundred degrees Fahrenheit to near zero, climbing twenty-degree gangways, pumping fuel from tank to tank by hand, lugging big oil drums of fuel, retrimming, groping around flailing bags of hydrogen gas they knew could easily ignite, and alarmed by noises that imagination invested with the dread onset of fire, they were near total exhaustion.

Lanni had borne up well. In her dungarees and sailor's tasseled cap, she seemed perfectly at home. Only the Kaiser's personal order had made her presence acceptable to Bockholt's chiefs in Berlin. She had won over his bridge officers by coaxing decent meals out of an icebox stuck in the side of the control car where the cold air outside kept the contents frozen.

Bockholt's plan was to come down in the high veldt between Kilimanjaro and the ABC wireless unit. A lot depended on weather conditions and how much Lanni could identify from the air.

On the fourth morning, making nearly sixty knots on a southerly course at 16,000 feet, LZ-59 caught the first rays of the sun over the Rift Valley on her ribbed skin. English settlers at Eldoret later described what appeared to be a ball of fire that slowly resolved itself into the strangest sight Africa had ever seen.

Chuck Truman, alone in his modified hydroplane, saw the torch-like spectacle. He had gambled on his own calculations and he had won. In front of him was the top of Kilimanjaro, pink and delicate as a flamingo's feathered breast. Beyond was the great Zeppelin riding in majesty and alone. He pulled the Stinkpot into a steep climbing turn to intercept the airship, and he checked the rolls of yellowish bark cloth he had placed under his legs. For the occasion he had pulled on several layers of thick English army sweaters, corded cavalry trousers, a riding boot for one leg, and puttees on the leg with the wooden foot. He wore a pith topee with a spine pad of quilted cloth interwoven with red material and buttoned to his shirt, the booty from a guerrilla strike.

He checked the horizon. No sign of English fighters. No risk of anyone getting up-sun of him. His service ceiling was 15,000 feet, and he was squeezing a little extra now to meet the Zeppelin. The opposition's BE2Cs were capable of 10,000 feet at most. The Royal Flying Corps had never bothered to send machines of a more advanced design to Africa, where there seemed no prospect of dogfighting.

Kapitänleutnant Ludwig Bockholt saw the sun strike the upper wings of the hydroplane ahead of him and a little below. He'd been briefed on what the English flew in Africa by meticulous experts originally appointed to cut heavy Zeppelin losses over England. If he held his present height, he should be safe. The dark hump spreading rapidly along the eastern horizon was Kilimanjaro, lapped on this side by a sea of cloud. He would have to valve gas and drop below the cloud to get his bearings. He rang the orders on the telegraph and felt his ship sink under him. He signaled the deck hands who doubled as searchlight and machine-gun operators to track the unidentified hydroplane coming up.

Chuck unfurled the long yellowish banner of beaten bark as he cut across the Zeppelin's path and turned gracefully onto a parallel course. He had daubed black lightning bolt signs along the fabric of the hydroplane's fuselage and on the reassembled floats. He was throttled right back. The Stinkpot overtook LZ-59 at a relative speed of twenty knots, slow enough for Lanni to identify the Thunderbolt insignia of Cornelius's forces. She clutched Bockholt's arm and shouted above the steady beat of the airship's four Maybachs, punctuated now by the stutter of machine guns. Bockholt jumped to the alarm bells. The firing stopped. Every man in the Zeppelin seemed to have a face pressed against the shuddering portholes as the hydroplane staggered, sideslipped, and then recovered. The unlikely figure of Chuck Truman in his spine-padded pith helmet gesticulated and Buckholt got out the binoculars. Chuck was signaling, Follow me.

"You are sure?" asked Bockholt, handing Lanni the glasses.

"Yes." She was focused on Chuck's face. "His name is Truman. His sister is married to the Kommandeur. Your gunners have put holes in his machine. I think they might have hit his shoulder. He's brave not to jump."

Bockholt bent over the navigation charts rather than explain that parachutes had yet to catch up with aviators in the colonies. He checked the data scribbled out by his observer. Nearly 20,000 pounds of fuel still. Enough for another sixty-four hours. He straightened up. "Where does he want to take us? In such a machine he cannot fly much farther."

Chuck Truman was thinking the same thing. The single savage ripple of the airship's machine guns had stitched his wings and engine and slashed his arm. He suspected a leak in the fuel line. He knew he was losing blood. He had no means of communicating Paul's location. Unless . . .

He was flying in close formation with the Zeppelin, forward of her main engine propellers amidships and almost abreast of the control car. If only he'd brought a passenger. Someone to clamber out on the lower wing. It could be done. Jacob would have managed it, would have worked his way between struts and crosswires and waited for the airship commander to slide open those side windows. The weight on the starboard wing would have to be corrected with some rough use of the control stick, but it could be done.

He was dizzy from the loss of blood and the high altitude. Why hadn't he brought a passenger? Of course. To take on more fuel. Increase range. If he opened the fuel taps, emptied the starboard tank, it would compensate for his weight. Then tie the stick so the Stinkpot was trimmed to keep up that wing. Why not? He began signaling again.

"He wants you to increase speed," said Lanni, still watching through the binoculars. "He wants to tell us something."

Bockholt had been watching the hydroplane with dismay. An airship was cumbersome compared to a small airplane. The maniac out there was close to stalling. "So he wants more speed? Yes, of course! Stupid of me." Bockholt rang for full speed ahead. The engines surged and the airspeed indicator crept up to seventy knots. Bockholt let the observer sing out the figures while he kept his eyes fixed on the hydroplane. It was too damned close! Did the fool know how inflammable this ship was?

Chuck knew. He signaled again. Hold course steady on the horizon. He motioned to open the side window and nodded encouragement when Lanni slide the big panels sideways. Now or never. The fuel was all on the port side. If he moved fast, his own weight would balance once he let go of the controls.

The noise outside the control car of LZ-59 was tremendous after Lanni opened the window. The ship's commander gripped the edges of the chart table in horror. There was absolutely no way of outmaneuvering the lunatic in the machine. If the airship decelerated and the hydroplane continued to keep formation, it would eventually stall and crash into the ship. If he called for an emergency valving of gas, the equivalent of a submarine's crash dive, he would drop below the hydroplane and run the risk of the pilot being unable to see the airship and landing on top. In either case, some two million cubic feet of hydrogen gas would explode and the LZ-59's girders and gondolas and machine-gun brackets and engine pods would slowly separate while the crew tumbled through the separating rings to become flaming torches slowly twisting earthward.

Bockholt issued orders in a tense low voice to his desk officers. Two stationed themselves by the open window, their cheeks pressed flat by the slipstream. The tips of the biplane's wings seemed close enough to touch. They saw the pilot stagger out. His helmet had been torn away and his matted hair gave him a demonic appearance as it flew out in the wind. He swung from crosswire to strut, one leg dragging, and slowly worked his way to the two men reaching out to grab him. The innately stable machine was so slow in responses that it had been discarded early in the war for aerial combat. Chuck's familiarity with it had been rewarded. He knew if he moved with all speed along the lower wing, the weight on the opposite side would not take effect until he jumped to the airship's control car. Then, relieved of the burden on his side, the Stinkpot would bank away and fall gently into a long shallow dive out of the Zeppelin's path.

It almost worked. Chuck braced himself on the outer struts and judged the distance. Even without the help of the airship's crew, he could leap to the side of the control car, arms through the window, one foot gaining purchase on the ridged metaling. But he needed all his faculties. His other foot was dead wood, insensitive, a club. At the crucial moment the artificial foot slipped off the shimmering fabric, Chuck lost his balance, and in that last desperate moment he threw himself toward the waiting arms. Other hands dug feverishly into his shirt, which ripped away. Fingers clutched his hair.

Lanni was half out of another open porthole farther aft. She saw Chuck grasp a stanchion with one hand. His legs flew away from his machine and banged against the side of the control car within her reach. The slipstream had plastered him against the pod while his other hand groped blindly until it curled around the strut beside the other hand.

The Stinkpot lurched. The torque of the engine exerted a new force now that Chuck was gone and the weighting was lopsided. The machine rolled slightly away from LZ-59, stabilized, and then veered toward the airship again.

Bockholt screamed orders, alarms sounded through the bowels of the ship, vents were torn open, and the Zeppelin seemed to shudder to a halt as the nose went up to present as small a target as possible to the pilotless missile. The desperate maneuver, worked out in actions over England by Bockholt, was used only in direst emergency. It tilted the airship at a steep angle. It was called "walking the tail." Men were tossed from the catwalks, lost their footing on ladders, and fell between girders. Lifting the nose of the airship was like stabbing the sky with a cigar, and reduced exposure to the bolting Stinkpot.

The roar of the Gnome engine and the rush of air carried away Lanni's shouts, but Chuck seemed to hear, for she saw him twist to face the bucking hydroplane. He was stretched horizontally with his legs within her grasp. He struck out with a booted leg, and she grabbed the other foot. His boot struck the hydroplane's wing tip. The slight jolt lifted the wing a few degrees. The machine rolled on its axis, the nose dipped, and the Stinkpot turned away from the Zeppelin in a slow descending arc, as ladylike in dying as she had been during her long affair with Chuck Truman.

The effort of kicking had loosened his hold on the handgrips. The ship was floating nose up. For a second his whole weight depended from the foot in Lanni's grasp, the wooden foot fashioned by his sister Kate's black nurses so long ago. Then the foot tore loose. He bounced along the Zeppelin's skin and was sucked into a whirling propeller. It happened so quickly that Lanni continued to stare at the artificial foot in her hands until Ludwig Bockholt pulled her back from the porthole.

The impact of Chuck's body broke a propeller blade, and the reduction-gear housing in the engine cracked. Bockholt rang for all working engines to be disengaged. While his officers checked the damage and brought the airship back to an even keel, he watched the long upward slope of Kilimanjaro drift closer. One of his eyelids had developed a bad twitch, and his stomach still churned. He turned to Lanni, supporting herself against a chart table. She had put Chuck's wooden foot between brass supports above the charts. She gave it a last look and shifted her gaze to his face. She was completely under control.

"Can you recognize anything? Anything down there at all?"

"Yes," she said calmly. "There. See? The English railway to Uganda." She was pointing eastward. She bent over the charts. "Von Prinz is here."

Bockholt marked the position she had indicated. His ship was drifting down through the mountain's plumes of cloud and mist. He lost sight of the higher peaks. Beneath, the ground tilted up to meet him. He was over the high slopes on the east side of Kilimanjaro. One of his engines was out. Another had water in the gasoline. Maneuvering would be awkward but possible. His altimeter read 8,000 feet, but the ground seemed now to be within reach of the tow ropes and landing lines. He was in danger of being carried against the mountain. Cautiously, he tested the effects of forward power on the remaining two engines. The big rudders and elevators of the Zeppelin's tail fin waggled and she turned slowly to parallel the slopes. He valved more gas. The ship wallowed through the murk over dark scree-covered ravines.

Lanni said softly, "We're close." She had studied the German *Schutztruppe* maps so often, and later, preparing for the flight, she had learned the navy's methods of aerial navigation. Now, a few hundred feet above her own people's land, she picked up familiar trails.

LZ-59, trailing ropes, sailed into an alpine valley with the serenity of a cloud. Bockholt knew how treacherous appearances were. He was not surprised when, valving gas fast, the Zeppelin struck with tremendous force the rocks at the head of the long valley. The snapping of girders and struts left him unmoved. He had judged the wind correctly, and the Zeppelin was held fast against the face of the mountain.

On that same morning Kate awoke to her first day on Portuguese territory. During the night Paul had led a platoon to reconnoiter the Portuguese post at Ngomano. Concluding that there were enough rifles, machine guns, horses, and medical stores to supply his army, he was preparing an attack. She heard the muffled sounds of preparation and then silence. Wearily she rose from her cot and paused at the entrance to the shelter they had built only hours earlier.

She was in a forest of great holy trees. She walked toward the river between the twisted trunks of two giant fig trees joined by aerial roots through which the browsing elephants had cut an arch. A strange formation of cotton plants appeared as dancing specters. She passed among feather-leaved acacias into a glade.

An unearthly light came from the cloudy sky reflecting a sun not yet risen. The spirit of the *bundu* seemed so powerful that she was prepared to hear voices. The sudden screech of a turaco, flaunting carnival feathers, made her jump.

A form took shape under a big sycamore fig tree. She frowned. Tall arum lilies stood sentinel before the shadowed outline of an intruder. She thought at first that she was staring into the blazing eyes of a lion; there was the suggestion of a mane sweeping back from the head and shoulders. She was aware of the warning bark of zebras, the rustle of tiny dik-dik, the ring of unseen birds.

She saw her brother. "Brer Fox! How did you get here?" He made no move, but his face broke into his most sweet and endearing smile. She said, "Chuck, dear, you cannot be here." Still he did not answer.

She felt a sensation of warmth and well-being. He remained fixed before her, bareheaded, and his hair now seemed touched with gold. He wore an expression she had known since childhood, of wanting her to understand him. She had no fear. She remembered the screech of the turaco and how swiftly it sped. She lifted her eyes from Chuck to look for the bird. When she looked back, the glade was exactly as before Chuck appeared.

She went cold with a sense of utter loss and emptiness. Had she been dreaming? She moved. No, she was still standing where he had faced her, but he was gone and she felt her limbs lose their strength, and a sensation like molten lead in her veins. She hurried back into the shelter and fell at once into a deep sleep. When she awoke, she knew without the shadow of a doubt that dear Brer Fox was dead.

Kate never mentioned this when Paul returned. He was triumphant after a day of skirmishes. The loot was phenomenal, more than he had expected: enough ammunition alone to last his men for weeks. This was how they would survive. She listened, but she did not exult with him. If a gun had been placed in her hand, she would have used it to save him but not herself. For the next month she slept always with a profound sense of emptiness, and she removed the pistol from under her pillow.

43

"So COME kiss me, sweet-and-twenty. Love's a stuff will not endure."

All day long the lines had run through Kate's head. It was ridiculous. She couldn't even remember where they came from. Love did endure. It had stood, for her, a terrible testing. This was her fourth Christmas with Paul. It would be their first Christmas together in conditions of reasonable comfort. For twenty-two days after crossing the Portuguese border, Paul's columns had marched six hours a day with half-hour halts every two hours, covering twelve kilometers a day. In striking distance of the Zambesi, Paul called a halt.

The drill was always the same. Kate's four askaris cut down

branches and made the frame for the tented sections of a grass hut. The bearers would come in from the march an hour later and cut firewood. More companies would be arriving while the camp grew around the Kommandeur's hut. A table was built from branches. There he skimmed through reconnaissance reports and messages. Around him machine guns were sited. He had split his army into three divisions, each with one hundred Europeans, six hundred askaris, and a thousand carriers. The additional numbers were *Schutztruppe* officers and men who had trailed him from the outposts and carriers picked up locally by Cornelius.

On December 25, 1917, there had been three days of respite from the harsh routine. The English had been left behind. Any fight with Portuguese units ended in the enemy running away. Like yesterday's lightning raid by a mixed group of Cornelius's men and askaris under Major Wolfe. He had come back with cigars and jars of Mateus for Christmas.

"How's the old lion?" asked Wolfe, ducking under an awning of boughs.

"Still sleeping," said Kate.

"We're ready to move him. To a four-poster with clean sheets and a tear-proof mosquito net for two. Fresh linen and one of those embroidered Portuguese counterpanes."

"It sounds inviting."

"Even a sort of mistletoe," crowed Wolfe, holding aloft a sprig with white berries. "Merry Christmas!"

She was surprised by the passion of his kiss. Even Wolfe looked flustered afterward. He stammered, "I brought these for you," and handed her a portfolio of sketches done on the march.

"They're—they're works of genius!" She was genuinely impressed. He had caught the feelings as well as the action of the men, and the atmosphere of Africa, in simple bold strokes. Her hand trembled slightly. One sketch resembled her nightmare long ago when, watching with Jacob the arrival of askaris at Tanga, she'd had the sudden vision of an army of skeletons led by a death's-headed general astride a pony of skin and bones.

"I'm sorry," said Wolfe. "I got carried away." He was referring to the Christmas kiss, but she thought he meant the drawing. His observation gave the moment a significance she otherwise would have dismissed. She closed the folio hastily.

"He's still sick," she said. "Can you carry him without a disturbance?"

"Positive! Kornatzki gave him an extra dose of his special 'quinine.' You'll see."

Kate watched doubtfully as he crossed the space to the large hut erected during the night. The day was scarcely born. The dew shone and spider webs sparkled. Morning doves cooed. She went back into the Kommandeur's hut. She had wanted Paul to sleep in his "office" alone. He needed long undisturbed hours of rest while he surfaced from another bout of malaria. This attack had been worse than anything before. For the first time he'd admitted defeat and let the Governor and Cornelius handle the administrative paperwork affecting the *Schutztruppe*. The Governor hadn't liked it much, but Cornelius understood military jargon still beyond Dr. Schnee's ken.

"Here we are."

She turned quickly at Wolfe's whisper. With him were Count Kornatzki, the sea diver Innocence, and Cornelius, all wearing large grins. Behind them stood four sergeant askaris. She stood aside.

They had worked out the procedure by numbers. Paul appeared to be in a deep slumber from the drug boiled out of wild nettles by Kornatzki. They lifted his cot between them. It rose, complete with the nailed uprights that supported the torn and stained netting. Kate thought of the Swahili name the askaris had given him: the shroud maker. There was something funereal in the white cocoon borne aloft to the new hut.

When she finally followed them in, Paul had been shifted to the double bed. Wolfe had been justified in his pride. His marauders must have carried the huge bed miles through the bush from the Portuguese settlement. It looked big enough to hold an entire family of little Portuguese.

"And on the menu," Wolfe was saying, "we've got haunch of piglet with crackling, sauerkraut, sweet potatoes, Mateus rosé, port, and cigars. A regular Christmas dinner, just whenever he wakens."

"I'll call you," she whispered and ushered them out.

"Love does endure," Paul croaked when she came back.

"You startled me!"

"I couldn't spoil their fun. I heard you earlier, talking to yourself. Love's very durable stuff where my poor Wolfe's concerned."

"Major Wolfe! He worships the ground you tread on."

"Mmmm." Paul lifted himself onto one elbow. He was laughing, and when he stretched out his arms, the skin had lost the damp feverish look. "He's faithful in his fashion. Merry Christmas, *Kätzchen*! The last one we'll spend in a state of war."

Minutes later Kate said, "Did you mean the end of war for every-one? Or just us?"

"Everyone. And if we hang on, whatever happens to Germany, there will be no question of our authority in Africa. The English cannot say we gave up and so surrendered our government."

"But if Germany loses?"

"It's what I had always anticipated. The best of what was Ger-many can be replanted here."

Kate shifted to the side of the bed at the sound of a cough outside. She knew that half-apologetic sound. "Come in, Your Excellency!" she called.

Dr. Heinrich Schnee appeared in the doorway, dressed in the starched white uniform of colonial civil servants, designed long ago by those who feared the sun. His cocked hat with a new set of ostrich plumes was under his arm. The hat, Kate noted, was riddled with tiny holes and coated in mildew.

"Season's greetings, Kommandeur!" The Governor gave a stiff little bow. "Dear lady, a most happy Christmas!" He jerked forward an involuntary step but recovered his balance with dignity.

"Reciprocations!" said Paul, falling back against his pillow.

The Governor advanced cautiously. In the still air of the hut, the fumes accompanying him were almost ignitable.

"I have, ah, been thinking," said the Governor, shyly withdrawing a hand from behind his back and revealing a liberated bottle of Por-tuguese wine. "But first, do you mind?"

"No. But not for me, Excellency."

The Governor nodded solemnly and took from his tunic pocket a small glass. Then, remembering, he said hastily, "Madame?"

Kate hid her distaste at the sight of the grubby glass. "Thank you, no." Then, to explain her cold stare, she added, "I was admiring your—your starched uniform. But *starch?*"

"Aha!" The Governor raised the bottle and pointed a finger. "The Kommandeur's wife is jealous." He giggled. "But you should know better than most, Madame, the ersatz talents of Etrich." Sensing a sudden tenseness, he said, "We must be ready for distinguished visitors at all times, isn't it so?"

"Is this what you were in the process of thinking?" Paul de-manded.

"Thinking? Ah, yes, what *was* I thinking?" Governor Schnee stared into his glass for inspiration. "We are perceived here as saviors from Portuguese officialdom. I see the natives rally to our side as an escape from the bastinado and the chain gangs. We are, dear Kommandeur, on a threshold—"

Paul wrenched his mind away from Schnee's peroration. Kate was still pale and shaking from the reference to starch, for she had used starch to restore the Uganda king's hat. From that small incident had evolved the melodramatic rumors about the kidnapping of Baby Paul by the king's men.

". . . and so rumors turn to facts," the Governor was saying. Paul's wandering mind caught on to the last few words. ". . . remarkable feat. . . . Marvelous to think the All Highest might soon be here among us."

"What feat?" Paul sat up. "Where's the Kaiser?"

"The Zeppelin," said Kate, summarizing the Governor's words, for she saw that Paul had not been listening, "LZ-59. They're saying it was a proving run."

Her words brought Paul out of the four-poster as if he had vaulted a horse. At the sight of his emaciated body, the Governor hiccuped and backed off.

"Will you never come to a point, Excellency?" roared Paul. "Send for Major Wolfe. Kate, my map case, please. What's all this about the Kaiser?"

The Governor crept nervously back. "One never knows, Kommandeur." He risked a roguish smile. "They *say* a test flight. But, of course, if the Kaiser's here, they would never tell us so."

"The Kaiser is not here!" Paul said flatly. He slid into his ragged shorts. "Really, Heinrich, you must keep a sense of balance." But his own face was shining with excitement.

Kate produced the maps and Paul held them close to his good eye. "Within a few kilometers of Tom von Prinz, eh? Excellent! Extraordinary! When?"

"The day we crossed out of German East," said Wolfe when he had responded to Paul's summons. "I just got the news."

"Thirty days after the Zeppelin landed!"

"Ease off, sir," said Wolfe angrily. "ABC intelligence takes two months at the best of times."

"Why the delay here?"

"My fault," the Governor owned up. "I requested administrative signals come to me while you were sick. It seemed kind to divide up the work. Unhappily, ABC thought it a civil matter since it involved the loss of a noncombatant, a neutral."

Kate gasped and turned white-faced to Paul, who had switched his attention. "We'll march straight north through the Livingstones."

"You're talking of seven, maybe eight hundred kilometers!" protested Wolfe.

"We can do it! Fast and straight as an arrow." Paul rubbed his hands. "Perfect! Splendid! To have both military and civil administration back where they belong, on the mountain."

Wolfe saw Kate covering her face with her hands, silently crying. "Come, now. Christmas is nothing but maudlin sentiment and false laughter to bring on tears."

She removed her hands. "Tell me, Major Wolfe. Who is the 'neutral noncombatant'?"

Wolfe was at a loss. "I've no idea."

"I have. My brother!"

Major Wolfe stood back, aghast. "My dear girl, you mustn't think like that!"

"Well, read your reports and we'll see," said Kate in a tired voice. "Go now. You've work to do." She pushed him gently away. A great load seemed to lift from her mind. The feeling of absolute loneliness that had engulfed her at the glen dissolved. She no longer wanted to understand how Chuck had appeared before her. Their meeting now seemed strangely perfect. She was left with the same exquisite mental pleasure with which he had irradiated her when he smiled. Paul had left the hut, and she stretched out on the bizarre four-poster and fell into the same oblivious sleep that had followed Chuck's appearance in the glen. This time she suffered no sense of loss. She was awakened by Wolfe stroking her face. She stared at him with large solemn eyes and said, "It is true, isn't it?"

"Yes," said Wolfe. "It's always the good ones who get killed."

Kate was constantly at Paul's side now. He was always in pain. She became his eyes and supported his rifle and checked the sights and range, for it was necessary for him still to squeeze the trigger, to feel he was sharing the danger and contributing to the larder. He liked the simple triumph of killing an antelope for the pot and fashioning from its skin a pair of ankle boots, all without the tools of civilization. What he most enjoyed was the calming effect of carving wood.

So days and weeks merged. Kate marched automatically, eyes half-closed at the start of the day, and came to when the tramp of feet settled into the monotonous rhythm of a quick shuffling through tick-infested grass or along sandy riverbeds, a muffled pounding of soft earth, a sighing beat like a giant earthworm twenty kilometers in length. She knew the goal was not the Zeppelin's precious cargo or a gathering of forces on the Kaiser's Mountain before Germany collapsed. Something obsessed Paul beyond that. She kept her own counsel and spoke neither of Baby Paul nor of Chuck's appearance at the moment of death. The vision had softened her outlook for a time, but now she felt herself merging with Paul each time she steadied his rifle.

Unpublished dispatch to The New York World *from Quentin Pope, Porto Amelia, Christmas 1917:*

> This correspondent arrived back on the English side to find this sleepy Portuguese African port the scene of another incredible English blunder. A massive troop and supply buildup has begun here despite news of a German airship's extraordinary feat in arriving on Mount Kilimanjaro nearly 1,200 kilometers to the north. The Germans have not only made aviation history. Their Zeppelin is the clearest confirmation that the elusive Paul von Lettow will race back to the Kaiser's Mountain with his remaining forces.
>
> His nine-company German guerrilla army is escaping through the dripping rain forest and across the vast savannah plains under cover of pounding rains normally starting in January. By my computation, the Germans will have struck nearly five hundred kilometers west of here into the heart of Portuguese Africa.
>
> But the base wallahs here, the red-tabbed administrative staff officers, will not accept that any army can move doggedly in this manner in these conditions. When they can tear themselves away from the pleasures of a Portuguese bordello town, they grapple with diversionary problems such as the difficulty of transshipping troops and supplies across Porto Amelia bay in small dhows and landing on open beaches (which becomes impossible if the wind blows the wrong way). A few eager young Englishmen dart in pursuit of the Germans along what they call the Tough Trail, TOUGH being an acronym for Trail of the Uncatchable Good Hun, a doubtful tribute to the German Kommandeur.

Quentin Pope had not been able to get his dispatches out of German territory because of the blockade. Now English censors held them up because of his frank criticisms. The exception was Myles Hagen, who agreed with the American and gave him as much information as he dared.

"You should know," he told Pope, "that Tom von Prinz is dead."

"And his wife?"

"Wife?"

"You know damn well his wife joined Prinz on the mountain."

"No." Hagen assumed his frankest expression. "The man I sent up there never came back. The post is too well defended to be worth an assault and our information is sketchy."

Pope knew how much Hagen would like him to discuss what he had learned inside Paul's camp, and he was resolved to say nothing that might imperil his former German companions. But his mind was racing now. If Magdalene was up there and Prinz was dead . . . ?

"Can't you negotiate a surrender?"

"You want to try?" asked Hagen, hiding his jubilation. Of course Pope would try. He'd do anything to get back with the Prinz woman.

"I can tell you where Paul's going," said Hagen to General Forget-Me-Not Gaunt, standing in a Portuguese customs hut above the harbor. "Back to the Kaiser's Mountain."

But the General was in full spate. "He raids a village here, he sacks a post there. Look at the colored pins on these maps, for the love of Moses! What blessed use are pins? I don't want to know where the German's been but where he's going."

"The pins come in gross lots from the War Office," said Hagen. "With them come fuzzy-cheeked schoolboys trained in, um, intelligence. They tell me the pins will indicate a pattern, sir."

"If they'd stop playing with their bloody crayons and get out there, they'd see the patterns all right. It's not as if the enemy's skulking. He's got machine guns, *our* field guns—" Gaunt broke off and glared down his long equine nose. "What did you say, hey? Kilimanjaro?"

"The Kaiser's Mountain," Hagen repeated gently.

If anyone else had made such a prediction, Gaunt would have had a doctor certify him as shell-shocked and sent him home. But this was Myles Hagen, the only Englishman who had insisted on passing up promotion and transfer to finish his feud with the Hun. General Gaunt said softly, "You don't have to tell me *how* you know. Just an opinion on how reliable *this* opinion is."

Hagen tapped his head. "I can read Paul's mind. He knows about the Zeppelin; he knows the crew got all the stuff up to the *Koenigsberg* gun. He wants to be with that gun when the Second Reich falls to pieces. For him, it's the people's gun."

"So?"

Hagen walked over to the map. "He's in there some place." He flattened his hand over an area about as large as England. "A direct path projected to Kilimanjaro narrows the cone of possibilities. Send a column here"—he pointed to a blank space on the map south of Lake Tanganyika—"and with scouts flanking the strike force for ten miles either side, you can't fail."

Gaunt stroked his long chin. "Forgive me, Captain Hagen, but that's *really* stretching things. Northern Rhodesia! I've chanced my arm with you so many times—and got my balls in the wringer for it."

"But I was always right."

The General nodded. "Aye, *after* I felt the pain."

"Well, if you'd acted faster, you wouldn't have got your bullocks crushed," said Hagen unsympathetically.

"I'll forget you said that, Captain."

Hagen leaned over Gaunt's desk. "You've forgotten and forgiven me a great deal, sir. You've given me freedom of action. Now give me that flying squad of horsemen." Hagen crouched like a bird of prey. His fingers on the desk were like talons, and in his eyes burned a fierce and watchful light. "Give me control of my own guerrillas."

"You're a ruthless bastard," said General Gaunt. "Are you asking for guerrillas or thugs?"

"Why split hairs?" asked Hagen. "We're all killers, thugs, tricksters. Remember the *Punch* cartoon? The field marshal asks the cavalry general what the purpose of cavalry is, and the cavalryman says, 'I suppose to give a little tone to what otherwise might be a vulgar brawl.' "

Gaunt allowed himself a bleak smile but refused to be diverted. "I don't sanction thuggery, Hagen. I don't like it."

"You'll like it less when Germany's defeated and the Kaiser still has his bloody mountain, sir."

Gaunt cocked his head on one side and studied the map again. "We'd look a pretty bunch of fools if the German heartland is torn out, eh? And we here still defeated by a few Germans, eh?" He sighed and fingered the forget-me-nots embroidered on his tunic. "From your own pack of hounds, then. Give 'em a code name. Then

I'll have some entry for the friggin' ledgers. Call it after the Trail Of the Uncatchable Good Hun: TOUGH—Tallyho. I'll spin some yarn for the chiefs of staff. Don't burden me with details. Just one thing."

Hagen looked up, unable to conceal the hunter's gleam in his eye. "What's that, sir?"

"When you make contact with Lettow, let me know. I want to be in at the kill. Or the promotion."

German forces seemed to have vanished into the unmapped interior by the summer of 1918. "They would appear to be hermetically sealed from the outside world," wrote Quentin Pope on his way to Kilimanjaro. "Yet their actions seem shrewdly timed to take advantage of the impending disaster in Europe, where Germany's days are numbered.

"The Rhodesian police report that a rabble in comic opera uniforms (made up from Portuguese tunics, Nigerian tarbooshes, and Punjabi puttees) raided a plantation railroad. A tall Negro, speaking American English, told the Englishmen on the train there was nothing to fear. His soldiers were all black and ransacked the freight cars with fastidious care. One bandit, injured by white guards, said the raiders were part of Lettow's army heading north to Kilimanjaro, a suggestion laughed out of court by English colonial officials."

This dispatch was spiked by a night editor on *The New York World* on the basis that if he did not know where the devil Rhodesia was, neither would the newspaper's readers.

44

MAGDALENE VON PRINZ shuddered in the first breath of the coming winter snows. Months on the mountain had not reconciled her to this unnatural withdrawal from life. The caves were gray tombs encasing the guns that occasionally spat death when the men of the garrison rose like ghosts in the gray mists of the long gray days. She had lost a husband in this place of barren ledges, so different from the Africa she had shared with Tom in life. The man who killed him was hiding somewhere by the ice-cold river hurrying down to the broad plains below. His name, she believed, was McCurdy. His relationship to herself, she supposed, was that of stepson.

"Keep out of sight!"

The words, uttered in a whispered snarl, left her unmoved.

Kurt Wahle watched her in helpless rage. "Get back. There's a truce team coming up. There'll be spies among them."

She nodded and stood back. Since Wahle had taken command in Tom's place, the bad feeling between them had grown. He seemed to hold her responsible for Tom's death. Even the arrival of the Zeppelin crew with Lanni and Elsa Looff had failed to ease the tension. The reinforcements only heightened her sense of trapped isolation, as if the impregnability of the bastion rendered her impregnable, too, and removed her from all sexuality. She had cut herself off from the possibility of love, and in her heart she knew it had nothing to do with the mountain. It was the desperate fear of never seeing Quentin Pope again.

"It's better if you give up," said Quentin Pope to the commander of the German bastion on Kilimanjaro. "The war in Europe can only end one way now. Why go on?"

"Because we have a right to be here," replied Kurt Wahle. "Regardless of events in another world."

Pope thought the choice of words strange. He glanced sideways at the impassive English sergeant carrying the white flag of truce and said, "Well, that was the message I was asked to convey. I'm here myself on another errand. Captain Looff of the *Koenigsberg* is in English hands. He is responsible for Elsa Looff, whose father has died. I have a note from Captain Looff imploring you to release his niece."

"A note written under duress!"

"I assure you, Captain Looff's concern is very real. He wishes her out of danger."

"She is not here against her will," said Wahle, taking the note but not opening it. "What else?"

"The wife—widow—of Captain von Prinz. Is she safe? Can I speak with her?"

Wahle stiffened, remembering this American long years ago with Prinz's wife at the razed farmhouse. "This request has nothing to do with truce procedures." Wahle tapped the unopened note against his other hand. "Come forward, alone."

Pope followed him a few paces up the chalk-white trail, leaving his escort out of earshot. The two men stood in a clearing between high boulders. The American could see nothing of the German defenses, but he was conscious of eyes watchful behind guns.

"Madame von Prinz will remain here to fight to the end," said Wahle, "as her husband wished."

"But that's suicide!" protested Pope. He thought for a moment. "You cut down the boy bugler at Tanga, I seem to recall."

Wahle stared directly through the American and tried to drive away the ghost of the child he'd killed because there was no alternative.

"There will be a call for eyewitnesses when this war is over," persisted Pope. "There are rules for the conduct of civilized peoples, even in war. You broke the most elementary rule when you shot a child in cold blood."

"He was in uniform."

"I say he was an innocent bystander out of uniform."

"Silence! I'm under no obligation to argue with an American civilian."

"No, an American war correspondent. A trained observer whose word carries weight in courts of law. In a trial for war crimes—"

Wahle turned on his heel and spoke rapidly to his escorts before marching back up the trail. Pope heard the click of rifle bolts. Bayonets barred his way forward, and at the top of the trail the snout of a machine gun poked through the scraggly bush. A German askari appeared. "Stay here!"

Pope shrugged. He knew he had put himself in danger by leaving the protection of the truce flag. He hoped his armed escort would keep cool. He stared at his own shadow in the chalky dust, idly noting how it shifted measurably during the long wait. There was still time to get back to his base camp before a patrol came out looking for him—and for trouble.

Suddenly the crunch of feet made him look up the trail again. He saw Elsa Looff and two guards who stopped at the top of the path.

"I was ordered here!" burst out the girl when she reached him. She seemed angry and frightened. "What is it?"

Before Pope could answer, a warning shot rang out. Wahle appeared again, standing above the LZ-59 machine gun. He shouted down, "Leave! At once! March!" Then he seemed to lose balance. Magdalene pushed past and sent him sprawling.

Pope moved toward her. A German askari's bayonet prodded him back. She spoke sharply to the askari, who turned doubtfully at the familiar voice. His hand trembled over the trigger guard of his rifle. "We are leaving," Magdalene said. "Do not stand in the way. Am I not the widow of the post commander? Then obey!"

Wahle was on his feet, his panther face dark with blood. He shouted, his voice rising to the Potsdamer-Ton level Pope remembered so vividly. Magdalene had both Pope and Elsa by the arms and was rushing them to the bend in the path. Wahle swallowed. "*Feuer!*"

The machine gun stuttered fifteen, twenty times. There was no shortage of ammunition since the Zeppelin's arrival. The gun traversed the path. Above it the shell-torn flag of Elsa's uncle streamed in the wind beside the *Koenigsberg* guns.

Pope felt one of the two women stumble. A few more steps and they would be around the bend in the path. He took a firm grip of Magdalene's waist and half dragged her forward, his other arm now supporting Elsa. Pain stabbed the lower half of his legs, and he thought he would collapse when suddenly the clatter of the machine gun stopped.

He pushed Elsa to safety and then sank down beside Magdalene, who had fallen to her knees, coughing blood.

"Run, you fool!"

Pope stared up into the face of a maniac whose hair reached to his waist.

"Leave her and run," the man repeated. He straddled the path between Pope and the German machine gun. He had two pistols in his hands, a rifle and bandoliers slung over his shoulders, and revolvers stuffed into his belt. Squinting beyond him, Pope saw the machine gunner draped lifelessly over the gun.

He turned back to Magdalene and held her as another paroxysm gripped her body. She trembled violently and her head arched back. "To lie in mountains . . ." She whispered the words, her eyes wide and shining. Even as he watched, the light in them faded. The body stiffened one more time and then became limp.

Part Eight

The Power of the Gun

45

From the war diary of Colonel von Lettow, somewhere in Rhodesia, November 1, 1918:

I am writing to Rachel's uncle, Walther Rathenau, at the War Ministry. God knows if he will ever get it, but these notes will serve as a copy to be delivered in the event the original does not get through. . . . If Rachel had lived, she would see that her dream of a Jewish homeland was not youthful nonsense. . . . She will never grow old as we who are left grow old, nor undergo the disenchantments that come with age. . . . But if the Zionist dream is to gain substance, you may need to re-examine the alternative path through English friends. Do not rule out this man Myles Hagen, who would substitute for the rich lushness of Uganda the wasteland of the Sinai desert as the land of Israel. . . . It is clear the war in Europe is lost to Germany. All the more important that we win it here! My Chinese hero, Sun-Tzu, declared that *"power grows from the gun."* I see the thought reiterated in an outdated Fatherland paper just to hand that quotes the famous fighter pilot Hermann Goering: "Guns will make us powerful, butter makes us fat." For the future of Africa as well as Germany, I must reinforce the Kilimanjaro bastion and the servants of the *Koenigsberg* guns, the people's guns.

From Quentin Pope in a dispatch to The New York World *(unpublished):*

Magdalene von Prinz was killed in the action. . . . According to Elsa Looff, the intervention came from an American notorious among Stateside police as Ace McCurdy, the train robber. Miss Looff said, "Magdalene always knew McCurdy was the bastard son of her husband. . . . She believed McCurdy shot him after weighing the rival claims of a father-son relationship and the vengefulness of a rejected bastard. McCurdy had been living like a savage and had probably 'gone bush,' lost his reason."

. . . McCurdy behaved in a crazy manner, but I disagree with Miss Looff about his going bush. The term is applicable to most of us who have survived African campaigns this long. When McCurdy held back the new German base commander and killed the machine gunner, he was acting rationally. . . . The circumstantial evidence indicates McCurdy killed Tom von Prinz, but we shall never know for sure.

. . . McCurdy probably saw the dangers inherent in a perfectly defended community based on total military discipline such as his natural father so fiercely advocated. That is the belief of this observer for reasons that are personal and therefore fallible. I believe McCurdy intervened, albeit unsuccessfully, on the side of life and love against the doctrines of death.

From Myles Hagen's The Bird Watching Notes of an English Country Gentleman:

These lines from Rudyard Kipling come to mind:
> For you all love the screw-guns—the screw-guns
> they all love you!
> So when we call round with a few guns,
> o' course you'll know what to do—hoo!hoo!
> Just send in your Chief and surrender—
> it's worse if you fights or you runs:
> You can go where you please, you can skid up the trees,
> but you don't get away from the guns!

Of course, the logical thing for us to do now is declare the war in Africa won and all go home, leaving Lettow to rot. But his use of the Kaiser's Mountain puts a different complexion on matters. It remains sovereign German territory until we spike those damned guns. They have a logic all their own. I still hope to capture Lettow alive, declare him a major general, even make him the Chief of postwar Germany. It all depends, however, on whose guns prevail.

Extracts from English propaganda leaflets dropped by air on Kilimanjaro:

[In Swahili] To the German askaris: Greetings from your comrades serving in the victorious English armies! German masters are full of lies. Germans know nothing. How can they, driven through the bush like wild pigs? The war is over! Our Bwana Mkubwa is chasing the Kaiser. How can the Kaiser pay you the gold you have earned with your blood? You are given bits of paper. What is difference between this paper and leaves on tree? Join us because your German masters are finished.

[In German] To the Kilimanjaro base commander: Your father General Wahle has laid down his arms in an honorable gesture to restore peace to the Africa we share. Your resistance has been magnificent! Your opponents salute you! Burn five bonfires on ledges marked with crosses and we shall arrange safe conduct out.

The accompanying sketch maps revealed the enemy's detailed knowledge of the bastion. But no bonfires burned.

46

KATE RODE loose in the saddle, enjoying the sensation of an animal between her legs again. She felt the movement of the saddlebags and remembered how she had put the buffalo's scrotum into them. Count Kornatzki had handed her the poison in the seamless testicle bag so long ago. She had learned such a lot since then, most recently that a girl like Celeste, carrying the baby of the dead Hammerstein inside her womb, became hard and unfeeling after seeing the fetus torn from her body. Was she, Kate, better for learning such things? She might be still running with the Fifth Avenue crowd, themselves so *maridadi*, so uselessly fancy, indulging their *mazigazi* hallucinations. You had to turn to African slang to describe them adequately. She could never go back to that other life without Baby Paul. Maybe she wouldn't go back *with* him, either.

The fresh ponies had been taken from the Rhodesian town of Fife. None of the askaris begrudged seeing Paul and his woman mounted again. The askaris were infected with pride. They had invaded another territory, the land of Nyasa founded by Rhodes. They had marched through the Zenj Empire of old, restoring the self-esteem of warrior tribes dazzled by white gods. None who marched with Paul considered himself white or black. "We are all Africans," he had said again and again.

But the three young English Zionists who turned up were only interested in getting home. They had rigged and operated the ABC wireless station and then dismantled it as the chase quickened. They had retained their streetwise sense of events, and they were afraid of being caught among Germans if the war abruptly ended. Kate had listened to them with intense curiosity. They talked with Cockney accents about the gossip they had picked up on the airwaves and through their black carriers. They had sought Kate for a last encounter. "We got this 'ere griff about yer baby," said one. "Take it wiv a pinch of salt, mum, but the locals say 'e's up north some place."

Paul reassured her. "I'm sending them to Broken Hill with Kornatzki. It's an English telegraph station. Like all the public services around here, it's run by the British South Africa Company whose disinterest in the war is monumental. Kornatzki will find out what's going on. They'll think he's a Boer."

Paul gave the ABC trio his letter to Walther Rathenau, to be sent on through couriers from South Africa to Berlin. He burned the last of the ABC intercepts. He told Kate, "If Baby Paul by some incredible chance is where these rumors say he is, we couldn't get there any quicker."

"The mountain's our objective," Kate reminded him coldly.

There were rumors, ugly and dispiriting. Elsa had fallen sick after coming down from the mountain with Quentin Pope, the sudden change causing a chest infection that turned into a form of influenza. If she had died, as the rumors claimed, Kate decided to say nothing to Celeste. But about Lanni, reported to be seriously ill in the Kilimanjaro bastion, Cornelius already knew.

"Hagen's behind these rumors," Paul told Cornelius.

"I wish you were right," said the rebel leader, rising wearily to his feet as the company commanders began shouting orders to resume the march. Clad in his Masai cloak, he seemed more remote now, older, and stooped.

Kate felt his indifference to personal tragedy. It resembled her own. She glanced at Paul, whose own armor she had spent so much time removing, and she suffered a pang of regret. His face was bathed in unnatural sweat. The skin had a yellowish tinge He hardly ate these days. They were living mostly on hippo fat and edible fungi. When raids yielded food, it was gone in a day. Black and white would picnic together, storing nourishment for the lean periods that always followed. Paul was beginning to look like the skeleton on the horse of her nightmares. She knew from his eyes that he felt the quickening pace, the time running out, the brush of cold steel at the nape of his neck.

"Take a look at the Governor. Persuade him to stay behind with the next lot of unserviceables," Paul told her one morning as they rode side by side behind the first column.

"I wish you wouldn't use that word."

"Unserviceable. Sick. Wounded. Useless."

She gave him a frightened look, and he leaned out of his saddle and stroked her cheek. "*Kätzchen*, I really think Schnee is sick."

She drew back and let the column overtake her. Paul spurred on ahead. They were entering a plain of thorn and tall elephant grass, perfect for ambush by the enemy. She saw Innocence trotting along and called to him.

"Take this horse." She dismounted and handed the reins to him. He jumped into the worn English saddle. She slapped the tripler's flanks and murmured, "*Pesi, pesi*," and watched it jerk forward.

She stood aside until Governor Schnee appeared on an ill-used pony with branded flanks, the body dumpy and scarred, the mouth hardened by the brutal frontier bits. Schnee bounced like a sack of potatoes. Her heart went out to the pony.

"Another halt?" Schnee stopped beside her. His helmet had shifted to the back of his head and was held only by a strap. His tunic, usually buttoned to the chin, flapped open. He slumped forward and she glimpsed his sickly white belly.

Celeste Looff drew abreast of them. Her section of the women's corps marched alongside litters of English wounded.

"We're making up another stay-behind party," said Kate, signaling the girl over. She spoke to them both. "Near a place called Kasuma. Paul doesn't exactly know where it is, with that ridiculous school atlas." The atlas showed the world on a scale of 200 miles to an inch. Nobody smiled.

Celeste still had the peaches-and-cream complexion of Alsace-Lorraine, the long black lustrous hair, and the amused cat's eyes. But she was no longer the beautiful long-legged tomboy in jodhpurs Kate remembered four years ago on her father's experimental game reserve at Kilimanjaro. Tragedy had marked her face.

"We can dump these English wounded any time. They're nothing but a burden," she said briskly.

Schnee must have had some idea of what was coming next. He did not wish to be left behind, not outside his own colony. He had asked for a captured Portuguese horse because he could better disguise his condition. Kate had seen his hands tremble when he leafed through dispatches at night. She knew he had hallucinations after a battle. He was speaking nervously now, uncorking the flask that was always tucked inside his bandoliers.

"We'll be back in German East by Sunday."

"Not you," said Celeste unexpectedly.

"I am not sick," said the Governor, holding the flask to his mouth.

"More shame on you," said Celeste. "Our hands are full enough with men who need care through no fault of theirs. Just look!" She gestured at the procession. The badly wounded were in the few stretchers. The sick were suspended between poles with slings to support their heads. Each man took the services of four carriers, some of whom were women with babies strapped to their backs. Celeste's black nurses filed on either side of this parade and were flanked by armed askaris who drove off scavengers when the column halted. The stench attracted a following of vultures and jackals, never visible until the litters were on the ground.

Celeste swung back. "Your sickness is in alcohol. You shake from delirium tremens. You should be shot!"

Kate stared at her in astonishment.

Schnee, calmer after his drink, said to Kate, "She's upset. Pay no attention."

"Why should I be upset?" flared Celeste.

"Your poor sister," murmured Schnee.

"What about her?" Celeste froze.

"To be killed in such a terrible fashion."

"Elsa's not dead! She is not dead. How *dare* you—"

The Governor gazed down at her, his mouth open, his mild blue eyes empty of expression, his pink hands clutching the flask. He had let the reins drop and was unprepared for the hysterical girl's attack, sudden and furious, startling the pony into flight. Schnee was thrown backward, and the pony shot away at right angles to the column as the Governor tumbled out of the sliding saddle.

Kate knelt beside the still figure. "He's unconscious."

"Don't move him," said Celeste. "He's probably broken his skull."

"I doubt it," said Kate, feeling the head with gentle fingers. "He's too full of alcohol."

"Don't make excuses," said Celeste. "He knows something about Elsa, doesn't he?"

"No. Only rumors. But you frightened him. He knows you can insist that he be left behind." Kate's voice was drowned in the noise of a gathering crowd. She saw the Governor's servants, his pen-pushing officials, his carriers, his keeper of records. They piled up a small mountain of open boxes filled with forms, and the hot noonday wind swept up some of the forms and scattered them like snowflakes.

She understood why Paul called the Governor a necessary totem pole, a cross carried by crusaders. Now, when the symbol toppled, a superstitious fear excited the procession. She looked around for her own horse. It must have bolted too. She felt dizzy, dismembered, as if all her faculties had been strapped inside her bedroll and saddlebag. Well, thank goodness, there was the bag on the ground. It contained all her worldly possessions now.

She saw General Wahle, better able to ride a horse than walk with his damaged legs, moving with the marching column that had divided around the Governor's retinue. Wahle wheeled beside her. "What's wrong?"

"The Governor," said Kate. "An accident."

"I'll stay." General Wahle glanced apologetically at his legs. "I'm not fit as I was. Excuse me, cemented up here like a blessed statue looking down on you. Not my wish, my dear. But once I'm down, I'll never get up again!"

The old man nudged his way through the crowd.

"Does he know about young Kurt?" asked Celeste.

"I doubt it," said Kate.

"Keep it from him. I'm going to catch up with my wounded and turn them back. We'll make a laager here, Major Wolfe says. The columns are raising a dust storm you can see for miles."

Kate squeezed her arm. The subject of Celeste's sister was closed.

Hagen was leading his TOUGH-Tallyho commandos, the only English force able to hang on to Paul's trail. Hagen's irregulars all wore the potato-sack uniforms invented by Pieter Pretorius after he had brought about the destruction of the *Koenigsberg*. The sacks were pure genius, blending into the landscape yet identifiable by other English-led irregulars.

A decent young intelligence officer from a Gurkha regiment inspected the potato-sack irregulars with Hagen. "Gad, sir!" he told Hagen. "What a remarkable fella that Lettow chap is."

"Really?" said Hagen. "And how would you know?"

"I read the files. Saw a comment written donkeys' years ago by old General Aitken explaining his own disgrace. He said England never kept faith on the gift of the mountain by Queen Victoria. Lor', she's been dead for centuries. And Smuts! Dammit, I never even knew old Smuts fought here. It all reads like ancient history, don't it?"

Hagen gave him such a withering look that the young officer fell mute.

On Monday, November 11, 1918, the Kaiser crossed from Germany into Holland and abdicated as Emperor of the Second Reich. Germany signed an armistice and the War to End Wars had ended. The news touched off a two-day drunk among the staff at the Rhodesian telegraph station on Broken Hill, and nobody thought of forwarding messages to the TOUGH-Tallyho squad operating under Hagen against a bunch of troublemakers up north. During that same Monday night, while the lights came on again in the capitals of Europe, Paul told Kate of his plan to trap Hagen and then win a clear run for the Germans to Kilimanjaro and victory.

47

KATE LAY in Paul's arms and listened in the darkness to his plan for trapping Hagen. It sounded infallible. The battle would be decisive. Her blood raced, and Chuck's description of her husband ran through her mind: "No single man ever held such authority. . . . He lives shrouded from view, armed with drawn weapons."

She would have struggled, once, to possess Paul against his being possessed by the smell of battle afar. Now she seemed almost to draw him to the final tournament, as if she had reached the end of a long journey and had crossed into the ranks of the warriors.

She had waited for a moment like this to tell Paul of her strange and reassuring vision of Chuck at the moment he had died. She said the experience had reconciled her to the loss of Baby Paul, adding, "I no longer fear death, but I fear parting from you."

"But I love you, *Kätzchen*. Love fuses our souls and we live in each other forever. If I die, you carry me within you."

"You love your askaris, too, and they love you. So you'll live as part of their lives, too, Simba. Only, you mustn't die tomorrow. You'll be needed, not only by Germany but by mankind." She moved her head on his chest. "Even your enemies will say this. I know it!"

At dawn Cornelius came to report that the English "potato sackers" were in the neighborhood. "Hagen can't be far away. We'd be wise to make this place the laager and operate from here."

He bent over Paul's hand-drawn charts. Kate hugged her waist and watched him trace the boundaries of the combat area in highlands west of the Livingstone Mountains and south of Lake Tanganyika.

There was a disturbance outside the tent. Kate looked up and thought she saw Paul entering. But Paul was on the ground treating the sores on his bare legs. She looked around again and studied the newcomer who wore a black patch and Paul's clothing.

"Major Wolfe!" She broke into a relieved smile. "The disguise is almost too real. You frightened me."

"Let's hope Hagen's as blinded by hate as you with love," said Wolfe. He added lamely, "For your husband."

Kate pretended not to notice the slip. "I wish you luck, Major," she said and kissed him lightly on the cheek. "Remember that I love you, too, though perhaps not in the same way. But remember it, if anything should happen."

Cornelius, circling with a piece of charcoal the tiny town of Kasuma, glanced at Paul, who shrugged and smiled as if to say, We're all tense today. Major Wolfe bent over the map to cover his reddening face.

"We're fifteen hundred kilometers south-southwest of Kilimanjaro," said Kate, joining him. "I prefer to work from this school atlas," she added, shifting from the roughly sketched chart to the dog-eared textbook. "It makes everything so wonderfully simple. The mountain's so close to us, and there's nothing shown between here and the mountain but pretty green plains."

She wrote "Laager-1500 SSW" onto the map already dotted with crosses marking the previous laagers. But this time she drew, instead of a cross, a circle with a dot, the African trackers' sign for "Gone Home," or *finis*. When Major Wolfe saw it, his face twitched and he straightened up abruptly, as if struck by some awful premonition.

Then he plunged into a discussion of the final preparations that kept his commander engrossed until it was time for their departure.

Major Wolfe, dressed to look like Paul and feeling like a cheap imitation of the Lion of Africa, led the first column. Paul rode out an hour later, concealed within a body of men mounted and on foot. His gun bearer this time was neither Kate nor Skaramunga but the cheerful sea diver, Innocence. There was time for a brief farewell.

"*Kätzchen.*"

"Simba."

She ran after him. "If it's a long siege, finish this. For me." She handed him the blocks of unfinished carving.

She stared into the rising sun that swallowed him, the blinding white light into which she had seen so many white figures dissolve and vanish. For the first time in a great while she was not with him to steady his gun and to merge her skills with his. She hoped he would complete the carving of—of what did she hope?

The spies placed inside Kasuma by Cornelius reported shortly after midday that Major Wolfe was taking tea and strawberries in the garden of the local magistrate, Edwin Croad, who thought he was entertaining the German Kommandeur. Warned the Germans were coming, Magistrate Croad had already opened the jail for a score of English askaris charged with desertion. The men had slipped away to be rehired by Hagen's guerrillas now sniffing around the edges of the town, and unknown to Cornelius they were put into potato-sack uniforms.

Governor Schnee snored most of the afternoon and in the tense twilight whined about the absence of askaris to guard the camp. Kate pointed to the large red crosses made from bark cloth, always kept ready and now displayed. "You can't claim immunity," she chided him, "and remain an armed camp." She moved restlessly among the litters of wounded and checked that bonfires were lit to illuminate the red cross flags.

The new potato-sacked guerrillas from the Kasuma jail approached secretly near midnight. They were fortified with native *pombe* beer, and they had helped themselves to weapons from the Kasuma armories. They were met by two of Hagen's scouts, also clad in sacks. "There's a white man wants to speak with you," they were told.

Hagen's horsemen moved in behind his outriders shortly after dusk. They probed down the rutted roads leading to the Kasuma town center, which encompassed the posts-and-telegraph office, the spired church, the courthouse and Magistrate Croad's bungalow. Under cover of an unusually black night, Hagen positioned his sharpshooters on the edges of the town square.

Then Paul's troops advanced to the rim of the town and quietly encircled Hagen's men. By midnight Paul's sole surviving artillery officer, the quick Captain Hering, had brought up two of the original 1873 field pieces and a *Koenigsberg* four-incher still trundling along on its handmade limber. At dawn the double siege began.

Pieter Pretorius, the surviving member of the two-man English assassination team, knew it was not Paul who was in the Kasuma town square. After questioning the new potato-sack recruits, he concluded that the German commander must be with the laager. He had no means of contacting Hagen. His assignment, anyway, was clear. His dead partner, Freddie Selous, had failed to kill the Lion of Africa. Therefore the job fell to Pretorius, who described the quarry to his irregulars. It was difficult in the dark. "He's not a big man," said Pretorius. "He has bad eyesight, and he wears a very old helmet, this Bwana Simba."

Kate thought Cornelius might have sent some of his own guerrillas back to protect the camp when she heard strangers moving through the night. Her bush sense told her they were not prowling animals. She had hoped for three or four hours' sleep before daybreak, but the demands of sick and wounded were never ending. She had made her rounds. She had admonished the bearers who crept inside the circles of stretchers, because even an injured soldier still had a gun, and the bearers never liked sleeping outside where they could be taken by beasts of prey.

She walked back to her tent and was astonished to see Paul's old helmet on the ground. She remembered the helmet was too large for Major Wolfe's head. She supposed Paul had gone bareheaded because he had not wanted to be recognized.

She picked up the helmet and at once experienced such a flood of sensation that she almost dropped it. It was very much like the first time she had been conscious of Paul's presence, as if all her senses were electrified.

She walked through the camp and found Celeste talking with General Wahle, who was an insomniac. "No matter what happens," Wahle was saying, "I'll die content. My only regret is I'll not live to see Kurt and make my peace with him." He sucked on his pipe. "Such a fuss I made that day. Pulled out my gun. Dreadful, dreadful. Boy must have thought I meant to shoot him because my gun went off, you know. He had to do something heroic to redeem himself. Who'd have thought, eh? My son holding the Kaiser's Mountain, the honor of the Second Reich in his hands—"

Kate touched Celeste's shoulder "I'm going for a walk."

Celeste looked up in alarm. "Then let me come with you."

"No, better you stay."

Oblivious to their whispers, Wahle said, "If I die before I see him, and I know I shall, tell Kurt I forgave, won't you? Give him my blessings if he marries your dear sister."

Celeste stared at him in silence, her eyes wet in the darkness.

"When I knew Elsa was there with him," the General said dreamily, "I knew it was God's will."

Kate left the circle of firelight. It would be typical of Cornelius's guerrillas, trained in bush fighting but ignorant of procedures, to sit outside the camp until first light instead of declaring themselves and coming straight in.

The soft air was fragrant with wood smoke and a kind of highland heather. Wild dogs yapped. She paused near a *donga* and peered into the pale rock-strewn riverbed, now reduced to a trickle. A sweet-sour smell reminded her of the native beer. She thought of the jackal, whose scent was the strongest of all the animals. She had long ago conquered any fear of wild beasts in the night. If you walked boldly and kept away from overhanging trees, you were safe enough. Animals were less prone to attack out of fear because darkness gave them confidence. She remembered walking with elephants peacefully browsing among the tents, picking their way with their trunks, considerate of the tenants. The one thing that scared her then was the feel of an elephant's trunk, the soft fleshy tip searching through her hair. The thought made her put Paul's battered helmet on her head.

She turned her back to the *donga*. She suffered then a curious lapse and imagined she heard the warning chatter of Skaramunga's monkey, Bamboo. As if Skaramunga's ghost had joined her, she seemed to hear the old gun bearer cry out. She reached for the revolver in her belt. A powerful blow between her shoulders knocked the breath out of her. Another blow behind her knees crumpled her to the ground. A stump of wood was rammed down into her mouth, which was open to scream. Fingers tore into her breasts, and there was a guttural shout of dismay that turned into angry mutters. She heard Paul's name and in Swahili some inflammatory growls that this was a woman who had fooled them. A potato sack was pulled over her head. Her legs were pinned apart.

48

HAGEN DISCOVERED too late that he was himself surrounded. His men had closed the circle around Kasuma center and the German forces there, but these were not led by Paul. Instead, Paul's main force encircled Kasuma and were squeezing Hagen into the bull's-eye.

Hagen had never known such savage hand-to-hand fighting. Spion Kop was never like this, nor the Khyber Pass. But still he kept a bull-dog grip on the town center, and by the second day he had crept as far as the churchyard and the courthouse. The streets filled with smoke as Paul's askaris fired bundles of hay upwind of the town. The sky at noon was black as night.

Thunderbolt couriers, directed by Cornelius, ran between Paul's siege force and Magistrate Croad's bungalow at the bull's-eye where Major Wolfe filled old cans of bully beef with dynamite. One of the homemade bombs was wired inside what Magistrate Croad termed his "thunderbox" in the outhouse: a toilet made from a Standard Oil kerosene can with a hole into which was fitted the "top hat," or pot. Wolfe prayed reverently that it would be Hagen triggering the explosion when he pulled the chain.

Wolfe escaped through the English lines back to the Kommandeur's post outside Kasuma on Wednesday morning. He found Governor Schnee there, reporting a massacre at the laager. Women had been raped by potato-sacked guerrillas. Celeste had been dragged away. General Wahle was dead.

"And Kate?" demanded Major Wolfe. "What of the Kommandeur's wife?"

Schnee turned large eyes on the adjutant. "God knows!"

"How in the name of all that's holy, then, did you get away?"

Schnee touched his bandaged head. "I was unconscious a long time.

The leader was polite and apologized for drunken behavior and said a mistake was made. He said I still had authority and I was to come here and inform you the war's over."

Wolfe swallowed his rage. He had a vision of Schnee groveling and then brightening when the enemy's lying propaganda was recited yet again. "The war's not over, Excellency," he said grimly.

Innocence appeared. "The magistrate's house made a very good bang," he reported with a grin. "The thunderbox is intact, though, and awaits the bwana with the red fur."

Innocence confirmed that Paul's men were now closing the circle like beaters moving inward on Hagen and forcing him into the abandoned town center. Major Wolfe thought tiredly, It's come right back down to Paul versus Hagen in hand-to-hand combat, the way it was in the beginning, is now, and ever shall be. He caught sight of the Governor's head lolling to one side, eyes fixed on a wicker basket enclosing a vat of raw Algerian wine.

"Give him a bucketful," commanded Wolfe. "Come to think of it," he muttered under his breath, "tip the bastard in and rename it Pumpernickel wine."

Hagen felt his forces being herded into the town center as his options closed. Two men he slipped into the bell tower of the church carried Mills Bombs and enough ammunition for their Lewis guns to hold off an army. He had ten veterans from the old Uganda Volunteers working their way into the magistrate's house. The post office, which incorporated the government telegraph service, remained in the hands of enemy guerrillas. He glimpsed their distinctive thunderbolt tattoo marks as they paced along the wire-netted counter, and he could imagine their taut nerves tortured by the incessant click of the telegraph key.

"If I can take the post office," he told Gideon, who was directing his potato-sack guerrillas, "I can telegraph for reinforcements."

The Kikuyu agent slipped across to the church. It had become very quiet in the town square. Hagen supposed that the same possibility had occurred to Paul, which would be why his best irregulars were holding the post office when the rest of the central area was being deliberately surrendered. Suddenly the click of the telegraph key was lost in a more rapid stutter of guns. Hagen's men in the bell tower were stitching a path to the post office door. The thunderbolt-marked occupiers hurled themselves out through a back window, then were picked off by one of Hagen's snipers.

Hagen moved into the building and, turning an attentive ear to the telegraph, began to copy down the constantly repeated message.

A stream of couriers jogged between Major Wolfe, on the outskirts of Kasuma and Laager-1500 SSW, four hours' jogtrot away, where Governor Schnee sprawled in the high-backed chair that must have belonged to some unsung English district commissioner. He heard the name *Simba* repeated many times. He heard the numbers of fatalities. He concluded, with a mind inflamed by alcohol, that his *Schutztruppe* commander had been killed. "So the Lion of Africa must be mourned," he said. In the hubbub Wolfe thought he had used some other word like "honored" and merely nodded impatiently. Schnee pursued the matter, his words slurred, "Would you consider,. Major, my duty lies back with those poor people in the laager?"

"You could take them food and medicine," said Wolfe, seeing the growing pile of booty. He should have thought of it sooner. But Schnee had said Cornelius had placed native guards over the camp. Still, Wolfe felt sick with fear for Kate, who was on his mind constantly. He said, "Take Innocence. Do it now. Get there before night falls."

The Governor stared tipsily into his wineglass and decided Wolfe was guilty of insolence. "I am not, sir, under your orders."

"You'll be under my fist if you don't move!" shouted Wolfe.

Schnee heaved himself upright. To preserve some dignity, he poured himself another drink. He did not think it fitting that, as the commander-in-chief whose Kommandeur was dead, he should have to be shepherded to the laager by a black ragamuffin. Another look at Wolfe's face, however, warned him to keep his objections to himself.

Kate had been lying under the burning sun all day. Her clothes had been ripped from her body. The open wounds buzzed with the bluebottle flies that always appeared from nowhere. She was too tired to brush them away. She lay in the *donga*, and the tall elephant grass on either side completed her concealment. She had no sense of how long she might have been there.

Innocence found her toward evening. Once he was under orders to go to the camp, he had moved like lightning. He cared little about the Governor. He wanted only to find the Kommandeur's wife. It took him less than an hour to read the signs and track her to this spot. He gently lifted her onto the bank. Then he called the medical orderlies and began carefully washing her body. When he was satisfied, he let the nurses take her away and went himself in search of revenge.

Schnee arrived on a horse. So long as he was in the saddle, he seemed sober enough. Someone helped him down. He trembled and remained rooted to the ground while he reviewed the scene. The English "potato-sackers" had killed most of the English wounded as well as Paul's own injured men. The guerrillas of Cornelius were chasing away scavengers and digging graves. When he saw Kate carried in, the Governor stumbled toward her. A gaudy sheet of cotton had been put around her by one of the surviving black nurses. Kate looked at Schnee with an expression of composure. One of the nurses carried her things and two more supported her.

Through Schnee's muddled brain ran the thought that he must comfort this girl. He swayed in front of her apologetically. He had not run away. She must not think him a coward. No more than the Kommandeur was a coward, poor fellow.

"What do you mean?" Kate demanded sharply. "Poor fellow—? Paul?"

Schnee tried to fit the pieces together. He remembered Major Wolfe and the messengers, the words "dying" and "the Kommandeur" and "the killing." He remembered the name *Simba* repeatedly mouthed.

"Your husband is killed," said the Governor and crossed himself.

Kate nodded. She called one of the nurses and while she waited, she sat on a soldier's bedroll. The girl returned with the saddlebag. Kate thanked her. By now Schnee was lying on a grassy bank with his limbs stretched out and his head thrown back, dead to the world. The light was failing fast. Camp fires were beginning to burn. She heard the low voices of sentries exchanging passwords. She said a prayer for Celeste, who had put up no struggle because the baby inside her had been destroyed and her man would never make another. She prayed for Baby Paul, who was certainly dead. She felt a strange warm glow like the one imparted by Chuck's ghost in the glen. Somewhere, a great distance away, a lion grunted like the little wood-burning train climbing the flanks of Kilimanjaro.

She felt inside the saddlebag until she located Count Kornatzki's gift of death. The buffalo pouch was wrapped in fibers. She had no difficulty finding the protruding needlelike bamboo shaft. She had tested the poison regularly; it had become a ritual. The poison was replaced from time to time. It came from the cherrylike fruit of a tree that Skaramunga, the soldier of God, had recognized. He would boil the sticks and roots into a sticky liquid, measuring the toxicity for her by making a cut in his arm and collecting a small amount of blood. A drop of the liquid was placed on the blood. If the blood turned black, the poison was good. Skaramunga had known why she carried the poison. Many of the askaris' *bibis* did that, he had assured her. If you were the *bibi* of an askari, the truly valuable thing you carried for him was his seed. If he was killed and your womb was barren, your purpose in life was ended.

She took a knife and nicked her wrist. She squeezed some poison at the foot of the rivulet of blood and watched the black discoloration rise rapidly to the cut. Already it was in her bloodstream. She stabbed the needlelike bamboo quill into the thick vein pulsing in the crook of her elbow. Nobody saw her lie back. She heard the same lion grunt again. She felt herself with Paul gazing down on the lions making love in the sun under a tawny sky. The last sound she heard was the lion's pulsating roar: *Whose land is this? Mine! Mine! Mine!*

Paul squinted through Max Looff's old telescope. The telegraph office was a blur. He wished he had Kate to tell him what was happening in this fading light. He wiped the blind eye and brushed moisture from the other. Two days and nights of fighting had finally broken something inside his head; whatever it was flooded his brain and filmed his eyes with red. Darling *Kätzchen*, I need your help. The gossamer lion needs his steel butterfly.

The world was reeling about him. A rising murmur of excited voices was followed by cheers that grew in volume until every other sound was blotted out. His askaris were chanting that ridiculous invention of theirs: "*Jambo Simba! Jambo Bwana Mkubwa General Kaiser!*"

Hagen was walking toward him, alone.

"Hold your fire!" Paul shouted to the men. A white flag was being waved from the flat roof of the telegraph office. So this was it! Final victory, four years after the Battle of Tanga. The rest of the English armies were of no consequence. It was Hagen's surrender he had wanted. That, and that alone, his Africans would understand.

Paul left the shelter of Magistrate Croad's bungalow and walked to meet his vanquished enemy. The chanting died down. A slanting ray of light from the setting sun broke through the dense overcast and bathed the town center in an unearthly glow. Paul unbuttoned the holster at his waist and stroked the butt of his revolver. With Hagen you just never knew.

They halted within a few yards of each other for the fourth and final time.

"Kommandeur."

"Captain."

"You have won a remarkable victory." Hagen studied the man before him, still handsome, effortlessly erect, without badges of rank on his ripped bush shirt, with nothing to distinguish him from his own askaris except the black patch over one eye.

"You are waiting to say something more?" asked Paul courteously.

Hagen glanced around the circle. The dead lay in the dust. The scavengers crouched in the shadows. The bloodiest battle was over, and the streets of Kasuma would stink of rotting flesh for many days to come. "Sir—" With an effort Hagen dragged his eyes back to the emaciated figure before him. "Sir, I have to inform you that Germany surrendered in Europe two days ago."

Paul heard the words after he sensed the news. He fumbled for the smudged and chipped monocle in his pocket. He removed the eyepatch and replaced it with the monocle. Now it was his turn to examine the enemy: a man turned gray since they had met in Tanga, bull-like and indomitable, crafty and grown old with the campaign.

"Sir," said Hagen, "it appears the telegraphists at Broken Hill have been attempting to get this message through to us for some time." He saw the suspicion in Paul's face and he added softly, "This is no trick. The message is countersigned by your Count Kornatzki." Hagen stared straight into the light reflected from the monocle. "I have the original message for you to read. Let me warn you, with all respect, it refers to a personal matter that will greatly disturb you."

Paul waited, impassive. The sun was dipping below the horizon, and the light now had a melancholy quality, irradiated from the heavy rain-filled clouds above.

"First, I should have congratulated you," said Hagen, surprised by his own jerkiness of manner. "The Kaiser appointed you to the rank of major-general as one of his last acts."

"Last acts? Where is the Kaiser?"

"There is no Kaiser," replied Hagen gruffly. "When Germany surrendered, he renounced the crown and is now a common refugee."

"Then who governs Germany?"

Hagen's expression changed subtly, and the hint of respect for authority entered his voice. "General, I am empowered by His Majesty the King of England to inform you that it is the wish of the British Empire's leading authorities to see you restore order to Germany."

"And where is the British Empire?" asked Paul with the barest hint of a smile.

"There is no empire. Though we won the war, we shall find we lost the empire. You, better than anyone, must know the reason why."

"Yet your King calls on me for help?"

"Sir, you are the only victorious general in Germany. Only you can restore order."

"Show me the telegram, please."

Hagen unfolded a piece of paper. "Your answer, General? His Majesty awaits your answer."

Paul waved the question aside. He brought the paper up so close to his undamaged eye that it almost brushed his nose. He moved the paper slowly from left to right, and the muscles in his scarred face began to twitch. To Hagen it seemed an eternity before Paul said, "And so, all else aside, my son—Kornatzki says my son may be alive in Uganda. Perhaps. Perhaps. Not an immortal soul yet. Not a ghost. My son." He lowered the paper. "A trick, is it, Hagen? Another of your tricks?"

Hagen tried not to see the tears running down Paul's cheeks. "No, sir! Lies are weapons of war. The war is finished, General."

"Then I must look for my son."

"If he's alive, my men shall find him." Hagen stopped for fear of pushing Paul the wrong way. Would Paul in this desperate hour turn his back on duty? His loyalty to Germany had been betrayed. It had cost him youth and middle age. It had cost him a war and a dream. It had cost him a child conceived in a love so rare that it was already a legend.

"Can your King wait a little longer?" Paul asked, his voice suddenly dry. "I must speak with my wife."

Hagen swallowed. "She is here?"

"A night's march away. I would like to go there now, alone."

Hagen stepped back a pace and saluted. In the deepening twilight, his white flag of surrender faded like a phantom from the roof above his head.

49

THE NEWS spread rapidly that England had won, after all. Stunned, the German askaris assembled along the trail back to Laager-1500 SSW, discussing the strange ways of the white man.

Paul paused to speak briefly with Cornelius, who later told his guerrillas, "Africans can take pride in our smashing victory in a war that for us is not yet over, not yet won. It is not yet clear if the Bwana Simba will continue to lead us." Cornelius allowed a new pain to show itself in his eyes, and he stumbled over the next words. "This is a man whose heart is fixed, whose hands thus remain free." Then he sent word ahead that Paul must not be disturbed during his solitary march.

Paul had laid aside his rifle and carried only the unfinished carving Kate had returned to him. His bloodstained shirt was open to the waist. His shorts were shredded. His mane of hair was tawny and black from battle. He walked barefoot like an askari, his body sloping forward. To see this lion pass, English and German askaris huddled under capes and palm-leaf hats in a drizzle of rain.

He fell into the rhythm of the march, to the soft chanting of his men. "*Heia Safari!*" they sang. "*Tuna-kwenda, tuna-shinda* / We go, We win." Shortly after midnight a thunderstorm broke that in ferocity seemed the natural finale to the previous days' fighting. The sky lit up from horizon to horizon, and Paul was almost continuously visible, even in the heaviest of the night's drenching rain. Now his men gathered in ever larger groups and, reinforced by the English askaris, raised their voices to be heard above the cannonlike thunder. All of them, English as well as German, knew the askaris' battle hymn.

The storm endured until dawn. The black cotton soil turned to gumbo and slowed Paul's march. His feet were torn, but he did not break stride.

Red and white flags began to wag, ordering the askaris back to their task of burying the dead. The voices faded and died. Paul moved between olive trees painted with the gold of the rising sun and came upon one of his men talking with an English askari, neither of them aware of his presence. He stopped, unseen.

His askari was looking at the other's uniform. "You wear an English medal."

"It is because I fought at Kilimanjaro."

"Would your king-emperor grant me such a medal?"

"He would need to know why."

"Why? Because I, too, fought at Kilimanjaro."

"But were you not on the other side?" asked the English askari.

"What other side?" The German askari turned to stare at the black corpses piled like logs. "Was it not the same war killed us all, brother?"

Paul slipped away, resuming his march. An unreasoning fear gripped his heart when he sensed the desolation of the laager ahead. He saw Major Wolfe standing before him, his hands hanging helplessly at his side.

"I see it in your face," said Paul, sparing Wolfe the agony of speech. "Where is she, old friend?"

And Wolfe took him to where Kate was buried.

A makeshift cross had been stuck in the earth between the aerial roots of a giant fig tree. Nearby, Paul found a rotting stump and brushed away the film of web in which a tiny crab spider trembled. Upon his face he felt the fresh cedary daybreak air she loved. Her favorite gold-backed weavers flickered between the swaying stalks of purple amaranth. Where he sat, the air grew heavy with the perfume of frangipani, so like her sweet breath that he half expected her to stand before him. His body was motionless, his eyes unseeing, as his mind roved the path of memory.

"Love is more powerful than any impulse to make war," Kate had once said.

He recalled Count Kornatzki responding with the warning, "You're too romantic!"

"You dare call me romantic," Kate had flashed back. "You poke among fossils and skulls here, trying to prove our ancestors progressed through violence, and that doesn't strike you as wildly romantic?"

"Conflict improves the breed," Kornatzki had insisted. "That's fact, not guesswork."

Their exchange must have taken place at Olduvai because Kornatzki had talked about Laager-120 W as the cradle of man, arguing that scientists could trace there the violent links between men and animals. Kate had retorted, "Where man differs from your animals, Count, is that the best and most successful men haven't always been the physically strongest."

"A leader fights his way to the top and only surrenders to superior force," insisted Kornatzki.

"Rot! You're a priest. Read your own Bible! 'Love bears all things, believes all things, hopes all things, endures all things—' "

" '—love never ends,' " Kornatzki had muttered. "My dear child, I can't argue against Corinthians. But what's love to do with the case?"

"A man can still win, even if he appears to lose."

"A formula for national suicide."

"A formula for human love," said Kate. "It grows naturally out of your friend Darwin's theories of survival. Every herd, every pack or pride, every nation survives by mutual concern and endeavor. That's the seed of love."

"Romanticism!" Kornatzki had declared. Now Paul realized how apprehensive the doctor-priest had always been, fearing Kate might soften Paul's will to win.

To win what?

Paul shivered inside the safari jacket, borrowed from Major Wolfe, with its royal crest of an English king faded to a khaki blur. He bared his hunting knife and took up the two chunks of wood he had been carving for Kate. Neither was finished, no clear image defined. The final outcome still lay beneath the surface. To Kate, one carving had seemed at times to be shaping into a *Koenigsberg* gun, eventually to fit snug into the other carving of a gun carriage. Was this what he had won, an argument for the gun?

He began to carve with the wood held close to his good eye. Kate seemed to guide his hand, to whisper to him in the soft murmurs of the forest. He carved paper-thin while the smoke of breakfast fires filtered through the trees and dispersed in the rising heat. The shadows shortened. The sun beat down upon his unprotected head. He carved with such precision that he seemed to whittle away each minute of the day. The long shadows were leaning away from the purple mountains, the light failing. The shapes emerged. The fit was perfect.

He held the two pieces together as Kate had once held them; he remembered the puzzlement Kate had felt. He was not ready yet to lock the pieces into the single indivisible carving for which she had waited. He put the pieces into his pockets and braced himself to find Hagen. He knew where his old enemy would be waiting.

A small knot of onlookers had gathered at a distance from Hagen. Hagen put his hand to his breast pocket and nervously traced the battered cigarette case. He knew General von Lettow better than he had known his own parents or his oldest friends. This man called Paul. This man who set duty above all things. This man so like himself they might have been opposite sides of the same coin. So like himself, except in one respect. Paul had loved a woman. Enough to cast duty aside? The man who must answer to a woman is unlikely to turn his back on his child.

Hagen straightened up. His face fell into professional lines of harsh indifference.

Paul stood before him and said quietly, "My wife is dead. She was right and I was wrong, and that is why she is dead."

Not the words but the sense of them reached the onlookers. They saw Hagen sag. They saw the big Englishman reach out and grip the General by the shoulder.

Count Kornatzki shouldered his way through the crowd, Governor Schnee at his heels. Kornatzki was covered in the red dust of a night-long ride, and his beard and face formed a single claylike mask.

"All I have left," Paul was saying, "is a missing son."

"An army too, still undefeated," said Hagen.

"And a country shattered and abandoned," interrupted Kornatzki. "Germany's without a leader, Paul. That's why Hagen wants you there."

"Hagen wants me out of Africa," said Paul.

"Aye," conceded Hagen. "I'll not rest easy while you command the loyalties of all askaris, yours and mine."

Kornatzki hurled down his knobkerrie. "It's yours at last, Hagen. Thine enemy, never to be loved."

The club lay in the dust at their feet. Hagen stared at it, unmoving. "Tyrants exercised power with that kerrie for as long as their followers made tyranny work." Hagen shifted his gaze quizzically to Governor Schnee.

"I'm here," said Governor Schnee, "to witness the Kommandeur's decision, officially."

"I'm returning to Germany," said Paul.

"And your son?"

"I must entrust the task of finding him to others." Paul glanced at each of them in turn and made his decision.

"I will do my best," Schnee began. "My German administration—"

"Is terminated," snapped Hagen.

"Responsibility for my son is in your hands, Hagen," said Paul with sudden finality. The words of rejection struck the Governor like a physical blow, and he fell back.

"And if I find him alive?" asked Hagen, no less surprised.

"Then I will come back to Africa."

A shadow crossed Hagen's face.

"A moral dilemma for you?" asked Paul.

"No, sir! I'll take the risk of your return." Hagen's face darkened. "You trust me with all you have, before your own countryman. I can only return the trust." He unbuttoned his breast pocket. "Here, sir, is my past. My guarantee of your son's future, should we find him."

He held out the heavy metal cigarette case with its indentations from bullets, shrapnel, and spear. Paul had no need to read the inscription: *"Never surrender."* He had known it since those days of chivalry in southern Africa when he'd first crossed swords with Hagen.

"Should you find him, Hagen, I'll come at once. Here's my token."

Hagen stared at Paul's hands holding the finished carving: a lion and a lioness. Paul locked the lion within the lioness so nothing would separate them.

"Love endures all things," whispered Paul. To the onlookers, he seemed to speak inaudibly to the wooden block in his hands. "Love never ends."

He held out the carving to Hagen. Their hands touched above the striped knobkerrie. It lay in the dust, its stains of blood and brain forgotten.

50

From Quentin Pope in a dispatch to The New York World, *datelined North Rhodesia, Tuesday, November 26, 1918 (published next day):*

A former policeman in Uganda, General William Edwards, yesterday accepted the surrender of the Lion of Africa, General von Lettow. We know of no military precedent for a victorious army surrendering to the generals who lost.

General von Lettow led the first detachment and halted his troops in close formation before advancing, alone, poker-backed and clothed in rags that lent him a curious dignity. He dominated the high-ranking English officers, though he wore no insignia save the now famous black eyepatch, and scarce could see.

General Edwards represented 137 English generals and 401,068 English troops, most of whom have quit this battleground.

The Lion led his command of thirty German officers, 125 German settlers, five German doctors, 1,100 askaris, and 819 women, white and black. Their total arms were 38 machine guns, a naval cannon on wobbly wheels, and 2,000 rifles. They made an impressive spectacle: the long motley columns, veterans of a thousand battles, askaris clothed in every kind of headgear, women who stuck to their men through four years of intense hardship and grueling marches, some with children born and grown during the campaigns, followed by porters chanting the famous *Heia Safari* song that is planting in Africa a legend that will not diminish until the Lion—so it is whispered—leads a black revolution.

From Myles Hagen's The Bird Watching Notes of an English Country Gentleman, *January 1919:*

The Lion of Africa is finally going home! Red tape delayed his departure. Ironically, the biggest red tape merchant of all, former Governor Schnee, still managed to race back to Germany ahead of General Lettow with his own version of events here. The General remained to keep watch on his askaris, decimated by influenza. Then arguments arose about their back pay. I was powerless to get the General out of detention camp once he'd walked in. Still no definite word of his son, though rumors abound. These are on a par with native stories that the Kaiser is on Kilimanjaro!

The gun on Kilimanjaro is silent at last. The Royal Navy loaded dynamite on an old Farnham Longhorn and flew it into the German garrison by remote wireless control. A fantastic experiment! It seems to have killed the few remaining brave young men. Agents report, however, the escape of the girl with the golden eyes, the stunning octoroon, Lanni. She received advance warning and is now with the Cornelius rabble again.

From the war diary of Colonel von Lettow, Berlin, April 1919:

A cold gray day for a victory parade, the only victory parade after this terrible war, known now as the First War of the World (are we, then, to plan for a Second and a Third?). Our battered African helmets and safari outfits looked offensively carnival. I rode a black charger at the insistence of the Mayor of Berlin. I wanted to walk. In light of later events, I wish I had overridden the Mayor. He was to honor us at a grand banquet. Then he got cold feet! Politics again. The chagrin of my men was dreadful. No wonder so many fine soldiers are joining the roving bands of self-styled vigilantes.

The new fight on my hands is the result of a powerful movement to discredit me. I had been urged by moderates to rally the veterans and appeal for national unity. Former Governor Schnee got back here ahead of me to publicize his version of events in German East. I burned the Treasury! I sought personal glory! I taught black Africans to fight and dream of revolution! Schnee is playing with the various nationalist groups, and they say he wants a political career with a bunch calling themselves National Socialists, inspired by an army corporal!

Rachel's uncle, Walter Rathenau, is under attack by these new elements for being Jewish. The Kaiser had put him in charge of organizing Germany's war economy, and now Rathenau is powerful and thinking of a new "Democratic Party" of his own.

Count Kornatzki is making an independent search for our son. Dear Kornatzki, at his age he ought not to be roaming Africa again! But he's obsessed with the rumors, and he does have unique contacts among all the tribes. Kornatzki did ask me to join him and Cornelius in the bush. I said Kate would wish me to fight the bigger battle here first. "The Second Reich is finished," I told Kornatzki. "We don't yet know what the Third Reich will be."

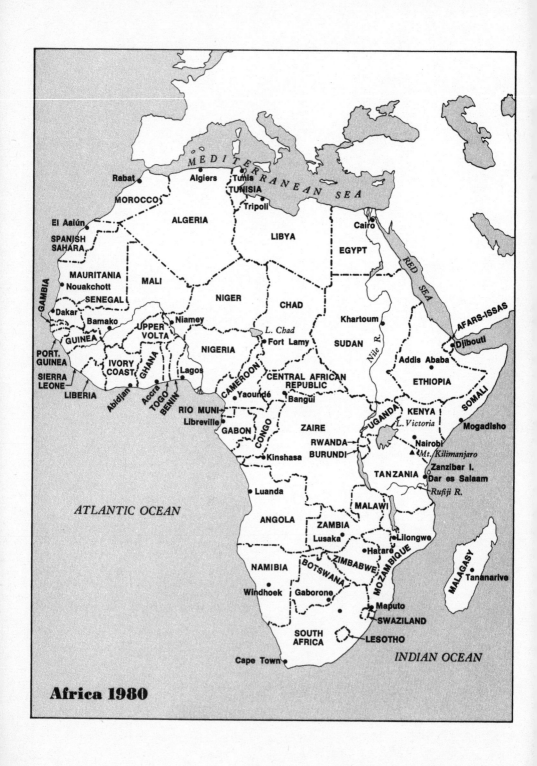

Africa 1980

Afterword

IN 1944, as the Third Reich entered its final year, a group of German generals plotted to assassinate Adolf Hitler and quickly end the wholesale bloodshed and devastation of a furious war turned hopeless. They called upon a seventy-year-old gardener who implemented his meager wages by carving pipes for sale to local tobacconists. This man was General Paul von Lettow-Vorbeck, the legendary "Lion of Africa," commander of German forces in East Africa during the First World War, and reduced by the Nazis to work as a menial.

The conspiring generals had requested material aid from American and British intelligence. They were told that they must first get a commitment from Lettow-Vorbeck that he would head an interim post-Hitler government. He replied, "No, the old Germany is lost and will not find its soul again until we pay the full price."

In 1953, after an absence of more than thirty years, Lettow-Vorbeck returned at last to Africa. The former German colony was then administered by the British, who welcomed their one-time enemy at a ceremony in Dar es Salaam. By chance, the grandson of the Kaiser, who had lived in England during the Second World War under the name of George Mansfield, was visiting Kilimanjaro at the same time. Mansfield, who could legitimately call himself Prince Frederick of Prussia, told Lettow-Vorbeck why the Allies had made that request: "If the rebel generals were sincerely anti-Nazi and were not just trying to weasel out of paying for their mistake in following Hitler, the British and Americans believed you would know. They trusted you."

These footnotes are fragments taken from the enormous store of evidence—military, political, social, and personal—that relates to the East Africa campaign of 1914–18. While this book is fiction, it is accurate in the portrayal of the pivotal military events that took place. All details of tribal practices and lore, of geography and climate, are authentic. The social and political attitudes expressed are derived from official records, eyewitness accounts, and scholarly retrospectives.

The interpretation of individual characters and their personal interactions are, of course, my inventions. Nonetheless, virtually every major role has a counterpart in real men and women. Who were they? What happened to them?

"Hagen" is, in part, fashioned upon Richard Meinertzhagen, the British spymaster who always referred to Lettow-Vorbeck as Lettow. In his *Army Diary* * the Englishman wrote how "the King in Buckingham Palace and Queen Mary were always more interested in Lettow than any other war figure and thought him a great man."

After the war, the real "Hagen" followed Lettow-Vorbeck's political struggle against Hitler. In June 1922, Walther Rathenau, the father of Lettow-Vorbeck's beloved Rachel, was murdered by anti-Jewish followers of Hitler. For those with eyes to see, this was a portent. Rathenau had, as foreign minister, played a major role in the Treaty of Rapallo that formally concluded peace with and gave recognition to Soviet Russia.

During the turbulent postwar decade, Lettow-Vorbeck clung to his elected place in the Reichstag. In 1929 "Hagen" invited him to meet Winston Churchill and General Smuts in London and discuss the rising power of the Nazis. Lettow-Vorbeck resigned from the German legislature soon thereafter.

A meeting took place between Hitler and "Hagen" on July 15, 1935. "Hagen" pleaded the cause of the Jews, already under the Nazi boot. He proposed Paul von Lettow-Vorbeck should serve as German ambassador in England. Nothing came of "Hagen's" attempts to influence the course of events, except that Hitler distrusted Lettow-Vorbeck more than ever. When the Second World War broke out in Europe in 1939, Lettow-Vorbeck was forced to eke out a living gardening and carving pipes. British intelligence kept track of him through his close friend Baroness Karen Blixen, the famous Danish writer who used the pseudonym Isak Dinesen and who was living in Germany.

Kate Truman was inspired by Karen Blixen, who had first encountered Lettow-Vorbeck on that 1913 voyage to Africa. Unlike

* Published by Oliver & Boyd, London, 1960.

Kate, Karen Blixen survived the 1914–18 war and during the Second World War she smuggled documents out of Germany and brought in small comforts for Lettow-Vorbeck from his old enemies in London.

Governor Heinrich von Schnee became Hitler's Minister of Colonies (In Waiting). I found a relic of the real Schnee in the old German farmhouse of Ngera Sera on Kilimanjaro's lower slopes. Schnee's family crest was stamped on an enormous pitcher for cooling bottles of wine, which seemed appropriate. Ada von Schnee, like her husband, really did exist and disappeared into the maelstrom of the Third Reich along with naval Captain Max Looff.

Reminders of them linger in the National Museum of what is now the Republic of Tanzania. To my surprise, I discovered their photographs in the museum, carefully preserved, as if nothing had happened since then. Indeed, glancing up from these faded impressions to look through the fretted museum windows at Dar es Salaam's slow traffic, I felt they might easily have stepped out from behind the huge fig trees shading the hot streets. Tom von Prinz is there, too, his image engraved upon a memorial plaque, and inside the museum showcases are Lettow-Vorbeck's pipe and his ceremonial sword.

Lanni survives in Tanzania's historical archives, among thousands of documents squashed into a bungalow of the German colonial era standing behind a monument to the askaris. *La fille aux yeux d'or*, the golden-eyed Lanni, is based on the daughter of Frau Emily Reute, the former Princess Salme, who so deeply offended the powerful overlord, Seyyid Said, that she had been smuggled to Germany out of the sultanate of Zanzibar by—of all things—the British navy. Lanni rejoined Cornelius, the leader of black guerrillas, whose nephew is well known as the first President of Tanzania, Julius Nyerere.

Cornelius did graduate from a Negro Baptist seminary in Virginia and indeed was involved in the first African National Congress, which took place in the United States in 1912. Senator John Morgan, pretending to be sympathetic, used the Congress to pursue his own dream of shipping all American blacks to Africa. From that time, Cornelius dated his distrust of whites. He was robbed of his chance of becoming the first black governor when he was killed by Ugandans in 1931. (Uganda has many tribes, but in the narrative I have simplified this confusing aspect by dropping the designating tribal prefixes.) I saw the last King of Uganda, properly known as King Freddie of Buganda, in the early 1960s when he was chased out of his Entebbe palace by warriors who finally gave allegiance to Idi Amin, the modern "Big O."

The Jews who considered making Uganda their home are epitomized in Jacob Kramer. Most Jewish nationalists were unsure about the proposal when it was first put to them by Dr. Theodore Herzl at the Sixth Zionist Congress at Basle in 1903. The Uganda dream died after Hitler came to power. Nonetheless, Chaim Weizmann won British support and a League of Nations Mandate for Palestine; eventually he became the first President of Israel. Serving in the Royal Fusiliers, that 1914–18 fighting unit of amateurs frequently used by "Hagen," were Jacob Epstein and David Ben-Gurion.

British War Office historians found that their records of the East Africa campaign differed "not only as to hour and even week when battles occurred, but also in every other possible detail." The diaries and memoirs of Richard ("Hagen") Meinertzhagen, Lettow-Vorbeck, General (later Field Marshal) Jan Christian Smuts, the white hunter Pieter Pretorius, and the writer Francis Brett Young (who is the model for Quentin Pope) convey better the feelings of those who fought. I have tried to reflect their sense of Africa, mindful that only "Hagen" among Lettow-Vorbeck's enemies recognized the German's prescience in matters of empire. "Hagen" believed that the myth of white superiority had been shattered by black Africans under Lettow-Vorbeck's command.

Was there a Baby Paul? Not according to British military records. Nor is there evidence of a lost child in the extensive German records now republished in several volumes jointly by the West German and Tanzanian governments.* However, in the remarkable photographs made by Walter Dobbertin, the official *Schutztruppe* photographer from 1906–18, a baby appears during the penultimate year of conflict, always in the arms of the tracker Skaramunga. We know Skaramunga died after the killing of Frederick Courtenay Selous. Perhaps there never was a Baby Paul, except in an imagination inspired in Dobbertin's unique photographs.

During one phase of my research, I was taken to the grave of

---

* Veroffenlichungen der Archivschule, 355 Marburg/Lahn, W. Germany.

Selous by my own son, Andrew. He is an expert on the German campaign and leads safaris along the old campaign trails. He is also the only white game warden in the largest game reserve in Africa, named the Selous after the famous man. The Selous permits no permanent human habitation, and there is accordingly a powerful sense of communion with nature. In that hot and lonely wilderness, I sensed why so many soldiers had reported experiences like that of Kate when she saw her brother's ghost. I remembered the moving account given by the brother of Wilfred Owen, the soldier-poet killed while the ceasefire sounded. Harold Owen, serving in the East African theater, "gazed in astonishment at my brother suddenly appearing . . . radiating a quality that made his presence absolutely right. . . . I loved having him there [but] I knew he was dead."

How the African bush does preserve the past and make it come alive! A friend of Paul von Lettow-Vorbeck, the white hunter Rolfe von Trappe, manages my son's camp. Not far from the camp, the steel skeleton of the *Koenigsberg* still rots in the Rufiji. The spoor of the *Schutztruppe* is still visible across that immense space from Kilimanjaro to what is now Mozambique and was then Portuguese East Africa.

In the British Imperial War Museum in London, I recently found records substantiating in specific detail the African voyage of the real Zeppelin L-59. The flight took place, as I have written, in November 1917. In ninety-five hours, L-59 traversed a total of 4,225 miles (6,845 kilometers), a distance equivalent to that from Germany to the midwestern United States—and enough fuel remained on board for another 3,750 miles. The mission, code-named "The China Matter," was by any standard an outstanding feat, but it was swallowed up in the secrecy of war. Count Zeppelin (who died before L-59 was completed) and the Kaiser, both deeply involved, took delight in proposing the component materials for use in Africa. The airship's covering was made of special cotton to be made into tents and tropical uniforms; the gas-cell containers were convertible to waterproof sleeping bags; the linen partitions would make shirts; aluminum alloy girders and struts were designed to be refitted into collapsible buildings and radio towers; the walkways were made of shoe leather.

This singular airship left its last European stop in Bulgaria on November 21, 1917, with a cargo for Lettow-Vorbeck's army, including 311,900 boxes of ammunition, 230 machine-gun belts with 13,500 cartridges, sacks of bandages and medical supplies, spare parts for guns, and mail. Over the Libyan desert, the rising air temperature forced some gas to expand and some to escape through safety valves; a ton of water had to be jettisoned to equalize that loss. The crew's personal diaries recorded problems never before encountered: clouds of flamingos threatening to block the engines; pot shots fired by duck-hunting British sportsmen in Khartoum; bottles of wine and cognac threatening to burst in rapidly changing temperatures and air pressure; and boxes of ammunition exploding when jettisoned to allow the airship to gain height.

The real L-59 was obliged to turn back after coming within a few hours' flight of Kilimanjaro. The reason has never been clearly explained, although it appears that German naval commanders, believing Lettow-Vorbeck had been defeated, signaled L-59 to return to base. In fact, the fateful message was radioed on the day Lettow-Vorbeck was invading Portuguese Africa. The Zeppelin arrived back in Bulgaria on November 25. It vanished without trace sometime later while en route on a bombing mission to Malta.

L-59 was unique among vehicles of the air. It began life as LZ-104 and was then *cut* in two, with additional compartments inserted to make it stretch to 750 feet, the better to fulfill its purpose in Africa. This masterpiece matched the ingenious improvisations of the colonial troops it was meant to reinforce, and it deserves a conspicuous place in aviation history.

Paul von Lettow-Vorbeck died at ninety-four. Among his papers was this extract from *Seven Pillars of Wisdom* in which Lawrence of Arabia describes Richard ("Hagen") Meinertzhagen: "A student of migrating birds [he] drifted into soldiering. His hot immoral hatred of the enemy expressed itself as readily in trickery as in violence. . . . A silent, laughing, masterful man who took as blithe a pleasure in deceiving his enemy (or his friend) by some unscrupulous jest as in spattering the brains of a cornered mob of Germans with his African knobkerrie."

That is one version of Lettow-Vorbeck's arch-enemy, his strangest friend. What did "Hagen" have to say about his foe beyond an obvious admiration? When Lettow-Vorbeck made that return visit to Dar es Salaam in 1953, the old askaris turned out to hoist the Lion of Africa on their shoulders. "Hagen" noted that the British administrators were apprehensive, recognizing Lettow-Vorbeck still

had the power to rally rebels. At the end of the visit, the old warrior took the salute at a march-past of *British* askaris who sang,
"*Heia, heia Safari!*" "Hagen" wrote: "Lettow stood erect, monocled.
The intervening years were cancelled. Out of the past, the ghosts
were made to seem alive. Old men picked up the threads of old
intimacies. Here we bled, here we hungered, here we feasted on
captured supplies and mastered captured guns. And now again
bleeding, again hungering, again confronting new ideas; only now
the faces grown haggard, wiry legs bent, all passion spent.

"Lettow alone seemed untouched by all the years."

It was Richard ("Hagen") Meinertzhagen who first interested me
in the Lettow-Vorbeck legend. The German's awareness of the
revolution in China and what it might imply for Africa had intrigued
me since my own time as a correspondent in China. In 1963, living
and working in East Africa, I visited the island of Zanzibar to find
that the Maoist Chinese were preparing a base there. The following
year, Lanni's nephew, the reigning Sultan, was overthrown and flew
into English exile. There began a lengthy period of Chinese revolutionary influence that spread over to the mainland. Sixteen years
later I can board a Chinese-built train to ride across the plateau
where Lettow-Vorbeck's troops once marched. This modern Chinese-
built railroad system was designed to help the black guerrillas fight
the whites in Rhodesia, where Lettow-Vorbeck fought his last battle.

Now, in late 1979, I stare at one of Dobbertin's photographs. It
shows Lettow-Vorbeck with one booted leg resting on the running
board of a magnificent staff car, circa 1914. This automobile is a
large, open landau with an enormous engine covered by a semi-
circular hood held down by a large leather strap. There is a folded-
back canvas hood behind the upholstered rear seats, making the carriage resemble a giant perambulator. There are big sweeping mud-
guards, huge headlamps, mighty spoked wheels, and a sense of power
and grace. Lettow-Vorbeck appears to be ready to jump into the
machine, behind the carved steering wheel, to drive off down the
unpaved street with its sloping palm trees and shuttered shops inside
the pillared colonnades.

Here, at this same spot, in the center of Dar es Salaam, there is
now a superb monument to the askaris of Africa. It must be Tanzania's best-known, manmade landmark; everyone gives directions
by reference to "the Askari Monument." It shows a native soldier in
full German battle kit, attacking with rifle and bayonet. Written
beneath it—in Swahili, Arabic, and English—are the words Paul

von Lettow-Vorbeck had drafted at the request of "Hagen" for inscription:

> In memory of native Africa
> troops who fought
>
> To the carriers who were the
> feet and hands of the army
>
> And to all other men who
> served and died
> In German East Africa 1914–1918
>
> Your sons will remember
> your name.

And so, speaking in the tongues of black and white and brown, with a warning we have yet to comprehend, the ghosts of Africa haunt us still.

Dar es Salaam, Tanzania